Catriona's past is about to collide with her present and make her future more uncertain than ever...

≪৯≪৯≪৯

From the darkness of the smokehouse Catriona heard her friend's call. Still wiping her hands on an already greasy towel, she stepped into the sunlight, finding herself momentarily blinded by the glare.

Adele caught her breath as she watched the woman in front of her raise her hand to her face to shield her eyes.

"Susan, I hear you, but I'm sorry I'm a bit troubled by the glare at the moment." Next to her friend, the grazier could just make out the vague outline of a woman. Blinking her eyes once again to try and focus she continued, "Sorry for keeping you both out in the sun, where are my manners? I'm sorry, but I don't think we've met."

"Don't you know me, Catriona?" Adele answered in a quiet voice. As she did she watched the emotions cloud across the other woman's features. They were a mix of confusion, memory, search, recognition, disbelief and desperate hope.

"Adele?" Catriona whispered, half hopefully, half fearful. As her eyes finally focused she took in the form of the woman in front of her. "My God, it's you."

And Those Who
Trespass Against Us

And Those Who Trespass Against Us

Helen Macpherson

Renaissance Alliance Publishing, Inc.
Nederland, Texas

ISBN 1-930928-21-1

First Printing 2001

9 8 7 6 5 4 3 2 1

Cover art and design by Talaran

Published by:

Renaissance Alliance Publishing, Inc.
PMB 238, 8691 9th Avenue
Port Arthur, Texas 77642-8025

Find us on the World Wide Web at
http://www.rapbooks.com

Printed in the United States of America

You know, one of the things that I've discovered about writing a story is that, when all is said and done, the author is merely one step in the process. What takes the story to the final product of a book is the support and teamwork provided by both friends and a publishing company. Without these people a story, no matter how captivating, would remain as just that. So, in some degree of chronological order I'd like to thank a few people. Firstly I'd like to thank Vanessa, Nicki, Sue, Selina, Carol, Kim and Megan. Thanks for not running when I asked you to read my story and, more importantly, thanks for the great feedback you provided; it helped the story to mature. Next I'd like to thank the RAP team and its CEO, Cathy, who accepted my script and set it on the path to publication. I'd also like to thank my cover artist Talaran who has really added polish to the final product. From the editorial perspective, I'd like to thank Barb and Linda who kept me on track, making sure that the storyline flowed as it should do. Finally, I'd like to thank my partner, Kate, who may have not been all that happy with all those hours I sat staring at a computer screen, however she supported me all the same.

— Helen Macpherson

Chapter
One

The moment Katherine Flynn stepped from the train she knew that something was wrong. There was no-one to greet her—no stationmaster, no porter. From what she could see of the station it seemed that the whole place was deserted. All was quiet, except for the wind that seemed to blow in a spiraling fashion down the length of the platform, spreading dust in its wake. Taking in her greater surroundings she realised not only the station but also everything as far as the eye could see was covered in a fine film of dust.

She'd heard that dust storms were a regular part of Australian country life, but up until now she'd never really witnessed the effects of one. It was said they were fiercer than the Reckoning itself. However she chose to dismiss such a description as the Australian way of over exaggeration, something they seemed prone to do. All the same it was a long way to come to be greeted by no-one except the wind. If someone had told her two years ago that she would find herself in the remote Australian countryside she wouldn't have believed them; for two years ago to the day had been her wedding day.

Katherine had been 22 when she'd finally succumbed to the pressure of her mother to find a husband. The threats she weaved around Katherine about a long spinsterhood were too much to bear. The problem was it wasn't marriage that worried the young woman. It was just that, in all honesty, she hadn't yet found someone who suited her. That was until the day her father had brought home a client who wished to continue business discussions not finalised at her father's office. Iain Riordan was the only person Katherine had met who came close to her expectations of a husband, and so after the acceptable months of courtship had elapsed, she consented to marry him.

The day of their wedding was no different to any of the many other days she'd passed in the countryside of Ireland. Gray and overcast, a light drizzle fell as the family coach approached the town church. Alighting from the coach, Katherine's hem dragged along the ground, causing a brown ring to form at the base of her white silk dress. On reaching the large wooden doors of the ancient church a flustered pastor informed her that the groom hadn't yet arrived but assured Katherine that there was a good explanation for this. Truth was—he wasn't coming. He had instead elected to elope with a younger woman who possessed not only good looks but also a sizable dowry. Thus, Katherine was left a somewhat non-plussed bride standing and listening to the weeping ravings of her mother in the minister's quarters of All Saints Church, in Kilmarney, Ireland.

Katherine's mother couldn't be consoled and talked of nothing but the disgrace that would be brought onto the Flynn name. In her unsettled way she seemed to have placed the guilt for the farce of the wedding at Katherine's feet. Katherine, unable to spend her days living with the ranting of an unrepentant mother, packed her meagre belongings and left her home the following day. She'd left no note, nor had she told anyone of her intended destination.

She walked out on her family and into a vocation that guaranteed never again would she be hounded to marry. This vocation, although not exactly of Katherine's choosing, provided a means of escape from her mother and the supposed shame she'd brought on the family name. And so, it was at Our Sister of Mercy Convent that Katherine spent her next twelve months. There she lived a frugal existence, no longer harassed by the social pressures that strangled a woman of the 1870's. The Sisters were a group who asked no questions, with most of their calling being of exacting work involving residence in countries far from the shores of Ireland.

Nothing could have suited Katherine better when her Mother Superior told her their work was again needed in Australia and that she was to replace the Sister currently there. It was made clear that she didn't have to go for the current Sister wasn't much of a correspondent, so no-one at the convent was fully aware of what life in New South Wales would hold in store for her. It was explained to Katherine that once she arrived it would be some time before the convent could raise the money and secure her a return passage if she didn't like her position in the remoteness of the flourishing State. What the Mother Superior couldn't know was that this opportunity presented Katherine with a chance to finally sever the tie with her old life, and so she grasped at the chance wholeheartedly.

After a relatively uneventful sea journey, save for the occasional bouts of seasickness, followed by an extremely slow four-day train trip, Katherine had eventually arrived at her destination—a deserted train station.

Chapter Two

It quickly became obvious to Katherine that God didn't have Australia in mind when he invented the nun's habit. She could feel the beads of perspiration running down the middle of her back and settling in a wet spot at the base of her spine. The sun was stifling, but not knowing where she should go, she had no choice but to sit and wait

Katherine had walked the length of the platform, trying the two doors of the cement-rendered building, annoyed at finding that both were locked. Bringing her hand up to one of the dust-covered windows, she rubbed at the glass to see if someone was indeed inside and merely asleep. The room she looked into was relatively bare. A bench travelled the length of the walls, before pausing for the presence of a fireplace, then once again resuming its journey. There was another door which obviously signalled the exit to the station. However, given where she was, there was no point in leaving the station and trying to find someone, for the place did truly look deserted. Despite the station's platform having a verandah to provide shelter from the sun, it was at a time of day when the direction of the sun was reflected off the muted tones of the building itself, and there was little shade to be found.

Moving down the small brick platform, she succeeded in the uneasy task of finding a place out of the afternoon sun. Sitting down in the small pocket of shade and making herself as comfortable as possible, she closed her eyes and promptly drifted off to sleep.

It was sometime later that she awoke with a start. Standing over Katherine was a man in uniform who by his dress could only be the stationmaster. In his hand was a flask, the contents of which he was attempting to pour down her throat.

"Thank heavens you're alive, Sister. Sitting here the way you were I thought you had fainted and died in the heat. Here take some water, but just sip it, don't gulp it or you'll find yourself bringing it up again." With that he offered the flask again to Katherine and this time she grasped at it.

As she quenched her thirst she took time to observe the man in front of her. He wore a deep blue jacket and trousers that, like his surroundings, were covered in a fine film of dust. It wasn't the uniform and the hunched shoulders of the man that struck Katherine; it was instead his face. She truly believed that she'd never seen so many creases on a man's face before. Even her Grandfather's face hadn't told the tale of hard years that this one did. It was as if the wind, that had weathered so perfectly the surrounding landscape, had created this face also.

Realising that she was staring at him much like an inquisitive nine year old, she uttered forth a word of thanks for his water. "Thank you. I don't know what happened. There was no-one here when I got off the train. At first I thought the Convent had sent me to a ghost town. I tried to get inside but all the doors were locked." Katherine's sentences were disjointed at first but as she became more aware of her surroundings her sentences became more coherent.

The stationmaster started to explain in an apologetic manner about the need for him to lock the station's doors when he was interrupted by a voice from behind him.

"The train; that would be the 1.15 weekly from Sydney. That was some two hours ago. If you're going to live out here you're going to have to learn not to fall asleep in the sun." Until that moment Katherine had been unaware of the figure behind the stationmaster who had stepped out from behind him and was now surveying her intently. "How can you be expected to bear the heat with all those clothes on? What's that cloth? It looks like wool," the person said, reaching forth to touch the material. The hands of the person in front of her ran the fabric of the habit between two dusty fingers. "If you want to survive more than a week out here you're going to have to find something lighter than that."

Katherine raised her face from the inquisitive fingers to the face of the person in front of her, only now realising that she was a woman. It wasn't that her manner of speaking was coarse, in fact it was impeccable, it was moreso her mode of dress and the shape of her body. She wore no dress, favouring instead a pair of pants and a shirt. The trousers were a dusty brown colour, which Katherine presumed were white when they were washed, and were the same width all the way down her leg. It was only later that Katherine learnt such trousers, called moleskins, were popular in the Australian Outback due to their resilience to wear. The shirt, also coated in a film of dust was of a blue colour and seemed to be made out of light cotton. In fact, the fabric of the shirt reminded Katherine of the light cotton used in undergarments back in England. This covered a chest, which was more like an adolescent's, and was accentuated by her slender hips, giving the woman an impish air, not like the nuns Katherine was more accustomed to at all.

Coupled with the effect of the clothes, the stranger herself seemed to be equally as interesting. She seemed overly tall for a woman with a slender build; her face was slightly square but this in no way made her appearance look harsh. Her face had been tanned by the sun but hadn't yet begun to show the telltale signs of weathering, like the stationmaster's. Her hair, which had been sensibly pulled away from her face and into a pigtail, was light brown in colour. The woman seemed to possess no physical similarity to the stationmaster who was standing quietly at her side and, as Katherine looked from one face to the other, it dawned on her that she was again staring. She also realised they had been standing there for a good three minutes and she didn't yet know their names nor did they know hers. Stiffly pulling herself up from her previously seated position and breaking her gaze from the younger of the two, Katherine extended her hand toward the stationmaster and introduced herself. "Excuse my rudeness, my name is Sister Flynn, Sister Katherine Flynn."

"James Nelson, Sister, and this is Miss Catriona Pelham. I know how tiring the journey is from Sydney. I hope it's left you with enough strength to have a cup of tea," Mr Nelson said, offering a steadying hand in view of Katherine's swaying form.

"Thank you very much, that's very kind of you. However, after the tea do you think you could tell me where Sister Coreen is? You see I was expecting her to meet me this afternoon, as she was to show me to my living quarters. You must know her—her full name is Sister Coreen Watson." Katherine paused as she saw the look that passed between the stationmaster and Miss Pelham. It was the type of look reserved for occasions when something was far from right.

"If it's Sister Watson you've come all this way for then I'm afraid your journey has been wasted." The stationmaster paused looking toward Miss Pelham for assistance. The dust-covered woman took up where the stationmaster had awkwardly stopped.

"You would have had to have been blind not to have noticed that everything is coated in dust; for earlier today we had a dust storm that went on for about an hour. Unfortunately, being the main market day there were a lot of people in the town when the storm hit. Most of those who were in from their properties, or farms as you would be more familiar with, took refuge in the Town Hall. What you must understand is that our Town Hall is— or should I say was—no more than a wooden shack. At the height of the storm the wind whipped though the town, uprooting trees and moving houses. Unfortunately the shops and houses that weren't strong enough either collapsed or just blew away."

Pausing in her story, the woman stared into the distance, recalling the next series of events with a clarity as if they were actually occurring all over again. "The Town Hall was one of those which collapsed, killing ten people and wounding many others. So you see that's why there was no-one here to meet you. Every person who could still walk has been down at the Hall sorting through the debris for bodies and survivors. Most of the job was completed with only a small section remaining when one of the workers heard the muffled sound of a crying child and when they removed the debris they found the body of Sister Watson and, under her, a relatively unscathed girl. It seemed that she'd shielded her from the falling roof, dying in the child's place. She was quite dead when they found her—probably killed by the impact of the roof." Catriona Pelham paused for a moment, much the way one does when telling of such an event. She momentarily gazed around her surroundings, composed herself, and then continued on. "So if it's Sister Watson you're waiting for, I'm afraid you'll be waiting a long time. She's dead you see; gone forever." At this Catriona Pelham turned and walked a few paces away from the small group before stopping and staring out at the gaunt landscape.

"But if you want to be of assistance there's something you could do," her voice carried back over her shoulder as she continued to stare into the distance. "Father Cleary who runs the church is away up north and is not expected to return for a week. We can't leave dead bodies in the open for that long, or they'll turn."

"Turn, what do you mean by turn?" Katherine asked.

"They will begin to, er, be fouled by the hot weather," the stationmaster said awkwardly, searching for the appropriate words.

Unsure of where the conversation was heading, the confused nun looked from one person to the other. "So what is it you want me to do?"

Turning, the tired blue eyes of Catriona met her own. "The dead need the appropriate prayers said over them after they're buried and, frankly, Sister Flynn, you're the closest we have to a town priest."

Her eyes widened in shock as her mouth formed a horrified "oh." "I can't pray over them. I'm not ordained to do that. I'm only a nun! Isn't there some way you can wait until Father Cleary returns?" She asked, tearing her face from Catriona to the stationmaster.

Leaving her previously contemplative position, Catriona strode toward the nun and grabbed her shoulder to wheel her around until Katherine was merely inches from her face. "Look around you, Sister Flynn. That shimmering effect you can see in the distance is the heat. If the bodies are not buried by nightfall they'll attract the flies that in turn will bring disease. It must be done now and you're the closest we have to a qualified person," Catriona replied belligerently, legs akimbo and arms folded.

Seeing the angered face of the woman in front of her, Katherine endeavoured to logically point out the religious scruples involved in such a matter. "I don't think you realise, Miss Pelham, that I can say nothing over them that will make their path into the hereafter assured. As a nun these words would have no religious significance."

"Do you think those people who are dead give a damn if it's you, me, or the town drunk who says final prayers for them? If I felt the matter could be resolved in this way, then I'd do it myself. This is for their relatives who are still alive. They're looking for assurance, religious assurance that their loved ones will be safe in the hereafter. You can give them that assurance. I doubt that in this time of their grief they care who you are, only that you're the closest they have to a priest. I suggest you realise that in Australia not all things fit the mould as they're supposed to. You're here for a long time if anything Sister Coreen said is true. If this is the case, you can endear yourself to the townspeople now or you can spend a very long and lonely time here," Catriona Pelham challenged, her eyes piercing Katherine's own.

"I understand what you're saying but when Father Cleary returns—" Katherine began to say.

"Sometime in the future the Father will be back and he can ensure that everything is remedied from a religious perspective. Now I think we should be making a move." Catriona grabbed Katherine's arm before she could object, propelling her through the doorway of the railway station, leaving the stationmaster struggling behind the two with the nun's meagre luggage.

Jim Nelson could think of nothing else but what a blunt woman Catriona Pelham was. One day her forthrightness would cause trouble and he couldn't help but think that when it happened it would make the effects of today's dust storm look like no more than a wind driven "willy-willy." Shrugging his shoulders, the stationmaster picked up the sister's bags and, placing the sister's meagre luggage in his own cart, followed the Pelham wagon into town.

Nothing could have prepared Katherine for the sight of a town destroyed by a dust storm, for it was as if a giant had stepped on the town, crushing it underfoot. It wasn't until she saw the desperation and pain on the townspeople's faces that she fully realised Miss Pelham's sense of urgency. She felt guilty about her stubbornness on insisting that she adhere so rigidly to the rules of the Church when it was obvious that what these people needed was comfort and reassurance. Katherine found herself spending her first day in her new town praying for the dead, comforting the survivors, and quietly mourning the heroic efforts of a nun she never knew. She wasn't sure what the Father would say of her actions upon his return, but she was ready to stand by the position she admitted she'd been unwillingly forced into.

When Katherine wasn't tending to the spiritual comfort of others, she found herself helping in the clearing rubble or attempting to sweep away some of the incessant dust which seemed to stick in the same manner as the flies in this country did. Through her work she found herself overcome with the most amazing feeling. For once in her life she felt part of something. It was more than that though; she was doing work that in Ireland would have been regarded as only men's work. Even in such frequent disasters as the mining disasters back home, a woman's duties would still be restricted to making tea and sandwiches. Maybe her decision to come to this land wasn't such a bad decision after all.

As she worked amongst the ruins of so many lives, the sun continued to work its way across the sky until the remaining people laboured in that time of day when shadows grew longer and the first hint of a full moon filled the sky. The tired group, having satisfied themselves that everyone had been accounted for and nothing more could be done for the day, collected the other members of their families and began to leave for their own homes. As they departed there were shouted goodbyes between the small crews, with guarantees to return tomorrow and complete what still had to be done. As they wandered away, Katherine found herself left with Catriona Pelham, wondering where she would spend the night.

Katherine attempted to wipe the accumulated dust and blood from the front of her habit but quickly abandoned the idea after realising that her hands were just as dirty as her habit. Wiping them in an attempt to dislodge some of the dirt, she looked at Catriona Pelham in the fading light. "Well, I expect I should be on my way home. If only I knew where my lodgings were."

"Though it mightn't be much of a comfort now, the town had planned a more appropriate welcome than the one you've received, but come to think of it, at least this one was more realistic." Catriona wiped her hands on the seat of her pants while looking around her for her hat. "Sister Coreen's 'lodgings' are on the same road to my homestead. I should tell you that she spent little time there and her reasons for this will become more apparent to you when we get there. Hop on the wagon and we'll be on our way. Don't worry about your luggage; I had Jim put it in the back of my wagon during a break this afternoon." Catriona Pelham busied herself with un-tethering the horse from where it had patiently waited throughout the day.

In the fading light Katherine could see little of the town that she was travelling through. The shapes that she could discern disturbed her. The Town Hall was only one of many buildings that suffered the brunt of the storm. She couldn't help but wonder if this were a regular occurrence, how could anyone endure this on a continual basis?

Heading out of town they entered another area that seemed detached from the remains of the main community they had just travelled through. The houses, or the structures that were still left standing, were a mix of whatever material was convenient. Their size reminded Katherine of the elaborate dollhouses she had been given as a child, rather than something that was lived in on a permanent basis. Although she couldn't readily describe it, the nun was unsettled by the uneasy silence of the area. What disturbed her more greatly was that Miss Pelham seemed to be pulling up the horse.

She slowed the wagon in front of what appeared in the early moonlight to be no more than a pile of tangled wood. "This is Sister Coreen's home, or should I say was." It was obvious the house hadn't escaped the storm that had devastated the town hours before.

When they came to a full halt all that could be seen in the gray light confirmed Katherine's initial assessment. Shaking her head, she found it difficult to believe that the mess in front of her had ever been anything that resembled a house; it looked more like a woodpile to her. The realisation of the mess in front of her dawned on Katherine, confusing her plans even more. This was where she was supposed to live, but it was obvious she couldn't do that. Katherine turned to the woman beside her for any suggestion she might have. "This may have been where I was supposed to live, but it's quite obvious this is no longer possible. If it isn't too much of an inconvenience, would it be possible for you to take me to the Father's residence? I'm sure he wouldn't mind if I spent a night in his home while he's away."

"Unfortunately the small home Father Cleary used to live in was accidentally burnt down last summer by an overzealous housekeeper trying to heat it for his return. Since then the committee, who oversaw the building of the first home, has been saving money to construct another. Not that it would be money missed out of their own pockets should they wish to open them," Catriona added with a derisive snort. "So Father Cleary's current residence is the unmarried men's accommodation in town. I'm sure he'd be quite shocked to find you spending the night there rather than sharing the hospitality of someone's home. But you don't have to worry, you can come and stay with me until a more permanent arrangement can be made." Catriona didn't wait for a response before motioning the horse forward.

"Are you sure that this wouldn't be inconveniencing you in any way? I don't wish to cause you—" Katherine found herself cut off in mid-sentence by the woman beside her.

"For heaven's sake, Sister Flynn, think of where you are and what time it is! It would be quite rude of me not to offer you my hospitality for the night. Why, if I took you back to the Town Hall or the train station my reputation with some members of the town would be worse than what it already is." Catriona clicked the reins, not breaking the forward movement of the horse and wagon.

Katherine wondered what sort of reputation this woman possessed, but had the sense to realise that now wasn't the time for the production of personal references. "In that case thank you for your most generous offer, although I won't inconvenience you for any longer than is possibly necessary." Katherine settled herself into the hard wood seat. "You said that house, or the remains of it, was Sister Watson's home although she didn't spend much time there. If she didn't live there and there's no convent, where did she live?"

"She lived with me; that is, my brother and I, on our property. As you're by now no doubt aware her house isn't located in the best area of town. Apparently during the tenure of one of the pastors, he decided that Sisters who came to work in this country should take their vows of poverty literally. While he was cloistered up in his comfortable residence, he supervised the building of the Sister's house in the poorest part of town. His idea wouldn't have upset the nun who was to be the recipient of the arrangement, except the house wasn't only situated in the poorest part of town but it was also located in the most drunken and thieving area. Not surprisingly, Father McGuire didn't last long and the current Father doesn't take the Sister's vows of poverty so literally. He had allowed Sister Coreen to live with my brother and I and she only ever used that house as a retreat for mothers from their drunken husbands." Catriona looked along the road in front of her. "However there'll be plenty of time to talk once we reach Gleneagle, but for now I need to concentrate on getting us home in one piece and before the bushrangers start their roaming. Hang on; if we keep going at this pace we'll reach home in time to turn around again and return to town to assist in tomorrow's cleanup." Finishing, she whipped the horse into a greater, yet controlled, pace.

Katherine found she was glad to have heeded the advice to hang on for this ride was nothing like the carriages of Ireland. She found herself hurtling along at breakneck speed, the cool evening wind picking up her wimple and flailing it in the breeze.

As the nun assessed her options of using one hand to hold onto the side of the wagon while her other steadied her wimple, one of the wheels of the wagon hit a rut, causing her to momentarily leave her seat. It was then she decided that to try and grab the headpiece would be against her better judgment; two hands were required to ensure she didn't fall from her already precarious position.

Katherine was amazed that anyone could drive at such a breakneck speed in merely the steel-grey light cast by the full moon. In her short time of knowing Miss Pelham, she knew it would be against her better judgment to ask her to slow down. After all, Katherine reasoned, this was her country—if anyone should know it then she should. Still, Katherine couldn't help but think that there was more to this woman sitting beside her. She turned to look at the profile of her in the moonlight and could see a determined woman, accentuated by the set of her jaw and the manner in which she sat forward in her seat, staring into the semi-blackness in front of her. Not once did Catriona's concentration wander, and the determination in her face made Katherine feel afraid. Was this what living in this country did to women? Katherine resignedly sat back and held on, waiting for their eventual arrival at their destination. Luckily she didn't have long to wait.

As the wagon slowed and turned, the wheels connected with something metal causing Katherine to yelp in surprise. "What was that?"

"It's nothing, just a cattle grid. It stops the small herd of cattle I have from wandering out of the property when they're in the lower paddocks." With that Catriona was silent and fully focused on moving up the driveway.

Katherine decided upon asking further questions and instead tried to make out what was in front of her. Except for the ambient light of the moon, the darkness had all but engulfed them now, and apart from the changed vibrations of the carriage and the changed feel of the ground passing beneath its wheels, Katherine could see no house. Catriona's stance seemed to have relaxed somewhat now as she slowed the horse's pace and as the animal slowed, Katherine began to make out the silhouette of a house in front of her.

"Well, we're here." Catriona brought the horse to a complete stop before applying the hand brake at her side. "If you just hang on I'll come around and help you off the wagon."

"No, that's kind of you, but there's really no need," Katherine started to say as she proceeded to fall off the wagon into the darkness. She hit the ground with a resounding thud.

"Are you all right?" Catriona asked with a note of frustration and concern in her voice. "I told you I'd help you off."

Katherine was somewhat taken aback. Catriona's words were somewhat stronger than before. "Yes, I heard you. I just wasn't expecting that alighting from this wagon could be so difficult." She found herself responding to the terse nuances of Catriona's voice.

"Well, you're off now. Let's hope that next time your landing onto *terra firma* will be a much safer one," Catriona replied in a more conciliatory tone.

Katherine was surprised that she knew Latin. "You speak Latin?"

"Yes, I do. Why do you sound so surprised? England isn't the only place where you can be educated." The irritation in Catriona's voice returned and was barely masked.

Katherine responded accordingly. "I didn't mean for it to sound as it did, and besides I'm not from England." The lilt in her voice matched the Irish anger that bubbled to the surface.

"Well, I must say, I'm surprised! A Sister with a bad temper. Such a temper should take you far in this country—about as far as the train station." Catriona stared through the darkness at the shorter silhouette in front of her.

"I don't believe this. You've brought me all the way out here and now you're going to take me back to the train station? That's absurd!" Katherine yelled, well and truly angry this time.

"If I was going to do that, I wouldn't have brought you out here. You've nothing to worry from me. I don't care how forward you are, but believe me the rest of the townsfolk may not be so receptive to your blunt tone and *Irish* anger." Catriona emphasised the country of the nun's origin. Realising the conversation wasn't travelling in any sort of positive direction she recovered herself. "Look, I don't think this is getting us anywhere and, besides, it's getting cold. Let's go inside and see if we can't start again."

Katherine realised the rashness of her actions. The Sisters had constantly warned her of her tendency of talking before fully realising what she was saying. "Yes, you're right. I'm sorry but it's been a long day for me. I think I'm a bit tired." Katherine turned and pulled her two small suitcases off the back of the cart.

"If you just wait there I'll tether the horse and be back. Then we can go inside and I'll fix us a brew or what you know better as a cup of tea." Catriona said as she turned to lead the horse into the moonlight.

"Is it possible that I could also have a hot bath? I don't believe I've had a good hot bath since leaving Ireland." Katherine called after Catriona who didn't seem to have heard her as both the grazier and the wagon blended into the shadows cast by the full moon.

It wasn't long before she returned with an answer to Katherine's question. "It might take a while, but I think it could be arranged." Catriona opened the front door of the house as Katherine followed, suitcases in hand.

Just inside the door Catriona reached for a lamp that would provide some light to the room and, leaving Katherine standing at the door, headed through the dark house to the kitchen where she hoped to find the fire hadn't completely gone out. The faint glow from the wood stove heralded that there was still enough hot coals to generate a light for the small taper Catriona had recovered from the top of the stove. Having lit the lamp she returned to find the Sister standing where she'd left her.

"First things first. I'll show you to your room. Now it may not be what you're used to, but it's a bed and a private space all the same." Catriona walked down the hall; the lamp cast a warm glow in front of her and the shadows played off the walls. Picking up her bags, Katherine followed her and stopped outside a door as Catriona opened it. She stepped aside and motioned the nun through the entrance.

Even in the light of the lamp, Katherine was aware that the room was more than she could have expected. "Thank you, this is quite nice and very spacious. If it hadn't been for your kindness I don't know where I would have been spending the night." Katherine moved to the bed and placed her bags on top of it.

"Oh, I do," Catriona laughed with an air of assuredness. "You'd have been put up with one of the fine standing families of the town and forced to tell them tales of the Old Country all night," Catriona finished, as she lit the lamp on the bed stand beside Katherine's bed.

"If that's the case, then thank you for rescuing me. You sound as if you don't have much time for the townsfolk. Have they done something to you to make you feel this way?" Katherine queried, feeling herself slipping into her more common role of religious confidant.

"No, let's just say that the fine, upstanding families' ideals of life and mine differ somewhat. Now if you like, I'll leave you to unpack your belongings." Catriona paused and looked at the two meagre suitcases. "That should take you all of five minutes. I've heard of travelling light but never as light as that." She turned to leave the room. "While you're doing that, I'll finish seeing to the wagon and then put some water on for that cup of tea," she called over her shoulder.

Katherine listened to the echo of Catriona's footfall as she moved through the house and turned back toward the room. She took time to pause and take in her surroundings. The overall size of the room wasn't readily discernible, for the fingers of the lamp's light failed to reach much further than its immediate surroundings. In an attempt to shed a greater light, she moved the lamp onto the dressing table, using the mirror's reflection to increase the beam of light. The result was the discovery of a room that was the most spacious Katherine had encountered since leaving her parents' home over what seemed a lifetime ago.

The room contained a bedside table, dressing table, hand basin, and a wardrobe. Sitting almost centrally in the room, and opposite a pair of full-length French windows, was a huge double bed. What luxury it would be to stretch her limbs in a bed this size! Being a Sister, and before that living with her parents, she'd never known the luxury of a double bed as such pleasures were normally reserved for only wedded couples. While she longed to lay her body full-length on the bed, the only thing that stopped her was the knowledge that if she did this she may not get up again. Shaking herself out of her self-indulgent reverie, she moved toward the dresser to unpack her clothes.

In another part of the homestead, Catriona, having finished seeing to the wagon and its contents and moving inside, placed a small kettle and a large kettle on the wood stove. Leaving both to boil, she moved out of the kitchen to retrieve the metal hipbath stored on the verandah. She paused and turned her face up to the night sky. It was a clear sky, lit by stars and a full moon. She sighed, finding it hard to believe the devastation that had been brought to bear on this part the country today. Although country born, she never ceased to be in awe of the way that nature could be so kind one moment yet in the same breath of wind, so wanton. Shaking her head, she bent down and grasped the lip of the metal bath and dragged it toward the kitchen door.

"Miss Pelham, where are you?" Katherine called out from inside the house.

"I'm outside getting the bath. The job would be done a lot quicker if you could please help me drag it into the kitchen," Catriona replied from outside the back door.

Moving beside her, Katherine grabbed the edge of the metal bath and proceeded to drag it along the verandah toward the back door of the house. "Where do we have the bath?"

"Well, as you can see it's too unwieldy to take too far so we usually bathe in the kitchen, but don't worry I'll close the back door before you start." Catriona continued to push her half of the lead-lined bath.

Katherine was surprised at this response. Things were done differently in Outback Australia. "I don't mean to sound prudish but didn't you mention you shared this house with your brother? What happens if he should walk in during the bath?"

"Then I expect that he'll see you in your full glory as God intended." Seeing the Sister's shocked expression, Catriona reassured her, "However you don't have to worry about him making an unexpected entrance. My brother's away up north and isn't expected back for a few weeks yet. Your privacy, apart from me, is therefore assured." Catriona brought the bath to a halt next to the stove. "Now while we're waiting for the large kettle to boil we'll have that cup of tea. If you don't mind we'll take tea in the kitchen. It takes a while to light up the parlour and I'm sure that at this time of night formalities can be disposed with. Truth be told, with just my brother and I in the house, the parlour is very rarely used." Catriona placed two mugs, sugar and a tin of biscuits on the table.

"I think you misunderstand me," the nun replied. "I'm more comfortable with this reception rather than one full of the social graces. After all I'm a Sister, not a social butterfly. I'm more used to this reception than you could possibly know."

Having allowed the tea to draw, Catriona poured the steaming liquid into the two mugs before handing one to Katherine. "Well, that's good. You'll get both out here so I suppose you can say you'll get the best of both worlds. Here, have a biscuit." Catriona motioned toward the tin. Katherine took one and sat silently munching on a golden coloured biscuit that contained oats and a great deal of something sweet. Both women silently reflected on the day's events before Catriona eased herself out of her chair.

"I hope you're ready for that wash. Your water should be just about ready. If you want to go and get your toiletries, I'll prepare the bath." Heaving the large kettle two-handed off the stove, she made her way toward the waiting bath. Pouring the hot water into the vessel in front of her, she straightened her back and watched the tendrils of steam rise from the surface.

Taking the lamp that she had earlier carried from her room, Katherine headed back through the house. She held the lamp to cast light out in front of her and was distracted by the light catching a painting that could have only been a portrait of the Pelham family. Pausing in an attempt to get a better perspective, she held her lamp to the painting. She could make out an elder couple, who she took to be Miss Pelham's parents, and sitting in front of the two were a girl and boy—these she took to be Miss Pelham and her brother. The dress the younger woman was wearing reminded Katherine of a time when she wore such things. It was a striking green that set off Miss Pelham's face in a much different way to what Katherine had witnessed since her arrival in the town. So engrossed in the painting was Katherine that she failed to notice the presence of Catriona behind her.

"What are you doing?" The voice broke the silence so suddenly that it nearly caused Katherine to drop the lamp she was holding.

Katherine, startled, jumped away from the painting before she managed to regain her composure. "I'm sorry. The lamp shone on the wall and I stopped to see what it had reflected off."

"As you've probably guessed that's my family. When we've a little more time I'll tell you about them but in the meantime your water is getting cold. If you collect your toiletries and head back to the kitchen you'll find that the bath is ready. I'll be in my room to allow you to bathe in private but if you need me just yell. The house is not so big that I won't hear you." Catriona moved around Katherine and continued down the hall.

Katherine's bath that night was just the cure for a long train journey spent bathing out of a bowl coupled by her day of hot and dirty work. It had been a long time since she'd been allowed so much time to herself. She took this as an opportunity to sit back and think about what sort of brother would go away and leave his sister alone on a farm for such a period of time. She was sure that Catriona could look after herself but this didn't quell Katherine's curiosity. However Katherine also knew it would be bad manners to ask.

Given that Catriona hadn't had a bath after the day's events, Katherine found herself feeling guilty about reclining in such liquid luxury. After satisfying herself that she'd removed most of the dirt and perspiration from her tired limbs, she alighted from the bath only to be shocked by the coolness of the evening and the realisation that she'd failed to bring her nightgown in with her. She had a towel, but this barely covered her and didn't shut out the cold night air.

Feeling a trifle embarrassed she called out to her host, "Excuse me, Miss Pelham, are you there?"

There was barely a pause before a reply came from the other side of the door. "Yes, what is it?"

"I'm sorry but I've left my night gown on the foot of my bed in the guest room. Could you get it for me please?" Katherine listened and waited for a reply but instead heard footfall moving away from the door. It wasn't long before Catriona returned.

"I have it here, do you mind if I come in?" She called from the other side of the door.

"No, of course not," Katherine replied, trying to ensure that she was as decent as possible given that her decency was currently restricted by the length of a towel.

The door opened slowly and wide enough to accommodate a head and a hand. "I hope this is what you wanted," Catriona said, her eyes downcast and her outstretched hand holding a threadbare nightgown.

"Thank you very much, it was silly of me not to bring everything with me." She paused as she realised that the other woman was looking decidedly uncomfortable. "Are you all right?" Katherine asked.

"Yes," murmured Catriona, "I think I'm just tired after such a long day."

"Well, I'm finished with the bath now and I expect that you'd like one too. If you could just wait while I get changed I'll help you empty the bath so that you can draw yourself a fresh one." Katherine turned her back to Catriona, affording herself some privacy as she slipped into her nightgown.

"There isn't any need for that, I'll just top up yours with a little hot water. Unfortunately we don't have enough water to afford the luxury of fresh baths all the time. And besides, as long as the dirt comes off it doesn't matter all that much." Catriona moved into the room and made pretence of busying herself with the fire.

As she finished lacing the front of her nightgown Katherine turned to Catriona, running her hand through her wet and short cropped curls. "In that case, is there anything else that I can help you with?"

Catriona seemed to baulk at this last question and, for a fraction of a second, Katherine had seen her features change. Her face seemed to have dropped its guard but, with the same speed with which it had dropped, her composure was quickly regained. "No, thank you, I should be right now." Catriona turned to draw the water kettle from the fire.

She looked at the back of Catriona with curiosity. She was sure that Catriona had meant to say something else but had for some reason stopped herself short and by turning her back to Katherine she'd effectively shut her out. Although her education in the convent had taught her to pursue such matters, it was late and at that moment Katherine didn't feel strong enough to listen to the troubles of yet another person. In all honesty, all she'd been doing that day was listen to the problems of others. Katherine was sure nuns weren't supposed to feel this way, but at that moment she couldn't help herself. "Well, I think I'll go to bed. Good night and thank you once again for extending to me the courtesy of your home." The nuns had taught Katherine the last phrase, and it was a convenient way to end a meeting. She wasn't sure she'd used it in its right context, but found again that she was too tired to care. Lifting her lamp off the table she wound her way back through the house and, upon finding her bedroom, said the necessary prayers before climbing into bed.

Catriona, having heard the footfalls of the Sister recede to another part of the home, trusted herself to turn from the fire and look in the direction Katherine had taken. Her cheeks were flushed, which was not that unusual when one stood so close to a fire. Only Catriona knew that the warmth of the fire had nothing to do with the heat radiating in her cheeks.

Chapter
Three

Katherine awoke the next morning to a cacophony of birds outside her window. Never having heard such a raucous noise in her life, she placed her shift around her shoulders before moving to the window, to see a tree outside occupied by what she thought to be at least a hundred white birds. They reminded her of a group of washerwomen on market day—all too preoccupied with shouting and singing at the same time.

With the morning sun's rays beaming through the opening in the French windows, Katherine at last had a clear opportunity to view her surroundings. The countryside around the home wasn't that dissimilar to what she'd witnessed on her train journey, and was as far removed from a soft Irish countryside as one could get. As far as the eye could see there was a brown-green grass interspersed with tall trees of white bark and green leaves, gum trees—as she'd so learned on her train trip.

Moving toward her dresser she felt a twinge of hunger; which wasn't surprising considering the small amount of food she'd consumed over the past 24 hours. That, coupled with the physical work she'd done the previous day made her quite aware that something more substantial was required. Deciding that a cup of tea was a good place to start, and mindful not to wake Miss Pelham, she walked quietly through the house only to find the woman in the kitchen, dressed and ready for the day ahead.

"Good morning, Sister. I was beginning to wonder if you were going to get up at all." Catriona stood and reached for an extra teacup.

Katherine took the empty cup from the other woman's hand, thanking her silently. "I'm sorry. I didn't know it was customary to rise so early."

"It's not so much that it's customary, but it's necessary. There are not enough daylight hours to get all the chores done and sleep in as well. My brother and I only employ additional workers for the harvest and divide the chores on other occasions between the two of us. On top of that, it gets so hot here in the summer that you can't work through the heat of the day. I could think of nothing better than to go to bed and not have to worry about what I had to do the next day." Catriona poured Katherine's tea.

"Well I expect that these early mornings are something I'll have to remember, Miss Pelham." Katherine smiled at the industrious air of the grazier opposite her.

"Before we go on there's something I must explain to you. As a child, a particular governess educated my brother and me. This continued until Alexander, my brother, was 17 and I was 14. For all the years she taught me she never called me anything but Miss Pelham. I didn't like her very much and I hated being called Miss Pelham. I'm somewhat older than 14 now, but I've never grown to like such a formal name. Sister, please call me Catriona."

"I'll do the courtesy of calling you Catriona only if you'll address me as Sister when the situation demands it. It would seem that in Australia people are more at home calling Sisters by their first name rather than their last. I'm more than comfortable with such an arrangement; after all Flynn seems far too formal for the Australian countryside. I'd be grateful if on all other occasions you'd call me by my Christian name—Katherine." She sat back in her chair and sipped her tea.

"Then it's a deal, Katherine." Catriona extended her hand.

"I expect it is, Catriona." Katherine placed her cup down and grasped the hand in front of her. "I hope you don't think me forward, but it seems strange to live in a house all by yourself. You mentioned a governess educated both you and your brother. You said last night that he lived with you. Where is he now?"

"Yes, I remember saying that I'd tell you about him at a more convenient time. Now seems as good a time as any, but it may be easier for me to start at the beginning." Catriona made herself comfortable before continuing, "First I should explain to you that we have two types of weather out here; one is drought and the other is flood. About three years ago we hadn't seen rain for ages and the whole country dried up leaving behind soil as hard as iron. Then one day the clouds gathered over, promising rain as they had done many times before. But unlike those other times, this time it rained. It wasn't the type of summer shower you'd be used to. The clouds weren't black; they were green— green and full of hail. The rain came down in torrents so thick that you couldn't see outside to the water pump. Flowing as fast and hard as it was, the ground had no time to absorb the water and so it ran into the creeks. The creeks couldn't hold the deluge and many rivers, already full of dead trees and branches, burst their banks.

"What you must understand is that, at first, the day seemed quite normal. Although there were sparse clouds, there was nothing about them to hint that they may hold any long awaited rain." Catriona shifted uncomfortably in her seat. "You see, it was my parents' anniversary and my father chose to take my mother for a picnic. From what we could piece together they didn't reach their picnic spot before the first light rain began to fall. Rather than have lunch they must have turned for home and they were almost there when the full fury of the storm hit. You may have remembered crossing a grate last night signalling the entrance to the property." Catriona paused to receive an acknowledgment from Katherine and take time to sip her tea.

"This grate covers a moderately deep ditch which must be crossed to gain entrance to the property. It's not a very deep crossing but on that day it must have been deep enough. As my parents were coming across it in the rain the horse shied, most probably from a lightning strike, and fell into the ditch, carrying the buggy and my parents with it. My father must have died almost instantly from a broken neck but my mother drowned. She'd broken both legs in the fall and had been unable to move out of the path of the rising waters. She was carried down the river a ways with her body finally being caught in a tree trunk.

"After their funeral my brother and I decided to stay on and work the property. My parents had been here the better part of their lives and so we decided that we'd also try to make a living out of the land. He looks after any long distance business, only because no man would be seen dealing with a woman, while I tend to the property when he's away. When he's here, we work as a team." Catriona stretched her arms out behind her before placing her hands behind her head. "My brother's much like me in looks except he's a few years older."

"Is he affianced or he visiting a potential wife now?" Katherine queried, attempting to redirect the conversation to a more pleasant topic.

"No, he's not visiting any potential wives for in fact he was engaged to someone, but not someone miles away; it was someone who lived in this town." Catriona brought her hands to rest on the table, choosing her next words carefully. "Her name was Coreen Watson, commonly known around here as Sister Coreen."

Despite her religious training which had taught her to maintain a calm countenance at all times, Katherine felt her jaw drop. Taken by surprise, it seemed that a thousand thoughts had entered into her head; thoughts that were quickly forming into questions. "I'm sorry, but I don't understand. A nun, when she's accepted into the Church, marries God. She wears the ring, which symbolises she's married to God, as I do. How could she have consented to marry your brother after already taking such vows?" The words, although not the right ones, were the first thoughts that entered into Katherine's head and they were out of her mouth before she could stop them.

Rolling her blue eyes and shaking her head in the same motion Catriona replied, "There you go again, getting on your religious high horse. It's different out here; things are not as cut and dry as they seem to be in England, excuse me, *Ireland.* It seems as if you think Coreen came all the way out here with the sole purpose of breaking her vows. It wasn't like that at all." Catriona leaned across the table. "In life no-one is perfect and nothing, excepting death, is permanent. There's room for a mistake in everyone's life and Coreen's mistake was marrying into the Church. Surely your all seeing and all forgiving God can realise that an honest mistake had been made and accept that it must be rectified?" Catriona asked with a tiredness that hinted this wasn't the first time she'd been involved in the same discussion.

Pushing the chair away from the table, Katherine stood and began to pace the room. Throwing her arms up she said, "I don't know what to accept. I come all the way out here from Ireland to arrive at a deserted train station, nearly die from the heat, spend the afternoon saying the last rights of a Father, find that I've no real lodgings, that the Sister who was supposed to help me settle has passed away, and even if she'd lived she wouldn't have been a Sister for long because she was getting married? It seems to me that this whole idea was one big mistake," Katherine said, thoroughly exasperated at the turn of events.

"I'm sorry you feel that way, you're sorely needed out here. I hate to throw your religion back at you, but isn't your first duty to others, not yourself? It seems to me that you're only thinking of one person at the moment." Catriona fixed her piercing stare in Katherine's direction.

Katherine was unsettled by the ease at which this woman could appear to see straight through her. What made it equally unsettling was the manner in which Catriona's blue eyes seemed to invade her very being. The woman was right—she was only thinking of herself and not others. "I'm sorry I didn't mean for it to sound like that but it's just, oh I don't know; what I've found myself in is as far removed as possible from what I expected it to be." Frustrated, Katherine sank back into her chair and threw her head in her hands.

Catriona paused in her attack and placed herself in the other woman's shoes. On top of the reception she'd received yesterday, the disorientation the Sister was feeling must be great. Most people in this world lived orderly lives based on set common principles and Katherine's set common principles had just been blown to the four ends of the earth. Reaching out to her across the table, Catriona's approach softened.

"I'm sorry I was so abrupt. I think I understand how you must be feeling and I'm sorry you feel that way. I know it must be a great surprise but please don't let it prejudice your overall opinion of Sister Coreen, my brother, and I," Catriona said, her face softening. "Let me get us some breakfast and we can talk some more." Despite coaxing, Katherine's head remained in her hands.

"Whether you believe it or not you're wanted and needed out here. I saw you working yesterday. You've a natural affinity with the people of this town. They opened to you and that's not something they do lightly. Please don't leave before you've had time to see the town in a better light." Catriona sensed the tension leaving the other woman's body. "And as for your accommodation, you're welcome in this house for as long as you wish. On behalf of my brother and I, let me extend to you an open invitation. Please just think about it while I make you some breakfast," Catriona rose from her chair and began to prepare the morning meal.

No words were spoken between the women as breakfast was

prepared. Sensing Katherine was preoccupied in her own situation, Catriona busied herself with frying up two generous slices of bacon, whilst searching her own thoughts. Why was she so keen to have this woman stay? Was it only because they were of similar age, or was there more to it than that? The only other woman she'd recently felt this comfortable with was Susan.

Catriona continued to absent-mindedly prepare a breakfast for the two of them; having done this so many times before for herself and her brother it had almost become second nature. Placing a plate of eggs, bacon and tomatoes in front of Katherine, she said, "I hope you're hungry. My brother and I usually only have two big meals a day—breakfast and dinner."

"Thank you. Yes, I'm quite hungry," Katherine replied, shaking herself from her previous pensive stance.

As Catriona busied herself with moving the hot fry pan off the top of the wood oven, out of the corner of her eye she saw that Katherine was waiting for her to take her place at the table. "Don't wait for me; please go ahead and start."

"I was waiting for you to sit down so I could bless the meal," Katherine replied.

"I suggest you start eating now. Since the death of my parents I've never had my meals blessed, nor have I entered a church. This is one lost soul that you'll never retrieve, *Sister,*" Catriona said.

"So be it. In that case, I'll bless my own," Katherine said as the other woman continued to clean up the breakfast mess that she'd made.

There was silence between the two as they ate. Taking the opportunity that the silence presented, Catriona's eyes took in the woman opposite her. She assessed her age as early to mid-twenties. Much of that assessment was based on Katherine's complexion. Such a fair complexion wasn't normally seen on women much past that age in the Australian countryside; for the sun was indiscriminate in the weathering caused to men and women's faces, aging it well beyond its years. If Katherine were to maintain such a complexion, she would definitely need greater protection than that offered by a nun's wimple. Katherine's face sported a sprinkling of freckles, the supposed bane of every good lady. Her brown, curly hair had been cropped in the manner normally associated with women in religious orders and Catriona couldn't help but think the cutting had been completed with a pair of sheep shears. However, by far the feature that lit up

Katherine's face were her eyes. They were the deepest green she'd ever seen. Looking into them reminded Catriona of emeralds in delicate settings, such as her mother used to wear on special occasions. Realising that she'd been caught staring, she started up a conversation, "So, how's your breakfast?"

"Thank you, it's fine. You're quite a good cook. Unfortunately I've never been able to master the art of cooking. The nuns who trained me found this out early in my training and ensured that I was never relegated to kitchen duties. Mind you, it took one meal to realise this." Katherine placed her knife and fork beside the plate and attempted some degree of reconciliation. "I'm sorry for my reaction earlier. I don't think I let you finish the rest of your story. How did Father Cleary react to the news that your brother and Sister Coreen wished to marry?"

"Well, at the beginning he was all thee's and thou's, fire and brimstone, just as you were a little while ago. He warned Coreen against the consequences of divorcing the Church to marry a man, and he informed her that under the rules of his Church he couldn't bless the marriage. It wasn't until he actually saw Alexander and Coreen together that he realised their relationship was more than just a stage in Coreen's life. Under the auspices of his own Church he couldn't condone the union, but he did begin to advise the two of them. He advised Coreen that she shouldn't rush into such a marriage, no matter how right it felt. He asked her to wait until you came out here and she could then discuss the consequences with you. His advice to Alexander was to try and find a church and priest who would be willing to marry them. Alexander found this hard to accept, but decided that it was best to go along with the Father's decision. In fact that's where he is now, attempting to find a priest to marry them.

"Don't get me wrong; he isn't some desperate man scouring the countryside. If problems arose and they couldn't find someone local, then they intended to go to Sydney and get married. Once they were, it wouldn't matter so much what the people thought. And if you really want to know, I don't think that it would have bothered them," Catriona finished.

Katherine shook her head. "I don't know what the Father expected to achieve with me. It seems very likely that she wouldn't have listened to me any way. What person would I have been to come this way and abuse your hospitality by stopping her from marrying your brother? I'm sorry about my abruptness this morning, given the loss that you must be feeling. Have you given much thought to what you propose to tell your brother when he returns?"

"With all that's happened in the past day I haven't given it much thought. I'm not sure when he'll be home, but I don't expect it will be for a while. Hopefully between now and then I'll come up with some way to break the news to him." Catriona rose and cleared the table. "But I expect that there are more immediate things to think about; like washing up and getting back to town as there's still a lot to do."

"Yes, you're right," Katherine answered. "Now if you like I'll help you with that and then I'll go and get dressed for the day."

Washing up for two wasn't like some of the wash ups Katherine had endured at the convent. It wasn't a chore she liked, but she didn't feel right leaving Catriona to look after the mess. Upon finishing she returned to her room with a pitcher of water and filled her hand basin to attend to her own ablutions. Having read her daily passage from the Bible, she turned, somewhat reluctantly, to place on her number two habit; her first one was still dirty from the previous day's efforts. Given the heat out in the countryside, she couldn't help but think that it wouldn't be long before this one was stained and dirty also. Using the remains of the water in her basin, she attempted to sponge off the stains on her soiled habit. Satisfied with herself that she'd done as much as she could, she carried both the water and the habit out the back of the house and looked for somewhere to hang the garment.

She watched as Catriona busied herself with hitching the horse to the wagon. Given that there was no produce to pick up, it seemed one horse would be sufficient for the task at hand. The wagon itself was indicative of most things Katherine could see around the farm. It was conventional and made to carry stores and produce, with its secondary purpose being the transportation of humans. Katherine hung her habit over a chair on the verandah to dry and headed toward the other woman to see if she could lend a helping hand.

"Right, well that's done," Catriona said to herself as she turned and careened into Katherine. "I'm sorry. I didn't hear you coming, are you all right?"

"Yes, nothing broken," said Katherine as she straightened the wimple on her head.

"Well, if that's the case, we'll get on with your education of the bush. I have to help this morning with the rest of the cleanup and this will give me the opportunity to introduce you to the town's matriarchs. However, I usually don't go into town on a regular basis and when I do it's normally astride a horse. You, on the other hand, will find that your trips around the immediate countryside will be a lot more frequent. So your first lesson will be how to manage a horse and wagon. I'll leave the more difficult task of preparing them for travel for a later time. For the moment though we'll concentrate on driving the rig. On the table on the verandah is a pair of gloves. I suggest you wear them as the reins can cause quite a few blisters on soft hands. Is there anything you wish to take into town with you?" Catriona queried, placing a mechanical implement in the back of the wagon.

"No, I don't think so," Katherine called over her shoulder as she looked for the pair of gloves Catriona had mentioned. She found them and put them on as she made her way back toward the wagon.

"The first thing you have to learn is that you use both hands when getting on and off. That was your mistake last night, trying to get off too quickly. Now hop up there and we'll start lesson number two." Catriona finished and made her way to the other side.

Katherine gathered her habit in her hand as she climbed aboard. "Yes, sorry about last night. I was a bit terse, but then I'm not used to falling off wagons."

Catriona grasped the reins with both hands. "Right, now the second thing to learn is how to hold the reins. Don't hold them too far apart or the horse won't know what you want him to do. He relies on you, through the reins, to direct him. If they're too loose he'll wander." Having given Katherine a practical demonstration, she handed over the reins to the nun. "Now you try. Hold them as I did and you shouldn't have a problem."

Katherine attempted to weave the leather through the third and fourth finger of her hands as Catriona had demonstrated. She found the procedure quite difficult but after some amount of floundering she was satisfied she'd succeeded in holding the reins as Catriona had. Turning toward Catriona for assessment proved to be the worst thing she could have done, as the motion of her turning body resulted in the lines of the horse being snapped accidentally, causing the horse and wagon to lurch forward. The horse, assuming they were on their way, started to break into a light canter.

"What do I do now!" Katherine cried, bringing her head and eyes around to the front.

"Well, I expect that unless you wish to go straight through the fence you'll have to wheel the horse's head," said Catriona, with a hint of amusement in her voice.

By now the reins controlling the wagon were being swung around in the air in time with Katherine's hands. "Wheel! Wheel? What's that mean?" the nun shouted.

"It means turn the horse, which you won't achieve with the reins above your head. I told you to keep your hands close together, not above your head like you were in a dance. Place them back down in your lap and move one of the reins slightly toward you and most of all don't shout, you'll scare the horse." The grazier calmly grabbed Katherine's hands and placed them in her lap. "Right, now pull the left rein toward you and you'll see that the horse's head will turn."

Katherine who had never controlled any form of gig was amazed. As the horse's head turned, so the wagon followed. Realising that they were turning in ever decreasing circles, Catriona eased Katherine's left hand back toward her right.

"Now that you've skipped a number of lessons, we will go back to your final lesson on the wagon and that's how to stop it. Slowly ease both reins toward you whilst at the same time tell the horse you wish to stop by saying 'whoa.' Then I'll put the brake on," Catriona instructed while guiding Katherine's hands back.

"Whoa!" said Katherine. The horse slowed down and then came to a complete halt. "Well, that was exciting. I've ridden in coaches before but I've never actually driven one. It can be most invigorating," Katherine said letting out a deep breath.

Catriona realised that although the wagon had come to a halt she hadn't yet released Katherine's hands from her grasp. They were so small compared to hers, and fragile, the way a woman's hands should be. Hers, in comparison, were broad with hard calluses forming a ridge below the fingers of each hand. So engrossed in what she was doing, she hadn't heard Katherine's question.

"Catriona, are you all right? Shouldn't you be putting the brake on now?" Katherine's eyes alternated between Catriona's face and her own hands, which were dwarfed by the larger and work-hardened ones.

Realising what she was doing, she dropped Katherine's

hands as if they were hot coals. "Yes, I'm all right. I was just daydreaming. Sorry about that," she said smiling. "Now I expect that based on the success of today's lesson I'll drive into town today. But don't worry, I'm sure you'll find yourself having to do this plenty of times if you're going to stay in Australia for any period of time."

Katherine smiled. "Thank you very much for the first lesson. I'm sure there'll be plenty of others, but in the meantime your driving will give me time to look at my surroundings. Last night it was too dark for me to see much of anything."

Leaving the property, Katherine noticed that the countryside to the right of the wagon was much like that which surrounded the farm. The gently undulating hills were covered with a brown-yellow straw like grass. This, Katherine was to later learn, was a crop known as wheat. As they passed she noticed that the wheat seemed to move in the wind's hypnotic dance, swaying in time to an invisible beat. It made the paddock come alive.

On the other side of the none-too-even road the grass was a green-brown colour. Remembering what Catriona had told her, the colour was probably due to the irregularity of rainfall in the district. Providing little shade in the paddock were groups of trees that couldn't really be called a copse in the Irish sense of the word, and grazing away in the middle distance were a group of the most unusual animals Katherine had ever seen. She'd first seen them on the train trip on her way to the town. Having stood up from the train seat to stretch her legs, she'd gone out onto the back platform only to see these great grey creatures with two legs and a massive tail bounding up the hill away from the train. It was at that moment the conductor had come through to the back platform and advised her that they were kangaroos, an animal that carries its young in a front pouch.

The kangaroos couldn't have sensed much danger from the passing wagon, as they seemed content to graze on what sparse vegetation there was. In deference to the wagon only one of the kangaroos paused from his repast, lifting his head and looking in their direction. Having contented himself that no threat was posed, he again lowered his head and continued to graze.

Catriona was also caught up in her own thoughts. She'd seen this countryside too many times to gaze at it longingly every time she headed into town. As a farmer she saw it as serving the purpose of maintaining cattle and growing a bumper wheat crop along with other crops, with the aesthetics of the countryside very rarely entering into the equation. However, if possible, this morning she paid it even less attention.

Although on the outside she was calm and composed, her mind was racing. It was happening again. It had seemed forever since she'd felt the same stirring of emotions she was experiencing. Although she'd hated her first governess with a passion, what she'd failed to tell Katherine were her feelings for her second governess. Adele Cooper had been employed by the Pelham family to refine Catriona after her mother realised that she wasn't growing out of the normal tomboy stage that most girls brought up on a farm go through. Elizabeth Pelham had realised that if Catriona were to have any chance of securing a husband, she would need the rough edges removed before too much longer.

Catriona at the time was seventeen and baulked at the idea of an old governess who would force her away from work outside and into the work of a housewife. However she was pleasantly surprised, for Adele being 25 proved to be not much older than her and they quickly became comrades in arms. Adele taught Catriona the finer graces of music, poetry, and art. While Catriona baulked at the first two it was the third — art that she seemed to have a natural affinity for. Her mother was pleased that she'd finally discovered a liking for something that was socially acceptable for a woman to do. Once such an interest in painting was awakened, Catriona and Adele would often spend hours in the countryside painting it from all perspectives. Over the months that followed, her skill with watercolours became quite advanced, creating paintings that seemed to come from a strength within.

However, overnight and without warning, Catriona again grew sullen and distant to her family and, in particular, Adele. Catriona's mother spoke to Adele in an attempt to discover the root of the problem but the governess advised Elizabeth Pelham that she'd done nothing to induce the young lady's present state. Her mother, concerned by her mood, confronted Catriona and in awkward sentences the girl explained to her mother that she was afraid she liked her new governess too much. Her mother assured her that it was natural for girls of her age to have such feelings for women close to their age. It was just a stage that all girls went through, which they quickly grew out of when they married. Her mother allayed her concerns by advising Catriona that she'd in fact had a crush on her governess when she was 15. This quietly confused Catriona, given that her own age was now closer to eighteen than fifteen. Rather than try to speak further with her mother about her feelings, which even at the best of times was a difficult task, she let the topic rest. She was satisfied that what she was experiencing wasn't out of the ordinary, and so she went back to her art classes with Adele.

As the weeks passed Catriona grew closer to Adele, who seemed at times at odds with how to deal with the situation. It wasn't that Adele was uncomfortable with the idea, but sensing the precariousness of the situation, she became more circumspect about the time and contact she shared with her younger charge. Regardless of her own burgeoning feelings, and in an attempt not to draw unwanted comments from the elder Pelham's, the governess forced herself to spend more time with Alexander.

Sensing that Adele seemed to be more content spending time with her brother, Catriona felt the need to draw her back into her own circle and so worked on a plan to do so. She'd often told Adele about a spot half a day's ride away that presented a wonderful opportunity for one of her watercolours. After repeated assurances to her mother that, as the place was still on the property, both women could cope with staying out overnight, they set off one morning for the spot that Catriona had often spoken about.

Catriona and Adele set out for their trip, the wagon packed as if they were going for a year, not just a couple of days. The sun was past mid-way when they eventually came in sight of the group of trees that surrounded a waterhole. It was just as Catriona had remembered it to be. It was hard to see the water through the surrounding trees for they served to create a hideaway from the outside world, a fact that Catriona most enjoyed. When life and problems on the property seemed to reach their limits, Catriona would often escape to this Shangri-La. It didn't seem to matter how bad things were in life as long as she still had this place to escape to, and now she was glad to be sharing it with Adele.

Searching along the outside of the trees, they eventually found the break that led them to the inside of the grove and the waterhole. It was hard going for the wagon and the team, as the trees had long since encroached on the path. This was what made it seem so dear for Catriona—it didn't matter what she tried to do to the waterhole and its surroundings; it essentially remained the same. She may have been able to temporarily tame nature and get it to bend to her will, but it wasn't long before nature came back to reclaim its own.

Breaking through, Catriona heard the governess catch her breath. The waterhole, fed by a small spring at one end, took up most of the enclosure. The surrounding trees were full-grown and healthy from the abundant water supply. To the left of the wagon was a clearing and traces of blackened ground, laying claim to human habitation in times past.

Catriona brought the horses to a halt next to the clearing. No longer encumbered by the noise of the constant movement of the wagon, Adele could hear the sound of the native birds that made the surrounding trees their home. She could just make out the sound of running water coming from one end. The elder woman shook her head, amazed that such a place could exist in such an otherwise bare area.

She scanned the area from left to right. "This is beautiful and so private. But how is it that it manages to survive in such a sparse country? The surrounding country is so dry; it's amazing."

"I'm not quite sure, but my father believes the area is fed by an underground spring. You see, ground in this area is well fed by artesian water and this point may be where the water is higher to the surface than in other places on the property." Catriona alighted from the wagon with one of the many blankets her mother had packed. "We'll have to set up a shelter for the night but first things first. I'll spread this so we can have some lunch; after all, it's been a long ride."

Aware that she wasn't being much help, Adele got off the wagon and grabbed the picnic basket, bringing it to where Catriona was preoccupied with spreading the blanket. Adele looked toward the spring that occupied the greater part of their hideaway and then back to Catriona. "Now I know you must be hungry but that long ride has left me quite hot. The water looks too inviting for words so I think I'll go for a swim. Are you going to join me?"

At the word of a swim the younger woman faltered. She loved the water yet she'd never learnt how to swim. While it was fine to wade her feet in the river near home, this was a deep waterhole in which a person could easily drown. Fearing that she

would be less in the governess' eyes she said the first thing that
came into her mind, "I can't go swimming, I haven't brought
anything to swim in." She took pains to adjust the blanket and
empty the wagon of more of its contents.

"Oh that's fine, neither have I," Adele answered. "There's
no-one here except you and I, so I'm going to bath in my chemise. We're not expecting visitors are we?" Adele challenged,
fully knowing that no-one was expected. Shrugging as Catriona
turned away, she continued to undress.

Catriona could feel herself being backed into a corner. To
try and delay the agony caused by her embarrassing secret, she
slowly removed her outer garments leaving herself in nothing
but her chemise.

Try as she might she couldn't help her eyes from wandering
in Adele's direction. She looked so different when she wasn't
wrapped up in lace and crinoline. She wasn't a fragile woman by
any means, yet she didn't seem to have the roundness that Catriona had seen in her mother. Stealing a look toward Adele's chest,
Catriona felt her breath taken away by what she saw. Her eyes
met a sight that was not as big and pendulous like her mother's,
yet they were full all the same. Catriona felt ashamed when she
thought of her own breasts for they had only just begun to fill
out, but they didn't show any such promise. They would never be
like Adele's; hers were beautiful.

Unaware of Catriona's shy curiosity, the governess called
over her shoulder as she walked toward the bank, "Well, are you
coming in?" Without pausing for an answer, she waded in until
all that could be seen of her were her shoulders. She then seemed
to pause, take her bearings before diving headlong into the
water. Catriona, who had been watching her up until that
moment, rushed toward the waters' edge. Scanning the top of the
waterhole Adele was nowhere to be seen. Becoming frantic she
began to wade into the water in search of Adele. What if she was
struggling caught in the reeds off the bank? She wouldn't be able
to help; she couldn't swim. Left with nothing but her voice
Catriona called out Adele's name.

Like a bolt out of the blue, Adele surfaced directly in front
of the younger woman, her hair clinging tightly to her shoulders.
But this wasn't the only thing that clung to her body. The plain
cotton chemise that had been so opaque only moments before
was now see-through and Catriona couldn't help but stare. The
lower part of the other woman's body was still concealed by the

water she was standing in, but her upper half was quite exposed. The damp cloth now outlined the breasts that to Catriona were so beautiful. Adele's brown nipples were visible as they pressed against the cotton material.

Her ogling was broken by Adele's voice, and realising her actions, Catriona blushed. Slowly she broke her gaze, moving it up the body and bringing her eyes to rest on the strange expression masking Adele's face, which seemed to be waiting for an answer to a question that Catriona hadn't heard. Adele seemed to be smiling but at the same time trying hard not to. Despite her efforts Catriona could still see the smile in her eyes.

"Well, are you going to stand in the water all day or are you going to come in for a swim? The water is lovely and cool, just what you need," Adele said enigmatically.

Catriona lowered her eyes, her mind in turmoil. She'd been caught staring but that didn't shame her and neither did the feeling created in her body as a result of the staring. What did humiliate her was, as a country girl, she couldn't swim. "I can't," she answered ashamedly, "I can't swim."

Adele folded her arms across her chest. "Oh, I see. Well, that's not a problem. The water we're standing in is only waist deep. Let me teach you." Adele could see the look of worry on Catriona's face, "What's the matter, don't you trust me? I won't hurt you, I promise."

Catriona avoided Adele's stare. "I'm sorry. It's not that. It's just you don't want to have to fuss over me. It will spoil your afternoon."

"You're wrong, Catriona, it doesn't bother me to fuss over you," Adele answered gently. Thinking that she'd said too much she rushed, "And besides, my afternoon would certainly be spoiled if I had to think of you sitting on the bank."

Catriona felt caught in her own emotions. She was heartened by the other woman's words and couldn't help but think that no-one ever worried over her—as a girl she was left very much to her own devices. At last here was someone who did care and Adele was right; the water was refreshingly cool. Head bowed she nodded her assent.

"There now that's better, I promise I won't let you drown. Now the way that I'll teach you is that I'll support you in the water by placing my arms under your waist. I then want you to concentrate on two things. First I want you to stroke the water like this." Adele paused to show Catriona what to do. "Then I want you to kick at the water with your legs like so." Adele demonstrated yet again. "Now you must trust me, I won't let you drown." Adele looked deeply into Catriona's eyes as she straightened herself.

At that moment Catriona felt that she could trust the other woman with her life. At first the lesson went quite well and she could feel Adele's strong arms supporting her in the water. The stroking with her arms was progressing and, with every stroke and Adele's reassuring words, she began to feel more confident. Catriona decided that it was the time to incorporate the kicking part of the lesson and it was then that things began to get out of control. She could feel her body rocking from side to side and felt that if she could only kick harder this would stop.

Catriona kicked so hard that she began to roll away from Adele's arms. Sensing that she was falling she panicked and wildly thrashed her arms about. Before feeling completely out of control, Catriona felt Adele's other arm encircle her waist in a vice-like grip and pull her upright. Leaning into Adele's shoulder she could feel herself crying as Adele's words of comfort reassured her.

Standing in the water which only moments ago had engulfed her, Catriona felt secure in the woman's arms. She clung onto Adele, afraid that if she let go she would fall back into the water. However, what held greater significance for Catriona was that she couldn't think of any place she would rather be than in Adele's arms. As she calmed down she began to feel an emotion surging through her that she'd never felt before. It was a tingling feeling, coursing through her body from her toes up to her fingers.

Breaking away from her own self-assessment Catriona remembered who the owner of the arms encircling her was—her governess—the same person who was now kissing the top of her head in between whispered endearments. Feeling a need to see her face, Catriona broke the embrace and looked up into Adele's eyes.

"Catriona, I should have never made you come out here. You should have stayed on the bank where it was safe." Adele reached up to wipe the moisture from the younger woman's tear stained face.

"I couldn't think of a safer place than being here with you now. I shouldn't have been so eager to learn; the fault was mine not yours," Catriona replied returning Adele's stare.

For a moment time and surroundings seemed to fade and all that mattered was the woman in front of her. She felt Adele bring her face down and ever so slightly brush her lips with her own, igniting a fire inside of Catriona. Reaching up, it was Catriona who eagerly sought Adele's lips. The feelings that coursed through her body were like nothing she'd ever experienced before. Wrapping her arms tightly around Adele, she moulded her own body into the other woman's. The feeling of Adele's hand playing up and down her spine sent another delightful shock through Catriona's body and, unsure of what else to do, Catriona began to stroke Adele in the same way. In response, the governess let out a deep moan that seemed to bring Catriona back to the present, and she drew back sharply. Startled by her withdrawal, Adele looked at Catriona with puzzlement.

"I'm sorry. I didn't know I was hurting you. It's just that, well I've never done this before and I don't want to hurt you." A reddened Catriona could feel herself stumbling over her words as she shyly lifted her eyes to Adele's. Looking back at her was a face lined with a smile and radiating warmth that only served to accentuate her already beautiful features.

"Oh, no, you didn't hurt me, that wasn't why I made that sound. On the contrary, your touch...er, pleased me greatly." Adele's face suddenly became serious. "I know that this is new to you but you must realise that I'd never do anything to hurt you." Adele paused as if searching for words, yet still looked at Catriona, "That's why I must ask you something. Catriona, now you know how I feel for you, but you must be sure that it's what you want also. You must be aware that your choice to continue won't be easy for what we have done so far is regarded by most as unspeakable and would cause great pain to both your family and us if it were ever found out. That's why I must ask you if you understand what you want." Adele looked down into the deep azure eyes of the woman she'd unwittingly fallen in love with.

Catriona was puzzled. She couldn't rightly understand why something so wonderful was so wrong and she creased her face in thought. "I'm sorry, I don't understand. I've never kissed anyone like I just kissed you and it felt wonderful. What's so unspeakable about what I feel for you?"

"It's wrong in the eyes of society. The way I feel for you, Catriona, is the way that a man would feel for a woman. Love of the same sex is an abomination in the eyes of the Church and society. I love you as only a woman should love a man, and I want to share that love with you, but not unless you also want the same. The decision is yours, Catriona," Adele replied, seeing the dawning look of recognition in the younger woman's eyes.

It was at that moment that Catriona stood at the gateway in her life. To open that gate and step through it would mean a different path. Adele was right—what they had done wasn't socially acceptable, but neither was Catriona with her tomboy ways. It may have been wrong but she'd never felt at such peace with herself and this was a feeling she liked. Reaching out, she took Adele's hand in her own before slowly looking up into her face. "I want you to share that love with me, Adele, and I want you to teach me how to love you in return."

Adele's face lit up in a smile as she took Catriona's hand and placed a kiss in its palm. Then she guided her out of the water to where the blanket had earlier been spread. Adele sat down with Catriona seated opposite her. Leaning over, Adele loosened the ties on Catriona's chemise. With tentative hands Catriona followed Adele's lead. Sliding her hands under the cloth onto Catriona's back, Adele could feel the softness of her skin. As Adele's hands continued their journey around to her front she raised them to cup Catriona's breasts. They were small and firm and responded well to Adele's touch. Adele reached down and peeled the wet chemise from Catriona's shoulders.

Catriona could feel Adele's eyes upon her. Afraid that she wouldn't be enough for Adele, she panicked and fumbled with Adele's chemise to hide her confusion.

Adele gently halted Catriona's hand with her own. "No, my love, let me love you first. There will be time for me later." Leaning over, she placed a tender kiss on Catriona's mouth.

Still kissing her, she lowered Catriona back onto the blanket and trailed her kisses to Catriona's eyes and throat. Catriona had never experienced such a sensation. She felt as if her heart had taken on a mind of its own and that she was no longer in control of her own rapid breathing. Soon all that she could concentrate on were the light kisses that Adele continued to tenderly apply to her body.

Catriona feared her heart was set to burst straight through her skin as again she felt Adele's hand cup her breast. The older woman's thumbs lightly traced the responsive nipples of the woman below her as her kisses followed a trail down Catriona's throat and across her shoulder to the breast that she was cupping. Catriona gasped as the older woman lowered her teasing lips to her nipple. Finding it hard to contain herself she instinctively moved her hand to grasp the thick tresses of Adele's hair. She couldn't help but think that if such an act were so wrong, who would want to be right? Adele's tongue played with Catriona's nipple until it blossomed in her mouth. Leaving a path of kisses across her chest, Adele paid the other the same amount of attention.

It had been so long for Adele. After Louise she'd felt that she would never find another lover, and now she had. Admittedly Catriona was young but her actions and her thoughts continually amazed her. Adele returned her thoughts to giving the beautiful and so responsive woman beneath her as much pleasure as possible.

Catriona felt as if her responses had refocused themselves to a deeper primal need and her body took on a life of its own. With every tease of Adele's tongue on her nipple, she could feel her body arch to meet Adele's. Her hands left Adele's hair as she clutched Adele to her so that when her body arched it moulded with her lover's. She could hear herself whispering Adele's name, but it was as if she was a spectator to all that was occurring. She knew she wanted Adele to continue her explorations but she didn't want this to end. In truth, she didn't know exactly what it was she wanted.

As Catriona's nipples hardened in response to her passionate onslaught, Adele kissed the hollow between the young woman's breasts and followed this path to reach the top of Catriona's bloomers. Momentarily easing herself off Catriona, she peeled the bloomers down to reveal a small crown of dark hair. Bending down, she kissed the crown causing Catriona to moan much like Adele had earlier. Pulling the cloth the rest of the way, she lifted them clear of Catriona and placed them to one side.

Bending over her, Adele kissed her gently on the lips. She could feel Catriona's rapid breath on her face and the beads of perspiration on her forehead. She, too, was hot but her heat was from her exertions, unlike that of Catriona's. Reaching down, she placed her hand on top of one of Catriona's legs and ever so gently she allowed her hand to follow the inside of the younger woman's inner thigh. She exerted a gentle pressure pulling her leg toward her and revealing Catriona's eager point of desire. Bending down, she kissed the soft flesh that nestled between the woman's thighs.

Catriona felt as if she was about to explode. Her breathing

had quickened and she knew that she was moaning, but it was like a dream. She could feel Adele's lips and the soft toying nips that she was placing on the inside of her legs. Her hands clenched the blanket in an attempt to stop herself from screaming out Adele's name as she felt Adele's tongue play on a fold of skin no-one, except for herself, had ever touched. As she parted the folds with her tongue, it seemed to Catriona that Adele was searching for something special. It wasn't long before she found what she was after and Catriona gasped, for it was as if Adele had found the centre of her being. Letting go of the blanket, Catriona placed her hands on Adele's head and arched her hips toward her busy mouth. Catriona felt as if a bright light was piercing the inside of her eyelids. Time seemed to stand still and then, in an eruption of pleasure, it was as if her lower body possessed a mind of its own. She continued thrusting her hips toward Adele's mouth until she could raise them no more. Finally spent, her body went limp.

Adele moved back up placing her body next to Catriona's. Leaning across, Adele kissed her on the lips and Catriona tasted what could only be a part of herself. Rolling across, Catriona wrapped her arms and legs around Adele. "Adele, I love you. I've never felt like this before and I love you for making me feel this way. Please don't ever leave me. I don't know if I could ever love or feel the same way again," Catriona pleaded, holding Adele tightly in her arms.

The romantic interlude between herself and Adele proved to be memorable, but all the same relatively short. For six months both managed to lead the dual lives of governess and student as well as lovers. However, during a period when her father and brother were away on business and her mother was supposed to be at afternoon tea, Elizabeth Pelham discovered them. Despite her pleas of love for Adele, her mother gave Adele her notice without reference. Her mother refused to speak to her, instead she sent her to her room. In her confusion, all Catriona knew was that she'd lost the one person she'd loved because of the bigotry of her mother. It was then that she decided she would never marry just to satisfy the social requirements of a female in the Australian countryside.

Since that time in her life Catriona hadn't met another lover.

Despite this she was still resolute for she knew what she wanted. It was just that in a small country town her celibacy was somewhat enforced. However, after such a long period of time she'd again found someone. The irony was that she couldn't have directed her feelings toward a more non-receptive person—a nun.

It would be so simple to introduce Katherine to the town matriarchs and then see her nicely settled in a well-to-do family, however she was uncomfortable with such an option. She felt there were redeeming features in Katherine—the main one being her ability to speak her mind—and living in a stifled town house would soon see this erased from her. Her work would become nothing more than a confidant to the daughters of the landowners and wealthy families. Despite all these smoke screen reasons as to why the nun should remain at the homestead, the main one was still left unspoken by the grazier. Catriona had again found someone that she liked too much.

Chapter Four

The ride through the streets of the town revealed a small
change to the devastation that they had left the afternoon before.
Small work parties were moving amongst the rubble that once
made up stores and homes, putting to one side items that could
be used again and discarding anything which couldn't into an
ever increasing pile on a cart. The nun watched as Catriona
acknowledged the calls of good morning given to her by the
small work gangs made up of men already dusty from the day's
exertions. She seemed to be well liked by those who acknowledged her but it was strange that the compliments paid weren't in
the same way as one would expect to be given to a woman. There
were no raising of hats or the use of the word "Miss"; moreso the
acknowledgments were like those given to a work partner or an
equal.

Katherine thought this strange but better judgment and second sense of propriety prevailed; deciding that querying the
workmen's manner was better done back at the farm rather than a
place where she risked the brunt of Catriona's tongue. *She's a
strange woman*, Katherine thought, for she didn't dress like any
woman she had seen before, yet she seemed unconcerned about
her attire. This morning she was again dressed, as she had been
when they first met, wearing dusty work boots and white pants.
The pants this day were complemented by a maroon shirt and a
broad brimmed hat. *She was a strong woman*, Katherine thought,
fortunate to be in the position where she didn't have to marry for

either the satisfaction of her parents or financial imperatives. For it was obvious that while Catriona and her brother didn't have the incredible fortune she'd evidenced in certain homes in Ireland, it was obvious that they did possess some degree of independent wealth. She couldn't help but wonder if she'd been given the same opportunities, would she have opted for the uncomplicated life of a convent?

Catriona drew the wagon to one side of the main street, interrupting Katherine's train of thought. Bringing the horse to a halt, the driver alighted from the wagon and came around to Katherine's side. With a rather impertinent grin she held her hand out to Katherine. "Now, I know you feel that you can get off this wagon by yourself, but based on your success last night I think it would be better if I helped you this time." Catriona stood poised to assist Katherine from her seat.

Deciding that discretion was the better part of valour, Katherine took the proffered hand and stepped down from the wagon. Steadying her as she alighted, Katherine was surprised at the strength she felt within Catriona's hands. Such strength would be well served on a farm, while hers in comparison weren't much good for anything at all.

Moving around to the back, Catriona reached in and picked up the mechanical implement she'd placed in the wagon before leaving the property and continued on toward one of the few stores left standing. Walking up the steps, she shifted the implement to one hip and turned toward the woman by the wagon. "I'll just be a few minutes; is there anything you need while we're here?"

Katherine couldn't think of anything she needed and besides she didn't have an overly large sum of money. The convent she'd come from had supplied her with just a little over enough money to see her to her destination and assured her that the local parish would then support her. However, by what she'd seen so far, with the exception of Catriona's home, the town in general was far from being affluent. How the population was supposed to support her she didn't know. "N...no, thank you, I came here with all I need; however, I'll come in to have a look around if I may." Katherine followed Catriona up the steps.

"Feel free, there's no need to ask. Besides I'm sure that the proprietor would be more than happy to see a new face in town."

Walking into the shop Katherine noticed that the interior was markedly darker than outside, and pausing a moment to adjust, she cast her eyes around a store which seemed to hold a little of everything. There were picks, shovels, and all sorts of weaponry, bolts of cloth, and provisions to name a few. Unlike the shops she was used to back home, it was quite conceivable that all the months shopping could be done through this one well-stocked store. Turning toward the counter, Katherine made an attempt to identify the proprietor of such a thriving shop. Standing behind the counter, amongst piles of stores and equipment, was a short woman with Germanic features. Her blond hair had been pulled into a functional bun, capably suiting Katherine's impression of what a storekeeper might look like. She had a friendly face that served to put the nun at ease and the pair of round wire-rimmed glasses that both suited her and added to her air as a proprietor of such a store. The dress she wore was a practical one, made out of a light blue cotton material covered by a freshly starched apron for the day's duties.

Catriona placed the metal implement on the counter. "Morning, Susan. You seemed to have been a bit fortunate in yesterday's dust storm."

Susan pointed to the implement dominating the bench top. "Before I answer you, miss, get that off my clean counter. I've got to lay cloth on this top and the last thing I want are grease stains caused by the bits and pieces you place up here. The last time you did that it cost me two yards of fine lace. Now put that thing down on the floor where it belongs."

Suitably chastened, and with a hint of mockery, Catriona touched her hand to her hat before placing the implement on the floor. With smiling eyes, Susan continued, "Now as I was saying, I'm glad this old building is made of stone rather than wood. It may be costly to maintain, but it's paid for itself after yesterday's storm. Unfortunately my laundry hasn't fared so well but it was really only a wood outhouse." Pausing in her discussion she turned to see the nun waiting by the store's entrance. "I see you've brought the new Sister in as well. As Catriona's manners seemed to have abandoned her, *as they often do*, let me introduce myself." Susan walked toward Katherine, hand extended. "I'm Susan Crosier; welcome to Australia."

"Thank you for the welcome, I'm Sister Katherine Flynn." Katherine took Susan's firm yet petite hand, shaking it in return. "Please excuse me for staring, but I can't get over the amount of goods you have in this one little store." Katherine's gaze again returned to her surroundings.

"Well purchasing goods out here is a little different to what you're possibly used to, I suspect. My store is patronised by people as far as 200 miles away and they don't get the opportunity to come in on a weekly basis. Why, there are some families we only see every six months or so. So you see it's important that they can purchase all their items at once so as to make things easy." Susan explained, proudly looking upon the varied items, uniformly arranged around the walls.

"Is there anything you see that you'd like to purchase, Sister Flynn?" Susan asked, patiently waiting to assist Katherine in any way that she could.

Looking around her, Katherine began to realise how difficult her stay in this country was going to be. There were a number of personal items she knew she required but at the moment she wasn't in any position to afford them. Hiding the shame she felt at not having the wealth to buy even the most rudimentary items she walked toward the far corner of the store. "No, thank you. I've more than what I require. I'm quite happy just to browse thank you." Katherine said a little too brusquely before turning in the pretence of looking around the store.

Susan and Catriona exchanged glances behind the nun's back. From the arrival of Sister Coreen they were more than aware that Sisters were sent out here with little or no money to fare for themselves. Pride was something someone in Katherine's position could ill afford and Catriona couldn't help but think that it was going to be a long road for Katherine unless she learned to deal with her pride and accept the helping hand of others.

"Well, if you're going to stay with me out on the farm, I don't intend to be responsible for your dying of heat stroke. As you must be aware from yesterday's near disaster, it's extremely important that you keep your head covered when you're out in the sun. So if you've no objections, I'm going to buy you a hat; as a welcome present." Catriona's tone left no scope for discussion. Without another word Catriona headed toward the corner of the store where such things were kept. "Now what size are you?"

Hearing the determination in the other woman's voice, Katherine knew that to refuse would only bring about an embarrassing scene. Resignedly she moved toward where Catriona was standing, a hat already in her hand. Katherine's hands unconsciously reached up to her wimple. "I'm not quite sure of my hat size; it's been such a long time since I've owned one."

Catriona handed a hat to the nun. "Well, try this one on. It has a nice broad brim and should keep the sun well off your face."

Placing it on her head, Katherine felt as if Catriona had made the perfect choice. Only then did she become aware of the silence in the shop. She turned in time to see that both Catriona and Susan were in the process of restraining themselves from bursting into laughter. Confused, Katherine asked, "What's wrong?"

"Have you any idea how silly you look with both your wimple and a hat on?" Catriona managed to say before losing control and breaking into gales of laughter.

"I'm sorry, my dear, it's not you we're laughing at, but I can't help myself when I think of the complete inappropriateness of your outfit for the Australian climate." The shopkeeper managed to say before she too joined Catriona.

Katherine searched for a mirror being keen to see for herself just what she looked like. Moving to one placed on the counter near the hats she soon realised how ridiculous she looked. Placing the mirror down she felt a flush colouring her cheeks. "Well, that settles it then. I can't possibly wear a hat with my wimple. Thank you for your generous offer, Catriona, but I'm sorry I can't accept." She removed the hat and handed it back to the now silent grazier.

Surprised at Katherine's response, Catriona's manner sobered. "Well, there's another solution, Katherine. Don't wear that ridiculous head covering." In turn she handed the hat back to Katherine.

"You know that's not possible, this is a part of my habit," the nun responded stubbornly, handing the hat back to Catriona.

"This is ridiculous, you're being silly. I don't care if that wimple is glued to your head. The simple fact of the matter is that if you don't wear a hat you'll suffer under the Australian sun. The sun out here does not differentiate based on religion, *Sister Flynn*," Catriona responded in an angry tone.

There they stood—Catriona having adopted the belligerent stance of hands on hips almost challenging Katherine to counter the logic of her argument, while Katherine stood, hands tightly clasped, calling upon all her willpower to keep her Irish temper in check. Susan, who thankfully was standing just out of the direct path of the confrontation, tried hard and managed to stifle a laugh at the two proud and stubborn women in front of her.

Such a situation, which was rapidly gathering momentum, meant that if the staring contest went much further there'd be no chance at reconciliation. It was at that point the older woman decided to intercede.

She shook her head and moved toward Catriona to remove the now crumpled straw hat from her hands. "For heaven's sake look at both of you. Catriona, you should know better. Katherine has barely been in this country a day and you're trying to map out her life for her. If she doesn't want the hat, then you may buy it, but you can't force her to wear it. And you, Katherine, should just step back for a moment. We're not trying to take your religion away from you, all we're trying to do is to point out that maybe your habit needs to be adapted to suit the different conditions out here. However, if you don't want to wear the hat, then so be it. Either way I cannot have the both of you standing in the middle of my store arguing—you'll scare all the customers away." She finished, reshaped the hat, and returned it to its original place.

Both women continued to stare at each other, realising the petulance of their situation but both unwilling to say so. Catriona seemed riveted to her spot in the store. Chin slightly forward and eyes afire, Katherine couldn't help but be angered by the woman in front of her. Coupled with this anger was a frustration that Catriona, with her family wealth, could afford to adopt such a position, while she, with little more to her name than a handful of pounds, couldn't. It frustrated her even more that one could afford to be stubborn and proud if you were self-sufficient.

Catriona, while still not shifting from her position, was regarding Katherine in much the same manner. She begrudgingly admired the nun's ability to mask her anger, although the whiteness of her clenched knuckles betrayed her real emotional state. Her facial features were like a mask, reminding Catriona of a mid-twenties version of her first tutor. With the exception of her green eyes, which had taken on a deeper glistening hue, Katherine's emotions couldn't be read on her face and this greatly frustrated the other woman. She was used to relating to her brother's moods that were easily read and therefore easily dealt with. Shaking out of her reverie, she realised such an impasse couldn't last. She definitely didn't have all day to stand here; there was too much to be done in the wake of the storm and, besides, Katherine still had to be delivered to the town's ladies for their inspection.

With prideful regret she was the one to break the silence between the two. "Susan, you're right. I've more important things to do than to stand around and crowd your store. As for Sister Flynn, she has an appointment with the gentlewomen of the town. Such a social event I'm sure she'll enjoy, and I'd hate to keep the Ladies Committee waiting. Sister Flynn, if you'll follow me, I'll take you to your appointment." Catriona made no attempt to return to the first name familiarity the two had shared earlier that morning, and with a nod toward Susan she strode out of the store, not bothering to see if the other woman was following.

Catriona took great delight in watching Katherine struggle with her habit to get onto the wagon. She knew that to watch her haul herself unaided and somewhat unceremoniously onto the wagon was inconsiderate, but she couldn't help herself. She didn't like to be bested by anyone, especially someone new to the town.

"Thank you for your help," Katherine said sarcastically, looking straight ahead. "I must refine my skills in getting on and off of this wagon, it's something that everyone should learn to do by *themselves*." Katherine straightened her skirt.

Damn it if that woman doesn't make me feel like a child, Catriona thought. *Yes, it was small-minded but she deserved it,* Catriona stopped herself. She sounded like a spoilt child. Masking her emotions, she used the whip perhaps a little too liberally to urge the horse forward. The result was a jumpy start causing Katherine to hang on, her lips pursed at Catriona's actions.

Little was said between the two during the short journey through town, leaving Katherine with time to view the structures left standing in the main street. *The work parties must have had an early start this morning,* Katherine thought, as the street began to regain some semblance of normality again. Like Susan's, the two main buildings still standing were also made of stone. One was a bank, which until yesterday, must have been complemented by two beautiful arched windows, now shattered. The bank's door was blown away by the storm so that the building more resembled a blind man, open-mouthed in shock. Katherine surmised that it would be quite a while before the windows would be replaced.

The next building, unlike the previous, had bars where windows normally would have been and it was obvious that it formed some sought of constabulary. *Well, at least the Superin-*

tendent wouldn't be preoccupied with the cost of replacing windows, Katherine thought. She idly wondered what sort of criminal problem they had in Australia and then remembered Catriona's passing comments on bushrangers the night before. She wondered if this had been said just to scare her or in fact if there was a genuine problem of highway robbery within the district.

As they reached the end of the street the wagon turned around a group of bedraggled trees before Katherine actually noticed the structure in front of her. It was a large two-story residence that looked completely out of place in the Australian countryside. Made mainly of red brick, it was completed by a verandah on both levels. Such a two-story house was obviously the real mark of wealth in the Australian country, but Katherine couldn't help but think how ridiculous it looked. Catriona guided the wagon up the gravelled semicircular driveway, halting at the front entrance.

Before she could commence her attempt to get down from the wagon Catriona was there offering her hand. Given the woman's reactions at the store, her actions now seemed to be a complete about face. *She is such a strange woman*, Katherine thought as she looked down at Catriona in a confused manner.

"I don't mind certain people seeing the more cantankerous side of my nature, but I'll be damned if I'll give a bunch of interfering, beak-nosed, old women more fuel for their fire. Please let me help you down," Catriona explained quietly, again offering her hand.

Katherine was about to baulk at this about face in Catriona, but given the sudden back down by the other woman, she thought the better of it. Besides, there was nothing to be gained by shaming her, and Katherine had to remember that she was a guest under Catriona's roof. Recognising the willpower it must have taken for her to do what she'd just done, she placed her hand into Catriona's gloved one and was gently assisted from the wagon.

"Well, I'll leave you in the hands of the town ladies' welcoming committee. I've some business to attend to and there's still a lot of work that needs to be done in the town." Catriona consulted a fob watch she'd pulled from her pocket. "If you don't mind I'll call for you again at, oh, about 4.30pm?"

Katherine hadn't realised that Catriona wouldn't be joining her and the ladies for lunch. She found such an action quite strange. Surely this woman, with her relative affluence would also be joining her. Besides, not knowing these people, she was at odds as to what she was going to talk about for the rest of the day. "You mean you're not coming in? I'm sure that the ladies won't be concerned by your attendance."

A wry smile tugged at the corners of the grazier's mouth. "To be honest, I wouldn't be caught dead in this viper's nest of gossips nor would they welcome my presence. Mind you, it would be worth it just for the look on their faces but maybe not on your first visit. No, Katherine, this is something you must do alone. They don't approve of me and I don't approve of their patriarchal attitudes. This is Australia, not Ireland, and every person is the same or at least should be, and should have the right to live their lives as they see fit." She placed her watch back in her pocket.

Katherine took some solace in the fact that Catriona had again resorted to using her first name. *However, why didn't these women approve of Catriona? She seemed respected well enough by the people they had met in town and the people she'd worked beside yesterday. What was going on?* Katherine started to ask but then noticed the front door of the house was opening. The sight of the woman at the top of the stairs was enough for Katherine to whisper in hushed tones, "I'm not quite sure what's going on here and I'd like some sort of explanation, but obviously now isn't the time. I don't like being a pawn in anyone's game and I'd like some answers. As for being here till 4.30pm, I don't think that's such a good idea; 3.30pm will be a better time to get home before it's too dark." Katherine hurried to finish as the woman moved down the stairs to meet her.

"Well, 3.30pm it is then." Catriona lifted herself back onto the wagon's seat, not waiting to acknowledge the other woman who also seemed to be doing her best to ignore Catriona. As the wagon pulled away, Katherine wondered what she'd gotten herself into. Watching the retreating horse for as long as was acceptable, Katherine then turned to face the woman in front of her.

"How do you do, Sister? My name is Mrs Muriel Greystone. Welcome to our little part of Australia. Please come inside out of the sun and meet the other ladies. It's far too hot for a lady of your breeding to stand out in such heat." Without waiting for a response, Mrs Greystone placed her hand under Katherine's elbow and guided her up the stairs and into the house.

Katherine found herself guided into a large entrance hall

where another five similarly dressed women awaited her arrival. She knew she'd been out of the world of fashion in Ireland for some time, but still these ladies were wearing fashions that were popular prior to Katherine even entering the convent. The dresses were tight-laced narrow waisted outfits that seemed to have outlived their era of fashion. They were obviously inappropriate for the climate, but seemed to suit this group of overly made up women perfectly. It seemed to Katherine as if walking into the house had signalled the halting of time and the reality of what was occurring outside. She kept her thoughts to herself, nodding politely as she was introduced to each of the ladies in turn prior to being marshalled through to the parlour where tea and cake awaited them.

The ladies were polite enough, if not overly so as they probed for news of what they termed "the Old Country." They seemed to be greatly interested in the current fashions, of which Katherine couldn't be of any great help. She provided them with as much as she could, excusing her ignorance due to her time in the convent where fashion wasn't at the forefront of her daily life. They seemed to halt at this comment, as if they had been chastised for forgetting the inappropriateness of their questions to a nun. Katherine was relieved when the conversation was steered toward topics that she was able to discuss. Fashion, in all honesty, hadn't held a great interest for her even before she joined the convent. Restricting their questions to her trip out to Australia, the weather, and how Sydney was looking, Katherine seemed to satisfy them with her responses. Many of the women professed they rarely travelled to Sydney with at least one saying her last visit was for her "season" which, from Katherine's assessment, must have been some time ago. The conversation then wound itself to Katherine's arrival and the lack of a proper reception committee, with the nun's response allaying their fears by saying that given the events of the past 24 hours, the lack of a reception committee was understandable. Not so subtly the conversation then turned toward Katherine's current accommodation arrangements.

"So, Sister Flynn, where are you currently residing?" Mrs Monteith queried, reaching forward with her gnarled hand to place another slice of cake on her plate.

Despite her absence from such games since joining the convent, Katherine inwardly smiled at this social game. Given that Catriona had deposited her outside the house, it was only natural that it was her she was staying with. Rather than point out the seemingly obvious, she decided she would also refresh her skills at how the game was played. "Well, I'm currently staying at the Pelham residence," she answered trying to make Catriona's house sound somewhat grand.

"It's a property, my dear." A patronising Mrs Greystone patted her hand, feeling it her duty to correct Katherine. "We very rarely regard all but the most affluent of houses on the land as other than a property. But no mind, this is all part of your education into our way of life. So do you intend to move into town once it's regained some semblance of order? I don't expect to have you live in that hovel on the outskirts of town and I'm sure one of the ladies here would be honoured to accommodate you."

Katherine found herself in a situation she didn't care to be in. To answer in the affirmative would see her moved into town, pandering to the whims of a select few, slowly losing touch with those she'd come out to help. And besides, what would Catriona think? She'd been polite enough to give her a room when she most needed one and she certainly hadn't seen any of these ladies yesterday helping in the town's clean up. It would be impolite to re-pack her belongings and move into town. Although all that they had seemed to do so far was disagree, Katherine felt she would miss the other woman's company if she was forced to move. But how would she extricate herself from this predicament? She was sure that if she declined this offer it would result in her offending the gathering. Seeking for a way out of the corner she'd been placed into, she hit upon a solution.

"I thank you for you most gracious offer; however, it's currently more prudent that I live out at the Pelham property. I'm most aggrieved by the loss of Sister Coreen and there are a number of her papers and small personal items that are currently out at the property that must be sorted out for return to her family in Ireland. As a fellow Sister of her convent, I feel I should be the one to do this. So, at least until the return of Father Cleary, I feel it's best I reside out there." Katherine responded as tactfully as possible. After all it wasn't that far from the truth as there were personal items of Sister Coreen's which would require sorting, and letters to be written to her family and the Sisters back home. However, this didn't seem to be the response the small gathering wished to hear.

The room suddenly fell silent as the women seated around her exchanged worried glances between them. *What was going on here?* Katherine wondered. *Why are they so keen for me to leave the property?* Katherine seemed to sense that asking this question wasn't such a good idea and so in turn she awaited a response to her answer. It was Mrs Cross who took the opportunity to speak.

"We're most touched by your need to place your responsibilities of caring for your fellow Sister's small belongings to the forefront; such a move is most Christian. But the environment out at the property is far from that of a Christian household. My dear, I feel it's our responsibility to advise you that the young Mr Pelham is currently seeking a Father who was to marry he and Sister Coreen. He's obviously not yet aware of her passing."

"Mrs Cross, I appreciate your concern and honesty on this matter, however Miss Pelham advised me of the situation between her brother and Sister Coreen this morning." Katherine, thankful for Catriona's honesty with her, sensed that the more formal use of Catriona's name was more appropriate for this gathering. "You must understand that this makes it even more important that I should be the one to see to her papers and belongings. Can you imagine the shock of the family or the Mother Superior finding something which could only bring heartache to those back home?" *Well I got out of that one,* Katherine thought, waiting for the inevitable response from Mrs Cross, but the response when it did come came instead from Mrs Greystone.

"Sister, I believe that the situation between Sister Coreen and Mr Pelham is the least of your troubles. I feel that you'll be badly influenced by the actions of Miss Pelham."

This was the first time that Catriona had been directly referred to during Katherine's short time in the house and she was curious as to what sort of influence Catriona represented. Playing the social game a bit further Katherine decided to play dumb and say nothing, which wasn't hard considering she really had no idea what they were talking about. The group seemed to be doing their best to speak around the root of the subject without actually raising it. Looking back at Mrs Greystone, Katherine tried to place on her face the best confused look she could muster.

Mrs Greystone chose her words carefully, "Well, as you can see she dresses very differently and entirely inappropriately for a woman with the assets she and her brother possess. And besides the fact, she's too old to be wearing the clothes of a tomboy; it's time that she was married and starting her own family."

So that was it! She didn't fit the mould of what this gathering expected of a woman. She dressed differently and refused to be bound by the ties of a marriage that may not suit her at all. Katherine suddenly found herself admiring Catriona for her refusal to surrender to the yoke of convention, wishing that she could do the same. Sensing again that it was time for a tactful answer, she replied, "I don't think you should be overly concerned by her influence on my dress as I already have my habit and this does not lend itself to wearing trousers. And as for her unmarried state, I'm sure that she has had plenty of suitors and is yet to find the one she wishes to spend the rest of her years with. Such a choice isn't one to be made lightly."

"But you see that's just it," Mrs Cross interjected. "She has never had a suitor. She seems content not to seek out the company of males for other than to discuss the cost of wheat or compare the latest new machinery which is entirely inappropriate for a woman of her upbringing." Sensing she'd said too much, she suddenly stopped, masking her embarrassment through raising her teacup to her lips.

"Ladies, I thank you for your concern, but I feel that it's most un-Christian-like to speak about someone who is not here to appropriately respond to your queries." Katherine tried to look as pious as possible. "I'll take heed of your generous proposal, and if I feel that my presence is not suited to the Pelham property, then I'll reconsider your magnanimous offer." Katherine endeavoured to make it as clear as politely possible that the subject was now closed, but this didn't help to answer the number of questions swimming around Katherine's head. *Just how old was Catriona and how was it that she'd escaped the marriage merry-go-round?* These were questions only the other woman could answer, but how was Katherine to broach them?

With the remainder of the afternoon passing uneventfully, the nun found herself tiring as the soiree came to a close. At precisely 3.30pm a servant quietly announced the arrival of Miss Pelham at the front of the house. Having said her goodbyes, she was again escorted outside by Mrs Greystone. Here the same ritual was played out as occurred in the morning, with no words being passed between the three of them, and Catriona saying nothing until the wagon was well out of earshot.

Catriona had known what the day would hold for Katherine. She would be bled dry on subjects she knew little about from a group of women who were living out a fantasy. They would banter casually, have lunch, and then the inevitable question would come. Catriona had steeled herself for Katherine's imminent departure and perhaps it was for the best. *Living on a property remote from the rest of population and prey to bushrangers wasn't the lifestyle for a Sister of the cloth and neither was being badgered by a quarrelsome female like herself*, Catriona thought. Unable to stop herself from not broaching the topic any longer, she queried in what she hoped was a casual tone, "So, whose residence will you be living in during your stay here?"

"I think you already know the answer to that question. I could no sooner see myself living in the household of any of those ladies than I could see myself living in the original accommodation meant for the Sisters during their stay. But if I'm to stay with you and your brother, I need to know what's going on. I don't know what one has done to the other, but both you and Mrs Greystone seem to be rather cool to each other. So what's going on?" Katherine asked turning to face Catriona.

Trying to answer as calmly as possible, Catriona replied, "I'll explain it to you when we get home," however inwardly she was elated. She felt sure her over-reaction that morning would have seen the nun more than eager to pack her belongings and move into town. Inwardly she rejoiced, but how had Katherine managed to do it, for the town matriarchs could be very convincing when they wanted to be. The grazier was as keen for an explanation herself, but how was she going to explain to Katherine just exactly what was going on?

As they pulled through the gate to the property, Katherine had her first real glance at the Gleneagle homestead. That morning she'd been too engrossed in preparing herself for her wagon riding skills and her trip into town to take much notice. To the front of her were two main buildings and a selection of smaller huts, with the smaller ones, as she learned later, serving the purpose of a laundry and smokehouse for dressing and curing meat. The smaller of the two main buildings, set a small distance away from the house, was of simple rectangular wood construction and was obviously the barn. Unlike the unwieldy house Katherine had passed her day in, this home seemed to be in greater harmony with the surrounding landscape.

The sun's rays reflected off the cream sandstone brick of the home, casting long shadows on the verandah that encircled it, affording a cooling shade to the heat of the afternoon's sun. The main door was flanked by full-length louvered French windows. These continued around the house at what seemed regular intervals. Katherine surmised that these were rooms and, having seen the effects of yesterday's storm, could understand the need for such a precaution for protecting fragile glass. The roof itself, which extended out from the house to meet the edge of the verandah, was covered in a corrugated iron sheeting, which seemed to be a popular roof cladding in Australia. The corners of the roof were met at a point, thus affording a great deal of shade from the afternoon sun. Nearing the home, Catriona slowed the wagon to a halt and helped Katherine to alight before continuing on to the shed.

Over a cup of tea, Katherine regaled Catriona with her tales of escape from the town's matriarchs. The grazier couldn't help but admire the quick thinking of this woman, wishing that she also could possess the same skills rather than rely on the sharpness of her tongue to resolve difficult situations. Catriona knew it was inevitable that Katherine wouldn't be satisfied discussing her own escape and would require some answers of her own. Fortunately, the trip home had allowed Catriona precious time in which to consider how she would field such queries and so she was ready when finally the question of her dress was asked by Katherine.

"As I explained to you this morning there are currently no workers on the farm, leaving just myself and my brother to manage the property in all but the periods of harvest and mustering. You remember I told you that he's often away on business and this leaves just me responsible for day-to-day management. It wouldn't be right for me to sit here in a dress all day and employ a man to do work I can easily do. That which I can't do awaits for my brother's return or I ask one of the men in town to help me," Catriona explained carefully in a non-committal tone, reaching for a biscuit.

"But there was another issue which the ladies seemed to be preoccupied about and that was your lack or absence of male suitors," Katherine mentioned innocently, taking a sip from her tea.

Catriona found herself nearly choking on her biscuit; for while she'd expected such a question, she hadn't anticipated it being posed so bluntly. She was more so prepared for a more obscure query regarding her age and the number of suitors she must obviously have. Fighting to regain her composure, she reached for her tea, making the pretense of washing down the remains of her biscuit in a throat that had suddenly gone dry. Placing her cup in front of her, she chose her words carefully.

"I know that at 28 I should have found someone to share the rest of my life with and there was a time when I thought I had. I was 17 and my mother felt that the age difference between my suitor and myself was...er, too great, so she forbade the relationship. Since then I haven't found any one else who I feel strong enough to commit a lifetime to." Catriona was pleased with her answer. It was as truthful as she currently cared to be. Given the chance, she was sure she would have been content to spend the rest of her life with Adele, except for her mother's interference. But now there was no-one to interfere, and her brother had long since learnt not to broach the topic of marriage with her. Her life was definitely her own to do with as she pleased, and if she was more at ease spending it alone then so be it.

Katherine was watching the other woman intently. If she'd been given the same opportunities in Ireland, she wondered if she would find herself still wearing the vestments of a nun. With that in mind, Katherine said to Catriona, "I understand completely."

Catriona was incredulous. "You do?" She barely stopped herself from spilling the remaining contents of her cup on the table.

"Yes, you see I was also in a similar situation. My family was forcing me into marriage based on my age—I was 22 at the time. As the situation unfolded, I was left at the altar by my husband-to-be who had eloped with a younger girl possessing a larger dowry. I really had no want to marry and found that I could find the solace I sought through taking my vows. This served to save me from a marriage that I didn't want and allow me inner peace," the nun answered feeling happy to at last be sharing her reason for joining the convent with someone else, albeit a relative stranger.

Catriona again masked her feelings, inwardly cursing herself as a fool to think that they shared the same reason for an unwillingness to marry. She was amused by Katherine's story all the same. Joining a convent would be one way to avoid an unhappy marriage; however, personally, the celibacy issue was something Catriona couldn't reconcile to, despite the fact that she'd been celibate for the last 11 years. Eleven years was such a long time that she'd almost forgotten what it would be like to hold another woman. Certainly this was something that wouldn't be resolved in the immediate future.

"So as you can see, Katherine, you've nothing to fear from my influence. The women in town find my values uncomfortable because I won't allow them to be compartmentalised like theirs. Ignorance will always breed fear and I think in their case that fear is masked through a dislike of anything different." Catriona moved to clear the table. "Well, enough said. There are chores to do in the yard which I would be grateful if you helped me with and, by then, I think you'll have earned your supper." Catriona lightheartedly finished, motioning Katherine to follow her into the yard and the fading light of an orange-red sunset.

Chapter
Five

As the days turned into weeks, Katherine found most of her time occupied with tending to the families of the district. She discovered that the surrounding area wasn't made up of a number of wealthy estates, as she first expected. The main landowners were free selectors living on selections of relatively small acreage and leaving only a handful of large properties in the district.

Katherine had been confused when Catriona had first referred to the small farms as "selections." She then explained to the nun that in Australia there had traditionally been three ways to secure land for farming. The first was through a land grant made by the Crown who, in reality, owned most of the land. The second was through "squatting" which essentially referred to finding a piece of land and claiming it for oneself, thus relying on possession being nine-tenths of the law. The third was through selection, which was the legal purchase of plots of land by someone for the sake of farming. It was this third means by which most of the struggling families of the district had purchased their land. Most of them had never been offered the opportunity to purchase land in the countries they had come from. Often the most they could have expected in England, Scotland and Ireland was to be made tenants, with the greater degree of their profits going to the landlord. At least here, no matter how small the plot of land, it was well and truly theirs, along with the accompanying profits or indeed debt, as was often the case.

Her work in the district was almost as a jack-of-all-trades. She offered spiritual comfort to those who needed it—mainly families on outlying selections who confided that there were just not enough hours in the day to go to church on Sunday. This surprised her at first, although it didn't take her long to realise that most of these families worked six days a week from dawn until dusk. It was understandable that the one day they had left was one on which the family was too tired to do anything but rest. However, most of the families found themselves getting into church at least once a month and Katherine supposed that she should be thankful for this. It was obvious to her these people retained their faith, for that was one thing needed by the families struggling to carve out a living on such small farms.

On top of the obvious spiritual comfort she offered, she also found herself providing limited medical aid and acting as a part-time teacher to the children of the outlying families. These children didn't have the luxury of a local school and, until they were old enough to work in the fields with their elder brothers, sisters and father, they required basic schooling. This was an easy and enjoyable task for Katherine who found the children she taught to be, on the whole, outgoing and inquisitive. She developed a method of leaving them small exercises that allowed them to use their numbers and letters in relation to farm life which would serve to benefit all. It also seemed this was the only way she could ensure that both the children and the parents were happy with the content of the lessons.

She was quite dismayed to discover that there was no library in the district and expressed such dismay to Catriona over a discussion regarding the children's schooling. It was only when she was gently reminded that it had been this way for many years that she stopped to think about the extent of influence she really had in these children's lives. She was sure that the richer families had their share of private libraries, but the likelihood of them sharing such knowledge with people so far below their social rung was out of the question. Resolving to at least try and change the issue, she sent a letter outlining her problem to her Convent's sister Convent in Sydney with a request for a range of children's books. Knowing how long this would take though, she used half of her meagre funds to also order books from Sydney, by placing an order with Susan Crosier at the local town store.

As the weeks progressed the town also begun to regain a sense of normality. People were still mourning the loss of friends and family but this was to be expected. This would go on for a long time yet, and Katherine found herself wishing for the Father's hasty return to ensure the proper blessing of the dead. As a consequence of the need to repair homes and businesses, Susan's local store seemed to be doing a thriving trade, however Katherine noticed that little money was passed over the counter to the shopkeeper. In fact the day that Katherine had placed her book order, Susan initially refused to accept her money despite the nun's insistence and eventual success at handing over the funds. The nun reminisced over their conversation that day, grateful for the assistance provided by the shopkeeper, as well as Susan's insightful comments regarding the workings of the small country town.

"I'm sorry, Susan, but I must ask you. Why do you seem so reluctant to take my money? After all, I was supplied with some funds by the convent before I was sent to Australia," Katherine asked in exasperation.

"Out here immediate payment isn't the only way I conduct business. Most of my customers must wait the outcome of the sale of their crops or their cattle before they can settle their accounts for the year." Susan added with a twinkle in her eye, "Besides, I've always had such a time of keeping my accounts, that the families always seem to be able to pay me in full with some money left over for the nice things in life."

"But how do you run a business in such a manner? Surely this must leave you for the better part of the year in poverty yourself. How do you manage to pay your creditors?" Katherine asked with a quizzical look on her face.

Susan inwardly smiled at Katherine, feeling a sense of amusement. She was so different from Sister Coreen, always asking questions, never quite realising what was impolite to ask. She couldn't help but think Katherine was wasted in her calling, but then who would accept such a questioning woman as a partner? Realising the woman was still waiting for an answer she provided her with one. "Well, there are three ways I manage to do this. The first and more widely used means is through a system of barter. I do this with families who wish to purchase something in exchange for produce such as eggs, milk, and sometimes cured or fresh meat from an animal they have slaughtered for the family table. I then deduct what we both agree is a reasonable sum from their final account. The second way I conduct business is that I treat the smaller families differently from the larger landowners that refuse to raise a finger for the smaller battling families. As far as I'm concerned, for such people there's only one mode of payment and this is payment on demand." Susan's eyes glinted with barely concealed anger as she referred to the richer families of the district.

"And, finally, you may be surprised to know that I'm a woman of independent means." Here she paused as Katherine's jaw dropped and allowed time for the woman in front of her to regain her composure. "I don't have a husband, but this wasn't always the case. A while ago, I was married to a man who loved money more than anything else. We arrived in Sydney when I was barely twenty and he immediately set about making money in any scheme that was profitable. However, his real luck came with the discovery of gold in Sofala just past the town of Bathurst. But he wasn't a man to be fooled, as many men were, by the lure of gold and hard work. He saw that there was a fortune to be gained in selling to those gold seekers the pieces of equipment they needed to find the precious metal. And so he sold these tools, but at exorbitant prices and, like most men, his greed consumed him. One day he pushed his luck too far and found himself killed by a miner down on his luck and desperate for just a small break. Unfortunately the miner got neither, ending his life at the end of a rope. As for me, I took the strongbox, which was rightfully mine, sold the store and the provisions within to another man eager to make easy money and left. Rather than return to Sydney, which I detested, I opted for a small country town, comfortable in the financial knowledge that I would never have to marry again."

"You've never seen the need to marry again? After all you're still a relatively young woman," Katherine queried looking at Susan, whose complexion hadn't yet experienced the ravages of years of some of the other women she had witnessed since her arrival. "I'm sure that there'd be many gentlemen in the district more than happy to marry a woman such as yourself."

Susan smiled enigmatically. "Well, let me say that everything you've said so far is correct and I've had a number of offers. However my memory of my marriage wasn't a happy one and my husband wasn't a kindly man, who found no wrong in hitting a woman. Nor did he seem content with the love of just one. He was a regular in the local watering hole, or as you would call it a tavern, and a favourite of the women who frequented the establishment. Now, I'm not saying that all men are cut from the same cloth, but my life now has different priorities and finding another husband is not one of them."

Katherine realised that her path of questioning was becoming far too personal and not befitting a nun—but being more in comparison with that of a fishwife. She deferred from asking any further questions, deciding it was best to ask such things of Catriona, who seemed more than happy to assuage her curiosity. Before leaving the store, Susan had convinced her to split the cost of the books for the children with her, in the name of kindheartedness for those who were less fortunate.

Katherine had found herself on two more occasions caught in the web of the town matriarchs. While she did find herself more at home with the hardworking families of the district, as a duty of her calling, she was still obliged to pay these women the same courtesy. Both of the visits lasted all day albeit at different residences. Despite the change in scenery, the visits always managed to leave her drained. This usually came from avoiding the continued polite but firm requests from the women to remove herself from the influence of Catriona, as well as the requirement to keep up polite, flippant and hollow conversation all day.

This was the only time that she found herself escorted by Catriona, who seemed to take a perverse delight in the looks on the women's faces as she dropped her off at the various residences. For, after a number of lessons, she'd become proficient at managing the wagon and had been given the free use of it. The only times the grazier now used it was when it was required for farm work and for picking up supplies in town, which she seemed to believe were far too heavy for Katherine to handle.

Katherine was astonished to discover that Catriona was more content with riding astride a horse rather than the more feminine manner of riding sidesaddle. However, she wondered if a number of the things that Catriona did were meant to shock, and so decided against the idea of adding fuel to the fire through broaching the issue. In fact it was at least one way of reducing the risk of falling off, which Katherine had managed many times whilst riding sidesaddle before entering the convent.

In the more quiet moments the nun found herself wondering if she'd made the right decision in joining an order. It served her purposes well indeed, but in her periods of reflection she found herself wondering what it would be like to be married, to have a husband, children, and a lovely house to live in. These thoughts were always short lived, quickly dispelled through taking in her immediate surroundings, as she realised such a decision wouldn't have found her in the company or country she was now in. Australia was a country full of beauty but harsh as well: the raucous noise of the white sulphur crested cockatoos landing in a tree, turning it from green to white; the early morning laughter of the Kookaburra who seemed to share a secret joke with others of its kind; the many different colours of green contrasting with the golden yellow of the wheat and the yellow-brown of the spinifex grass; and the skies at night that first heralded a myriad of colours in a sunset only to be followed by the night sky with stars she hadn't known of in Ireland. Catriona had patiently explained that the constellations were different for the northern and southern hemispheres, taking time one night to sit out under the stars pointing the more common ones out to the Irishwoman. The stars Katherine liked the most were the Southern Cross, as it reminded her of a kite with its tail blowing in the wind. It wasn't so dissimilar to the kites she'd marvelled at as a child with their freedom only restrained by the string tying them to their owner.

The number of shooting stars occupying the night sky was more than Katherine could ever remember seeing in Ireland. One night while sharing conversation and a cup of tea, they had the fortune to see two shooting stars running parallel to each other. Instinctively the nun closed her eyes to make a wish; something she hadn't done since she was a child. She was relieved with the night's darkness, as it concealed the redness of her face for indulging in such a pagan and childish act.

However, the moment wasn't lost on Catriona who turned to the other woman's profile and made light of the situation. "I don't believe what I just saw, Sister," she chided in a mock scolding tone. "Please correct me if I'm wrong, but I'm sure that I just saw you close your eyes after the passing of that shooting star. Perchance you weren't indulging in the act of making a wish, were you?"

Katherine couldn't help but laugh at the mock severity of Catriona's tone. "Yes Miss Pelham, indeed I was. As one of many of God's spectacles I was in fact thanking him for the opportunity to view such a rare event," Katherine replied as she faced Catriona, masking with words her embarrassment at being caught. How could she tell Catriona her wish involved hoping the women of the town would soon tire of the constant requests that she leave the property, as she truly enjoyed the life out here and the company of someone relatively close to her age? Hoping to detract further questions regarding her wish, Katherine decided that the best form of defence was attack and turned the question back on the woman beside her. "And are you telling me that you didn't let such an opportunity go unnoticed to make a wish?" She asked flippantly, looking back at Catriona.

"I never let an opportunity go unnoticed if the time is right," Catriona said quietly, staring back into Katherine's eyes. For a moment neither spoke and, for Catriona, time seemed to stand still. She couldn't read the nun's features for it was too dark and thankfully so, for neither could Katherine read hers. Uncomfortable with the path the conversation was taking, the grazier fell back onto safer ground.

Catriona eased herself out of her chair, throwing the remains of her tea into the inky black of the night. "Well, if you'll excuse me, I'm off to bed. I've a long day ahead of me tomorrow. I have to check fences in the top paddock as well as going into town."

Katherine hadn't yet seen the complete property and, knowing her day tomorrow was free, asked, "May I come along? I'm keen to see the property and besides I'm sure that I can help you with whatever it may be, even if it means just holding the hammer. Besides, how can you do all this by yourself?"

Catriona was touched that Katherine should feel so keen to see the rest of the property. She saw it everyday and so to her it had become, in places, uninteresting. But she would be happy for the company. "Feel free to come along but we won't be alone. Mr Connor and his sons from the adjacent farm will be helping me. The fence stops their cattle from straying onto Gleneagle and ruining my crops. I pay them for the work but I'd be happy if you didn't mention the fact that the job could just as easily be done by two than by five, for all the sons will be there tomorrow. I'm sure that they're also aware of this but they're not so foolish to refuse money they sorely need. I suppose it's a private game we indulge in. They'll provide lunch; that's the way of their family showing their skills. Their mother is one of the better pastry makers in the district." She picked up the lamp to move inside.

"Yes, I remember them now. Four sons, two daughters, and another baby on the way. I couldn't fathom how they managed but it's understandable when they've a neighbour like you," Katherine said, touched at a side that she hadn't seen in this woman. For all her brashness, she seemed to share a true affinity with the people of the land. Maybe this was why the men treated her with such respect.

Fighting to cover her embarrassment, Catriona responded in a brusque manner, "Well, it's something that any good neighbour would do for another, and besides it's a reciprocal arrangement. I don't wish to light the lamp in the kitchen so if you'd like I'll take you to your room and light your lamp for you. It will be a long day tomorrow." She raised the light they'd been using and walked through the house with Katherine in tow. After arriving at Katherine's room and lighting her bedside lamp, Catriona said her goodnight and waited for the door to close before heading toward the sanctuary of her own room.

Catriona sat on her bed and undressed as she cursed herself for the comments she'd made on the verandah. She had to be careful as such comments, if read true by the Irishwoman, may well force her into the town, just where those old matriarchs wanted her. She felt they had established a good friendship and it was unlikely to continue if she scared her away with spoken thoughts and actions that weren't likely to be ever reciprocated. She was also glad that Katherine hadn't asked her to expand on her wish regarding the shooting stars. After all, how would she explain that her wish involved getting closer to Katherine?

Katherine hurriedly dressed into her threadbare shift; glad that it was so light for at the moment the nights seemed to be so balmy. Undressing, she couldn't help but think about the woman of Gleneagle. She seemed to take great pains in hiding the good she did for people, but there was more than that. She also seemed to take great pains in masking her own emotions. She could only think that this was a defence mechanism after losing her parents. She seemed to want to keep everyone at arm's length, never letting down the shield she'd created for herself. Katherine just hoped that if she ever needed it, she could repay Catriona for the kindness she'd shown her. Climbing into bed she quickly fell asleep, her dreams full of shooting stars and town matriarchs hot in the pursuit of a laughing Catriona who seemed to remain just out of their grasp.

Katherine awoke the next day to a knock on her door and the sound of footfall continuing down the hallway. In the still muted greys of dawn Katherine moved to her bedside table to light her lamp. Catriona had casually mentioned the evening before that their start would be an early one. It was better for her and the Connor's to get the best working use out of the daylight hours and, to that end, the grazier didn't want to spend the majority of them travelling. By the time the nun had washed, breakfast had been made. Hot tea, bacon, and eggs awaited her as she came through the kitchen door. They ate the meal mainly in silence and shared the task of washing up prior to setting out for the day. On the end of the table were two hats, as Catriona was still hopeful of getting the other woman to wear one. Regardless of this act, no more was said concerning the hat and, as usual, as they passed out of the house one remained untouched by Katherine.

The ride out to the boundary was uneventful, with the scenery resembling much of what the rest of the district looked like. The journey would take two hours Catriona had said. Much of the time was spent discussing the work of the day and the resurgence of bushranging activity in the district. The grazier explained that despite the constabulary's best efforts, they were yet to catch the bushrangers. She surmised that it was quite likely that they were being given protection by the poorer families of the district, who seemed to both rejoice in the fleecing of the rich while also benefiting from such forays. Given their manner of operation, it was unlikely that they would be caught in the near future and Catriona warned Katherine about her movements, suggesting she leave a note of her comings and goings at the house. Given the unknown intentions of a group of marauding men and her memories of highway robbers in Ireland, the nun accepted this as an imminently sensible idea and both fell into silence as the trip continued on.

As they topped the rise of one hill, Katherine noticed in the very far distance a group of trees that couldn't readily be called a copse in the true sense, but seemed a strange presence on such a landscape. She pointed in their direction. "What's that group of trees over there? Is it still part of the property?"

Every time Catriona rode out this way she passed the trees that dredged up memories of happier times. She cursed herself for bringing Katherine this way and, looking straight ahead, replied, "Yes, it's still part of the property, but it's nothing now but a dried spring. I don't think it's run for years."

"How do you know it's dry?" Katherine asked enthusiastically. "If it's not, it would be a wonderful place for a picnic, would it not?"

"It's not nice and it's probably overgrown. Where there's overgrowth there are snakes and besides I've hardly the time for picnics. I don't want you going there by yourself either. If you hurt yourself you may not be found for days." Catriona's reply was in sharp clipped tones. Refusing to even look in the direction of the trees, she whipped the horse into a faster pace, making it difficult for the nun to look behind her at the trees and hold on at the same time.

It was obviously something that the grazier didn't want to discuss and Katherine, who didn't feel like starting their day on a bad note, let the matter rest. There would be plenty of time to ask her about it when she wasn't in such a prickly mood. She attempted to steer the conversation onto safer ground, "You mentioned you had cattle on your property?" She waited for the other woman's reply.

Catriona's features relaxed a little as she nodded. "Yes, we run a small herd of beef cattle in the top paddock. It's one close to a gate connecting this property to the Connor property."

Katherine creased her forehead in thought. "Why do you need a gate between the two farms?"

Catriona took a deep breath, realising that while these were relatively banal questions for a person borne on the land, for the woman beside her the answers weren't so obvious. "This allows a business arrangement between both families regarding agistment of the Connor's and Gleneagle cattle. We can switch between properties when the grass gets a little low on one."

"Correct me if I'm wrong, but I didn't think the Connor selection was so large." Katherine paused as puzzle pieces came together in her head. She answered her own question, "You do this for them, don't you?" Catriona's only answer was a somewhat shy smile as she pretended to occupy herself with the handling of the wagon and horse. "Why are you so uncomfortable with the assistance you provide others?"

Catriona shifted in her seat. "It's not that, it's just that the less people who know about it the better. I trust you not to say anything to them, as I'm sure that if Mr Connor found out he would have the incessant need to pay me for the agistment on my property. And besides, in times like this when Alexander's away, it does help to have another pair of eyes on the cattle."

The nun smiled, nudging the other woman in the ribs. "You can't fool me, you're just overly generous." Her answer was a grunt from Catriona as she urged the horse forward.

The rest of the journey was conducted in relative silence with the Irishwoman choosing to look at the surrounding countryside rather than engage in conversation when Catriona clearly didn't want to speak. Catriona was lost in her thoughts of her time with Adele and her new found friendship with Katherine. Things were so difficult at the moment and she was slowly losing the fight over her feelings for the woman beside her. She wanted Katherine to stay with her, but seeing her everyday created such a painful wound. For all the pain it caused though, she knew she wouldn't have it any other way.

With six pairs of hands working on the fence repairs, it didn't take long to get the job done. Katherine spent the first part of the morning entranced by the way that the previously felled trees were stripped of their bark before the logs could be split into the right size for fence posts. In between the activity Katherine queried the grazier as to why the trees were not just felled as part of the morning's activities. In patient tones, Catriona explained to the nun that it was necessary for the trees to be felled and for the wood to dry out for a while before they were made into posts. To use green trees would result in warped posts, and indeed a warped fence line.

While some of the workers barked the trees, another split the logs, whilst another prepared the hole for the post to go into. When finished with the construction of the fence, they placed a wood structure on both sides which the nun, upon asking, was told was a step-over system used by neighbouring farmers to effectively eliminate the need to travel the extra distance by road. Roughly hewn, it looked like a stepladder erected on both sides of the fence so as to stop clothing being torn in trying to climb through barbed wire. Again Katherine was amazed at the simplicity of the invention and its extreme versatility in such a situation.

What also never ceased to amaze her was how well Catriona worked beside these men. She didn't have the obvious strength

they possessed but she held her own all the same. Her movements seemed graceful amongst the men, with a surety of purpose Katherine hadn't seen many other women possess. She was
very casual and not afraid to share a joke or laugh at her own
misfortune when one of her axe swings missed its intended target. Her face took on a completely different aspect when she
allowed herself to smile. But it was her azure eyes that Katherine
was so enthralled by; they seemed to take on a different light,
leading her face through the humour of the situation. *She has
such a natural beauty*, Katherine thought, *and it is such a shame
that she chose to live her life alone.* Shaking herself back into
the present she decided to occupy herself in a more practical
manner.

Rather than waste the time of one of the men, she prepared
the lunch that was more than an ample fare for the seven of them.
Catriona was right; Mrs Connor had prepared a number of sweet
and vegetable pastries that could easily be eaten on the run and
with the tea she had also prepared, it reminded Katherine of the
ploughman's lunches she'd often eaten in Ireland. But unlike Ireland in late October, the sun here was truly shining and reminded
her of the heat created by her woollen habit. She could feel the
sun beating down on her face and couldn't help but think what
her complexion would look like once she got home. She ruefully
thought back to the hat she'd left untouched on the table and
wished that for once she'd swallowed her pride and worn it.
Well, it was too late for that now. As the men and Catriona finished their work she motioned them over for their meal.

Lunch served as an opportunity for Katherine to question
Mr Connor as to how his wife's health was keeping. Fortunately
after six children already it seemed that the pregnancy, as far as
he was concerned, was progressing fine and Katherine promised
that, if he didn't mind, she would visit the family to see how
things were going. With the lunch finished, both groups said
their goodbyes and were on their way. On such a fine day, there
was no time to be wasted on pleasantries when there was more
work elsewhere to be done. The nun remembered that Catriona
had mentioned she also had business in town.

The return trip to the homestead was a quiet one and especially strained as they again passed by the trees in the distance.
Catriona again concentrated on the task at hand rather than even
acknowledge the copse of trees. The mood didn't change as they
crossed the grate out of the homestead on their way to town.

Deciding to lighten the situation, Katherine attempted to strike up a conversation. "That was a lot of heavy work today. I suppose you're grateful for the assistance you received."

"Yes, there are times when I'm grateful for their physical assistance. I know my brother and I could have managed it by ourselves, but it would have taken such a long time. Sometimes I wonder if it wouldn't be just as easy to employ permanent workers, but in truth I enjoy the solitude that being out here gives me." Realising that she'd been holding hard onto the reins, Catriona eased her grip as she was spoken to.

Katherine turned in her seat and placed her hand on Catriona's arm. "You know, sometimes there's more than just physical assistance that you can ask for. If there's ever anything you want to speak about, you know you can talk to me. What ever we speak about will remain private between us."

Catriona hurried to hide the fact that she was momentarily taken back by the comforting hand of the woman beside her. "Thank you, I'll keep it in mind. However, at the moment I think I better concentrate on the trip to town or we may not get there. Is there anything you want in the store? That's where we'll be stopping."

"Yes, I'd like to check with Susan on when the children's books from Sydney will be arriving. I can't wait to see the look on their faces when they get the opportunity to read something different than rain calendars and agricultural manuals. So, what are you picking up in town?"

She smiled a secret smile. "Nothing much really. Some farm machinery and a parcel that Susan has for me. It will only be a quick stop for it's been a long day and I'm eager to get home and into a bath for a good soak. If we're lucky we won't run into your old age group of admirers and by the look of your face we better pick up some malt vinegar as well—you're as red as a beetroot."

Katherine brought her hand to her cheeks and felt the warmth there. As she did she smiled at the other woman's restraint. She knew what Catriona really wanted to do was give her yet another lecture on the downfalls of not wearing a hat in the country. She resolved to speak to the Father on his return. By all accounts she had been given, he seemed like a reasonable man and hopefully he would approve of a change to her habit. Katherine begrudgingly admitted to herself that it would be infinitely more comfortable than continually getting sunburnt.

Susan was busy when they arrived at the store and stopped only for enough time to hand Catriona a large brown paper parcel and to direct her to where her repaired farm implement was on the store's verandah. Calling over her shoulder, Catriona invited Susan to dinner when she felt that she could spare the time. She jokingly added that they might use the formal dining room in celebration of her visit.

Arriving home almost at dusk, their time was taken up with the ritual positioning of the bathtub in the kitchen and the filling of the large kettle on the stove. Both were thankful for the bath that night. For both of them it had been a hot day and for Catriona quite a sweaty one. After such a heavy lunch all they could manage was a small tea of sandwiches. Katherine treasured these as they usually involved thick slices from a smoked ham and hot tea, and that night was no different. Their dinners had developed a welcomed casualness about them that gave them time to talk about the day's activities and what was planned for the next day.

Katherine took the time to towel her short hair whilst Catriona used a small clasp knife to clean the dirt from under her fingers. Seemingly occupied in her task, she said, "We'll have to put that malt vinegar on your face once you've finished with your hair. You'll find the vinegar will help to remove the sting. Tomorrow we'll put some cream on it to stop it from drying out. You know this could have been avoided if you'd decided to wear a hat. It's not as if you're committing a mortal sin or anything." She folded the small knife and placed it back into its leather holder before putting it on the table in front of her.

Katherine placed the towel aside on the table and looked at Catriona. She knew the last comment had been a bait and she chose to ignore it by answering in a rational manner. "I'm aware that it's not a sin, but you already know my reasons. Besides, at least your hair is shoulder length. Mine looks as if a madman has taken to it. And believe me when I tell you that it isn't normally this long, the Sisters in Ireland kept a strict regime of haircuts. While vanity isn't something expected of a nun, I'm still a woman and I can't abide people looking at me as if I were half bald."

Catriona unconsciously reached out as if to touch Katherine's hair, but managed to redirect it to the towel to place it over one of the chairs. "Honestly there's nothing wrong with your hair. I think I've told you once before that you should be glad you've the freedom to wear it so short. I barely get away with the scandal of wearing my hair this length as it is, be happy that you can. And besides, such curls aren't done justice beneath that stifling habit. Talking of which, I've something for you." She rose from her chair and moved into the hallway. It wasn't long before she returned with the parcel she'd picked up from the store. "Now before you open this let's get one thing straight. This isn't charity, nor is it a hat. I know you've your own money and I don't want any of it. I'll not take this back and I certainly can't use it if you don't want it. Think of it as my thank you for not only being my champion with the town matriarchs but also for the company that you've given me out here. I had forgotten how lonely it can get without female company." Catriona placed the package in front of the other woman.

Katherine first looked at the brown paper wrapping held by a string and then at Catriona. She was right. It would be rude not to accept a present given in friendship; however, she couldn't think of anything she truly needed. As she untied the string, the paper fell open to reveal two complete habits on top of each other, but unlike hers these were made of black and white cotton. She was at a loss for words as she held them up to the front of her chest where they seemed to make a perfect fit.

"How did you manage to do this? You barely have time to clean the house let alone time to sit and sew. And by my estimation they should fit me perfectly. Thank you very much." Katherine stood and hugged Catriona in gratitude.

That was the last thing that she'd expected, but everything she'd wanted, and in response Catriona closed her arms around Katherine, neatly encircling her waist and back. She had long thought about what it would be like to hold Katherine, but this far exceeded her expectations. They were almost the same height and she could feel the touch of the nun's hair upon her face. It was overpowering, but she could no sooner break away than cut off her own hands.

Katherine in her thankfulness was unaware of the effect that her expression of gratitude was having on the grazier. But she did notice something she'd never experienced before. She didn't know the proper words to express it, but one word kept rebounding in her head—security. She felt secure in the other woman's arms and rightfully so as Catriona was such a strong woman. But something wasn't right and she consciously broke the embrace. "How did you manage to do this?"

Catriona had found herself caught up in the moment and,

realising the spell was broken, she stepped back grabbing a chair to steady herself. This was the second time Katherine had asked her the same question and was now waiting expectantly for an answer. "It was easy. If you remember your first day here when your habit was too dirty to wear regardless of your attempts to sponge the stains from it, I told you that I'd take it into town for washing, which I did. I also took the opportunity to ask Susan to have her laundress make up two more habits in a more conventional fabric. You'll find they're exactly alike, including that infernal wimple of yours. Really these are much more functional for the hot summer weather. You can always get good wear of your woollen ones in the winter time," she replied, managing to seat herself before she fell down.

Katherine, for a reason she couldn't readily fathom, didn't move toward Catriona to again hug her for her thoughtfulness. Instead she smiled and thanked her once again, conveying her gratefulness and saying that she would start the day tomorrow in her new habit.

It was only then that Catriona remembered her promise to dab malt vinegar on Katherine's face to remove the sting of her sunburn but, in all honesty, at that moment in time she didn't trust herself or her hands not to betray her own emotions. Feigning tiredness, she instructed the Irishwoman on how to do it before bidding her a goodnight and retiring to her bedroom.

It didn't take Katherine long to complete the task, smelly though it was. However, she still found herself sitting at the kitchen table long after she'd finished. Catriona's reaction and her sudden distance confused her. What confused her more was her own inability to describe or understand adequately her reactions to the hug she had given Catriona. Going over it in her mind didn't seem to help and in fact only served to remind her of her own fatigued state. Taking the lamp from the kitchen table she rose and found her way to her own bed and a restless night.

Chapter Six

The following day Katherine woke regretting her stubborn attitude over not wearing a hat. Her face had been sore yesterday, now it was not only sore but also her skin felt as if it was stretched taut against her face. She peered into the mirror. She looked as if she'd spent too much time cleaning linen in the boiler room of the convent with her complexion taking on a shiny red hue. Taking pains not to aggravate her sunburn, she finished her toilette before moving through the house and into the kitchen, where she placed the kettle on the stove.

Standing at the back door she could make out the figure of Catriona, already deeply preoccupied in repair work to the curing shed. Her preoccupation gave Katherine the opportunity to unobtrusively observe this somewhat enigmatic woman. Despite the early hour of the morning, her shirt already carried the telltale signs of dirt and perspiration that accompanied manual work. Her sleeves had been rolled up to her elbows, revealing slender yet well-formed, brown, sinewy arms more commonly seen on a man. Occasionally she would raise one hand to her face in an attempt to shoo away the flies, which seemed to thrive in the country sun. She swung the hammer in tune to a song she was contentedly whistling, oblivious to Katherine's curious stare. *Maybe she's just as happy on her own,* Katherine thought, and as she absentmindedly wiped a cup clean of its dirt, she began to think about their friendship. As a child and even at the convent it had been difficult for her to make friends, but in Catriona she'd found a true confidant. She couldn't help but think that if she and her brother were alike, then it wouldn't be difficult to see why Sister Coreen had been so attracted to him.

The whistle of the kettle served to break her reverie and interrupt Catriona, who turned toward the house in time to catch Katherine move from the door and into the kitchen. Placing the hammer on the wood block beside her, she moved toward the kitchen. Her pace was a controlled one, for fear of again betraying the emotions she'd shown last night. Breaking stride, she quickly washed her hands in the verandah hand basin before joining the other woman inside.

She was touched to see that Katherine had wasted no time in discarding her old woollen habit for the more conventional cotton ones. Katherine, sensing Catriona's pleasure, said, "Thank you once again for these. I can't believe how well made they are, and so like my woollen ones. The seamstress who created these should be congratulated." Seeing the smile on the grazier's face, she chided, "And to think, they even came complete with wimple. Weren't you just a little tempted to have them made less the article you seem to dislike so much?"

Catriona laughed as she pulled out a chair and seated herself. "Well, I'd be lying if I told you that the thought didn't cross my mind. However, given your predisposition to not see reason, I was afraid that you might not wear them at all and the gift would have been a waste."

Katherine responded to the light-hearted barb by throwing a dishrag at the seated woman, who easily fended it off with her hand. Picking it up from the floor, Catriona laughingly continued, "And I thought nuns weren't supposed to resort to violence. I'll have to be wary of you in the future." Seeing the nun stretch her arm back, ready to launch another rag in her direction, she held her arms up in mock surrender. "Okay, enough, you win this round. Now if I promise to behave may I have a cup of tea before I go back into the yard?"

Katherine returned the rag to its original place. "Well, that was the general idea. In fact, if you hadn't been so quick about it you may have got one delivered to you on site. So, what else do you have to do today?" she queried, pouring two cups of tea.

Catriona nodded her thanks and took the cup from the proffered hand. "I lost a great deal of time yesterday, with the fence and all, and there are a number of small jobs around the yard which must be done. So, I expect that the better part of my day will be spent close to the house. How about you?"

"I've some lessons I've got to plan and then I thought I might start with the Farrell selection, work my way to the Dawson farm, and finish with a call on Mrs Connor to see how her pregnancy is going," Katherine answered, taking a sip of her tea.

"Don't wait too long before you start out for home or you'll be hard pressed to be here before it's dark." The grazier paused in thought. "In fact, if you get to the Connor place and the sun has begun to set, wait there and I'll come and get you. I'm not particularly happy about the idea of you travelling these roads unaccompanied."

Katherine's immediate response was to ask who was to accompany Catriona, but on reflection realised that she was right. She wasn't familiar with the roads and tracks of the district, and it would be too easy for her to guide the horse and wagon in the wrong direction and get hopelessly lost. Swallowing her pride she advised Catriona that she would wait and, satisfied with the response, Catriona returned to her work outside.

The lessons Katherine prepared were relatively straightforward arithmetic and reading exercises incorporating life on the farm and so, in a relatively short period of time, she was on her way. With a last wave to Catriona, who had moved onto repairing the front verandah, she headed toward the gate and on to her visits for the day.

Due to the Farrell's having just the one child, Katherine's visit to their selection took up very little of her time and by late morning she left their small farm and headed toward her next stop. Unfortunately the Dawson's, unlike the Farrell's, were prolific breeders, and Katherine found her hands full managing five inquiring minds ranging in ages from six to twelve while becoming painfully aware of her meagre breakfast. She was grateful for the offer of lunch. It never ceased to amaze her how the families managed to cope in such an unforgiving environment. Despite their lack of resources they would go without food themselves rather than turn out a visitor. The nun made a mental note to make sure on her next visit to bring something for the family.

The sun was still reasonably high in the sky when she made her final call of the day to the Connor farm. As her wagon came to a halt she was greeted by the noise of Mrs Connor's youngest son, Liam, eager to tell her about the lessons she'd previously left them. Gently extricating herself from his grasp, Katherine made her way toward the tired figure of Mrs Connor waiting in the doorway of their small one bedroom hut.

"Sister Katherine, what a relief it is to see you," Mary Connor said, in a lilting Irish brogue. "While I love my children dearly, between them and the babe on the way, there doesn't seem to be enough hours in the day."

"Oh, don't you worry about that now. Let me have some time with your children and before long they'll be too absorbed in their work to worry us while we have some tea. Why don't we go inside and I'll get the kettle started and then give the children their lessons for the day?" Katherine was painfully aware of the tiredness portrayed in Mary Connor's eyes and stature.

Moving inside out of the sun's rays, Katherine's eyes took time to adjust to the room. The hut itself wasn't much larger than the curing shed she'd seen Catriona repairing that morning and yet it accommodated such a large family. Katherine marvelled at the strength required in a woman to raise a family under such conditions. All the same, she surmised that it was possibly better than what the Connors' had left behind in Londonderry. At least in Australia they were free selectors, owning their land. She quickly placed a kettle on the wood stove before busying herself with the children.

It wasn't long before a temporary silence descended on the room, giving the two women time to talk about the pregnancy without interruption. So engrossed was Katherine in her discussion with Mary and her teaching of the children that she lost track of time. It was only when Mary rose to light another lamp within the hut that she realised she may have left her return home too late. Although remembering Catriona's words, she was also aware that her wait would mean sharing the scarce food that the Connor household barely had to offer. Despite the welcome hearth and promise of food, Katherine graciously refused the offer rather than delay her home journey any more, hoping that it wasn't taken in offence. With the shadows from the eucalyptus trees growing longer, she boarded the wagon and turned the horse for home.

All too soon she regretted her rash decision to leave the warmth of the Connor household. Despite the heat of the day, the clear twilight sky heralded the promise of a cool evening; one that Katherine was quickly becoming aware of through her cotton habit. As her body rocked in time to the motion of the wagon, the hairs on the back of her neck rose. This was the time of the evening during which a symphony of nature could be heard, echoing the calls of native birds and the sounds of insects settling into their evening song. However, with the exception of the sound of the movement of horse and wagon, the countryside was silent as if it was holding its breath.

Her eyes squinting in the last traces of the setting sun, she scanned the road ahead, for what she wasn't quite sure. Suddenly the horse raised its head, ears pricked, innately aware of another horse not far away and, by straining her eyes, Katherine could just make out the silhouette of a rider and horse on the bend ahead. Remembering Catriona's words to wait, she felt that this was one lecture she wasn't easily going to get out of.

Frightened and annoyed by the manner in which Catriona had chosen to greet her, Katherine decided to speak her mind. "Yes, yes I know what you're going to say. I should never have left the Connor home. I'm sorry. I didn't appreciate how fast the shadows fall in this country. But you should be ashamed of yourself. Sitting there, on a bend, not even telling me you were there. You scared the daylights out of me! You scared the horse, you know. He could have bolted and heaven only knows what might have happened as a result." Despite the warmth now generated from her indignation, the words that followed chilled her to the bone.

"Sister, I don't know what or who you're talking about, but I'd lay odds it's not me." Riding out of the slowly disappearing glare of the sun rode a man, his hatted face covered and a pistol on each of his hips.

The words Catriona had spoken and those that Katherine had heard in town over the past few weeks came rushing back into her mind. Bushrangers! Riveted to her seat with fear she rapidly assessed her options. She could hardly run the man down for he obviously had the advantage of both speed and weaponry, even though she was aware that both his weapons were still holstered. She remembered Susan relaying a story on the gallantry toward women of the local bushrangers and she prayed that there were more to those words than just the beginnings of a legend. The bushranger had now halted just in front of her horse and was casually leaning forward in the saddle, like someone who had stopped to pass the time of day.

Katherine summoned up the courage to speak. "If you're who I think you are, then I'm sorry but you've picked a very poor target. I'm Sister Flynn the local Sister, and I'm sorry to disappoint you, but I have nothing of worth to you. The best you can expect from me are children's school primers and I doubt that even you would lower yourself to rob from children," she said with nervous defiance, pulling the reins toward her.

Her reply was met with a deep throaty laugh. "But that's where you're wrong, Sister. There is something you have that I need." With that, man and horse advanced toward her.

In panic Katherine managed to wheel the horse and wagon slowly back toward the way she came. Turning her head toward her new direction she tried but failed miserably in stifling the scream that arose in her throat. Behind her was another man, bareheaded but his face was also masked.

In fear of the words uttered, she turned back to the man who had initially spoken and, summoning up all the courage she could find she spoke, "I had heard that your type are not violent toward women or was I wrong?" Barely giving him time to reply and bolstered by her own words, she blurted, "I'm a nun, and even you must know what awaits you not only in this life but the hereafter should you harm me."

The two men laughed in unison, enjoying a joke at the nun's expense. "Firstly, Sister, let me tell you that I'm already damned by my actions, so it's no good you trying to frighten me with your sermon of eternal damnation. Besides, there's greater pain awaiting me in the world of the living should I harm a hair on that Irish head of yours. My leader would have me skinned alive for even a scratch," the hatted man replied.

A spark of hope crossed Katherine's features. "So you're going to let me go then? I'm late as it is and I'm expecting someone to come looking for me any minute." She swallowed, fervently praying for Catriona's speedy arrival.

"Well, I'm sorry but that's not exactly the case. You see we do need you and we've been waiting all day for you to come back along this road. I can't let you go because if I return to camp without you my leader would have my head on a plate, if not other parts of my anatomy. Now I can promise you that you'll come to no harm if you do as you're told and, when we're finished, I give you my word that I'll bring you right back to this spot. However, I'm going to have to cover your eyes, just in case you feel the need to bring anyone back to where we're taking you. Don't worry though, honest Ben will ensure that your horse doesn't stray."

Before Katherine could protest the hatted man leaned forward and in one deft movement snatched the reins from her hands. Holding tightly onto her hands, he firmly bound them before placing a hood down over her head. Whether it was from the sudden onset of darkness or her own fright she didn't know, but Katherine promptly fainted.

She awoke some time later to the scent of hay assaulting her nostrils. She'd no way of knowing how long she'd been unconscious, but it was obviously time enough to have removed her from her seat on the wagon to where she was now—lying on its boards, where provisions were normally stored. The wagon was moving, obviously driven by one of the bushrangers, but to where? Despite her previously unconscious state, her hood had remained in place and her hands tied. Frustrated but aware of her inability to escape, she allowed herself to think on why the bushrangers had taken her in the first place. She didn't have long to think before her ears and nose made her aware of their arrival at what could have only been the bushranger's camp. The smell of smoke and cooked food announced that they had arrived around suppertime, making Katherine uncomfortably aware of the time since she'd last eaten. She again heard the voice of the hatted bushranger as he shared a joke regarding what booty they had caught today. Katherine could feel herself blushing, angry to be the brunt of someone's joke. The jibes continued with the raucous laughter of other men in the camp joining in the merriment. However this was cut short by the voice of who Katherine presumed was the leader.

"What the hell do you think you're doing! Are you the least bit aware of what you've got in the back of the wagon? It's not some whore you've brought back to have a little fun with; it's a bloody nun! It may have been a while since any of you've had any religion, but I won't have her treated in this manner. Besides, have you forgotten why we brought her out here? It certainly wasn't for your bawdy entertainment." Katherine, shocked by the words spoken, could hear footsteps approaching the side of the wagon and the sound of disgust uttered by whom she presumed was the leader. "Take that bloody hood off her head and for Christ's sake untie her damn hands. What did you expect her to do? Attack you with her cross? Once you've done that give her something to eat; she looks like she needs fattening and then take her to where Joshua is lying."

Katherine heard the footsteps recede, shortly followed by a flurry of activity as she was helped into a seated position on the wagon's floor boards before her hood was removed and her hands untied. In front of her, silhouetted in the fire's glow, was the hatted bushranger who had kidnapped her earlier. Looking around him she could see a man spooning out a portion of what looked like stew onto a plate while another cleared a seat for her by the fire.

"I'm sorry, Sister, about the hood and all," the hatted man said awkwardly. "And we didn't mean no disrespect with what we said, we was just havin' a bit of fun that's all." He helped her down from the wagon and led her toward the fire.

"If that's your idea of a joke, I'd hate to see what you're like when you're serious." Seating herself before the fire, she graciously accepted the steaming plate offered her before continuing. "Now that I'm here, will someone tell me what it is you expect from me?"

The man who had offered her the plate of food spoke first. Dipping his hat in deference to her position, he introduced himself. "Jim Barrett, Sister. It's Joshua, you see. He was winged yesterday in a job we did over at the Moreshead Downs property. We can't take him to a doctor, as all he'll do is fix him up so he can be hung. We've heard about you helping others and we thought you might be able to help him."

Katherine paused the spoon to her mouth. "You say he's been injured since yesterday and he's yet to be treated?" She placed the plate down in the dirt in front of her and rose. "My supper can wait. If you're aware of my assistance throughout the district, then you must also be aware that my medical skills are rudimentary to say the least. However, if you take me to him I'll see what I can do." Looking around in an attempt to locate the wagon and her bag, she became aware of a figure watching her from the shadows. Pausing only long enough to ensure the figure was aware that it had been seen, Katherine turned and, aided by Jim Barrett, went via the wagon to where Joshua lay.

The word "winged" was an understatement. It was obvious that the property owner's gun had at least gained some revenge from the bushrangers, hitting Joshua low in the leg. By torchlight Katherine was able to ascertain that the leg, whilst it had a rather large hole where the bullet had passed through, wasn't broken. What concerned Katherine most was the slight odour coming from the wound and the glazed look of the young boy's eyes. These told her that the leg was infected and he had a fever. Issuing orders to Jim to find both hot and cold water, clean rags, and alcohol, Katherine set about her task, all the time aware of a figure in the shadows behind her.

By his still smooth face, she surmised that Joshua couldn't have been more than eighteen and, as she cleaned the leg with water and alcohol, Katherine wondered what caused someone so young to get caught up in such a group. She checked herself, realising the decision Joshua had made may well have stemmed out of necessity rather than idol curiosity. She had only to think about the families she'd visited today to realise that the life of bushranging presented an escape from a life of living from hand to mouth.

"Well Mr Barrett, I've done all I can to help Joshua. He has a fever from the infection and, unless it breaks, I'm afraid my efforts may well have been in vain. It's obvious that I'm going nowhere tonight, so if you don't mind I'll sit with him." Seeing Jim Barrett's tired face she realised he was weighing up the options of doing the same. "There's no need for you to sit up also. I have no idea where I am, so the chance of me escaping is non-existent. And besides, I wouldn't leave a person in need. Go and get yourself some rest; I'll look after him," Katherine said, returning her attention to the young man in front of her. She was aware of Jim Barrett's shuffling feet of indecision before he turned and made his way into the darkness.

Despite being alone with Joshua, she felt no fear. Having heard the voice of the leader earlier today; it was unlikely that any of his gang would risk attacking a nun. She began to wonder if it had been the leader who had silently watched her ministrations throughout the evening. As if reading her thoughts, she was startled by the sudden presence of someone beside her.

"I figured by now you'd be pretty hungry. Jim managed to hold some supper for you and some tea as well. I told him to go to bed and that I'd bring this over. After all, not only do I owe you my gratitude, but we've not yet been introduced." Crouching down in the shadows the leader offered the plate and tea to Katherine before extending a gloved hand. "I'm Mary Carraghan and you might say I'm the leader of this unruly crew."

Katherine felt her jaw drop in surprise. It seemed that when-ever she was beginning to become adjusted to the many differ-

ences of this country another came along. In her wildest dreams
she wouldn't have imagined the possibility of a female
bushranger. "But you're a woman!" she managed to stammer,
still in shock over the recent revelation.

Mary chuckled and sat herself on the ground beside the nun.
"Well, it's good to see that some people still know the difference. After living with this bunch for so long, it's easy to be mistaken for a man. I know you sent Jim packing, but if you don't
mind I'd like to sit with you a while. Joshua hasn't been with us
all that long and I have a responsibility regarding his welfare."

Katherine, too stunned to reply, managed to nod her head.
Taking a sip of her tea she composed herself before inquiring,
"How is it that a woman finds herself tied up in such a venture as
this?"

Lighting a cigarette from the coals in front of her, Mary
removed her gloves before replying laconically, "How is it that a
man finds himself caught up in such a venture? Poverty is no dis-
criminator, Sister Flynn. It hits women as hard, if not harder,
than it hits men."

"How did you know my name?" the Irishwoman asked in a
flustered voice.

"It would be surprising if I didn't know your name. You're
becoming quite well known around the district for your kindness
to others. Had that not been the case I would never have had my
men, shall we say, invite you to our camp." Seeing the anger in
Katherine's fire-lit features, the bushranger held up her hands.
"I'm sorry for the manner that the invitation was served, but I've
a responsibility to my men and myself. I still can't be sure that
you won't leave this place and lead the constabulary right back
here."

Katherine's face lit up at the thought of leaving the camp.
"So, you're going to let me go?"

Mary raised her face to the stars in exasperation. "For
Christ's sake, of course we're going to let you go! If we didn't
I'd have more people on my heels than I could poke a stick at,
and no doubt led by the determined figure of Catriona Pelham."

Katherine choked down her food at the thought of Catriona
scouring the countryside in search of her. However, it stuck in
her throat when she thought of what she would do to her when
she finally caught up with the nun. She should have waited at the
Connor place rather than risk the journey home. However, for the
moment she didn't know what was the better option—remaining

here or returning home to face the wrath of Catriona.

She ate her meal in silence, watching the woman in front of her finish her cigarette. The figure Mary cut in the shadows of the fire was that of a short woman dressed in men's clothes. Her hair was as short as her own, which had aided Katherine in her initial belief that Mary was a man. She seemed at home with the silence, content to let Katherine finish her meal. Mary got up once to check on Joshua and sponge the sheen of sweat from his brow, before returning to the close proximity of the fire.

"Sister, you're going to burst any minute if you don't get off what's on your mind," Mary said taking a sip from the flask which moments before had been attached to her hip.

"I'm sorry, I was just wondering if there were many female bushrangers and whether you really like such a lifestyle," Katherine stated, attempting to hide the unfamiliar feelings that Mary was evoking in her.

"Well, I can't say that I've done much socialising outside this gang, so I don't rightly know if there are any other female bushrangers. As for liking the life, well it's better than what I left. I was in love and married young to a man who unfortunately took a greater interest in the bottle than he did his land. Despite its hardships at first, this has been an escape that I've grown used to. There are many women who are in my predicament and I'm sure that if they knew about this life they might be tempted to also leave their husbands. I try to do my best to help them with the little money we get from our bushranging but in truth for them it's just a vicious circle, of which I was lucky to escape." She took another sip from her flask before offering it to a shivering Katherine. "Where are my manners? Have a sip of this; it will warm you."

The nun hesitated before reaching to take the flask from Mary's outstretched hands. As her fingers grazed Mary's she felt the same unfamiliar feeling she'd felt earlier in the evening. It was as if her stomach was still hungry and yet she was full. Covering her confusion by raising the flask to her lips Katherine swallowed what could only have been rum. After a great deal of spluttering, and annoyance at the look of laughter in the bushranger's eyes, she attempted to return the conversation to familiar ground.

"But don't you miss being with your husband? I mean, I know that there are men here but, well you know, don't you miss being with him?" Katherine queried in her normal forthright manner.

"Let's just say I was in love with the idea of being in love, and no, I can't rightly say that I've missed him. As for the men out here, they don't interest me either. My interest lies, you might say, in ones of the fairer sex," Mary replied casually, lighting another cigarette.

Katherine took a few moments to digest Mary's words before realising the implications of what she had said. When she was still at home Katherine had heard, by way of gossip with the servants, about people who shared the love of the same gender, but she'd never actually met one. Shocked and confused, she fell back on familiar territory. "How can you when the Bible clearly foretells damnation for those who engage in such acts?"

"Unless you haven't already noticed, I think my actions as a bushranger have already damned me to Hell. I see that the issue of whom I wish to live with as already covered by that previous damnation. After all, Sister, how many times can you be damned?" Mary's challenging eyes gazed back at the woman opposite her.

Katherine fought to understand the actions of the woman in front of her, as an unfamiliar feeling again entered her stomach. "Mrs Carraghan, damnation is not a matter of one bad covering a series of other bad actions. How can you think of living in such a manner with another woman?"

"Why don't you stop for a minute and think about what you've just said? As you're aware, your reputation of good deeds is known throughout the district. I was fully aware of who you were and where you lived long before I had need to seek your services. Do you not live out on the Pelham property? Is that not where the Pelham male is currently away, as he is for the greater majority of the year? Does that not leave you living with a woman? If you weren't a nun, what do you think would be said about you?" Mary replied, throwing her cigarette into the fire and standing to stretch her legs.

Shocked by what Mary had just said, Katherine also stood, toe to toe with the woman in front of her. "How dare you! How dare you even insinuate that, that the life you pursue and the fact that Catri...Miss Pelham and I share the same house are even remotely the same? We're nothing but friends, and she has been gracious enough to let me stay with her after my home was ruined in a dust storm. How dare you insinuate such impropriety!" An outraged Katherine was now standing decidedly close to a smiling Mary. Katherine was aware that her breathing had quickened and again her stomach seemed to be drumming out a tattoo of its own. Pride and anger forced her to remain in her spot, demanding a reply from the woman directly in front of her.

Like the sun's rays on a cloudy day, Mary's face changed from one of humour to one of logical challenge. "If that's the case, then why, all of a sudden, are you so angry?" Mary stood her ground waiting for an answer.

Stumped for words Katherine turned on her heel, angrily muttering something about checking on Joshua. Mary watched after her before taking out her hip flask and once again seating herself by the fire. Shaking her head toward the nun, she raised the flask to her lips and drank in the temporary warmth the rum provided.

Katherine returned to the fire to find that the other woman had made herself comfortable for the evening. In deference to the nun, the previous discussion wasn't raised again, and Mary seemed content to instead regale her with stories of bushranging and narrow escapes. The Irishwoman listened inattentively, a part of her mind still playing over the words Mary had uttered regarding her and Catriona, while another part tried to rationalise her body's reactions to what had been said between them. How could she even think that the friendship she and Catriona shared was the same Mary shared with other women? As the time stretched on, both women took turns between sleeping and watching Joshua whom by early morning had conquered the fever of the night before.

Good to her word, once Mary was content that Joshua would live, she directed that the nun be returned to where she'd been abducted yesterday. Before the sun had yet risen Katherine's hands were again loosely tied and a hood placed over her head before commencing her homeward journey. It was Jim Barrett who led the wagon this time, all the while thanking her for helping Joshua. Upon reaching the road her hands were untied and, as the sound of horses receded into the distance, she removed the hood from her head. Taking her bearings and the reins, she turned horse and wagon for home and lost herself in own thoughts of the events of the night's events.

As Katherine's journey took her up the path to the homestead, she could make out a number of horses tethered by the barn. A man, up early and checking on the horses, turned to see the wagon coming up the drive. In his apparent shock, he dropped the bundle he was carrying before running at high speed toward the house.

Catriona, having spent a sleepless night worrying about Katherine, was confirming the scope that the search would take when she became aware of a man yelling inside the house. Breaking through the door the man skidded to a halt on the polished wooden floors, barely managing to keep his balance. "She's back! Sister Flynn's back! Coming up the driveway as bold as brass you might say." With that he turned again skidding on the floor, before returning from where he came.

Catriona's heart leapt with relief at the news the man had brought. The relief however was short-lived and replaced with anger. Clenching her jaw in an attempt to not swear in front of the group of men, she turned on her heel and made her way out the front door. Coming up the driveway in the wagon was an obviously tired yet safe Katherine.

Seeing Catriona on the steps reminded Katherine of the words Mary had spoken the night before. *Surely no-one thought of Catriona and me in that manner?* Climbing down off the wagon she made her way to a stationary Catriona, legs akimbo and her blue eyes on fire with anger.

"Where the hell have you been! Didn't I tell you to wait at the Connor place? Do you ever listen to anything I say! I told you if it became dark that I'd come for you, but no, that wasn't good enough for you. I rode over there last night to have Mrs Connor tell me you had left just on dusk. Dusk, Katherine, when it's getting dark for God's sake! I've been up most of the night as have a number of the men from nearby farms waiting to start a search party this morning. And you ride up here as if you've been to town and back, instead of being away God only knows where all night!"

For once the grazier's anger had the opposite effect on Katherine. Rather than rise to the bait she instead composed herself by first tying the reins of the horse to a nearby tree and checking the brake of the wagon before replying. "I'm sorry, I know now that I should have listened. I was taken by the bushrangers." Katherine paused as she saw the other woman's hands clench into fists. "But as you can see I'm all right." She looked past the stoic figure to the men who were now standing behind her on the verandah. "Gentlemen, thank you for offering to help look for me. I'm eternally grateful and touched by your actions. However, as you can see I'm back and unscathed. Now if you'd like to move into the kitchen, I'm sure I can prepare some breakfast for all of us." The men turned and headed back inside the house speaking between themselves. As she passed Catriona on the steps, she briefly met the eyes of the other woman. "This is not the end of this."

"You're damned right it isn't!" Catriona forced her words through gritted teeth, following Katherine into the house.

Katherine, despite her tiredness, prepared breakfast for the group of ten while politely answering the questions of the town's police constable. No, she didn't recognise any of the people who had abducted her; yes, she'd been treated well; and, no, she couldn't lead the constable back to where she'd been, due to her being hooded during the journey. Disappointed that again the bushrangers had escaped his grasp, the constable sat down and sullenly ate his breakfast.

The group of men was barely out of eye and earshot when Catriona again turned on Katherine. "Inside, now!" was all she uttered before grasping the nun's arm and wheeling her forcefully into the study.

In spite of pacing the floor of the study in an attempt to check her temper, Catriona found she was losing the battle. "Do you have any idea what sort of danger you were in last night? You could have been killed or injured and left for the wild dogs to finish! Bushrangers are not some romantic vision you may have inside that head of yours. They're desperate men," Catriona said, trying to impress on her the danger she'd been in the night before.

Katherine took a deep breath to calm her own exasperation at being talked to as if she were a child instead of the adult she was. "As you've already heard, I wasn't in any danger, they needed help that's all. And given that the leader stayed with me all night, I doubt that any of the men would have thought the risk of assaulting me worth the reward."

"Well, that's just great, the leader spent the whole night with you! And who protected you from him? That damned habit of yours won't protect you from everything. You could have been raped for God's sake!" She placed her hands on the arms of the chair Katherine was seated in, effectively trapping her.

Katherine thought back to her discussions and the unfamiliar feelings she'd experienced the night before with Mary and a smile broke from her lips. "Catriona, I've no doubt the leader protected me through the night and as for the leader raping me, well that's extremely unlikely—the leader was a woman, something I neglected to tell the good Constable Ford." She watched as the grazier's face registered surprise at her last words.

Breaking her grip on the chair, Catriona put her hands to her head in exasperation. "I don't care if it was a man, woman, or well trained monkey! You can't go running off to help someone without leaving some sort of message."

"Haven't you been listening to me this morning? I didn't run off, I was abducted! Between, having my hands tied behind my back, a hood placed on my head, and fainting, I barely had the time to leave you a note! Be reasonable for heaven's sake. You can't always be running after me, making sure I'm alive and safe. I have my own responsibilities to the families of the district." Standing up, she moved to where Catriona had her back to the Irishwoman, her hands gripping the mantelpiece. "I know last night couldn't have been easy, but you must understand that I need my freedom just as much as you do. Freedom to come and go as I please without taking you away from your work here on the farm. If you can't respect that then I'll have to take a place in town," she finished quietly.

Catriona turned, her tortured eyes seeking the green eyes of the woman in front of her. Gently reaching for Katherine's hand she continued, "I'm sorry if you feel as if I'm smothering you. I didn't mean for you to feel that way. It's just that, well, I care for you. I would hate to see you come to harm in a place you're still learning about. It's just," she paused, searching the Irishwoman's face, at a loss for words. Shaking her head, she dropped Katherine's hand and walked out of the study silently closing the door behind her without another word.

Katherine stood where Catriona had left her, the words spoken by Mary the night before echoing in her mind. Again she'd felt the same unsettled feeling in her stomach—this time caused by the touch of Catriona's hand upon her own. Shaking her head in an attempt to clear her thoughts, she left the study and moved quietly to her room for some well deserved, albeit restless, sleep.

Chapter
Seven

By the following week both women had negotiated a silent truce regarding Catriona's over-protectiveness and Katherine's demand that she not be mothered as if she were a child. Once the agreement was reached, the nun found herself well and truly settling into a routine involving visits to the small farming families in the district and the occasional trip to the local store to share a cup of tea with Susan. She found herself developing a good friendship with the shopkeeper who, like Catriona, was more than happy to educate her on ways of the surrounding district.

Such friendships were a new experience for Katherine. In the convent in Ireland, most of the nuns were either old women who had been in the calling for a lifetime, or painfully shy teenage novices—both of which she shared no close friendships with. And before entering the convent, the number of childhood friends she had she could number on one hand. She felt with Susan and Catriona a friendship with women who were at least close to her age and shared similar interests. Susan also seemed happy for the additional female company and had promised that she would pay a visit to the property as soon as she could find a spare moment.

A less savoury aspect of her time involved having to contend with the painful process of maintaining regular contact with the more affluent families. They were a persistent group, and having heard second-hand about Katherine's adventures with the bushrangers and Catriona's subsequent outburst on her safe return, continued to politely suggest to the nun that it would be easier for her if she lived in town. Her replies remained polite but unwavering. Since resolving their differences she felt more than comfortable where she was, although she didn't discuss the recent problems between her and Catriona with these women.

In truth, she wondered what would have been the outcome had Catriona refused to give her more freedom. She doubted that any of these women she had to endure would have let her travel unescorted within stones throw of their homes, let alone roam the district alone. She shuddered when she thought what might have occurred had the grazier not offered such hospitality, or if she'd indeed been afforded a proper welcome by the town on her arrival. She doubted that Catriona would have been central to such an event and her assimilation into the town, and surrounding community, may well have been different.

Strangely enough, she couldn't help but think that the recent disagreement between the two of them had strengthened rather than compromised their friendship, one that seemed to grow stronger each day. As a result of the farmer returning to her routine, the two now very rarely spent the whole day together, as both had different work to attend to. But in the evening, over dinner and a cup of tea they always found time to discuss the day's activities. This was the time she enjoyed the most, as it seemed Catriona was the least guarded. There were times that she felt Catriona held her at arms length and this confused her. Occasionally, she found the woman staring at her in an enigmatic way as if she was measuring her against someone else. Without any obvious reason for the other woman's actions, Katherine decided that she was probably comparing her way of pastoral care against that of Sister Coreen.

Despite the subtle prompting of Katherine, Catriona had said little more on the type of person Sister Coreen had been other than what had been said in her first few days after her arrival. She had found no answer in Sister Coreen's goods either. There were scant few of her belongings and it didn't take long for her to collate that which belonged to the Church and what was Sister Coreen's Australian part of her life. Looking amongst the few items that were part of the previous Sister's personal life, Katherine also found a parcel of letters bound by a ribbon. These, she surmised, were personal and should be sorted by Catriona's brother, not herself. She often found herself wondering how long it would be before the return of Alexander Pelham.

Catriona realised with a sense of foreboding that her brother had been gone for over six weeks and knew it would be only a matter of time before he returned. She knew that it would be up to her to break the news of Coreen's death to Alexander and she wasn't looking forward to the painful task. He had never been one to display his emotions, but he had been different with Coreen. It was as if for the first time in his life he had found something to live for, rather than just exist. It was this strength of emotion in her brother that scared her, as she had no way of knowing what his reaction to Coreen's passing would be.

On a lighter note, to the great humour of Catriona, Katherine had tried her hand at cooking with some disastrous results. It became patently obvious this was one thing she'd never mastered either at home or at the convent. Her first batch of scones was greeted with solemnity by Catriona, who used an increasing amount of jam and tea to wash them down. She managed to eat two before Katherine tasted one to determine what the problem was. With one poised between her teeth, Katherine looked at Catriona for a long moment before they fell into laughter. They were as hard as a rock. The grazier joked that while they were maybe a bit hard, they did have a purpose. She suggested they place them outside where they could be used to pitch at the crows when she was dressing meat. Katherine's second attempt at cooking resulted in the cremation of two perfectly good pieces of breakfast steak and a smoky haze that persisted in the house for the rest of the day. Despite what Katherine felt was a terrible waste of food, Catriona took it in her stride.

Catriona was amused by the Irishwoman's attempts at cooking and had finally resolved herself to teach her the basic arts, lest she come home one day to find the house in ashes. What gave her greater joy, however, was the warmth that the other woman exuded. Like Katherine, she too felt a strong bond of friendship developing between the two of them. There had been no further close contact between them since the morning Katherine had returned from her episode with the bushrangers. Catriona didn't trust her emotions with such close contact and had been careful to ensure it didn't occur again.

Casting her mind back to that morning, she shuddered at how close she'd come to telling Katherine the truth—that she cared for her more deeply than she had for anyone in a long time. The restraint she maintained on herself resulted in restless nights with dreams invaded by thoughts of Katherine. She was at least thankful for the stone walls of the house and her closed door. She was sure that on more than one occasion she'd awoke calling the other woman's name.

Realising her sleepless nights were affecting her daytime work, she sought to do something about it and thus decided to talk to the only other person in town who she had confidence in to keep her secret. So, after finishing breakfast one morning, she told Katherine she'd business in town that would keep her there for the most of the day. During her ride into town she cast her mind back to the first time she and Susan had met and begun a friendship, which had steadily grown over the last three years.

Susan's initial arrival in the town had caused its own share of excitement, consternation, and curiosity for she'd arrived without a husband. Instead she'd arrived with her luggage and a slight Chinese woman who was short on words. What surprised the townspeople most was that Susan had bought the local mercantile shop off the old owner outright, and in cash—a feat rarely seen in the town. She then proceeded to launch a large scale expulsion of years of slow moving and useless stock. Once that was accomplished, she had given herself enough space to clean and repaint the store in one process. The restocking of her store caused a great deal of interest amongst the local community, especially the women. For the first time the mercantile had not been stocked only for men, but there were bolts of cloth, soaps and perfume for the women. In addition to the store, Susan cleaned and repaired the small outdoor laundry, which was run completely by the Chinese woman who had arrived with her.

The grazier had taken an immediate liking to the shopkeeper, who seemed not at all perturbed by her insistence on wearing men's clothes or her blunt manner. She found herself spending quite some time helping Susan at the store as well as trying to strike up a friendship with the quietly spoken Me-Lin. One day, Catriona came into the store to find the main counter unmanned. Being the normal hour for lunch, she presumed that the other woman had stepped out to the back of the store to make something to eat. Striding through the store and into the kitchen, Catriona found Susan and Me-Lin in each other's arms. She was momentarily alarmed, for aside from her time with Adele, she'd never seen two women in an intimate embrace. She stumbled backward, hoping they weren't aware of her entrance, only to trip on the kitchen rug and fall awkwardly to the floor. The cou-

ple, startled by the noise, separated instantly and moved around to ensure that she hadn't done herself any serious damage.

Assured that Catriona was all right, Susan helped her into a chair, whilst Me-Lin quietly left the room for the private upper rooms of the store. Susan busied herself with lunch preparations, avoiding Catriona's gaze. Having made a plate of sandwiches, she sat down and faced the woman opposite her. "I expect you're somewhat confused by what you just saw and I wouldn't be surprised if you felt the need to never speak to me again. However, I'd like to try and explain something to you." Sensing no objection she continued. "Sometimes people can be happy by their own company, as you seem to be. Most of the time women are happier by finding a male partner to share the rest of their life. Occasionally this isn't the case and people find happiness in their own gender. I'm one of those people, as is Me-Lin. Both of us have been married and never shared the kind of happiness that we've experienced together. I'm aware of how society and how this town would view such a relationship, but we're happy and there aren't too many people out here who can say that. Now, if you feel that the relationship between Me-Lin and myself may jeopardise our friendship then I'll understand. However I ask that if this is the case that you go and do so in silence. Such news in a town like this would force me to move yet again and that's something I don't really wish to do." The shopkeeper waited for a reply from the other woman. She didn't expect the tears that came instead.

Moving around the table, Susan comforted Catriona until she was coherent enough to explain her emotional outburst. Catriona explained the friendship she'd shared with Adele and the shame her mother had made her feel over the affair. She explained how her mother had called the governess an abomination and told Catriona she was doomed to Hell if she followed along the same path. Her mother led her to believe that what she'd committed was unnatural and not an act condoned by society or God. Catriona explained how her mother had made her feel; that the feelings between her and Adele were wrong, and that they were best reserved for when she married. Despite her mother's words, deep down she knew her feelings to be true and that she would never waste such love on a man. Unfortunately such a position in a small country town was a difficult one. She'd never really found anyone else who felt the same way and so she kept a tight rein on such emotions. And as the years had *passed, she had begun to wonder if she'd ever be able to speak to anyone about her innermost secret. Now she had found that person. They were tears of relief she was crying, not tears of disappointment. Catriona assured the other woman she wouldn't disclose her relationship with Me-Lin to anyone else. Susan responded by telling her that if she ever needed to talk, or if she wanted to ask her any questions, she should feel free to do so.*

It was an offer Catriona had rarely taken up, but one she was going to hold the woman to today.

Arriving in town Catriona seemed reluctant to go immediately to the store. Instead she occupied her morning discussing crops and the latest harvesting devices at the farmer's co-operative and then moved on to the local foundry where she had her horse's shoes checked for any need of repair.

This confused the blacksmith, Mr Young, as he had only re-shod the horse the month before and he doubted that the horse would need to be re-shod so soon. All the same Catriona was a nice woman, who had quietly helped him and his family through some rough times, and so he advised he would check them. However, because he had only recently worked on the horse, there would be no charge. They passed the time during his ministrations sharing the local news. It was always interesting and relaxing to do this as, unlike most people, the local blacksmith knew a bit about everything in the district. Most of the information was only of passing interest and they shared a joke at the constable's ongoing efforts to catch the successful yet elusive bushrangers. Despite all his news, there was only one item she felt she must pass on to Katherine. It seemed that the town Father had been spotted in a town less than 30 miles from theirs, not more than two days ago. This was a sure sign he was on his way home. So, having managed to forestall her true reason for coming into town, Catriona thanked the blacksmith and left the foundry for Susan's store.

Walking through the front door she acknowledged the shop-keeper who was in the process of discussing cloth with Mrs Greystone. The conversation amused Catriona while she made the pretence of occupying herself at the other end of the store. Despite the fact that Susan worked in the store, in terms of relative wealth, both of the women were on reasonably equal footing. This was lost on Mrs Greystone, who continued to treat the shopkeeper as if she were one of her house servants rather than a businesswoman of means. It never ceased to amaze Catriona how Susan managed to keep her temper when dealing with such a pretentious woman. Catriona was aware that Mrs Greystone knew she was in the store, however neither made any attempt to exchange pleasantries on her departure.

As Mrs Greystone left, Susan said, "Good morning. It's nice that you managed to maintain a sense of silent composure with my recent customer. I know for you it couldn't have been an easy task." She folded the bolt of cloth and replaced it in its compartment.

"I don't know how you do it. You always manage to remain so polite with those women. You're right. I couldn't do it. In fact I think I would have ended up strangling her with the bloody cloth." Catriona laughed at the thought of seeing Mrs Greystone strangled in blue watered silk.

The other woman shared the joke. "Well, you can't make money by strangling your customers. Word gets around, you know. But I'm sure you didn't come in here to view the rudeness of old woman Greystone. How can I help you?"

Unsure of where to start the grazier made a pretence of looking at the various jars and utensils on the shelves. Looking at the hat stand she picked one up and idly tried it on. "Oh, I just thought that I'd drop in to say hello."

Susan managed to smother a laugh. Catriona wasn't one known for idle chatter in the middle of the day. *Sometimes this woman is so easy to read.* Catriona had very rarely approached Susan with questions regarding her and Me-Lin's relationship, however her approach was always the same. What surprised the shopkeeper was this current discussion had taken so long for Catriona to broach. For this was one she had been expecting— only the time when it would occur had been unknown to her. Susan moved around the counter to lock the door. "How about we go to the kitchen for some lunch? We had a rather small breakfast this morning and I'm starved."

Catriona was relieved to have the opportunity to talk uninterrupted with her friend. For a woman of her years, it always frustrated her that she never knew how to start such a conversation and she was still unsure how she would manage this one.

Settling down to tea and sandwiches, Susan waited patiently

as Catriona searched for the right words with which to start. "I think I have a problem, well not really a problem, but something I need to speak to someone about. I don't exactly know how to put this but...oh, damn it! How do I tell you this?" Standing up, she walked in ever decreasing circles around the kitchen.

Susan usually took time to tease the other woman when she paced the kitchen in such a manner, but on this occasion she sensed it wasn't a good idea and she decided to take the lead. "Can I presume that you've found someone?" She asked knowing all along that Catriona had.

"How did you know? Has someone been talking to you?" Catriona accused, staring at the shopkeeper with a worried look on her face.

"Oh, yes, of course they have. It's all I've heard in my store during the last week." Seeing the shocked look on the younger woman's face, Susan hurried on. "Of course no-one has spoken to me but for God's sake, woman, have a look at yourself. You're pacing around the kitchen with your hands in your pockets. And I swear in all the time that I've known you I've *never* known you to try on a lady's bonnet covered with flowers, as you did in the store a little while ago. I have to tell you it definitely didn't go with the moleskins."

Catriona blushed, not realising how preoccupied she had been when she entered the store. Sometimes it frustrated her that her friend seemed to know what was going on long before she was told, but sometimes this made the telling easier. Taking her hands out of her pockets, she sat opposite Susan and looked at her. "Yes, you're right. I have found someone, but I don't know what to do about it. I mean it's not as easy as it seems. We seem to have a lot in common, but I don't know if she realises that my feelings run deeper than just friendship." She ran her hands through her hair in an unconscious gesture.

"Well," Susan began, "has she given you any indicator that she wants more than friendship?"

"No, not really. But she seems so happy and I think I am as well if I wasn't so frustrated," Catriona said as she began to raise herself again from her seat.

"Sit down. You make me dizzy moving round the kitchen like a willy-willy blown about by the wind. Perhaps you should tell me who this person is. I can't possibly help you if I don't know her name," the shopkeeper instructed, bracing herself, somehow knowing the name that was about to be uttered.

"It's Katherine. Don't look at me like that, Susan! I didn't plan it this way, it just happened. I can't help myself, but every time I look at her I want to take her in my arms and kiss her." Looking at shocked features of the woman opposite her, she hurriedly added, "But rest assured, I haven't done anything."

"It's a good thing you haven't. Something tells me she wouldn't have taken to the idea of being kissed by a woman too lightly. After all, you must remember where she's come from and what she is."

"Don't you think I'm aware of that? Everyday she gets up and puts that damned habit on. It's like a full body chastity belt!" The grazier growled in frustration.

Susan laughed. "Yes, I suppose it is. On a more serious note, when did you decide that you liked her?"

"I felt something on the first day I saw her at the train station. You should have seen her; slumped asleep against the wall covered in dust. She looked like a long lost treasure you find that hadn't been touched in years, like the ones you read about in books. But I think I began realising how much I really felt as she started working with the families of the district. They talk so well of her and she works so hard at helping them and their children. And she's so excited when she talks about them as if they were really part of her family. But it's not only this or her natural beauty, she has the most wonderful stubborn streak I've seen." Catriona stared into space, oblivious to the gushed praises coming from her mouth.

"Ha! Stubborn streak my backside! Obviously you haven't looked in the mirror lately. But I'll agree with you, she does seem to have her own way of doing things. Tell me, you say she hasn't given you any sign that she wants anything more than friendship, but are you sure of this? Why does she persist in living out there with you rather than living in town? Has anything happened that may have given you even an inkling that her feelings go deeper?" the other woman asked leaning forward to top up their tea.

"Well, I think she stays out on the property because she can't see herself living in any of the households of the town's wealthy." Given the goings on of the past week Catriona chose her next words carefully. "And in relative terms, her living out there allows her to basically come and go as she pleases to tend to the families of the district as well as her own affairs. She has also told me that she left such pretensions of the comfortable life back in Ireland and feels that the farm life suits her." Again Catriona paused collecting her thoughts. "As for whether her feelings run any deeper than friendship we seem to share an intimacy, but this could be that of close female friends. I haven't had many so I really can't tell. Recently there have been a couple of times that caused me to wonder. You remember the cotton habits that Me-Lin made?" Susan nodded and the grazier continued. "Well, the night I gave them to her she hugged me. At first I wasn't sure what to do but then I hugged her back. She has such a small waist that my arms seemed to go right around her. Now I've hugged both you and Me-Lin as well as my brother and this seemed to be different. You see, it seemed to go on for longer than I suppose what you would deem proper. She eventually broke off the hug, but she seemed different for it."

"Are you sure it wasn't just confusion she was feeling? After all, you must admit that she wouldn't have been exposed to too much body contact behind convent walls. Did she discuss it with you at all?"

Swallowing a bite from her sandwich Catriona answered, "No, she hasn't but her actions toward me didn't change after the incident. And then there was something that happened a week ago. I don't know if you heard but I was a little cross with her after that business with the bushrangers." She paused when Susan laughed uproariously.

"A little cross! That's not what I heard. From what Mrs Connor relayed to me from her husband, it was lucky she didn't end up over your knee for a good spanking." Seeing the other woman blush, Susan tempered her words and reached across the table. "You must be careful, Catriona. It will do you no good to be seen arguing with her; and in front of so many of the men— when will you learn to curb your temper?"

"Yes, I know my actions were a bit rash, but she worried me with her disappearance. Anyway, as I was saying, we had words in the study after the men were gone and I impulsively grabbed her hand. Susan, there was a tangible change in the room. I felt something, I'm sure of it."

The shopkeeper's brow furrowed and she concentrated on choosing her next words carefully. "You must be wary, Catriona. Are you sure you're not looking for something that isn't there? If so, any actions on your behalf to make your feelings obvious may be disastrous."

"But I don't know what to do, Susan. I crave her company

so badly it's like a continuing ache in the pit of my stomach and it's only made worse through knowing that she's almost untouchable. I know the ache would be taken away if she weren't at the property but this would only be replaced by another pain—that of distance and longing to see her. I really can't see myself strolling up to the front door of the Greystone mausoleum, knocking on the door, and asking for the town's nun."

Susan made a face at the suggestion. "Yes, you're right, you couldn't do that." Susan carefully offered her opinion. "I'd like to say to you that everything will be all right and that she does or will grow to like you. However, in relationships like ours, romantic endings are the essence of what fairy tales are made of. I can't give you any quick solutions to this as any such solution is just as likely to unravel. I'd again caution you on pressing your hand. Take things slowly, Catriona, for both yours and Katherine's sake." She looked at the other woman's face shrouded in disappointment. "I know I've said this to you before, but have you given any further consideration to leaving town and moving to the city? There at least you've a greater sense of anonymity than you have here. I'm not saying you'll find anyone any easier in a city than here, but it's not as likely to raise as much attention."

Catriona vigorously shook her head. "I could no sooner leave the countryside than have her move out of the house. Besides, that would leave my brother to manage the farm alone and that's not fair on him. I hear what you're saying though and I'll tread carefully. You never know, things change, maybe she'll change as well. I expect that's the only thing I can hope for." She fell silent, her face downcast and her hands flat on the table.

Susan reached out and took the grazier's hands in her own. "Just remember, Miss Pelham, that there's no need to keep this bottled up inside. If you want to speak again, as I've told you before, I'm here." She tilted her head to the side in thought. "However, what might be a good idea is to show Katherine another perspective of life. Now take that horrified look off your face. What I mean is that maybe you should have Me-Lin and I out for dinner. This may serve to prompt her to ask questions about us. If there's one thing she's not short on it's forthrightness. If she docs, I give you permission to answer her questions or redirect her to me, whatever you feel most comfortable doing. Something tells me that what's told to her in confidence will remain that way. I'm sorry, but aside from that, there isn't much more I can offer you."

"Thank you for listening to me, I feel that by just talking to you a weight has been lifted. And I'm grateful for your suggestion about dinner; it's a good idea," Catriona said as a solemn look cast itself over her features. "I very much appreciate your offer of allowing me to talk to her about Me-Lin and yourself. I realise it's no small offer, and you must know the risk you're taking. Just remember, I may not have the wisdom in life that you do, but should you ever wish to speak on anything be assured I'll be there for you also." Catriona squeezed the other woman's hand.

Susan laughed. "Rest assured that I will, miss. I don't easily forget the first woman who showed me friendliness in this town. You made my acceptance into this little community easier than it may well have been. But that's what friends are for, best you remember that." Rising from the table, she placed the crockery in the washbasin. "However if I'm to stay in business, I'd better reopen this store."

Catriona rose and followed Susan out to the main part of the mercantile. There was only one customer who seemed to be just making his way up the steps, but all the same he managed, through his sheer presence, to stop Catriona in her stride. Susan stepped aside as he came through the door.

"Good afternoon and welcome back from your trip, Father Cleary. It's no doubt good to be back home again," the shopkeeper said as the Father strode through the door.

"Thank you, Miss Crosier. It is indeed good to be back. I've been made aware that while I was gone there's been a great tragedy in the town. I'm truly sorry I couldn't be here, but the news took some time to reach me, as it usually does in this country," Father Cleary replied as he took off his hat. "It's also my understanding there were many lives lost including Sister Coreen. I can't begin to express how much she will be missed. She was truly well liked within the district," he said with emphasis and then turned to Catriona. "Hello, Miss Pelham. I believe that Sister Coreen's replacement is currently residing with you and your brother?" He moved closer so his next sentence couldn't be over heard. "Is your brother aware of Sister Coreen's passing?"

"No, Father, he's not," Catriona answered in equally quiet tones, despite the fact that she'd already spoken with Susan about Alexander and Coreen's relationship.

"No doubt he'll be returning home soon. If there's any

assistance I can give you in this matter, please let me know."
Raising his voice to its normal tone he added, "I expect that I'd
better meet the new Sister, Sister Flynn, but not today. Is it possible that I can call on you tomorrow to talk with her? There are
many things we need to discuss."

The grazier's throat became dry with the last comment and
she found herself having to swallow before answering. "Of
course, Father, you're always welcome. Would eleven o'clock be
suitable for you?"

"Yes, that will be fine. It will give me a chance to pay a
quick call on Mrs Greystone and her Ladies Committee. Eleven
o'clock it is then." Father Cleary moved toward Susan to discuss
some purchases he wished to make.

Catriona and Susan exchanged a quick glance before the
shopkeeper's attention was interrupted by the voice of Father
Cleary. Knowing that she had no further reason for being in the
store, Catriona said goodbye, walked down the steps and
mounted her horse.

The trip home gave her ample time to think on her discussion with Susan. The shopkeeper was frustratingly right when it
came to the situation that existed between Katherine and herself.
It was a matter of waiting, but the difficult thing was, despite all
the waiting in the world, there was no guarantee the nun's feelings would change. Catriona was reluctantly resolved to this fact
and agreed with Susan's observation that at least they shared a
sound friendship. Maybe Susan was right when she suggested a
dinner between the group of women might help the situation
along.

As for the return of Father Cleary, Catriona wasn't sure
what to expect from him. He had strong ties with the town's
matriarchs and this was understandable. Living in such a country
town wasn't easy and money wasn't readily parted with. It was
important he maintained a financial patronage from the richer
families. Without their monetary assistance neither he nor the
small town church would survive. But did his familiarity with
the families go as far as sympathising with their attitudes as
well? If this was so, then Catriona was sure that it wouldn't be
long before Katherine found herself in the home of one of these
families. Although, maybe that wouldn't be the case, for despite
his refusal to bless the marriage of her brother and Coreen, he
had shown a surprisingly liberal view in not dismissing it completely out of hand. Although a glimmer of hope for Catriona, it

still brought her worry. Maybe Father Cleary would remember what happened to the last Sister who resided at the Pelham property and, with that in mind, would be reluctant about the possibility of the same situation recurring. She could see the irony in this thought because, in essence, at least on her private behalf, that was exactly what was happening.

Her thoughts reached no greater resolve the closer she got to home and only resulted in tying her stomach in knots. The situation wasn't made any easier as she unsaddled her horse and brushed her down by Katherine coming out of the house to greet her. She masked her feelings, attempting to greet the nun with a friendly hello, and decided to tell Katherine about the Father's return later. As the Irishwoman approached, Catriona noticed that the front of her habit looked as if she'd engaged in a wrestling match with the flour sack.

"You'll never believe it, but I think I've mastered the art of making scones." Katherine attempted to dust the flour off the front of her habit. "Mind you, I did use a little bit more flour than I thought I would in the process so I may have to buy some more. You finish up and I'll pour us a cool drink and you can tell me what you think. By the way, did you get everything done in town that you wanted to? No need to answer now, there'll be plenty of time over that drink." She continued to dust the front of her habit as she turned toward the house. As she approached Catriona, she had sensed she was preoccupied. She found at those times it was easier to give Catriona a little time to herself to gather her own thoughts. If she wanted to speak about it she would, but Katherine never pressed Catriona for her problems.

Catriona was aware that she'd done little to acknowledge the other woman other than her half-hearted hello and a brief nod of her head. She felt guilty, especially given the enthusiasm with which Katherine had greeted her. It was obvious she'd spent an afternoon and possibly a bag of flour baking scones for her. She finished brushing down her horse and resolved herself to being a little more talkative and thankful for the efforts Katherine had put into her day. Dusting off her shoes, she entered the back door. "Should I get the hammer and chisel for this batch or is the dynamite more appropriate?" She sat down at the table, smiling at Katherine.

"Oh, ye of little faith. No more will you be able to use these as cannon balls against the crows for I believe I've truly mastered the art of scone making. Today scones, tomorrow sponges!" Katherine reverently held one of the small brown cakes high in her hand. "Here we are, try one of these. How was your trip today? Any news to speak of?"

"Please, one thing at a time. I must concentrate on the official tasting of this manna." Catriona laughed as she raised one of them to her mouth. In actuality this also gave her time to consider how to broach the issue of the Father's impending visit. She was pleasantly surprised, as the scones were indeed edible; not Town Fair standards but were more than adequate for entertaining at home. Swallowing the scone Catriona said, "I do believe you're right, these are quite nice. Thank heavens for this as your use of flour was beginning to be costly. Mind you, Susan is happy for the business," she added with a twinkle in her eye.

"Miss Pelham, you're a most ungracious host. How long has it been since you've made scones?" Katherine asked jokingly. "So, now tell me how was town, still there?

"Yes, it was. I had lunch with Susan and we spoke about some future issues that may need addressing. I've also invited her for tea and she will let me know when she and Me-Lin can come out." Catriona casually introduced Me-Lin's name into the conversation.

"I'm sorry, but who is Me-Lin?" Katherine asked, not aware of meeting or being introduced to a person by that name.

"Me-Lin shares the store with Susan; she's the laundress and the lady who made your cotton habits. She's a Chinese woman and that's why you haven't been introduced. Whilst her race bothers neither Susan nor myself, the town isn't as accepting of her presence. Mind you, they're happy for her to do their laundry and mend their clothes but not happy enough to invite her into their homes." She held a bitter note in her voice.

Katherine couldn't recall ever knowing or speaking with a Chinese woman or man before, however she found herself frustrated but not surprised by the prejudices of a small town. "Where did Me-Lin and Susan meet? Did she come from the gold fields with her?"

"Yes. Me-Lin lost her husband on the gold fields during a riot by the white men who felt that the Chinese were making more money than they were and thus their reaction was to stop them any way they could. It wasn't an unusual occurrence and unfortunately the apathy and the lack of constabulary meant that such incidents usually went unpunished. Susan and her husband employed Me-Lin as a laundress and seamstress after her husband's death, mainly so at Susan's insistence. Me-Lin's only other form of employment in such a rough town would have involved selling her body to the town drunks. So when Susan's husband died, she left the gold fields and took Me-Lin with her. Me-Lin has maintained a low profile within the town and in doing so they have left her to her own devices. Whilst this is far from ideal, it suits both Susan and Me-Lin," she explained, reaching for another scone and the jam.

"We must indeed have them out to dinner. It's been so long since I've had a dinner party. I suppose I shouldn't think like this, being a nun, but there are some elements I miss from my previous life. Mind you, I don't know whether we can manage such an affair. I don't mean to be presumptuous, Catriona, but I don't think your steak and eggs lends itself to fare for a dinner party any more than my scones could make a suitable dessert."

Catriona was heartened by the other woman's comments. She liked the way she'd used the word "we" rather than "you." She also wondered what else Katherine missed from her time before she joined the convent. Did she crave personal company? Realising that Katherine was awaiting her reply, she said, "No, it will be fine. When my brother and I entertain we call on the services of Mrs Johnston. You must have met her by now. She is more than happy to help on such occasions in exchange for the assistance my brother and I give her family." She paused realising now was as good a time as any to let Katherine know of Father Cleary's morning visit. "But enough of dinner parties and the like. There was another person I ran into while I was in town today. He's keen to see you and will be visiting tomorrow at eleven o'clock."

There was no need for her to spell out to Katherine the name of her visitor for, as a nun, there could be only one man calling on her. "You mean Father Cleary has returned and is visiting tomorrow? Did he say anything to you? Did he seem disturbed by my actions on my arrival? Is he happy with my work so far?" Katherine pounced on the news, a thousand questions rushing into her mind at once.

"Whoa! I said I bumped into him. I didn't interrogate the man. He was coming into the store when I was on my way out. He said he was keen to meet the new Sister, but other than that little else was said. He did mention however, that he'd be visiting the Ladies Committee prior to his visit. Now don't worry yourself; you've done nothing wrong by anyone. How could he not be satisfied with your efforts to date? If you start worrying now you'll be a nervous wreck by the time you meet him tomorrow and I doubt that you'd want that to occur." She reached across and reassuringly grasped Katherine's forearm.

"Yes, I suppose you're right, but I wish I knew what his visit with Mrs Greystone and her committee will involve. You'll be here during his visit won't you?" Katherine looked with pleading eyes at Catriona.

The grazier found herself swallowing at the eyes pleading with her. They were emerald eyes that she felt she could happily drown in. What made it worse was what she had to say next. "No, I'm afraid I won't be as I've work out at the Johnston farm. If I'm to convince Mrs Johnston to cook for us in the near future it's only right that I avail my services to them. Besides I know they're in the process of mustering cattle and an additional horse and rider is always handy. Don't worry. You'll be okay. I'll be home in time for dinner, and if you're not here then I know the Father has dragged you into more appropriate lodgings." Her attempt at humour was met by a look of horror by the nun. "He's not likely to do that. I think it would be best if you occupy your thoughts on other things than his visit, like helping me in the yard. There's some hay I want to load and deliver to the back paddock. I could do with the extra pair of hands. Now let's clear this feast and make a move before it gets too dark." Catriona picked up her plate and glass and delivered them to the large washbasin on the bench.

Katherine moved to do the same, but her mind was still occupied with Father Cleary's visit. Despite her worry, Catriona was right; there wasn't much she could do before his visit, and worrying about it would only cause her to be even more restless when the actual event arrived. Following the other woman out of the kitchen Katherine tried to focus her thoughts on other matters, something that was easier said than done.

Chapter
Eight

Katherine woke the next morning to what she fondly called nature's alarm clock, as the native birds outside her window again signalled their presence. She couldn't help but think what the nuns in Ireland would make of this wake up call, rather than the ringing of bells up and down cold corridors. Taking a moment to soak up her surroundings, she spread her limbs to their furthest extremities on the bed in an attempt to take up as much space as possible. This was yet another luxury she'd left behind on becoming a nun that Catriona had kindly offered her. Smiling to herself she wondered what type of lodgings she would have been offered in town. Yes, they may have been materially just as nice; however, would they have afforded the kind of company Catriona did? It was sometimes nice to have someone to come home to and talk over the day's activities. Thinking of activities, the nun sat up with a start. Today was the day she would finally meet Father Cleary. Fearing what today's meeting would herald, it had taken her quite a while to fall asleep last night. Had she done everything she was supposed to do and would he be happy with her performance? Realising that she was again working herself into a state of panic, she swung her legs over the bed and got up to start her day.

She poured water into her hand basin and removed her nightgown, putting it on her bed before turning around to the mirror in front of her. Tentatively placing her hands on her slightly rounded stomach, she realised that the country life had caused her to gain a few pounds. Blushing, her eyes followed her hand's trail up her body where they halted to rest on her breasts. These hadn't been affected by her extra weight and were still their same full size; not that any of what her body looked like mattered. As a nun it was unlikely it would serve any of the purposes that God had designed it for. Katherine's face burned at the blatant vanity of her last thought, for as a nun these weren't concerns that were supposed to cross her mind. Inwardly shameful, she realised it had also been over a week since she'd last read her morning passage. In fact, without the presence of the Father and her habit, Katherine felt that she could easily be mistaken for no more than a Good Samaritan to the people of the town. Conscious that she'd let the religious side of her life take a back seat, she made a silent promise to remember her calling. Dropping her hands to her sides, she turned to the hand basin to commence her morning's ablutions.

Catriona had risen early and was occupying herself in the study with a list of the accounts requiring payment and the calculation of the extra help that would be needed for the wheat harvest. Despite the pain that Alexander's return promised, she needed him to return soon for decisions had to be made on what was to be planted next year. She glanced up as she heard the other woman enter the room and smiled at Katherine's appearance in one of the cotton habits Me-Lin had made for her. Her smile quickly broke into barely restrained laughter when she looked at Katherine's face. Her serious countenance resembled that of a woman about to meet her maker in person and she found herself chuckling at the thought. "Good morning, Katherine. I'd like you to remember something about your meeting this morning. The Spanish Inquisition has been over for years. Besides didn't that involve a different religion?"

Realising how severe she must look, the nun smiled. She liked when Catriona laughed; she didn't do it often enough. "That's easy for you to say. I feel like a novice meeting the Mother Superior because of a misdemeanor I've committed. Didn't you ever feel reluctant about being chastised by your governesses when you were a girl?"

Catriona smiled a secret smile. "Well, I suppose that depends on which governess you're referring to." She cast her mind back to her time with Adele, who never had cause to really chastise the young woman. "But yes, I can understand your predicament. I've these accounts to finish and then I'll be out until mid-afternoon. That should give you time enough to expunge your sins to Father Cleary. Oh, bloody hell, I'm only joking, Katherine!" She looked at the storm that had started clouding the Irishwoman's features.

"This is a serious meeting! He may not be happy with my work at all. He may not be happy with what I did with the bodies on the day of the storm." She felt her anger grow, frustrated that Catriona seemed not to have realised the seriousness of their meeting. As her ire crested, she searched for words to make the grazier understand that. "He may not be happy given the current arrangement of me boarding with you! Given your family's record with nuns to date." She realised her arrow had found its mark; the words out of her mouth before she could halt her tirade.

The air between the two seemed to noticeably chill, almost as if Coreen was standing in the room. Catriona said nothing, but rose out of her chair and shuffled her papers into a neat pile before placing them in the top drawer of the desk and locking it. Katherine felt ashamed at what she'd just said for there was no reason or logic for it; she'd again allowed her anger to get the best of her.

Moving toward the now silent woman she gently took hold of her elbow. "Catriona, I'm sorry. I didn't mean what I said. They were harsh and cruel words. I should never have used them. It wasn't fair to you and definitely not fair on a woman who isn't here to defend herself."

Saying nothing, Catriona carefully removed the nun's hand from her arm. She walked steadily toward the door and then paused, her back still to the other woman. "I'll pretend you never said what you just did, and we'll speak no more on it. I'm going outside where I'm going to prepare my horse for the ride ahead. I'll be gone until mid-afternoon at which time I'll return. I hope your meeting with Father Cleary goes well."

Catriona's clipped words to Katherine were formal and struck her more deeply than any emotional outburst could have done. She made no immediate move to follow Catriona, feeling as if she'd been dismissed in a manner similar to a child who had done ill. Regretting her outburst was one thing, but regaining the grazier's full friendship would be another. She only hoped her meeting with the Father would go a lot easier. Nervously smoothing the front of her habit, she made her way out of the study closing the door behind her.

Katherine spent the rest of the morning preparing for the visit, but she found her mind still occupied on the words she'd said in anger and she vowed she would do her best to make it up to Catriona when she returned home. In an attempt to keep her mind off such matters, she prepared the parlour by opening the curtains and windows to let some air into a room that obviously didn't get a lot of use. It was only a small room, dominated by typically Australian cedar furniture, a small pianoforte, and a watercolour landscape above the fireplace. This simplicity complemented the room, unlike the dark and intensely cluttered Victorian influenced rooms of the Ladies Committee. Despite how unfashionable furnishings like the Pelham's were supposed to be, Katherine liked them. She had barely finished her preparations when she heard a horse and carriage moving up the driveway and, peering out the window, she realised Father Cleary had arrived. Hastening to the hallway, she paused to check her habit before opening the door in greeting.

Father Cleary had been the town's cleric for the past ten years. He had first arrived at the small outpost full of idealism and righteousness, which wasn't unusual for most new religious types who found themselves in the outlying diocese of New South Wales. It hadn't taken him long to realise that things were different in the remote countryside of New South Wales to what they were in the city. Most of the people were common folk who relied on the comfort he could give them. Despite the patronage provided to him by the richer families of the district, he soon realised he would never have the grand church he dreamed of building and, as years passed, he became content with the life he led. He'd watched the progress of three nuns and the work they had performed in the district in his time. He had sometimes wondered how he would have reacted to Sister Watson's revelation had she been the first nun rather than the most recent one, not counting Sister Flynn of course. He knew he shouldn't have approved and had said as much to Alexander Pelham and the Sister. However, in reality he was silently pleased with the happiness they'd found together. This countryside with all its hardships seemed all too short on happiness.

Katherine looked at the man in front of her. He wasn't an overly tall man and, unlike the church Fathers in Ireland, had a wiry build. His face, similar to that of Mr Nelson the stationmaster, had just begun its process of physical erosion but this didn't detract from his grey eyes. They were eyes that seemed to mirror the many hardships he had experienced with little gain except guaranteed entry into heaven when his work on earth was complete. This caused her some comfort as she realised the visual image she'd created for the Father was something far different to the ecumenical one was standing in front of her now waiting to be invited in.

"Good morning. My name is Father Angus Cleary and I believe you're Sister Katherine Flynn. Welcome to Australia, Sister." He took her hand before adding, "It's been a long ride, do you mind if I come in?"

Katherine stepped out of the doorway and allowed him to enter. "I'm sorry, Father, my manners seem to have temporarily deserted me. Thank you for your words of welcome. I must admit, it's truly a remarkable country, full of many extremes that I'm sure you're more than aware of. One thing I must say though is its climate is at least a lot warmer than that of Ireland." Slightly nervous, she took the hat of the cleric before moving toward the parlour.

"Yes, I expect you're right. I've never seen England or Ireland as I did all my theological studies in a seminary in Sydney. Mind you, the previous Sisters all remarked on the change of climate. Some dealt with it better than others and I'm happy to see that you've realised the conventionality of wearing cotton rather than wool. I've no doubt that it's much more comfortable. Come winter wool may be of benefit but definitely not during any of the other seasons of the year." Father Cleary seated himself, smiling at the nun reassuringly.

"Yes, it was Catriona, er, Miss Pelham's suggestion actually. I must admit she was right. I honestly don't know how long I could have lasted on my visits to the families of the district wearing those hot woollen habits." Katherine realised that it was perhaps better she refer to the grazier by her surname in the presence of the Father.

"Yes, an eminently sensible young woman, somewhat too sensible." He cleared his throat. "However, if I can add one more suggestion. Get rid of that infernal wimple and find yourself a hat to protect yourself from the sun. I'd hate to send you back to

Ireland at the end of your tenure with your face resembling a prune," Father Cleary declared, flexing his hands in front of him.

She acknowledged his suggestion, laughing to herself while thinking of the look on Catriona's face when she realised that she'd won that battle. *She'd probably known all along that she would win this battle of wills.* Realising that Father Cleary was waiting expectantly for her to say something she found her voice. "Father, I'm sure there are a number of things you wish to discuss with me but could I first offer you some tea and refreshments?"

"God be praised! I thought you were never going to ask. I'd dearly love both as I always find my trips have a tendency to work up a thirst." The Father rubbed his hands together in anticipation.

"Father, if you'll wait here I'll bring it in to you. I'll only be a minute." She excused herself and made her way to the kitchen.

It wasn't long before she returned to the parlour with tea and a batch of the scones she'd made the day before. She was happy she'd experimented with them on Catriona previously. She would have hated to think she gave the Father food poisoning because of her shortfalls in cooking.

Having fulfilled the social requirements deemed of a visit, the Father relaxed into his chair and looked at the deep green eyes framed by deceptively delicate features which were mostly hidden by a wimple. From what he had been told by various people the previous day, she'd made quite an impression in the past two months or so and, unlike two of the three Sisters who had worked here previously, her acceptance into the community had been almost immediate. This acceptance he believed was in some way attributable to Sister Coreen, God rest her soul, who had done some remarkable work among the less fortunate. He just wondered how long Sister Flynn would want to stay in a country which was so unforgiving.

Placing his scone back on his plate, he sat forward and addressed the woman opposite him. "So Sister, it would seem that you've had an unusual introduction into the district. From what I'm told, you nearly died at the train station only to recover sufficiently to tend to those of the town who were in need."

Katherine looked down at her hands, unsure and embarrassed at his words. "I think, as seems to be the case in Australia, someone has been indulging in over-exaggeration, Father.

Really I'd only fallen asleep at the station. Despite the tragedy that had occurred that day, I'm sure that sooner or later they would have remembered my arrival, as they eventually did. As for my actions, I'd like to say that I would have never shriven the dead as I did if you were here. It was just at the time there was no-one else to do it. It did seem to give the families who had lost someone comfort, and I did assure them that you would visit them on your return." She knew her words were flowing freely, like water from a water tank's faucet, but she couldn't turn them off.

Father Cleary, realising what was occurring held up a hand to halt her ramblings. "Sister, don't mistake my comment. I'm appreciative of what you did on your arrival. You're correct, there wasn't anyone else to help in such religious matters and your decision to give comfort to these people was the right one. I'll ensure I conduct a memorial service for the dead just to put at rest any doubts any of the families may have on their lost loved ones. But rest assured, your decision was correct given the circumstances." Father Cleary smiled reassuringly.

Katherine felt guilty in accepting the credit for a decision she'd been virtually forced into by the grazier. She felt ashamed at how the Father had applauded what he thought was her decision for had it been left up to her, she would have done the opposite. This made the morning's outburst between the two even more painful. *Why do I have to be so prideful sometimes? Father Cleary is right; Catriona is an inherently sensible woman and a thoughtful one at that.*

Father Cleary was somewhat taken aback by the nun's sudden silence but took a moment to finish his scone before saying, "Apparently you've been very busy working with the less fortunate families within the district. I'm glad that you've taken to this task so well as you'll find it will occupy a great deal of your time. One of the requirements that I ask of the Sisters who are sent here is that they have a modicum of knowledge on the treatment of minor ailments and the like. Our closest doctor is in the next town. Even though our town has the new modern telegraph, it still takes half a day's hard ride to get here from there. As you can see, our tyranny of distance still makes the physical trip for the doctor a long one. Tell me, Sister Flynn, were you given any medical training by your convent?" he asked, buttering yet another scone.

"Yes, I was, but only for minor ailments. This training has

been supplemented by Miss Pelham who has provided me with advice for the treatment of heat sickness and snakebite; two maladies we're unfamiliar with in Ireland. I'm grateful that you're happy with my work with the families. It's certainly a delight to get around and talk with them especially the small children. Speaking of which, I hope you don't mind, but I've sent for some children's books to assist in their learning. It seems unfair that they shouldn't have access to the readings more suited to their age group." Her eyes lit up as she spoke of the children and the work she'd done with the district families. It was one thing that gave her a sense of worth and she felt she'd made many friendships in carrying out those tasks.

Father Cleary was relieved to see the Sister come alive at the mention of this work. The literacy and numeracy of the children had been an ongoing concern of his, but there never seemed to be enough hours in his day to attend to it. The fact that her education was greater than what would normally be expected of a nun was a great asset. "Yes, I've heard of your book venture and I must say it's a wonderful idea. Miss Crosier asked me to mention that she's not yet seen your shipment, but she'll keep you in touch with its arrival. I've always believed the children out here grow up way too fast, with the responsibility of adulthood being thrust upon them before they barely reach their teens. Such a cycle is repetitive and must be broken. I strongly believe your endeavours may well achieve that, Sister." The priest smiled broadly.

"Thank you, Father. I've managed to incorporate my teaching with their farming tasks so as to not make their parents suspicious of their learning. It seems to be working out well for all concerned." She reached for her tea feeling much more at ease.

Father Cleary followed her lead and did the same. Draining his cup, he placed it down and then wondered how to broach the next topic. It was a situation that he didn't like being placed in, but after his meeting with the Ladies Committee that morning, he'd been placed squarely in the middle. "Yes, I'm happy with your progress, Sister Flynn, and I'm more than pleased that you're also enjoying yourself. However, I feel I must speak to you in regards to a meeting I had with the Ladies Committee this morning. I'll preface my comment by saying that I'm not comfortable with their discussions but you must accept that I rely primarily on the more affluent families of the district to assist me in my Ministry. Therefore when they raise a concern I'm obliged to pursue the matter." The Father paused, looking at Sister Katherine's face that was masked with worry, and he chose his next few words carefully. "Mrs Greystone is beside herself with worry over you accommodating yourself so far from town. She feels you'd be much better suited by staying with one of the committee families. Her concern is the influence that you're receiving out here. Now before you answer, I've no doubt that by now Miss Pelham has discussed with you the situation involving her brother and Sister Watson. I'm sure you're not surprised that it caused a great deal of discussion amongst the town gossips. However, her main concern is the influence of Miss Pelham and her rather unorthodox ways. Additionally, she told me of the rude manner in which Miss Pelham addressed you after your return from your, er, bushranging adventure. She said she'd heard that her actions bordered on physical violence. Is this correct?"

Katherine wasn't a fool and knew that the ladies would grasp at any opportunity presented to extract her from her current accommodation. It angered her that after making it politely clear to them of her refusal of their offers to reside in town, they persisted by getting yet another reluctant party involved. She inwardly cursed herself and Catriona for allowing themselves to become embroiled in a disagreement on the morning of her return from the bushrangers. Katherine contained her anger before responding to the Father's comments. "I'm sorry Mrs Greystone has seen fit to discuss this with you and I realise that it's put you in an unfair situation. The disagreement that Miss Pelham had with me on my return after capture was warranted. She, in looking after my safety, had advised me to wait with the Connors' so she could escort me home. If any one was at fault it was my own pride; had I waited, she would have had no cause to get as angry as she did and I can't say I blame her.

"As for Mrs Greystone, I've already politely declined her offer for practical reasons. It's easier for me to administer care to the families of the district from out here. They're more accessible and what is even more important is my accessibility to them. You've mentioned, Father, that your day is full with the tasks required of you which means families who need to see me need to do so free of any incumbency which may come from me residing in town. If I may speak freely, Father, I can't see the more eminent families being too receptive to the less fortunate families being on their doorstep at all hours of the day. Moreso,

if I resided in such a manner they're unlikely to approach me
anyway and this defeats the purpose of my work out here." She
paused as she felt her anger rising and was consciously aware
this would also be obvious to Father Cleary through her flushed
cheeks. Forcing herself to unclench her hands, she smoothed the
front of her habit before she continued.

"Mrs Greystone also warned me of the unorthodox ways of
Miss Pelham and I've discussed these with her. It's true she
doesn't dress in the way a woman should, but given her work on
the land a dress would be no more suitable than my woollen habits and wimple. I'm also aware she currently doesn't have or
hasn't had in the immediate past any male suitors, and I again
can see the reason for this. After all the work she does in a day
there's hardly time left for entertaining. If I may be so bold to
add, Father, that in the immediate district her choices are rather
scarce. She told me she had a suitor when she was 17 which
wasn't approved by her family because of the age difference. It's
my belief she has never recovered from this and would be naturally reluctant to seek out another suitor." She paused as she saw
the pallor of the Father's face pale from its normal browned
appearance.

Gripping the edges of the chair he leaned forward as he
said, "Did she ever mention to you the name of the suitor?"

Katherine sensed something wasn't quite right. "No, she
hasn't and given the sensitivity of the subject I've seen no reason to pursue the matter. Father, I know this puts you in a rather
delicate situation, but under the circumstances I'd sincerely like
your assistance in allowing me to stay out here. Please rest
assured I'm not likely to take to wearing trousers and I promise
you I'll still maintain regular visits with the more affluent families." She found herself still unsure of what to make of the
Father's previous reaction.

Raising himself from the chair, he moved to the fireplace.
Above the mantelpiece was a watercolour that had been painted
by Miss Pelham about eleven years ago when he first arrived. He
recalled one of his first visits involving the Pelham family, at the
behest of a worried Mrs Pelham. He barely remembered the
vague concerns Catriona's mother had voiced over her reluctance
in accepting any of the many male visitors of the district and Mrs
Pelham called upon him to discuss with Catriona the sacred bond
that existed between woman and man. He was somewhat confused at the time since he felt it was a subject that could have

been more capably handled by the child's governess, or the mother herself. However, strangely enough at the same time he had been called upon to perform the task, the governess had left the family unexpectedly and never returned. He remembered his discussion with Miss Pelham that was mainly received with a polite silence. He also remembered her polished thank you at the end of his speech, but what struck him most were her last words that she would never marry as she saw no need to be burdened or comforted by a male.

He now wondered whether or not it were the actions born of these sentiments which disturbed Mrs Greystone. As a young preacher he hadn't thought much on the subject and was greatly relieved when his task was completed. Now, in retrospect, he couldn't help but wonder if Miss Pelham's interests lay else-where. Shaking his head as if to dismiss the thought, he turned and faced Sister Flynn who was waiting for an answer, with full knowledge that her argument was a logical one that couldn't be faulted. He was trapped, deciding whether he should leave her in the current situation or move her on the whim of Mrs Greystone and his own unfounded suspicions. Making up his mind he answered, "Yes, you're right in what you're saying and it's diffi-cult for me to be caught in such a situation. I've very little authority over your presence here beyond that of a Father to a Sister. However, under the circumstances I'll speak to the ladies and explain to them it would be better that the 'dirty and disease ridden' families visit you out here, rather than have you drag them into their sitting rooms." Seeing the look of relief on the Sister's face he diplomatically chose his next words. "As for Miss Pelham's unorthodox ways, I'm aware that she's, er, differ-ent. I must say that if I feel the influence she's having on you is detrimental to your calling out here, then I'll personally see to your relocation closer to the main part of town." Father Cleary attempted to utter these last words in his most foreboding Sun-day Church voice but the impact was lost on Sister Flynn who was already rushing to grasp his hand.

"Thank you, Father, I won't let you down. I feel there's so much I can do out here for these people, both through your guid-ance and some ideas I have of my own. I feel Miss Pelham is someone who does not have a lot of female company and she may well benefit from my presence out here. You never know, it may well serve to soften her a bit." Katherine was enthusiastic that she'd faced the last hurdle and overcome it. She couldn't wait to tell the grazier about the visit and the success she had; however, she remembered her first duty would still remain in apologising for this morning's unseemly behaviour.

Father Cleary had made no effort to sit back down and, turning toward the table beside the door, he retrieved his hat. "Well enough of the morning's pleasantries, I've families to visit also. If you'd please, give Miss Pelham my regards and my wish that she's in good health. I think you and I should meet on a weekly basis when I'm in town. You may reach me at the Percy's accommodation hotel." He opened the door to the hallway, paused, and again looked at the watercolour hanging over the fireplace. "One more thing before I go. When you speak to Miss Pelham next, you may wish to ask her about the watercolour." He motioned to the one in question.

Katherine's face creased in a puzzled frown, but she nodded anyway. She managed to skirt around Father Cleary and opened the front door before he could do so. "Thank you, Father, I will. I look forward to speaking with you next. Again, thank you for explaining my situation to the Ladies Committee."

Father Cleary climbed onto his sulky and grasped the reins in preparation of leading the horse on its way. "Goodbye, Sister Flynn, and thank you for the scones they were delicious." Turning the horse's head, he pulled away. He had enjoyed his morning; for once he felt the convent had got it right. Now his only problem was Mrs Greystone.

Katherine waited until the wagon was well on its way toward the gate before closing the front door. Moving into the parlour, she closed the windows and drew the heavy drapes before any more flies or the oncoming heat of the day could get in. Picking up the tray that had carried the successful morning's scones and tea, she made her way to the kitchen.

As she heated water to clean the morning's dishes, she couldn't help but feel that at last she had somewhere she could stay. Despite the difficulties Father Cleary would face, she was confident he'd be successful in his endeavours. She was certain that despite her rudeness this morning Catriona would be happy to have her stay.

Katherine paused in her motion of pouring water into the large wash basin to think of Catriona and she wondered whether the protestations she'd made this morning solely revolved around her necessity to tend to the families of the district. If Katherine was honest with herself, she had to admit part of her strong wish to stay had a lot to do with the closeness that had developed between them. For the first time she felt she was in a household where she was welcomed and sharing a friendship with a female closer to her age. She wondered if the relationship that Susan and Me-Lin shared was as strong as the one she and Catriona seemed to be developing and she found herself looking forward to having them to dinner. It would give her the opportunity to relive such occasions that, now she was a nun, seemed a lifetime ago. Shaking herself out of her pensive mood, she turned and began on the dishes.

After preparing herself a small lunch, she spent the rest of the afternoon doing minor cleaning around the house and preparing vegetables for tea; for while she hadn't yet mastered a full evening meal she could still assist in its preparation. With the vegetables completed, Katherine decided that given the other woman's mustering activities of the day, it was most likely that one of the first things she'd do on her return would be to have a bath. Moving out the back door onto the verandah she grasped the high edge of the bath with both hands and dragged it slowly toward the house. She'd almost completed her task when she heard the sound of hooves heading up the driveway. Pausing in her ministrations, she straightened up and moved to the end of the verandah so as to look down toward the entrance to the property. Bringing her hand up to shade her eyes from the brightness of the afternoon sun she could make out a person on a horse. She presumed it was Catriona. *Given her terse words before her departure this morning, she is due home around about now,* Katherine thought. She raised her hand in greeting, which was acknowledged by the rider, and turned toward the back door to finish dragging the bath into the kitchen.

She'd barely finished when she heard the horse come to a halt and the footfall of boots on the verandah. Straightening and bracing herself for the apology she knew she must give, she turned toward the back door. When it opened, she grasped for a chair as she realised the person standing in front of her wasn't Catriona. Katherine was in shock, for all intents and purposes the man in front of her was obviously Catriona's brother, the resemblance to Catriona was definite. His shock was equally so and for a moment silence passed between the two. It was obvious he had mistaken her for Sister Coreen.

Having mastered her emotions, she introduced herself. "Good afternoon, my name is Sister Katherine Flynn. How do you do? I'm sure there's no other person who you could be other than Mr Alexander Pelham. You and your sister bear a striking resemblance to each other, but I'm sure many people have told you this." The nun managed with a nervous smile on her face.

Alexander strode across the kitchen toward her with an extended hand. "Yes, Sister, you're right, but I'd prefer if you call me Alexander. Mr Pelham makes me sound older than my years. I expect Catriona has told you that I've been away for the past couple of months but welcome to our house. I'd presume that Cat has made you welcome, despite her sometimes brittle and explosive nature. Please excuse me, but I must see to my horse and then wash up outside. I've been away for so long, but I'd like to talk to you about issues I'm sure you've been made aware of." Alexander looked down at Katherine with a pair of sky blue eyes, which were obviously a strong family trait. He silently regarded the woman's lack of response as shyness. After all, it couldn't be a normal occurrence for the Sister to have a male in such close proximity. He nodded his head, turned, and strode out the door to tend to his horse.

As the back door closed Katherine's shoulders slumped and she snapped out of her reverie. She could now understand why Sister Coreen had fallen for such a man. His and Catriona's features were so alike with the exception of a height advantage that he had over his sister. She judged him to be over six feet given she had to look up to speak with him, not eye to eye as she did with Catriona. His eyes were slightly lighter blue than Catriona's, but both had the ability to hold a piercing stare. Again she found herself thinking back on the times she'd looked into Catriona's sometimes happy, sometimes angry deep blue eyes. However, if they were the mirror to ones deepest secrets, she was still yet to truly discover the inner secrets so well concealed by Catriona. Jumping at the sound of the barn door being opened, she realised Alexander may well be both hungry and thirsty and so moved through to the pantry to prepare him lunch.

As she did so she suddenly halted in her tracks and raised her hand to her mouth in horror. Alexander had mentioned he wished to speak with Katherine and, with a sense of foreboding, she realised the discussion would involve Sister Coreen. Given the manner in which he had entered the house it was obvious he didn't yet know about her death and Katherine started panicking. She definitely didn't want to be the one to have to tell him and she found herself wishing that Father Cleary hadn't left so soon.

And where was Catriona when she is most needed? Katherine thought. How long would she be able to avoid questions on the issue until the other woman came home? Katherine's range of social discussion skills was out of practice and she wished she'd paid a little more attention to the ramblings of the Ladies Committee. At least she could postpone the issue by preparing him lunch. Katherine just hoped that Alexander would take an inordinate amount of time in seeing to his horse.

She'd spent the time with one eye on the barn outside and both ears wishing for the sound of hooves heralding Catriona's return. She was thankful Alexander obviously shared the same caring nature for animals as his sister did, as he had taken the last half an hour to see to the horse before moving to the outside pump to wash up. Stripping down to the waist, he washed the dirt accumulated in riding from his body. Katherine's mouth dropped as he headed toward the house half-naked. In almost synchronisation with her reaction he stopped, seeming to realise there was a stranger in the house. He returned to the barn to get a shirt, Katherine surmised correctly, before entering the house.

She had decided she wouldn't give him time to commence a conversation and in that way she hoped to avoid the obvious questions about Sister Coreen. With that in mind she said brightly, "Alexander, sorry for my reaction earlier. It was a bit of a shock to see someone new at the house. Mind you, Catriona had said she was expecting your return and I believe she's left some papers in the top drawer of the desk in the study for you to review. But before you busy yourself with those, I'm sure you're hungry, so I've prepared you some lunch." She motioned Alexander to the table where there was enough food for both her and Catriona. He began to utter words of thanks but again the nun interrupted him. "No, there's no need for a thank you, I'm more than happy to prepare you lunch, given you and your sister's generosity to me. And I'd also be grateful if you'd call me Katherine. Catriona has taught me that sometimes formality isn't required this far out in the country, and besides it would be foolish if I'm to call you Alexander that you call me Sister all the time. Now I'll leave you to your lunch as I've some religious reading and passages I've to prepare for the children of the district."

Alexander, who was halfway through a sandwich again endeavoured to swallow so as to pose a question, Katherine presumed.

"Please excuse me, but I must get this done today. I'm sure there'll be more than ample time to talk later on this evening but for now I'll leave you to finish your lunch." Before Alexander could respond Katherine turned and left for her room.

Alexander watched the retreating figure of the nun. She seemed to be nervous over something, but on first meeting he dismissed this as her nature. He was grateful for the lunch she'd prepared and the advice he had been given regarding the impending business matters. However, in reality, there was only one question he wanted an answer to: where was Coreen? Smiling, as he thought of her tending to the families of the district, he assumed she would be at home in time for tea and the wonderful news he had for her. He had found a Father who, after much persuading, had consented to marry them.

Katherine retreated to her room and closed the door firmly behind her. Convinced Alexander wouldn't follow, she paced the floor, her hands nervously clasped in front of her. She paused only long enough to look out the window, as if willing the figure of Catriona and horse to appear. She hoped she would return soon for Katherine was sure she couldn't stay in her room all day and night or Alexander would indeed sense something was amiss. Realising the sound of her leather-heeled shoes was making from her pacing she went to the small dresser and opened the drawer containing her religious documents and Bible. Placing them on the dressing table, she sat down and tried to concentrate on reading, just for the sake of trying to take her mind off the other occupant of the house. Despite her attempts at concentration, she gave this up after a very short period of time. She rose again and moved to check the view out the window. The scenery was no different to what it usually was, and it certainly contained no hint of Catriona. Realising she couldn't concentrate, nor could she pace the floors, she took to her bed. Although this was unusual for her to do in the middle of the day, she felt maybe some spiritual meditation would help calm her. Lying down, she concentrated on relaxing her breathing.

It was some time later that she woke with a start. Listening for sounds inside the house and realising there were none, she surmised Alexander was still engrossed in the study. What had awoken her were the footfalls of a horse approaching the house. Katherine flung herself out of bed, opened the French windows to her room, and ran outside in vain hope of seeing Catriona. She said a silent blessing as she saw the almost unmistakable figure move toward the barn and, hoping that Alexander would be too preoccupied to investigate the noise, she ran in the direction which Catriona had taken.

Arriving out of breath and gulping in air, Katherine found she couldn't find the words to tell Catriona the news. Catriona, tired from a day's riding had dismounted her horse and, occupying herself in unsaddling it, hadn't visually acknowledged the Irishwoman. Rather than waiting for her to speak Catriona pre-empted her. "It's been a long day and whatever it is it can wait. Right now all I want is a hot bath and bed. No arguments please, just let me..."

She turned and paused mid-sentence seeing the look on Katherine's face as she sensed there was more to this look than a batch of burnt scones. *Had Father Cleary ordered her out of the house?* Rather than prolong any further Catriona grabbed her arm and asked, "Katherine, what is it? Has the Father ordered you into town for if he has you need to know he doesn't have the direct authority to do it. I've half a mind to ride into town and have words with him." Catriona released the nun's hand to recommence the process of saddling the horse.

The sight of the other woman's apprehension touched Katherine deeply. Despite the harsh words spoken earlier, it was obvious Catriona still cared for her welfare. Afraid that Catriona was about to launch into town on an unfounded goose chase, Katherine grabbed the saddle to halt her actions. "No, it isn't that at all. In fact, I think it's much worse. Your brother's returned and I've managed to stall him all afternoon in the study." The nun looked into Catriona's eyes. "He's very happy and that would lead me to believe no-one has told him about Sister Coreen."

Catriona closed her eyes and bent her head as if to gather her thoughts. Handing the reins to Katherine she said, "Then I expect it's up to me to break the news. I'd ask that you make yourself scarce as I'm not sure what his reaction will be. If I need you, I'll call." With that Catriona turned toward the house to break the news to her brother which she knew would emotionally rend him in two.

Chapter
Nine

Catriona entered the back door of the house and paused to gather her thoughts; for despite the fact she knew this day would eventually come, she hadn't really prepared herself for it. The arrival of Katherine and her work on the farm and surrounding district hadn't given her the time needed to really sit down and think about how she would give this news to her brother. She'd never seen him as happy as when he was with Coreen and now she was about to completely ruin his world. All at once she felt very old for her twenty-eight years and longed just this once to have someone else bear the responsibilities that came with being an adult. Lifting her head she reluctantly made her way through the house to the study where Alexander was waiting. Steeling herself, she grasped the handle and quietly opened the door.

Alexander, who had been resting in one of deep leather chairs, jolted awake. He was momentarily confused as to exactly where he was and scanned the room to re-establish his bearings. It was then that he met the guarded eyes of his sister standing at the door. She'd a strange look on her face of mixed emotions, as if she was happy for his return but at the same time wasn't. Shaking himself out of his sleepiness, he rose out of his chair and strode toward his sibling. Encircling her in his arms he said, "Hello, Cat, you look as if you've been wrestling cattle again. Dare I ask who won?"

The woman returned her brother's hug. "Need you ask, big brother, when you know a Pelham always succeeds at what ever endeavour they begin?" Catriona held her breath, realising her brother's most recent endeavour could only be one met with bitter success. In an attempt to redirect the conversation she said, "Welcome home and how are you? What business stories of the world do you have this time?"

Leading his sister to the fireplace they sat in seats facing each other. Alexander eased himself into the comfort of a soft chair. "Oh, not much really. The price of wheat has picked up a bit but not half as much as barley has. They tell me that, as far as crops go, barley is not an easy one however its financial benefits are enormous. I think next year we'll plant a paddock to see if it will take or not. If it does then, my dear Cat, I think that we'll be well established as one of the most affluent families in the west." He smiled, locking his hands behind his head, a smug look upon his face.

"Not that we really need it, Alex. We're more than self-sufficient here. There are certainly a lot of people in far worse situations than we are." Catriona gave her brother her most serious stare.

"Yes, I know, but don't you think it would be nice just to well and truly rub it in the faces of those rich impostors in town? I'm sick to death of being looked down by them every time we go into town. I would like to establish this property as one of the most modern properties in the district. With the returns I envisage, no-one would dare treat us like just farm trash." Alexander fought to keep the bitterness from his voice and lost. Calming himself, he redirected his conversation closer to home. "So, tell me what's been happening around here?"

Catriona swallowed not ready to raise the topic of Coreen just yet. She raised herself from her chair and moved toward the liquor cabinet. "Before I start, would you like a drink? I've been riding all day and need something just to quench my thirst. I could think of nothing better than a whiskey and water." Not waiting for his reply, she poured two generous helpings of scotch into the glasses in front of her.

Alexander uncrossed his legs and sat forward in his chair. "Sister, I don't believe my ears! You consuming alcohol is surprising enough, but even before the sun is set? You must have had a hard day. Yes, of course I'll join you and then you can tell me all about what's happened since I've been away."

She moved toward the door. "I'll just get us some water and then we can sit down and have a good old talk." Closing the door behind her she moved through to the kitchen to find Katherine seated at the table.

"How's everything going in there?" Katherine asked, a concerned look on her face.

The grazier busied herself with getting a small pitcher of water from the larger one on the benchtop. "Everything's fine so far, but then I haven't told him anything yet. I think it's going to be a long night so please don't wait tea for us. I intend to get him a little drunk, at least enough so that, once I begin to tell him, hopefully the pain won't be too great." Catriona replaced the large pitcher on the bench.

Katherine rose and moved to stand beside the grazier and placed her hand over Catriona's. Catriona paused in her actions, first looking at the hand and then at the nun whose face seemed perilously close to hers. "Just remember that if you need me, I'm here. Please don't try to break the news to him all by yourself."

Catriona looked deeply into the other woman's eyes, too moved to transfer into words what she felt. After their morning argument she'd been so angry with this woman, but how could she maintain anger with someone who was so beautiful? Placing the smaller pitcher on the table she placed her other hand over both of theirs and without breaking eye contact she squeezed the hands as she tried to manage a small smile. Remembering the original purpose of her mission, she reluctantly removed her hand before raising the pitcher and again returning toward the study.

Opening the door, she found her brother had already helped himself to one of the glasses of scotch. Moving toward him, he held it out and she topped it up with a scant amount of water and then moved toward the liquor cabinet to do the same to hers albeit with a more generous amount of water. Taking her seat, she took time to take a large sip before placing it down on the small table beside her. Before she could commence with her sanitised version of what had passed during his absence Alexander cut her off. "Oh, by the way, I met the new Sister this afternoon. Katherine, I think she said her name was. She seems to be a very nervous sort of person. Mind you, I got the impression that I surprised her with my sudden entrance. Tell me, Cat, is she always like that?"

Catriona took time to choose her words carefully. She could hardly tell him her feelings for Katherine raged between the impetuosity of love tempered strongly by the sensibility of friendship. "Oh, no, she's not usually like that. In fact, she's a stubborn and proud woman." Catriona paused as her brother started laughing.

"Then you two should get on famously then. Why come winter with both of you and your stubborn pride, there may not be any need to light a fire in the house. So tell me, Cat, how many disagreements have you had so far?" Alexander smiled at his sister's face adorned by a distinct red tinge.

"Well, yes, you're right. But I'm not the only one in the family with that trait, brother. As for Katherine, well, yes, we've had our disagreements but we still seem to share a lot of common ground. She has a desire to help the less fortunate families of the district which she has been doing very well. They seem to have accepted her quite well also." Catriona took a sip from her scotch as she watched her brother smiling at her.

"I didn't think I'd live to see the day when you said you had something in common with a nun. There must have been changes around here since I was gone," Alexander said good-naturedly. "So tell me, what else has been happening?" Once again he relaxed in his seat with his drink in hand.

Catriona paused, trying to marshal her thoughts. She decided that rather than start from the time her brother left she would work backwards. This would give her enough time she hoped to find the words to explain to her brother what had happened. He seemed to listen contentedly to the occurrences of the town, stopping her occasionally, asking her to expand on some small point or another. She told him about the first visit Katherine had made to the ladies of the district and Mrs Greystone's reaction to Catriona's presence.

Alexander laughed. "You can't help yourself, can you? You seem to take a great delight in upsetting the woman."

"No, I don't. If I didn't carry on like I did, what would she and her old cronies have to talk about? After all, there's very little other excitement out here, and besides she deserves it," Catriona added, a cheeky gleam in her eye and a smile on her mouth.

Her news had now brought itself to the day of Katherine's arrival and the dust storm. Realising the time of telling was almost upon her, she swallowed the remains of her drink and rose to make another one. She picked up her brother's glass, which was also empty and refilled it, again with a greater portion of whiskey than water.

Watching his sister's actions, Alexander frowned. She

seemed somehow reticent about something and it was unusual for her to be drinking. She did it so very rarely and usually only when she was in a melancholy mood. At such times, he found it best to leave her to drink herself senseless before carrying her to bed. The result was always the same with protestations by his sister that she would never touch another drop. Trying to inject an air of casualness into his voice he said, "Things must have changed, Cat. Two drinks in quick succession. Don't tell me that Sister is driving you to it." He took his glass from his sibling, carefully studying her reactions to his words.

"No, Alex, I just thought it would be nice for us to share one together. We very rarely do, what with you touring the country all the time and me stuck here," Catriona explained as she took a long sip from her drink.

Alexander looked at his sister's guarded features quizzically. There was something wrong with her, he was sure of it. Rather than wait for her to raise the subject in conversation he leant forward in his chair and, looking straight at his sister, said, "Cat, you're hiding something, what's wrong? Have those ladies in town been at you again with their gossip? I've told you before to ignore them; they don't even deserve a response from you. Now tell me what's wrong?"

Catriona placed her drink down and also leant forward in her chair, so that her and her brother's faces were very close. "No, for once it's nothing to do with them. Alexander, there was a dust storm shortly after you left. It wasn't like the usual ones we have. This one caused untold devastation to the town. I gather you didn't return through town on your journey home?" She paused as he shook his head. "Then you haven't yet heard what it did to the place. Most of the shops made of wood were blown apart." Seeing the look of concern on his face she again took a sip from her drink before continuing.

"At the height of the storm a lot of people sought refuge in the Town Hall. There was so much being blown about in the street outside that it seemed a natural place of refuge. Alexander, the Town Hall collapsed, killing most of the people inside of it." She halted, finding it hard to proceed any further while looking into his eyes.

Catriona noticed the slightest twitch occur below her brother's eye. Breaking away from the piercing blue that matched his own, he rose from his seat and walked toward the windows. Thrusting his hands deep into his pockets, he kept his back to her. "I'm terribly sorry it occurred while I was away; however, if there's anything we can do for the people who have suffered then we will." Alexander paused before turning and staring straight at Catriona. "Cat, where is Coreen?"

Catriona tried to speak but found the words wouldn't come. She felt the silent tears begin falling down her cheeks as her brother crossed the room and knelt before her. He held both of her arms with his hands and looked steadily at her. Again he asked, "Catriona, where's Coreen?"

She lowered her face trying to regain her composure but with little success. Lifting her face, she looked directly at her brother and said in a quiet voice, "Alex, she's gone."

Alexander's face ran a gamut of emotions from disbelief to anger. "What do you mean she's gone? Please tell me, Cat, that she's left. Please tell me that the Sister out there convinced her to return to Sydney for I can be packed in the hour and ready to follow her." He paused, looking at her face for a response. "You see I've wonderful news for her, Cat. I've found someone who will marry us." He desperately searched her face for an answer.

She wished she could tell her brother what he wanted to hear but to prolong the moment any more would only be painful to them both. Reaching up, she gently grasped his hands from her arms. "Oh, Alexander, you don't know how much I wish I could tell you that, but it's not true." Looking at his face, which had seemed to take on the features of a child's whose Christmas was about to be ruined, she continued, "She was also in the Town Hall on the day of the dust storm. I'm sorry, Alex, she was gone by the time they found her."

Alexander pushed himself away from his sister, causing her to fall back against the chair. She watched him as he paced the room like a caged animal. He said nothing, as if he was searching for words to say and then turning toward Catriona, he closed the distance between them, grabbed her roughly, and shook her. "No, it's not true, you're hiding something. That nun out there has convinced her to return to England. That's it, isn't it? That's why she was sent out here I'll bet. Well, I won't have it I tell you. And I won't have that woman staying in our house!" Loosening his grip on her, he turned toward the door.

She barely caught his hand in time, holding it in a vicelike grip. "It's nothing to do with her; it wasn't her fault!" She had realised that she was shouting. Maintaining a grip on Alexander's hand, she said more quietly, "She's dead Alexander; you can't begin to imagine how I wish it wasn't so, but it is. Katherine arrived on the day of the dust storm—it's not her fault or any one else's. There's nothing anyone could have done to save any of them in the hall."

She watched her brother's face as he fought a losing battle to maintain his composure. She watched as his eyes crinkled and his face puckered up much like a child's does only seconds before they begin to cry. Collapsing to his knees on the floor, he wept silently. Catriona followed him to the floor still maintaining a hold on one of his hands. Unable to offer any words of comfort that would ease his pain, she put her arms around him and rocked him gently—as he had done for her the day their parents died. Thinking back on that day, and on Coreen, she too silently wept.

During the course of the late afternoon, Catriona managed to gently move him from his position on the floor and back into one of the chairs in the study. She'd only left the room twice—on both occasions to get more water for the scotch. On her first trip, she'd run into the nun, who was sitting in the kitchen making notes. On her second journey, which was late in the evening, a trimmed lamp solemnly lighted the empty kitchen and it was obvious the other woman had retired for the night.

Over the ensuing hours and varying measures of scotch, brother and sister spoke about Coreen and the time she'd spent in the small country town. They spoke of her reaction on her arrival, which had been an attempt to re-board the train that was already pulling away from the station. Alexander spoke fondly of her and the realisation between the two that their friendship had developed into something a lot deeper. Not that he couldn't have had his choice of any of the girls within the district; instead, he was happy to wait for what he termed the right girl to come along. This, Catriona believed, angered the affluent families of the district; for he had shunned their entire match making schemes in preference for a nun.

During the evening there were many more tears shed, as both came to terms with the gap Coreen had left in both of their lives. Catriona shed tears not only for Coreen but for her brother also. He was a kind man who wouldn't willingly hurt another human being and he had never berated her on her lifestyle,

whether it be her dress or her lack of suitors. Just as he had made
the decision to marry late, after his initial attempts regarding her
unmarried state were met with stubborn silence, he had never
pressed the issue with his sister.

Being the one bestowing the scotch, she had managed
throughout the evening to regulate the drinks she gave to herself
and her brother. As the shadows grew longer his held a greater
percentage of scotch while hers contained only enough to colour
her water. As the drinks got stronger, his voice became more
slurred and the pauses between his comments more prolonged.
Eventually, Catriona knew she'd achieved her mission as her
brother had fallen asleep and she was relieved for the both of
them. After the day they had both experienced, she was also
fighting a battle to keep her eyes open. Rising out of the soft
depths of her chair, she linked her hands under her brother's
arms to lift him, intending to assist him to his room. Unfortunately a combined day's effort of cattle mustering and emotional
efforts with her brother had also drained her. This, in addition to
him being a six-foot dead weight, made it near impossible for
her to do little more than move him forward in his chair. Realising that she would need help, she left the room to find Katherine.

Katherine spent a long time moving silently throughout the
house, listening to the muted sounds of weeping and words
which came from behind the closed doors of the study. Occasionally she could make out the lighter lilt of Catriona's emotionally
charged and pained voice sharing in her brother's sorrow and
longed to give her comfort from the burden she was currently
bearing. In an attempt to occupy her mind with other thoughts,
she wrote out a series of lessons for the Connor brood, who she
hadn't visited since the incident with the bushrangers. Pausing in
her efforts, her mind's eye was suddenly occupied by the smiling
face and challenging words of the enigmatic Mary Carraghan.

At that moment a silent Catriona entered the kitchen and
refilled the pitcher before wordlessly returning to the study. The
nun watched her actions with a heightened sense of awareness
regarding her own emotions and again the laughter and challenging words of Mary Carraghan invaded her thoughts: *"Does that
not leave you living with a woman? If you weren't a nun what do
you think would be said about you?"* Despite her endeavours to

return to her lessons, the words of the bushranger circled her mind like carrion to a prey. That night she'd remembered her own shocked refusal at the mere mention of such actions between two women, but what concerned her more was the unfamiliar emotion that Mary had evoked in her—one that she'd also felt with the grazier. Realising she was fighting a losing battle, she placed down her pencil and retired to her room where she fell into a restless sleep.

Katherine found herself in a dreamscape back in Ireland, in the evening mists of her family's country garden. The sounds of a string quartet wafted through the open French doors of her father's house, across the grass to where she was dancing in the shadows with a stranger. They danced with a familiarity which could only be borne by a knowledge of each other, however try as she might she couldn't make out her partner's face. As if to assist her in her efforts, a shaft of light fell between them and Katherine realised that she was looking into the face of Catriona.

"I'm sorry to wake you and sorry to intrude, but I need your help." Catriona paused to allow the other woman to fully regain consciousness.

Katherine wasn't sure if she was still in her dream and if the face in front of her belonged to her dance partner. In confusion and in a sleep muddled voice she asked, "Catriona, what are you doing here?"

Aware the Irishwoman must have been dreaming she again spoke this time with a degree of impatience. "I'm here because this is my house, why else would I be here?" Mindful of the harshness of her voice she continued softer, "Please, wake up, I need your help."

"What time is it?" She queried, shaking herself from the tendrils of her dream and rubbing her hands in her eyes.

"I'm not sure. But I've a feeling it's well past midnight. I've managed to put Alexander asleep with the assistance of two decanters of good scotch but now I can't move him. I'm pretty sure between the two of us we could move him from the study to his room." Despite her care with her consumption of alcohol, Catriona realised that her own voice was less than steady.

Katherine had also noticed the change in the other woman's voice but chose not to comment. *After all*, she thought, *Catriona couldn't be expected to go through the afternoon she'd just gone through without some assistance as well.* "Yes, I'm sure between the two of us we can move him, but maybe we should prepare his room first." Katherine pulled back her bedcovers as she lifted herself out of bed.

"You're right, of course. Has your lamp got any light on it? I'd prefer not to go back in the study to get one of those lamps until we're ready to move him," she queried, moving toward a dim glow beside Katherine's bed. Fortunately the nun had only allowed her lamp to burn low and the wick, once raised, cast its light around the room. Katherine took the lamp from Catriona, assessing that if her speaking was a little unsteady then her feet may well be the same. Following Catriona down the hall they entered her brother's room and Katherine lit one of the lamps from her own while the other woman turned the bed down.

Catriona grabbed the edge of the bedspread and pulled it down. "I've managed to remove his shoes and belt. This will allow us to lay him fully clothed on the bed and just cover him. I don't wish to do anything else than that, just in case it wakes him." Having prepared the room she turned toward the door and motioned the nun to follow her.

Halting in front of the study, Catriona quietly opened the door to check on her brother. Fortunately he was just as she'd left him—sleeping soundly. She motioned for Katherine to take one side as she took his other arm and placed it around her shoulders to raise him out of the chair. He was heavy and his height didn't make the task any easier, but all the same, between the two of them, they managed to half-carry, half-drag him down the hall to his room with him rousing only once before dropping his head again. Katherine heard the sound of tearing material during the process of their actions and knew that her cotton nightgown would be in need of repair in the near future.

Once in his room, they lowered him onto the bed. With support from the Irishwoman, Catriona moved around to the other side to drag him further toward the centre. After much pushing and shoving they had achieved the task between the two of them. Katherine straightened as she closed her eyes and placed her hands in the small of her back, which was aching as a result of her efforts. Catriona having pulled the covers over Alexander on one side of the bed moved around to do the same on the nun's side. Katherine, too preoccupied in the pain in the small of her back, hadn't pulled the covers forward and allowed the grazier to complete the task.

It was the sudden sensation of someone very close which caused her to open her eyes and Katherine found Catriona standing within arm's reach, looking toward her chest. She followed the other woman's gaze and realised that the ripping she'd heard earlier was the front of her nightgown. It had slipped in the process of their activity and silhouetted in the light of the lamp was one of her breasts, the curve of it very obvious with just the hint of a nipple showing.

Catriona couldn't drag her eyes away from a sight which, aside from her own body, she hadn't seen in such a long time. Sensing something was wrong, she raised her eyes to meet Katherine's stare who, by her look, was well aware of Catriona's preoccupation. Her features were unreadable in the light, but Catriona sensed there was no anger radiating from her, moreso an unreadable calm. Ever so slowly, and without breaking eye contact with the other woman, Katherine raised her hand to the torn fabric and pulled it back onto her shoulder. Quietly she said, "I think it's time for you to go to bed." Trimming the lamp by Alexander's bedside, she raised her own lamp and motioned for the other woman to follow.

Katherine had barely taken ten steps from Alexander's room when she heard a muffled sound behind her. Turning, she found that the grazier had caught her foot on the hallway runner and had fallen. She was attempting to get up with a degree of difficulty given her unsteady state as the nun rushed to her aid. "I'm sorry. I didn't see it there, which is funny as I suppose it's always been there. I'm so tired I think I could sleep and never want to wake up."

Katherine precariously held onto her lamp in one hand while attempting to hang on to Catriona with the other. "I think that's understandable given the day you've just had. I'd like to tell you things will be easier when you wake in the morning but something tells me that both you and your brother may not feel the best. Can you open your door for me? I've run out of hands."

Catriona reached forward, opened her door and promptly collapsed on her bed. The nun again straightened her nightgown and placed her lamp on the bedside table, before moving forward to centralise Catriona on the bed as they had done with her brother only moments ago. Realising Catriona still had her boots on, Katherine removed them with a fair degree of effort before placing them to one side. Remembering the sister's removal of her brother's belt, the Irishwoman began to do the same. She'd managed to manoeuvre the buckle, which was no easy feat given her inexperience with such items of clothing, and was in the process of removing it when Catriona sat up suddenly, eyes opening, her hands going to where Katherine's already were. "What are you doing?" she asked.

Feeling as if she'd been caught doing something wrong, Katherine could only manage to stammer. "I was loosening your belt so that it didn't dig into you during the night."

Catriona let go of one of the nun's hands in order to manoeuvre the belt through the loops in her trousers and placed it beside her on the bed. Again neither woman broke eye contact, both masking their own emotions during Catriona's actions. With deliberate slowness Catriona raised the other woman's hand to her face, cupping it on her cheek and letting it rest there only fractionally before turning her head to place a soft kiss in the hollow of Katherine's palm. She returned her gaze to the face of the Irishwoman who was riveted to the spot, unsure of what was occurring between them. Realising the effects of the alcohol and the drama of the day had resulted in her acting more than her normal cautious self, Catriona lowered the nun's hand back toward the bed before saying as levelly as possible, "Thank you for your help today. I doubt I'd have been able to move Alex without you." The other woman had yet to break her gaze with Catriona and was at a loss for words. Tiredly the grazier lay back on the bed and closed her eyes. "Go to bed, Katherine; as you've already reminded me, tomorrow is going to be a long day."

Katherine said nothing but, picking up her lamp, she left the room and upon entering hers closed the door behind her. Mechanically placing the light on her bedside table, she lay down too confused to sleep. It was only then she mastered her breathing, which until a moment ago had been a rapid accompaniment to the staccato beating of her heart. She wondered if she'd really been a part of what occurred that night or if indeed it had been the epilogue to her strange dream. Raising to her face the hand that Catriona had kissed, she then knew it had occurred. Her own face was on fire, her feelings in turmoil. At first she'd been shocked when she saw the other woman looking at her as she had in her brother's room. She couldn't precisely read Catriona's features in that light but nor did she need to—the palpable exchange between the two was enough.

Her thoughts became more confused as she realised that once she'd recovered from her initial shock, she was flattered to think someone was looking at her the way that Catriona was at that moment. She was also aware of a feeling that such an incident shouldn't be happening; yet she had taken her time in covering herself. She was still a relatively young woman, but she knew, despite this short period, she'd never experienced the strange feelings she'd encountered that night with Catriona. Trimming her lamp, she rolled over and lay in darkness, trying to calm the confused emotions that were rushing through her.

Catriona, too tired to change, lay on her bed as the Irishwoman had left her. She wasn't sure if it was the emotions of the day or the influence of alcohol that had caused her to act so brazenly. She couldn't tear her eyes from Katherine's body and was slightly embarrassed when caught in the act; yet this turned to surprise when the Irishwoman made no immediate attempt to cover herself up. As for her actions in her own room, they were more of a reaction to waking up and thinking the other woman was undressing her. Katherine was so close and she couldn't resist placing a kiss in Katherine's palm, but it had taken all her willpower to release her hand rather than pull Katherine down onto the bed with her. She closed her eyes trying to will herself to sleep. Her thoughts were constantly interrupted by what might have happened had she not managed to control herself.

Catriona awoke the next morning feeling as if she'd fallen off her horse headfirst and it took her a moment before she realised the thick furry object in her mouth was actually her tongue. Endeavouring to sit up in bed was only met with a sharp reverberating pain through her head, as if she'd been too close to an explosion. It soon became obvious to her that, despite her efforts last night, she'd consumed more alcohol than she had in a long while. Laying back did little to alleviate her head's throbbing and placing her hands on either side of it, she recalled the evening's events after they had managed to get her brother to bed. She winced, closing her eyes and recalling her actions with Katherine. The worst thing, she thought, was at some time she was sure the Irishwoman would ask for an explanation and she wasn't quite sure how she would explain to Katherine she'd wanted her physically last night, as a man wanted a woman. One thing was sure and that was she couldn't remain in her room all day—there were issues that still had to be resolved with her brother.

Gingerly hopping out of bed she shed the clothes she'd now

been wearing for over 24 hours. What she really felt like was a bath but at this moment in time that seemed like far too much hard work considering how she felt. Splashing water into the hand basin, she began rudimentary ablutions in an attempt to make herself at least presentable. It was only when she was again fully dressed and a little refreshed by her wash did she feel strong enough to open her curtains. This turned out to be not a very good idea, as the bright light shining through the window only brought her headache on yet again. It was obvious she'd well and truly slept in, as she judged the time to be at least mid-morning. This was confirmed by the fob watch she pulled from the pockets of her soiled trousers. It was 11.30am! She couldn't remember sleeping so late in all her life and she opened her door to a silent household.

Moving toward her brother's bedroom she found the door open, his room empty and the bed made. She tiptoed past Katherine's room, assuming her to be still asleep. Opening the study door she found it too had been cleaned up after the previous night's activities in there. The empty decanters had been returned to their correct place and the glasses, now clean, were beside them. Suddenly she felt her stomach grumble in protest at the fact that it hadn't eaten in 16 hours and closing the study door, she quietly made her way to the kitchen to make herself some lunch. Reaching the room she halted as she saw Katherine sitting at the table, calmly mending the nightgown that had been torn the night before.

Looking up at her Katherine smiled. "Good morning, sleepy head. I was beginning to wonder if you were ever going to wake up."

Catriona moved around the back of the nun to cover her embarrassment. "Yes, I don't think I've slept so soundly for a long while. Mind you, I also know I haven't had a headache such as this for a long time and I need a cup of tea. Do you want one?"

"Yes, thanks. I've cleaned up the study and tidied your brother's room. I too slept in; not rising till eight o'clock. By the time I was up your brother was already gone. He doesn't seem to have left a note so I really don't know where he is." Katherine placed the nightgown down, and moved toward the cupboard to retrieve two cups for their tea.

The grazier frowned. "He may have gone into town. I have to go there later myself so I'll check on him while I'm there." She seated herself as far away as possible from Katherine.

An awkward silence descended over the table and realising something had to be said Catriona decided she should start. "Katherine, about last night, I'm sorry for my actions and I hope you don't take offence by them. I can only say in my defence that I think I had a little too much to drink. I'll understand if you wish to move out of the house, all I can offer you is that I'll watch my drinking in the future," she finished quietly and looked at the woman opposite her.

"I think we were both a little tired last night. There's no need for an apology and, as for moving out of the house, I think that's a little extreme. I'll leave if you want me to, but I'm happy to stay. And besides, I believe you may need a little more assistance with your brother over the next few days." She smiled at the other woman's embarrassed face.

In ironic retrospect, Catriona couldn't help but think how correct Katherine had been, for that day heralded the beginning of a repetitive cycle with her brother. He would rise early in the morning, ride into town and spend his day propping up the bar at the local watering hole. He soon became withdrawn and sullen, not caring for the opinions of his friends or Father Cleary. Catriona soon found a regular part of her day involved riding into town, wagon hitched, to retrieve her brother. Once arriving home she would bath him and prepare him a meal, which he barely touched. Despite her hiding all the alcohol in the house, he still managed to find it and top up his drunken stupor. The result was always the same, with Katherine helping Catriona to get him to bed. The only difference being that Catriona never again allowed the Irishwoman to see the same emotions she'd witnessed on the first night of Alexander's return.

As the first week passed, there was no let up in his actions. Alexander seemed to be on a cycle of self-destruction which neither Catriona or anyone else could deter him from.

Chapter
Ten

As Alexander's return entered its third week, fatigue began to show in Catriona's features. With Catriona's increased responsibility, as well as the tension in the house, it fell on Katherine to take a greater charge of the domestic tasks of the household. Gone from their everyday life was the routine friendliness between the two women. It was as if the only issues their lives revolved around were Alexander and the running of the farm; something that normally absorbed Catriona's working day but was now overshadowed by the need to care for her brother. Privately shared moments between the two few and far between.

Gradually Catriona realised that she couldn't wait for her brother to recover from his drunken state, there was work to be done. She could no longer wait for his advice and her intentions for the following day involved the purchase in town of seed for the next season's sowing. This year she would rely on the assistance she knew she could receive from the farmer's co-operative in town. She also needed to talk with Susan on some business issues. Katherine had asked if she would mind company, given the fact that she'd seemed to have spent a great deal of time avoiding it. The grazier nodded her assent, choosing to ignore the other woman's comment regarding her aloofness. If she was honest with herself there were two reasons for her remoteness. The first was that her brother's current demeanor left little time

for social interaction. But in all honesty, it was the second reason that caused her to maintain her distance and that was her fear
of again letting her defences down in front of Katherine.

As the nun entered the kitchen Catriona murmured a quiet
good morning, her eyes still fixed on the view outside. Chastising herself for the rudeness of her greeting, she turned to find
the Irishwoman standing, hair uncovered and a smile upon her
face. Without the wimple Katherine's curly hair complemented
her green eyes perfectly. Instead of looking stern and reserved,
she radiated a presence that almost encircled the older woman.
Katherine found herself pleased at last in getting a reaction from
a distant woman in front of her.

"Where's that thing you normally wear on your head?" The
older woman questioned, seeing a wry smile light the nun's features.

"Well, *that thing*, as you so politely call it, has not been
worn since Father Cleary's visit." Katherine paused as she saw
the look on the other woman's features.

Catriona felt like kicking herself. Her time had been so
absorbed between looking after her brother and managing the
farm that she'd missed a change that had been going on for some
time. She closed her eyes and dropped her head, rubbing her
hand across her forehead as she did so.

Katherine was momentarily stumped in her attempts to give
Catriona at least some respite to the drama that she currently
lived. Rather than offering comforting words she decided
humour might be the best medicine. "You were right, as you so
often are, and what's more Father Cleary agreed with you about
the wimple. In fact, during his visit here one of the first things
he said to me was, 'Sensible things cotton habits, and get rid of
that infernal wimple.'" Katherine tried her best to impersonate
the walk and mannerisms of the Father.

The grazier lifted her head and laughed, something there
had been little of since her brother's return. Katherine had managed an impersonation of the town priest rather well and was
continuing to strut around the kitchen, as he had a tendency to
do. *She is such a beautiful woman*, Catriona thought. She
couldn't help but wonder if the other woman had any idea of the
effect she was having on her. Since the incident on the night of
her brother's return, she had kept her distance while Katherine
had seen no great issue in it and instead seemed more intent on
getting closer to Catriona. She'd noticed that while there was no

increase in the physical closeness they shared, the Irishwoman's actions bespoke of an awareness that her presence had on the grazier, and in a sense seemed to enjoy the response it evoked in Catriona.

Catriona wasn't sure whether this impersonation of Father Cleary was an attempt to raise her spirits. However, despite Katherine's actions she was careful not to indulge her, as she was sure that the nun wasn't truly aware of the fire she was playing with. She responded to the imitation of the town's clergyman, she stood, performing a mock curtsy. "Father Cleary, I wasn't aware of your presence today. Please be seated and I'll fix us both some refreshments."

Laughing at each other, both women took their seats. Catriona felt a load temporarily lift from her shoulders, allowing her to relax more than she had done in a number of days. She smiled at the woman opposite her. "I'll be honest with you. I was almost completely sure that he would usher you out of the wimple and into the hat, as he had done it with all the previous sisters."

Katherine's mouth dropped open, a look of surprise on her face. Catriona had known all along that he'd recommend the change and had been content to fool her. "You rude woman! You let me wander around in the blistering heat with that wimple on knowing what the outcome would be? Why I could have died and then what would you've done?" she asked in a mock scolding tone.

The grazier responded with laughter in her eyes. "Yes, I'm sorry, you're right. I knew what Father Cleary's actions would be. In my defence I'd like to add that I tried to buy you a hat and you would have nothing of it. And that same hat has watched you proudly stride out of the house on numerous occasions. Yes, I could have forced you to wear it if your life was at risk but there's one thing you must remember about the way that business is conducted out here. No-one can make you do anything—the decision must be yours; you must be the one to take the first step."

Katherine seemed to pause for a moment, measuring the intent of the other woman's words. Catriona was right; she'd been stubbornly proud and foolishly so. She was also right about decisions that had to be made—they *were* sometimes difficult to make. "Yes, as is often the case, you're right." She watched the other woman lean back in the chair, giving herself a superior air. "I also understand that the decisions I make have to be my decisions and all I can say to you is that life is a continued learning experience, and I've learnt from this one. Maybe I'll learn to be more willing to listen in the future." Katherine finished by rising and moving to the end of the table to try her hat on. "Hmm, perfect fit don't you think?"

The hat suits her very well, Catriona thought, *it almost makes Katherine look like just another woman of the town and not a nun.* She wondered how she would have conducted herself with the Irishwoman had that been the case. Looking at Katherine's face shaded by the hat she replied. "Yes, admirably so. I can't wait to hear about the reaction you have when you next visit the Ladies Committee. Your new attire should be worth quite a bit of mileage I should think. But enough of frivolity, there's breakfast to make and work to be done." She rose to continue preparing breakfast.

With the nun's assistance, the task was completed in short time. She was grateful for the help Katherine provided around the household and realised this couldn't have been easy given her own work commitments. Despite such commitments, in the past week Catriona always managed to come home to find a meal prepared for both she and her brother, and the bathtub in position by the fire. Despite her own attempts to keep her distance from the nun, she couldn't begin to imagine how she would have coped without Katherine's presence.

Having tidied the kitchen after breakfast, Katherine returned to her room to collect the notes she required for her day's work while Catriona prepared the wagon. Given that this was becoming an almost regular occurrence in fetching Alexander of an afternoon, the task was one done in little time and by the early morning they were on their way. Wanting to maintain the air of closeness they had re-established that morning, Katherine questioned the other woman on the crops they would plant for the oncoming season.

"To tell you the truth, I'm not all that sure. This is an area Alexander usually deals with but obviously at the moment he is in no fit state to do so. I'm fortunate that the town has a farmer's cooperative that provides advice on what crops to grow and how to achieve the best yield. It's something that was introduced only two years ago but its membership is continually growing. I'm looking toward them for some of the advice with the intent of trying at least one paddock of barley. It's the only crop that Alexander suggested we should plant before his current state,"

Catriona quietly finished, her emotions in turmoil over her brother's current condition.

Alexander wouldn't listen to her when she attempted to ask him to curb his drinking, instead he became surly and arrogant. It was a side she hadn't seen in him before and it served to remind her how relieved she was that she hadn't harnessed herself to a husband who might have turned out to be a drinker. Yet at the same time she felt pity. It was obvious he was mourning his loss which was still relatively new. *But how long could he continue on this way?* Catriona thought. Shaking herself out of her reverie she turned to the woman beside her. "So, what business do you have in town today? Not another death by boredom with the Ladies Committee I hope?"

"No, nothing of the sort. Father Cleary and I have matters which need to be discussed."

Before the grazier could restrain herself the words were out. "Yes and I've no doubt the news on the situation at the Pelham household will figure prominently in your discussions." Immediately regretting the harshness of her words, she rushed to apologise to Katherine's stiffened and angry figure. "I'm sorry, I didn't mean to say that. I know you wouldn't do anything to hurt my brother or myself. Those words were spiteful and inconsiderate."

The nun relaxed her shoulders and her grip on the wagon. "I'd be lying to you if I said that the current situation between you and your brother won't be discussed by Father Cleary and I. However, by now you must be aware this isn't for the sake of gossip alone; both he and I care for you both and would do anything to see the current situation resolved. Your apology is accepted as long as you remember that if you want to discuss anything there's no need for you to travel all the way into town to discuss it with Susan." Katherine was surprised at her last words. For no rational reason she was becoming annoyed at the way the woman beside her seemed to continually confide in Susan. After all, she was a nun and not one prone to repeating the confidential conversations of others.

Catriona was equally surprised at the nun's last statement as she sensed a touch of jealousy on the other woman's behalf. Despite this she was in no position to tell Katherine that what she discussed with Susan directly involved her feelings for the nun. Rather than verbally respond to the topic she nodded and they both rode on in silence.

Katherine, feeling that her last comment was petulant, endeavoured again to start up a conversation, "Catriona, I couldn't help but notice the number of lovely watercolours around your house. There are a number of beautiful countryside landscapes and their similarity would lead me to believe that the same artist created them all. Tell me is it someone local?"

Catriona relaxed and was quietly pleased that Katherine had noticed the works. "I'm glad you like them and you're right, they are locally done. You never know, I've a bit of influence with the artist, I may be able to have one painted for you."

"I'm afraid you'll have to tell him that it may well take a while for me to be able to pay him for the works for my funds are rather scarce." Katherine found herself excited at the prospect of a purchase, yet at the same time frustrated that she couldn't afford to pay for one outright.

"Oh, I'm sure that a mutually agreeable arrangement can be worked out between you and the artist. Say, paint in return for favours perhaps?" The grazier looked away to conceal her grinning features. Stealing a glance at the other woman's shocked expression she continued with a chuckle. "There's no need to worry. I think you've already treated the artist more than favourably—you see, I'm responsible for those works. I used to paint when I was younger."

Katherine was fascinated, as she'd never really known an artist before. Her father had regarded such people as frivolous and bohemian, not the sort of people she should mix with socially. "Catriona, you *are* a mystery; they're quite good. Are you a natural as they say or did someone teach you?"

Catriona stifled a laugh at the innocent double entendre and found herself thinking back to the excellent teaching and advice she'd received from Adele during their time together. "No, I didn't even know I had an artistic bone in my body. It wasn't until my mother employed my last governess to teach the finer arts of being a lady that I discovered I had a talent for it."

"You haven't said much about her to me. Was she as awful as your first governess?" the nun asked innocently.

"Oh, no, we got on very well. She was much closer to my age than my first governess and we were more like friends sometimes than teacher and student," she recalled fondly.

"That must have been a great comfort for you to be that lucky. All my governesses resembled religious relics. Tell me, is she still in the district? I'd like to visit her." Katherine found herself interested in meeting someone who had managed to coax such a talent out of the usually pragmatic woman beside her.

Catriona's features fell at this question, something that didn't go unnoticed. "No, I'm afraid she's not. Adele left the district after my mother and she had a disagreement on the curriculum that she was teaching me. As far as my mother was concerned her methods were somewhat unorthodox," she chose her words carefully.

Sensing the other woman's discomfort at her questioning, Katherine relented. She sensed that Catriona had been fond of her governess and obviously upset at her premature departure. Rather than continue the conversation, and given their close proximity to town, she chose to spend the remainder of the journey in pensive silence.

Catriona dropped Katherine off at the steps of the accommodation motel, agreeing to call for her again in an hour. This gave the grazier the time to discuss and purchase the best seed for planting before paying a visit on Susan. Little was mentioned to her about her brother on her visit to the cooperative. Many of the men went out of their way to help her. This touched Catriona as she realised what a tight knit community she lived in and that the men were only too grateful to help a family who had never once said "no" to their calls for assistance over the years. After leaving the co-operative she halted the wagon in front of Susan's store.

The shopkeeper was glad to see her friend; there had been little time for them to speak over the weeks since Alexander's return. The problems at home were obviously affecting her friend as reflected in the dark shadows below Catriona's eyes and the set of her body. Moving silently around the counter she locked her front door before escorting Catriona to the rear of the store. Catriona had barely managed to make it to the chair offered to her before she started weeping. Susan wrapped Catriona in her arms and held her until she was ready to speak.

"Oh God, Susan, it's so hard. Alexander seems intent to drink himself into an early grave and the farm is suffering as a result. I spend my days working on the land and my nights playing wet nurse to my brother," she managed, sobbing into Susan's shoulder.

"You've Katherine there to help you. She's helping you, isn't she?"

"Oh, she couldn't have been better what with her work

around the household and her cheery disposition. Sometimes I wonder if I wouldn't have joined my brother if it weren't for her," she replied wiping her nose on her handkerchief.

Susan attempted to make her next question as casual as possible. "So, how are things really between the two of you?"

Catriona spent the next 20 minutes describing the events of the night of her brother's return. Susan listened in silence, nodding occasionally to show that she was listening. "But she's changed, Susan. It's as if she realises something happened on that night and the effect it had on me. I can't rightly describe it but her actions have changed. If it were a normal situation I'd almost say that she's naively flirting with me, for I sense a change in her. Not that there has been any further physical contact between us—I hardly trust myself."

"Yes, well I don't rightly know what to say and I can only add to what I've already said. The way she treats you may well have changed, but I'll wager my life savings she still has no idea or is fully aware of the impact she's having on you. And given the current circumstances with your brother, I suggest you tread carefully." The older woman wished she could offer Catriona more.

The remainder of the conversation alternated between her brother and how things were between Me-Lin and Susan. Realising the time had come for her to pick up Katherine, Catriona stood and again thanked the shopkeeper for her help. She was happy she'd the chance to show her real emotions to someone. Over the past few weeks she felt as if she'd been vested with the responsibility for holding up the whole world. With a final wave to her friend, she pulled away from the store and continued down the dusty street to collect Katherine.

The ride home was uneventful, with both women very much occupied in their own thoughts. Katherine had spent the morning being gently chided by Father Cleary for the lack of attentiveness she'd paid to her religious endeavours in the past week. He was sympathetic given the circumstances in the household and agreed that, in retrospect, it was a good idea that she was staying at the Pelham farm to offer assistance. In turn she promised him that she would make every attempt to get back into her routine of tending to the families of the district. Catriona spent the time carefully measuring Susan's words and taking the occasional opportunity to glance sideways at the woman beside her. She was extremely grateful for Katherine's presence on the property and was glad she hadn't tried to lecture her or her brother on the evils of drinking. She wished that there was more time for the two to spend alone for there were delicate matters that she wished to discuss with Katherine—matters involving the two of them.

Returning home, Katherine made her way to the house leaving the grazier to tend to the horses. *The day is going to be a hot one*, Catriona thought, *and it would be a nice day to do nothing but sit in the shade.* Even the distance between the house and the barn was shimmering in the afternoon's heat and, raising her face to the cloudless blue sky, Catriona could feel the sun beating off it. Shaking herself out of a reverie she could ill afford, she continued into the barn and the work that awaited her.

Katherine, who had spent the past three hours in the house preparing lessons, had almost been too engrossed to hear the sound of a wagon coming up the driveway toward the house. It was strange to receive visitors so late in the afternoon but maybe it was something Catriona had purchased in town being delivered by a kindly neighbour. With her curiosity getting the better of her, she put down her quill and moved to the window. In retrospect, she was glad that she did.

Opening the French doors she could just make out a figure on the wagon, who could be no-one else but Susan. However, it was the person riding behind her who caused Katherine more concern. There was no mistaking the black garb of Father Cleary astride his ever-suffering chestnut horse. As Katherine walked around the verandah to the front of the house, she raised her hand in greeting. This wasn't returned and it was then that her stomach lurched in uncertainty. Innately she sensed something was wrong; otherwise why would both the Father and Susan be out here when both had been visited just that morning?

Katherine caught movement out of the corner of her eye and turned her head to see that Catriona had come from the front of the barn to see what the noise was. The grazier's relaxed form was suddenly rigid as she strode down the driveway toward the oncoming wagon. Katherine, sensing something was terribly wrong, did the same. As Catriona broke into a run so did the nun. However, hampered by her unwieldy habit the distance between the two women was increased and it was Catriona who arrived at the wagon first. Katherine was still too far away to make out the words being said but nothing could stop her from hearing Catriona's cry of anguish as she headed toward the rear of the wagon.

Susan had been quick in dismounting and following the now distraught woman, and despite her size disadvantage she was making a good effort of restraining Catriona as Katherine eventually approached. Instinctively moving toward Catriona, Katherine halted seeing the look on her face and turned toward the wagon. Katherine felt her blood turn cold at the sight of a pine box similar to the ones she'd seen on her first day. In the back of the wagon was a coffin and the shopkeeper was doing her best to restrain Catriona from opening it.

So engrossed in the anguished features dominating Catriona's face, Katherine hadn't noticed Father Cleary dismount behind her and she jumped when he spoke in hushed tones. "There was an accident in the town this morning not long after you had left. Alexander had staggered out of the hotel straight into the path of the weekly coach. There was no way the coach could have avoided him; the horses were on him before he knew it. I've said prayers for him and will prepare a service for tomorrow at the family graveyard. I'm so sorry to see him come to an end like this. He had so much to live for."

Looking toward Catriona, she could see that Susan was managing to guide the now robotic figure toward the house. Her heart went out to her—she'd been brave and never really shown her emotions, but this was just another tragedy in a long line of tragedies for her. She couldn't help but empathise with the pain Catriona was going through and wished that it was she who was placing her arms around her and telling her that the pain would pass. *They seem hollow words now*, the nun thought. Yet they were the same comforts she'd offered on the day of the dust storm. *What spiritual comfort could I really offer to a woman who was now alone in the world?* she thought. She was jogged back into the present by words from Father Cleary. "I'm sorry, Father, what were you saying?"

"I'm sorry, Sister, I know this isn't easy for you either, you two are such good friends. But we must get the coffin inside before the heat affects it. I think it would be appropriate if we lay it in Mr Pelham's room. Do you think you can manage one end? I'm reluctant to ask for Miss Pelham's or Miss Crosier's assistance, given the current circumstances."

"I'm not sure Father, but I won't know until I try. If you like

I think the best way would be to drive the wagon to where Mr Pelham's room was and carry the ... him through the French windows entrance. It's much easier than carrying it through the house, and then we can see if we can be of any assistance to Miss Crosier." Not waiting for response of the Father, she climbed onto the wagon and urged the horse forward toward a spot adjacent to Alexander's room.

In the parlour of the house Susan sat on the chaise lounge, holding securely to Catriona and trying to comfort her, but to no avail. Susan was concerned, for after her initial outburst of grief, her friend's tears were silent ones but she seemed to draw comfort in the security of the shopkeeper's arms. Temporarily releasing her grip, Susan pulled back and looked at a grief stricken Catriona, her face pale and her eyes red. "Catriona, is there anything I can get you?" Susan asked, trying to search for suitable words to console the woman beside her.

Instead of responding yes or no, Catriona searched Susan's face for an answer for what had happened to her brother. "How did it happen? What was he doing? He knew that I'd come and get him. God, why didn't he just wait?" Her last sentence was uttered in a voice choked with emotion.

Susan gathered her back into her arms. "No-one really knows. From what the barman said Alexander was going to get some lunch when he stumbled out of the hotel. He was down the steps and in front of the coach before the coachman could rein in the horses. I know this can be of little comfort to you, but I don't think he would have felt much pain. He was gone before they lifted him from the ground." Susan felt the other woman's body shake with grief. "I can't begin to tell you how sorry I am. I wish there was some way to make things better again, but I can't. All I can say is that you must allow yourself to grieve, and as time passes the ache will grow less. Please don't bottle it up or it will tear you apart. Remember there are friends here to help you." She paused as she heard the door open. She continued to hold Catriona close, not caring for the image they would be presenting to the two other people in the house.

Stepping through the door Katherine was momentarily taken aback by the intimacy Catriona and Susan seemed to be sharing. She strangely felt that it should be her comforting the distraught woman. Father Cleary was close behind her and, despite his silence, she'd heard his sharp intake of breath. Recovering herself, she realised the futility of words she might offer to someone she felt so close to and moving forward, she reached out and silently placed a hand on the woman's shoulder.

Father Cleary had also moved from his position in the doorway as he began to speak. "I'm truly sorry, Catriona, for your brother's death and there's little I can offer you in your time of grief. But I hope you can take comfort in knowing that your brother has gone to a better place and I'm sure that God..."

But having gotten so far he got no further. With her hand on Catriona's shoulder Katherine could feel Catriona body stiffen with each of the words he uttered. Tearing herself from Susan's grip and Katherine's hand on her shoulder, Catriona wheeled on Father Cleary and the nun, her face red, eyes on fire. "Look at you both! You're like a pack of religious vultures waiting to swoop in for your prey! And you," She stabbed her finger at Father Cleary, "How can you stand there and honestly tell me that this fits somewhere into the scheme of things! Come on, Father, explain to me about the all-loving, all-forgiving, omnipotent God of yours. How can he take my mother and father, Sister Coreen, and now my brother? They were good people, not evil. All their loss has created was more pain or is that what your religion feeds upon—the pain of others? You do what you have to do but don't stand here and lecture me on the benefits of my brother's death for there are none." She paused, taking in both the nun and Father Cleary, her breathing ragged from her outburst. "You bury him or do what you like, but don't offer me religious platitudes. Get out, get out of my house the both of you!" She shouted and raised her clenched fist at both of them.

Stepping backwards out of the parlour Katherine found herself in shock. She'd never seen Catriona so angry before and so vehement in her words. Katherine found herself amazed that Catriona could turn upon them so. Father Cleary seemed to feel her concern and he said, "It's the grief; some people react to it in different ways. She's never been an overly religious person, but I never knew she felt so strongly about the Church." He shook his head in amazement before turning to the nun. "Under the circumstances, Sister, I think it would be best if you moved into town for a few days, at least until the initial shock has passed."

The nun vigorously shook her head in disagreement. "No, Father, on the contrary I think my place is here where I can do most good. You've said it yourself that she's obviously grief stricken. What happens when she comes out of her present state to find no-one around? Do you want to be burying another Pelham by week's end?" She realised her last words were said in criticism to the clergyman's suggestion, but she didn't care. Her place was more than ever with Catriona. Her current state would pass and Katherine dreaded what Catriona might do if left alone to her own devices.

Father Cleary was surprised at the passion of the nun's response and he baulked at her last question, "I think you're being a little melodramatic suggesting Miss Pelham would do something drastic, but I understand what you're saying. Stay if you wish, I'll be out here for the funeral tomorrow. If you've changed your mind, then you can return to town with me. Please excuse me, but I've matters I must attend to prior to tomorrow's service. I can't offer any suggestions but tread warily, Sister, Miss Pelham's emotions at the moment are less than under control." Taking his hat he quietly showed himself out of the house.

Katherine occupied her time with un-harnessing Susan's horse from the wagon. Having achieved that task she moved silently through the house alternating between her room and the kitchen. She'd paused frequently outside the door of the parlour, listening to Catriona's sobs and the muted tones of Susan, longing to go inside and be of any assistance. It pained her to think of what the grazier was going through but, given her last reception, she reluctantly left the door unopened and returned to her room.

With the approach of darkness came a light knock on the nun's door. She moved quickly from her dresser and upon opening it found the tired face of Susan staring at her, a tired smile lighting her features. "I knew you were made of stronger stuff than that. I knew you wouldn't leave. The words Catriona said, they were said in anger, she didn't mean them. She has no time for the Church but with you Katherine, it's different. Over the next few days she'll need your help to get through this." The shopkeeper reached for Katherine's shoulder, grasping it as a friend would. "I don't mean to sound rude, but do you mind if we have something to drink?"

Katherine, touched at Susan's words, managed a surprised yes and they moved toward the kitchen. Whispering over her shoulder she asked, "Where's Catriona?"

"I've put her to bed with a small dose of laudanum to help her sleep. I can't seem to find her bedclothes, so I've left her in just her bloomers. Mind you I suppose it doesn't matter, after all we're all women." The shopkeeper took a seat at the table.

"Surely it's too late for you to return to town tonight. Will you stay? I'm not quite sure what sort of reception she would give me at the moment. I can make up her parent's room if it's not too inconvenient for you." Katherine hoped that the other woman would accept her offer.

Looking at the Irishwoman, Susan could see the attraction Catriona saw in her. Her green eyes and innocent face shrouded in short curly hair belied a beauty that under other circumstances, well... "I think you'd be surprised at the sort of reception you'd receive; however, you're right it's too late to return. I advised Me-Lin before I left that I may not return tonight and she'll bring me out appropriate clothing for tomorrow's service. Thank you for your offer, I'd be more than grateful to spend the night," she finished, looking at the relieved face of the woman opposite her. Smiling her thanks, Katherine set herself to the task of preparing a small supper for the two of them.

Given the suddenness at which the incident had occurred, the funeral the next day was attended by a great many people. It didn't surprise her that the Ladies Committee wasn't in attendance, but Katherine was quietly pleased at the attendance of many of the Committee's husbands. The smaller families made up the greatest representation, having taken time out of their busy day to pay their last respects to a man well liked within the district.

It was on this occasion that the Irishwoman experienced another tradition linked with country Australia, for not one family had turned up empty handed despite the difficulties that some of their offerings of food would have cost them. Susan had advised her that this might be the case and it was considered rude to refuse, despite the lack of wealth of the family. It didn't take long for both the smoke house and the pantry to fill. Men who had arrived with their families also approached a staunch Catriona, hat in hand, and offered her pledges of assistance whenever she should need it. Despite her grief, Catriona had a kind word for each of these men who dealt with the grazier with a form of awkward gentleness which made Katherine, at times, swallow back tears.

Catriona didn't detract from her normal dress and attended the funeral in trousers which were more cut for a formal occasion than work. Not that anyone seemed to notice or care, so great was their respect for the man they were burying and the remaining family member standing by the graveside. As the afternoon shadows lengthened, groups paid their last respects before starting the long journey home. Katherine again reasserted her insistence to Father Cleary about remaining at the house and this resulted in him leaving alone. The last to leave was Susan, who explained to her that she'd again undressed Catriona and put her to bed, but she couldn't afford to stay another night and have her store closed for three days in a row. Katherine understood her predicament and, upon saying her goodbyes, closed the front door to what was now a very silent house.

The house, which had seen so many people in it during the day, seemed now unnaturally quiet. Making her way to the kitchen, Katherine completed the clean up after the day's activities, her mind preoccupied on thoughts of Catriona. *She'd looked so proud and yet so lonely standing by the graveside. Why was it that God saw it so necessary to cause such pain to such a lovely woman?* Here she caught herself, realising that her thoughts were preoccupied not with the other woman's spirit but with the woman herself.

She cast her mind back to the night when Catriona had kissed her hand and to the thoughts that had run through her mind at that instant. It scared her to think of the moment now in retrospect, for only now could she admit to herself that she'd liked Catriona's kiss. Again she heard the mocking words of Mary and raising her hands to her cheeks she could feel that they were flushed.

Deciding her thoughts and emotions has also been jaded by the day's events she moved through the dark house only pausing at the other woman's open door to reassure herself that she was still asleep. Susan had told her that she'd again given Catriona a small dose of laudanum to help her sleep, but this had been quite a few hours past. Moving to her own room she only hoped that the dose would last until morning.

Katherine had no idea of judging how long she'd been asleep when she awoke to the cries of Catriona calling out to a number of people including her parents and her brother. There was a silence, as if she realised that they were gone, before again she called for Adele, her last governess. Katherine was out of bed attempting to raise the wick in her lamp when she heard Catriona calling her name in what was now a frantic voice. Cursing the lamp's reluctance to fully light, she grabbed it and made her way down the hallway toward the distraught woman's door.

Moving through the entrance she found Catriona sitting up in bed, her face contorted with fear and tears coming from her eyes. On seeing Katherine she turned to her, arms outstretched in a gesture of supplication. Disregarding the distraught woman's nakedness, Katherine lowered her lamp to the bedside table and went to Catriona and took the woman in her arms. Rocking her gently, she allowed the woman's sobs to abate. "It's all right. I'm here. Everything's going to be fine. Today was the first day in the healing process. Now why don't you lie back down and get some rest? I'll be here. I'm just next door if you need me. I'll leave both our doors open just in case you call," she said attempting to lower Catriona to the bed.

Her attempts were to no avail, for at the mention that the nun was about to leave Catriona clung to her even harder. "No, please don't leave me alone. I don't want to be alone, not tonight. Stay with me, please. Don't leave me, Katherine. I need you," she said through a voice choked with emotion.

Katherine, her own emotions in turmoil, hugged Catriona hard before whispering into her ear, "I'm here and I won't leave you. But if I'm to stay with you, you're going to have to let me put the lamp out and move over." She talked to the other woman as she might have done to a child. Catriona released her and provided a space in the bed for the Irishwoman who, having extinguished the lamp, climbed into bed and was again subjected to the vice like grip of Catriona. It was some time later before the nun had reassured Catriona enough to have her release her so that they could both get some much needed sleep.

Katherine awoke the next morning as she always did to the sounds of the cockatoos heralding the start of the day. Laying on her side and taking a moment to relax, she felt a reassuring arm around her waist and a body spooned up against her own. Remembering the events of the previous night, she tried as gently as possible to remove Catriona's arm from her waist. Pulling back the bedcovers ever so slightly she managed to extricate the woman's arm before rolling over and facing her. As she did so she was reminded with surprising clarity the way she had found Catriona the night before. Raising the bedcovers to remove Catriona's arm resulted in Katherine again seeing the grazier naked from the waist up.

Shocked, her immediate thoughts revolved around raising the blankets to cover the other woman's nakedness. *But what happens if I wake her up?* Katherine thought as she shyly took in the body in front of her. Even on her side it was obvious Catriona's shoulders were broader than that of a normal woman's. These were complemented by strong arms that, even in repose, hinted at the muscular strength hidden just beneath the skin. Her eyes followed the trail of one of the grazier's arms and looked at her waist that was indeed as narrow as her hips. Slowly and shyly she raised her eyes to look upon Catriona's chest. Unlike her own that were well rounded, Catriona's breasts were small but well suited to her physically toned body. Again, like those other moments, Katherine sensed her breathing quicken as she found her eyes glued to the body of the woman in front of her. The sensations in her stomach were as if she hadn't eaten in days but she knew this wasn't the cause. Whether it was in curiosity, or something else that she couldn't describe, Katherine felt a compelling desire to reach out and touch one of Catriona's breasts.

She didn't know what made her look, but on returning her eyes to Catriona's face she realised that she was awake and that she'd been caught staring, much like Catriona had been on the night of her brother's return. She could feel her face redden but couldn't break contact with the mesmerising azure eyes of Catriona.

Time seemed to stand still as Catriona appeared to be struggling with a way to deal with the situation. Very slowly Catriona raised her arm and brushed a curl from the Irishwoman's forehead. Katherine's breath stopped and where the grazier had touched her felt like it was now burning.

Catriona lowered her arm to the other woman's shoulder. "Katherine, I'm sorry for what I said in the parlour. I meant what I had said about religious platitudes, but not what I said about asking you to leave. I'm glad you didn't leave; for last night when I woke up and couldn't find anyone I thought I was all alone. Thank you for coming to me and staying with me through the night. It makes a change waking up with someone beside you."

Katherine was still trying to calm her emotions that had gone haywire at Catriona's gentle touch and before she could reply her thanks, Catriona closed the small distance between the two of them and lightly brushed Katherine's lips with her own. The beat of Katherine's heart had now become a roar and she felt that it could be heard clearly in the room. She felt a strange warmth begin between her thighs as if a fire had been ignited. The grazier's lips had barely touched her own, but she was very aware of the mark that they had left. As if by some unknown strong emotional force Katherine tentatively moved closer to Catriona, till once again they were kissing each other.

She felt Catriona's hand encircle her waist to pull her even closer and, as if by instinct, Katherine felt her own hand go to the well-toned back which, she was reminded, was bare. Placing her hand across Catriona's shoulders Katherine could feel the play of muscles under the pressure of her hand. She felt her lips part slightly as Catriona's tongue slowly entered her mouth and the sensations that Katherine was feeling were like ones she'd never experienced before. She wondered if this was what it was to be drunk and not responsible for one's own actions. Taking her lead from the other woman, Katherine tentatively used her tongue to explore the inside of Catriona's mouth.

Catriona's hand, which had so skillfully played along the spine of the Irishwoman's back, now manoeuvred its way to the front, eager to feel the fullness which were Katherine's breasts. Drawing a slow line up from her waist she cupped the breast in her hand, gently using the fabric between hand and breast to tease the nipple. At this Katherine gasped and broke contact. Looking at the nun's confused face, Catriona asked, "Katherine, are you all right?"

"No, I'm not. I don't know. I'm not sure." Flustered and confused, Katherine sat up in bed. *What do I want?* She wasn't sure. Her eyes widened in sudden realisation, aware that these were the unorthodox ways the Ladies Committee had referred to when they mentioned Catriona. While her time in the convent and her relative inexperience with men didn't make her an expert on intimacy, she knew that what the two of them had just done was socially taboo. Her confusion was multiplied by her private acknowledgment that she'd enjoyed it and had in fact returned the other woman's kiss.

Catriona had made no attempt to re-establish contact with the woman beside her. She was elated when Katherine had returned her kiss and was careful in not taking things to quickly. She had been aware of the Irishwoman's eyes upon her when she awoke and her heart had quickened at the prospect of taking her in her arms. Now she realised that maybe she'd expected a little too much.

Sitting up in bed, Catriona made no attempt to hide her nakedness, "So, now you know why the richer people of the town shun me. I don't think they know I like women as I should like men. Although I've no doubt they have their ideas. Believe me when I tell you that I didn't mean to hurt you or force myself upon you. You confused me when you returned my kiss." She looked at the nun's flushed face. "You'll remember that I once said that no-one can make you do anything. The decision must be yours." Seeing the other woman's nod she continued. "There's something between us. I know there is, but you have to work out in your own mind if it's what you want. My actions have revealed to you what my feelings are for you. However, I'll not destroy a friendship with something not reciprocated," she finished watching the other woman's confused face.

"I don't know what I want any more. I'm not sure. I need time to think about what has happened between us. I'll not lie to you. I also feel that something has occurred between us, but I need to search my own feelings on what has happened. I don't know where this leaves me as a person or as a nun. I don't know." She placed her head in her hands.

After a short silence, she looked up at Catriona. "As for the town's thoughts on the matter, I've already told you, their opinions are of little relevance to me." Katherine moved her feet to the side of the bed, stood up, and turned to Catriona. "I need to look at myself and what I should do. Please give me the freedom to do this."

"You've all the freedom you want, Katherine. Whatever your decision, I'll abide by it. But I ask two things of you; first, that you search yourself to find what it is you really want, not what others expect of you. And the second is that you tell me your decision. I'll not ruin a friendship by pressing you for more. You're welcome to remain here. I won't compromise our friendship until you know your decision and have told me either way." Catriona finished, quietly looking into Katherine's eyes.

Not sure if she could form the words given the indecision

she was currently feeling, Katherine nodded her assent before leaving Catriona's room for the comfort of her own. The grazier lay back down on her bed, her emotions scrambled. In a matter of days she had lost someone dear and yet found another. But had she lost this one as well?

Chapter
Eleven

In the ensuing days Catriona continued to mourn the loss of her brother in her own silent way. Under the pretence of checking both the cattle and the young crop in the paddocks, she spent a lot of time away from the house and Katherine, reminiscing and shedding tears in her brother's memory. But Australia was an unforgiving country that didn't allow the luxury of long and drawn out displays of mourning. It continued to grow and change, not waiting for anything in its path. Despite the pain she was feeling, the grazier knew that she must continue on or risk seeing the paddocks engulfed by weeds and with that the possibility of damaging her livelihood. With some crops the invasion of weeds was not such an issue, however, at least two of them would be sorely affected by the presence of such a menace. She knew she would need a lot of help to weed those particular crops that needed it, let alone prepare the unsown paddocks for the oncoming season. She was grateful for the words of assistance that had been given to her by so many on the day of the funeral; she just hoped that they weren't hollow promises.

It still came as a surprise to her that on the second Sunday following her brother's burial, a wagonload of men and farming equipment arrived at her house ready to assist in the task that lay before her. Like Catriona, they too accepted that life must go on, no matter how hard it seemed at times. Their arrivals were shortly followed by their wives ready to prepare lunch for the hungry hoards around midday. This was a relief to Katherine who, although having ample food to feed to the workers, had problems with preparing the amount for the mouths needing feeding. Taking over from the nun, and thus allowing her time to teach the children, the women prepared lunch for all.

By the sheer weight of their numbers and working into twilight, they achieved alone what would have taken Catriona weeks to do. So now, like everyone else, all she could do was sit, wait, and pray that the rains would come and assist her young crops to their maturity. Before their departure she thanked the families for the assistance that they had given her, telling them she was unsure how she could ever repay them for the help they had given.

It was Mr. Connor who, having been chosen as the spokesperson, stepped forward and removing his hat from his head responded to her words. "Miss Pelham, there ain't one person here today who is not somehow beholding to you and your family over the years. There are many of us who would have been turned out of our homes and forced to go elsewhere for work at one time or another if it hadn't been for the generosity of you and yours. Why both you and I aren't fools, either of us, but how many times have you offered my whole family work which could have easily been done by just a few?" Turning to the silent group behind him, he continued, "And how many of us have found presents and food for our families at Christmas when we ourselves didn't have two pennies to rub together?" A number of heads nodded as he again faced the woman in front of him. "So Miss Pelham, don't you stand here and tell us you've no idea how you can repay us for what we done here today. In truth this is our repayment to you for treating us as if we was equals; not like that lot that live in those fancy places in town." Sensing he had said enough, he placed his hat back on his head. "We best be on our way now, but rest assured we'll be back come harvest time." The families behind him joined his voice, uttering the same sentiments.

Catriona stepped forward too choked with emotion to utter words of thanks. Where words failed her, her actions didn't. Grasping the man's hand, she shook it vigorously. As the last of the wagons pulled away, she moved inside to where Katherine was battling with putting away the dishes and plates which had been used during the day. She too had heard the speech but had moved inside as the crowd broke up. That was Catriona's moment she felt and besides, it wouldn't have seemed proper to see the town's Sister standing on the steps of the house with tears of gratitude flowing down her face.

Catriona had been true to her word and hadn't again broached with the Irishwoman the intimacy they had shared on that morning; but despite this, the interaction between the two had subtly changed. There was a closeness between the two that hadn't been there before. Where once the grazier had jumped at the nun's touch, she was now more relaxed when by chance they happened to brush against each other during the day. Katherine in turn was more aware of the effect she had on the other woman and seemed to be struggling with how to deal with this new found emotional bond holding the two of them within its circle of influence.

Aside from these subtle changes, both still continued in their every day life as only could be expected. As the grazier felt the wound of her brother's loss start healing, she paid greater attention to the day to day maintenance of the farm, while Katherine continued to spend the better part of her time tending to the educational needs of children. The return of Father Cleary had meant a reduction in the number of summons she received from the Ladies Committee and this suited her well. However, she did on a regular basis drive herself into town to meet with Father Cleary to discuss religious matters and her work in and around the district.

It was one such day that Catriona accompanied the other woman, for she had business in town. A delighted Katherine had received the news she'd waited for. After what had seemed like a lifetime, the children's books she'd ordered had finally arrived and she was eager to take delivery of them. As for Catriona, she needed to purchase a new blade for her plough. Susan looked up as both women entered the store. The grazier stepped to one side to allow the Sister to enter first. A look of thanks passed between them that made the shopkeeper grateful no-one else was in the store to see it. For it was obvious to her, if not to anyone else, something had happened between the two.

Katherine moved to the counter, a brilliant smile on her face. "Susan, how are you? Thank you for your message about the books. I thought they'd gotten lost somewhere. Why I believe that in the time it's taken for them to arrive I could have written one or two myself."

The shopkeeper laughed at the light-hearted tone that accompanied the nun's relaxed features. "Yes, they may have been a long time in coming, but I don't think you'll be disappointed." She motioned to the box in the corner. "You see that tea chest over there? Well, that's yours and it's full to the brim with books. Go on, take a look."

Susan need not have bothered with the last statement as the Irishwoman was already crossing the floor to where the tea chest stood. "Oh, this is just wonderful!" Pulling out the books, she examined their covers before placing them on the floor. "I think there's something here for everyone. Just think; if I could get regular shipments of these I could almost start up a library," she said over her shoulder, somewhat preoccupied in the contents of the chest.

Satisfied that the nun's attention was focused elsewhere, Susan now turned to Catriona, who was watching the nun's reaction from the end of the counter. She moved toward the preoccupied woman. "So, what news do you have, Catriona? As for town gossip there's little to tell—the Ladies Committee is on a righteous campaign at the moment and have set up shop outside the local pub, chastising any man caught carousing with the local women." The shopkeeper laughed as she folded a piece of cloth in front of her. "Oh, and I hear that our bushranging friends have been active again. Last week they entered a grazier's property not ten miles from here and held the family at bay before making off with a substantial amount of jewellery. I'd hazard a guess that they're getting a bit too bold. It shouldn't be long before they find themselves caught." Pausing in her ministrations she realised she'd only half of the other woman's attention and so endeavoured to elicit a response which went beyond a nod and a grunt. "I hear you had a number of helpers last week out at your property. I'm happy for the assistance they gave you, for it would have taken you days by yourself."

Realising that Susan was waiting for her input to the conversation, Catriona broke her gaze from the nun now covered in books. "Yes, I never realised my family had done so much until I saw those people out there. It just shows that good deeds and kind words do count for something. Unfortunately though, in the course of the day, one of my plough blades has broken and it's beyond repair. I normally loan it to the O'Hara's for their planting so I'm keen to have it replaced before he asks. You wouldn't have one would you?" she queried, her mind on the task but her eyes lingering back to the nun.

Susan brought her hand down hard on the counter to again

gain the grazier's attention. "Yes, as a matter of fact I do. Now tell me," she insisted, lightly touching the other woman's arm to gain her attention, "what other news do you have for me?"

Returning Susan's stare briefly Catriona blushed and made a pretence of cleaning an invisible spot off the glass counter. "Oh, um, I'd heard about the increase in bushranging, but other than that nothing much out of the ordinary has happened," she replied still avoiding the shopkeeper's questioning stare.

In a pig's eye, Susan was sure just by viewing the interaction between the two that something had happened since she and Catriona spoke. Eager to find out what was going on, but reluctant to ask in the nun's presence she said, "Well, I'm sure any news that you have for me is better than none at all. How about you join me for some morning tea?"

Suddenly reticent at the woman's insistence, Catriona began to search for words to hide her confusion. "I'd love to, but I've got to take Katherine to her meeting with Father Cleary—" Before she could go any further Catriona was aware of the nun's presence beside her.

"Oh, there's no need. He's really only up the street, Catriona, and even for someone as soft as myself it's definitely within walking distance." Katherine moved toward the door, unaware of the colour that had risen in the grazier's cheeks at her unintentional mention of her softness. "You two have morning tea and a talk; that's unless you wish to come and discuss religious issues with Father Cleary and I?" She smiled at the other woman, knowing full well what her answer would be.

Just as she recovered from the first onslaught, Catriona's face reddened again and realised she was caught. A smiling Katherine had paused at the door waiting for an answer when Catriona replied, "Thank you for your offer, but I think a cup of tea is more appealing. I'll pick you up in an hour if you don't mind. Is that enough time for the two of you to finish your discussions?"

Nodding her head in assent Katherine left the store on her task and, as she did so, Susan swept around the counter and locked the door before anyone else could enter the mercantile. Turning to the grazier with hands clasped in front of her, she said, "Now how about you come out the back and tell me exactly what's been going on?"

Moving to the back of the store, Catriona took a seat and relayed the incident that had occurred between the two of them

in Catriona's bed. The shopkeeper's face was inscrutable
throughout the telling as she non-verbally acknowledged the
story told to her. She was happy for her friend to think that she
had found comfort so soon after her brother's death, but she was
also concerned. Even though Katherine hadn't again approached
the grazier regarding their intimacy, it was plain to see that there
was now a definite closeness between the two. What greatly concerned Susan was that if she could sense a closeness between the
two, she was sure others could see also. In the nun, Susan could
see a difference. Her actions reminded Susan of the skittishness
of a young colt, dancing about the field sure of its ability to gal-
lop on such fine legs, but afraid to take the first step.

Catriona finished her story and with a mouthful of cake
asked the woman opposite her, "What confuses me is your sixth
sense. How did you know that something had changed between
Katherine and I?" She reached for her tea to rinse the cake.

The shopkeeper leant forward in her chair. "Sixth sense be
damned. I would have to be blind not to notice a difference. Why
it's written on both your faces. She looks at you with a softness
that could melt anyone's heart. And you! Your preoccupation
with her makes me think that any moment you're going to sweep
her up into your arms, take her somewhere and ravish her," she
finished looking at the shocked look on the other woman's face.

Catriona scratched her head in concern. "Is it that obvious?
I wasn't aware."

Leaning back in her chair, Susan folded her arms smugly.
"If your feelings were any more obvious you could bottle it and
sell it." Susan gently slapped the grazier's hand. "All I'm saying
is, be careful of who's around you when you look at her like that,
that's all. Most of all, be careful when you're in town—this
place has eyes everywhere."

The women spent the intervening time discussing
Katherine's reference to a library. Both women laughed at the
enthusiasm she possessed, agreeing that a library would go a
long way to giving the opportunity of education to all who
needed it, rather than just a selected few. Glancing at her fob, the
grazier realised that time had gotten away from them, and she
still wished to visit the cooperative before picking up Katherine
and returning to Gleneagle.

They moved out into the main part of the store where Catriona easily lifted the heavy box of books for Katherine. She was
happy they'd finally arrived for she was aware that the nun was

beginning to lose hope of ever seeing them. Placing them in the back of the wagon, she returned once more to the store, picking up the new blade for her plow, which she also put next to the tea chest of books. Waving goodbye to Susan, Catriona made her way to the farmer's cooperative where she occupied her time before picking up the Irishwoman for the journey home.

The discussions between herself and Father Cleary had more than occupied Katherine. It was almost two weeks before she could fully concentrate her efforts on what she really wanted to do—sort through her box of books. Catriona, sensing that she wanted the space to do this without interruption, elected to check on the progress of her crops. A storm had passed through the district the previous night with distant lightning worrying the grazier; and she was keen to ensure that the crops hadn't suffered as a result of the deluge and that the cattle were still safe. After packing herself a lunch of sandwiches and cold tea, Catriona said her goodbyes to the other woman, advising her that she would be home before dark.

Occupied in her task of allocating books according to children's needs, Katherine wasn't aware of someone else's presence in the house until she heard the study door open. Not looking up from her efforts she said jokingly, "Catriona, you must have galloped around your crops." Raising herself on her knees, she turned and faced the grazier, "I was sure you'd be gone for much longer—" Her features froze. Standing in front of her wasn't Catriona—it was Mary.

"Hello, Katherine." Mary smiled as if this was a visit she made everyday.

The nun again sensed the uneasiness in her stomach that she'd come to associate with the bushranger's, and lately that of Catriona's, presence and tried to appear calm. "What are you doing here? It's not safe for you to be this close to town and Catriona could return at any minute," she said, looking over Mary's shoulder as if willing the other woman to materialise.

The emotional shadow that had played across the Irishwoman's features wasn't lost on Mary. She'd seen shock and fear in the other woman's eyes, but had she seen excitement also? Casually dropping herself into a chair and crossing her legs, she looked up at the standing Katherine. "Yes, and it's nice to see

you too, Sister. As for Catriona's early return, well that's doubt-
ful. She's currently heading toward the paddock which borders
the Anderson property and that's, oh, a good 2—3 hours there
and back. And as for being this close to town, well I've been a
lot closer and escaped. So, why don't you sit down and make
yourself comfortable?" She eased herself deeper into the chair.

Trying to keep her conflicting emotions in check, Katherine
remained standing. "You still haven't answered my question.
What are you doing here?"

Mary silently chuckled at the nun's unease. "Well, it's nothing sinister if that's what you're thinking. I was up north when I
heard of Alexander Pelham's death. I just wanted to ensure that
you were all right and, of course, pay my respects to Catriona."

Unsure of how the other would react at the woman who had
abducted her, Katherine stifled a laugh, confusion still evident in
her features. "I'm sure you meant well and I'll pass on your
regards. However, I don't think you'd be well received by her."
Looking around again as if she expected the grazier to come
bursting through the door any moment, she advised, "Having
passed on your message, I think it would be best if you'd leave."

Mary eased herself out of her chair and started toward the
nun who in turn moved behind the box of books to place a physical barrier between the two of them. "What's the matter? Don't
tell me you're afraid of being in the house with a desperado? Are
you afraid I might ravish you or something?"

The nun's eyes widened at the suggestion and she felt her
cheeks blush as she remembered what had occurred between her
and Catriona. "How dare you! Of course I don't think that. It's
just for someone, who has such a high price on her head, you're
not very careful are you?" She struggled to regain her composure
in the face of the bushranger.

The bushranger laughed at the Irishwoman's tone. "Life is
one big gamble, Katherine. I've raised the stakes by following
the profession I do. My time will come soon enough and it's
nothing I can run away from. There are many places I'd not feel
safe in, but this isn't one of them."

Katherine watched Mary's easy manner as she spoke and
realised with a shock that she was comparing the woman opposite her to Catriona. They both had the same pragmatic outlook
on life and were both strong, independent women. Yet that
wasn't all. Both of them had the ability to evoke a response in
her that she seemed to have no control over. She returned her

thoughts to the woman who was now staring quizzically at her. "Well, if you insist on risking your own neck, the least I can do is offer you something to drink." Taking a wide berth around Mary, she moved out the door toward the kitchen, not bothering to see if the bushranger followed her.

Mary's brows knitted at the interplay of emotions that had crossed Katherine's face. Her sixth sense had never let her down before, and if she was reading the other woman right, she could feel that she was excited by her presence. Yet accompanying such feelings was a fear not associated with Mary's safety—it was a fear that the nun held within. Easing her creased brows, she shrugged her shoulders before following the other woman to the kitchen. Taking a seat at the table, Mary silently watched Katherine as she busied herself with making a pot of tea.

Finally as the nun sat down opposite her, Mary became aware of a difference in the nun's demeanour—a difference she couldn't quite put her finger on. "Is everything all right?"

Katherine sat back in her chair. "What do you mean? Aside, that is, from the fact that I'm sitting down drinking tea with a bushranger?"

Mary smiled at the other woman's response. "No, that's not what I mean and you know it. You seem very evasive about something. It's as if you've changed somehow," she said, scrutinising the nun's reaction to her question.

Katherine again felt her cheeks redden as she thought first of Catriona and then of Mary. Ashamed by what the bushranger might see, she stood and made a pretence of busying herself with something in the pantry.

What's going on here? Mary thought. *She's being very secretive about something.* As her mind played with the possible reasons for Katherine's reaction, she stopped at the thought of Catriona. She hadn't met this woman and yet she was aware of the good Catriona had brought to the families of the district. She'd heard of her kind-heartedness, yet could it be possible that something more sinister lay beneath a veneer of such largess?

Following Katherine, she stopped at the door to the pantry, effectively blocking the other woman in. "Has Catriona been kind to you? I know the death of her brother hit her quite hard and I've heard of her temper. She hasn't hurt you, has she?" Mary asked, surprised at the interplay of emotions on the Irish-woman's crimson features.

Slowly the kernel of a thought took seed in her mind as she

watched the other woman's reactions. She cast her mind back to the night of Katherine's kidnapping and her reactions to Mary's questioning about her and the grazier's relationship. *Could it possibly be that I wasn't too far from the truth?* Folding her arms across her chest and leaning her frame in a knowledgeable manner on the doorframe, she probed again, "I think my last question well should have been what's going on between you and Catriona?" The bushranger let a knowing smile tug at the corners of her mouth. So pleased was she at Katherine's reaction to her last comment that she nearly didn't catch herself as she was forcefully pushed out of the way by a now indignant woman.

"How *dare* you!" Katherine yelled, her green eyes afire, her chest heaving in barely suppressed fury. "How dare you speak to me of such things? You may be comfortable to live your life in that kind of manner, but need I remind you I'm a nun and answer to a higher calling? I won't have you discuss either myself or Catriona in such a manner!" She finished angrily and her body now dangerously close to that of Mary.

Undaunted and also thrilled by the other reaction, Mary quietly laughed. Stepping ever closer to the inflamed figure in front of her she met the Irishwoman's eyes with her own. "Well to paraphrase a great man, 'Me thinketh the lady doth protesteth too much.'"

Katherine, although silent, became frighteningly aware of her closeness to Mary. As the other woman's words were spoken she could feel the rush of breath on her face. Looking into the bushranger's eyes, she was close enough to witness the excited reaction of her pupils. Her own breathing was equally as heavy and despite her indignant response she could feel a warmth in the pit of her stomach which could only have been caused by the outlaw's proximity. Katherine said as levelly as she could muster, "I think that you should leave. You've more than outstayed your welcome."

Never breaking contact with the set of excited, fearful and deep green eyes, Mary replied, "If that's what you want."

"Yes, it is. Now please go," the Irishwoman answered, attempting to regain her composure. Breaking contact with the other woman's eyes, Katherine turned to move away from the almost hypnotic presence of the woman. As she did so, she felt her arm caught in a viselike grip before she was propelled even closer to where she'd been standing only a moment before. The bushranger's other hand locked itself around her waist, drawing her in close until Mary's lips were almost brushing Katherine's cheek.

Looking into her eyes the bushranger no longer saw fear— she saw excitement, an excitement borne of an expectation that she hadn't seen with Katherine the night of her kidnapping. Without breaking eye contact she trailed her fingers down the nun's arm to reach the woman's soft pliant hand. Leaning forward until Katherine could feel the closeness of Mary to her ear, the bushranger breathed, "So now I see, and now my questions are answered. It would indeed seem that your protests were too great, but don't let that bother you for they have fallen on deaf ears." Stepping quickly out of their embrace the bushranger was gone before the other woman had much time to rationalise about what had just occurred between the two.

Groping for a chair Katherine sat down and willed her breathing to return to normal. She'd felt the same feelings in Mary's arms as she'd felt during that morning in Catriona's.

Katherine placed her head down in her hands and wept. What was she doing here and what had she come to? *I'm a nun here to do God's work,* she answered herself. *This is not happening to me, I don't have the same feeling for Catriona that Mary has for other women. But if that's the case why did I react so with Mary and why did I react so with Catriona?* Her emotional turmoil raged throughout the afternoon as she sat, almost statuesque at the kitchen table. As the afternoon shadows lengthened she at last knew what she had to do.

Arriving home well after dark Catriona found the other woman in the study staring at the delicate watercolour landscape above the fireplace. Characteristically running her hands through her hair she took in the nun's silent form. "Well, it looks as if you bit off a little more than you could chew. I swear this mess is much the same as the one I left you in this morning," she finished with humour in her voice. Her humour, however, was cut short by the nun's non-responsive form. Moving quietly to her side Catriona frowned, "Katherine, is everything all right?"

I wish everyone would stop asking me that, Katherine prayed silently. Turning to the grazier's concerned face she replied, "Catriona, I think you should sit down." She motioned her to a chair and took the one opposite.

"I must speak with you, but I'd ask that you let me finish without interruption. What I'm about to say is not easy; however, I've given it a lot of thought. Catriona, you're the closest friend I've ever had. You're considerate and funny, patient and kind. What happened to us that morning has never happened to me before and I can now admit that it's shaken me." She raised her hand as Catriona started to respond. "Please, don't misunderstand me. I'm not passing judgement on the way you live or who you are. In honesty, I'm passing judgement on myself. I need space and time to think. While I stay here with you, I can't do this with any degree of clarity, not with you so close. I'm sorry, but I think it would be best for both of us if I moved into town."

With these words, the grazier's face fell and her form slumped in her chair. "I'm sorry, but I don't understand. I've been good to my word and given you space and not touched you since that morning. I feel a difference between you and I, and I know you must feel it, too. But I've given you my word. Is that not enough for you? Don't you trust me?" She searched the Irishwoman's tortured features for some sort of reprieve.

If I'm honest with myself I trust you implicitly; it's myself I don't trust. "I trust you, but I need time and distance to put this in perspective. I'm sorry, but I can't do that here." Leaning forward at the anguished look on the other woman's face, she continued, "But don't mistake me, just because I'm moving into town doesn't mean I won't still visit you, does it?" She realised the presumption of her final words.

Reaching forward Catriona clasped her hands in her own. "No, it doesn't mean that at all. You'll always be welcome here either as a guest or as an occupant again, should you wish. I know what you're doing is reasonable to you, but please don't ask me to openly accept your decision because I can't. However, if this is what you want to do, then the decision is yours. But please don't tell me you're going to move in with one of the Ladies Committee." She finished, as a desperate look crossed her face.

Seeing the pain in Catriona's eyes was almost too much for the nun to bear. Swallowing her own emotions she said quietly, "No, not at all. In fact, I was going to ask Susan if she would mind if I stayed with her for a while."

The grazier choked back a laugh at the irony of the situation. She wondered if Katherine would be so keen to move in with the shopkeeper if she were aware of Susan's own circumstances. Aware that the Irishwoman was awaiting a reply, she redirected the conversation, "How are you going to explain this to Father Cleary?"

"I know it's going to be hard for him to understand, but I'll use a similar reason for originally wanting to live out here. The circumstances haven't changed and I'll still be tending to the ill and poor of the town. Something tells me that while this will bother the town's ladies, if I've read her correctly, this won't bother Susan."

Releasing her hands the older woman again slumped in her chair, a defeated look on her face. She knew Susan wouldn't turn Katherine away and maybe what she said was for the best. Maybe with time the Irishwoman would realise how she felt about her. *But what happens if she doesn't?* Catriona thought.

Within a few days the arrangement had been made. A slightly confused Susan was happy to welcome the Sister into her home above the store, even though it was obvious that Catriona was less than wedded to the arrangement. The shopkeeper showed Katherine to her small quarters, explaining the house's other occupant, Me-Lin, was currently visiting relatives in Sydney and wasn't expected to return for a few weeks at least. The absence of any amount of space necessitated the nun continuing to store her books at Catriona's and for this she was glad. This at least gave her a reason to visit the other woman; for despite the change in living arrangements she was adamant that their friendship wouldn't suffer as a result. Father Cleary had been somewhat confused by the turn of events but was surprisingly accepting of the nun's request. The only person who seemed not altogether accepting again found herself alone, with only the echoes of an empty house to keep her company.

Within a couple of weeks, Katherine seemed to have settled into her routine at the store. While she was still a willing aid to the families of the district, at least twice a week she conjured a reason to pay a visit on Catriona. And when this wasn't the case, it seemed that the grazier's second home had become the store; all of which was beginning to play on Susan's progressively stretched nerves. However, unbeknownst to Susan there was still more to follow.

It was a rare afternoon that the shopkeeper had the store just to herself and her customers. Katherine had her teeth-pulling afternoon appointment with the Ladies Committee and this, of course, meant Catriona was nowhere to be seen.

As she quietly took stock of the provisions she was running out of, the door of the store opened to admit an exceptionally well dressed, yet dust covered, woman. It was obvious to Susan's eye that she'd recently arrived on the stage and, as the woman took time to avail herself of some of the dust of travel, Susan appraised the woman before her.

She was the same age, if not slightly older than herself, with raven hair that cloaked the delicate features of a handsome face that bespoke English drawing rooms, rather than the Australian Outback. Her well-proportioned features complemented a dress of what could have only been the latest fashion. As if aware of someone's stare, the woman raised her smiling face and her violet eyes stared into Susan's hazel ones.

The movement caused the shopkeeper's heart to lose a beat. *Who was this advancing woman and what was she doing here?* It wasn't long before Susan's curiosity was assuaged.

"Good afternoon. I'm wondering if you can help me?" said the woman, still smiling, her eyes keenly appraising the woman in front of her.

Susan shook herself out of her reverie. "I'm terribly sorry, I seem to have lost my manners somewhere." Extending her hand she continued, "I'm Susan Crosier, the owner of this store. If you don't mind me saying you're obviously not from around here, are you?"

"Well, yes and no," the woman replied. "I used to live here but it's been a few years since I left. However I've come looking for someone by the name of Catriona Pelham. You wouldn't know her would you?" The woman replied, taking in the shop-keeper's frozen features. Seeing no immediate response she persevered, "I'm sorry, how rude of me.   I haven't introduced myself. My name is Adele, Adele Cooper." She extended her hand toward the other woman.

Chapter
Twelve

"I'm sorry, what did you say your name was again?" Susan attempted to buy herself precious time to gather her thoughts. She knew quite well who the woman in front of her was. She was more than sure that there was only one other person who would register greater surprise at her return and that was Catriona.

"Adele Cooper. I used to work out here on the Pelham property as the Pelham children's governess. I left some time ago and returned to England. It's only recently that I've returned to Australia," she replied in a soft English accent as she studied the features of the woman in front of her. She could have sworn that at the mention of her name there had been a flicker of recognition in the other woman's eyes. She had also been aware of the shopkeeper's appraisal of her as she entered the shop and she was sure that this went beyond idle curiosity on her behalf.

Aware of the sudden silence, Susan shook herself out of her reverie. "Would I be correct in assuming that Catriona isn't aware of your arrival?"

"Yes, you're right. I happened to be in Sydney when I literally ran into Mrs Greystone at the emporium." *Pursued by the curious witch was more like it.* "She mentioned that there had been a great deal of tragedy with the Pelham family with the most recent being the loss of Catriona's brother. My plans were fairly open and so I thought I might take the time to come out and pay a visit," she finished, removing her hat from her head.

Sydney was a long way to come for merely a visit, Susan speculated, looking at the woman on the other side of the

counter. Again she smiled; if there was one thing Catriona
seemed to possess it was an impeccable taste in women. This
woman had a quiet assuredness about her that seemed to place
the shopkeeper at ease. She would definitely be an interesting
person to hold a conversation with, but for the moment Susan
was postponing the inevitable. Clearing her throat she said,
"Although there have been some changes in town, they haven't
extended to any form of coach service within the immediate district. However, if you give me a moment to close up, I'll be
happy to drive you to Catriona's place. She's a very good friend
of mine and it would be remiss of me not to deliver you to her
doorstep."

The emphasis on "very good friend" wasn't lost on the
woman in front of her who, at its inference, smiled enigmatically. "Thank you, I'm grateful for your help." With that, Susan
locked the store and, after preparing the wagon, both women
headed toward the Pelham homestead.

During their short journey Susan took the time to fill Adele
in on the news of the past 10 years or so. The woman laughed as
she discovered that the town Ladies Committee was as strong
and vocal as ever. She took time to tell her of Catriona's parents'
death and the shocking turn of events that had fallen upon her
brother's unhappiness. The governess was genuinely shocked at
his loss, for even in her time the presence of the town's Sister
had played a key part in the community. Waiting for a break in
the conversation Adele queried, "So has the local Sister been
replaced? In my time they were made to live in the hovel just
outside of town, but the dust storm seems to have put an end to
that disgrace."

Susan took an inordinate amount of time in rearranging the
reins within her hands. Making pretence of her actions she
answered as noncommittally as possible. "Yes, in fact the Sister
arrived the day of the dust storm. It was fortunate she arrived
after the event or we may have lost her as well. Her name is Sister Katherine Flynn and she's worked miracles with the children
of the district." *Not to mention Catriona.* "As for her accommodation, she lives above the store with me." She felt no need to
explain to the other woman that this was only a recent arrangement and for a reason the nun refused to share.

"Well, with a little luck I hope I'll get to meet her," Adele
replied, sensing that what she'd heard wasn't the total sum of the
story.

"Well, she does get around and, due to the lack of space at my store, Catriona has graciously allowed her to keep her children's books out at the property. So I've no doubt that you'll catch up with one another sooner or later." Susan found herself wondering whether the other woman's return was merely a passing visit or a more permanent one.

As they arrived at the homestead, she drew the wagon to the rear of the house and, reining in the horse, both women alighted from the wagon as Susan called Catriona's name.

From the darkness of the smokehouse Catriona heard her friend's call and, wiping her hands, wondered what would bring her out here so late in the afternoon. Still wiping her hands on an already greasy towel, she stepped into the sunlight, finding herself momentarily blinded by the glare.

Adele caught her breath as she watched the woman in front of her raise her hand to her face to shield her eyes. *The years have been kind to her*, she thought. For where once dwelled the awkward body of a woman-child, now stood the assured body of a grown woman.

"Susan, I hear you, but I'm sorry I'm a bit troubled by the glare at the moment." Next to her friend, the grazier could just make out the vague outline of a woman. Blinking her eyes once again to try and focus she continued, "Sorry for keeping you both out in the sun, where are my manners? I'm sorry, but I don't think we've met."

"Don't you know me, Catriona?" Adele answered in a quiet voice. As she did she watched the emotions cloud across the other woman's features. They were a mix of confusion, memory, search, recognition, disbelief and desperate hope.

"Adele?" Catriona whispered, half hopefully, half fearful. As her eyes finally focused she took in the form of the woman in front of her. "My God, it's you." Shaking her head, her mind still refused to believe that Adele actually stood in front of her. Instinctively she moved to hug her and checked herself as she remembered Susan's presence.

"How are you? What are you doing here? What have you been doing all these years?" A myriad of questions spilled forth from Catriona as she drank in the features of the apparition before her. Indeed, Adele was obviously older than she remembered, but if anything this enhanced her beauty rather than detracted from it.

Adele laughed at the disbelieving look on the younger

woman's face. "Well, how about we all go inside and I'll answer that for you?"

Susan interrupted her, "I'm sorry, but I'm going to have to pass. If I don't return soon I won't be home before dark and, with the increase in bushranging activity in the district, it's a risk I don't want to take." The shopkeeper finished as she pulled herself onto the wagon. "But I'm sure there'll be time for us to speak more when you're better settled. I'll see you soon. Oh, and Catriona, I do have some stores arriving on this Friday's train. Don't forget to come and pick them up, will you?" Her last comment was a well-known code between the two that Susan wished to speak with her about this recent development. Nodding and waving goodbye, Catriona then picked up Adele's bags and they both made their way to the back of the house.

As Adele closed the back door, she turned to the other woman who had placed her suitcases on the table. Looking at her with a smile in her violet eyes she opened her arms. "Now, are you going to finish what you almost started outside?" Catriona needed no more prompting, and moved toward her to find herself blanketed in the other woman's embrace.

"God, it's so good to see you." Catriona said, revelling in the feel of being in another woman's arms. "But what brought you here? How did you know that you'd be welcome out here?" she queried, intimating at her less than warm departure ten years ago.

Adele laughed as she released the grazier. "Still the curious mind, I see. Before we sit down, could I have a few moments to wash up? I see the roads out here are as dusty as ever."

After refreshing herself from her journey, the older woman spent the afternoon relaying to Catriona what she'd done with her life in the ensuing years since her banishment from the Pelham household. After that most unfortunate event of being sacked without references, she had found herself at pains to find a placement either in the country or in town. Out of ideas she'd decided to return to England and was booking her return journey when, by chance a young family had been doing the same. In assisting the family with their two unruly children, the suffering mother had commented on her skill with the two and Adele had leapt at the chance, explaining what her employment was and the fact that she was returning home to seek a position there. The woman, who was none too keen on the idea of a long sea voyage with the two young children, had offered her a job. As she expected, Adele had proved her worth over the voyage and had consequently remained with the family over the ensuing years. It seemed only natural that when they returned to Australia that she would return with them.

It had only been by sheer coincidence that on her second day in Sydney she'd been shopping in the emporium and had run into Mrs Greystone who had treated her like a long lost friend. She'd spent the afternoon filling the governess in on the last 10 years, but it was the more recent news that had shocked Adele into action. Mrs Greystone had advised her of the Pelham family loss and she'd decided that it might be a fortuitous time to visit Catriona to see how she was faring.

In exchange, the grazier filled Adele in on the last 10 years of her life, explaining to her that she'd never gone back on her word to her mother, refusing to conform to her expectations of a daughter. In fact, as the years passed she found herself more comfortable living as she did, away from the pretensions of town.

Choosing her words carefully, Adele asked, "So, Catriona, what we shared, was there ever anyone else?"

Catriona's thoughts were immediately crowded with the elfin features of a smiling nun. *Was what they shared the same as that between her and Adele?* As much as she wished it to be the case, Katherine had virtually made her position clear when she'd moved into town. Despite this she seemed to spend an inordinate amount of time at the house. Realising she was taking far too long to reply to Adele's last question, she raised her eyes to the other woman. "No, nothing that's been reciprocated." *Well that's the truth isn't it?* She felt a little guilty at her lie by omission. Rushing to hide her embarrassment she asked Adele the same.

"I expect I've been more fortunate than you, for in London society a woman who does not have close female friends is considered unusual. There was someone before I left. She was an older woman of independent means and our arrangement suited her," she replied a wistful look on her face.

Strangely enough, Catriona felt a pang of jealousy for this other woman. However as quickly as it surfaced it was chided by her own acknowledgment that she had no more control over Adele's personal life than the older woman did over hers. Still, it felt unusual to be discussing things in such a casual manner. Bringing her thoughts back to the present she heard the other woman say, "I don't think she was all too pleased to have me travel to Australia, but I'm sure that should I never return she'll find someone else." Catriona's breath caught at this last disclosure. Did this mean that Adele wasn't committed to returning to England? What did this mean for the two of them? She was cautious to not read too much into Adele's comments, but felt a flicker of hope all the same.

Adele looked at the clock above the wood stove. "Heavens, look at the time. I don't believe we've been talking for that long. I expect that if you're going to get any sort of an early start tomorrow that we best call it a night."

"You're right," Catriona answered, looking at the fob she'd drawn from her trouser pocket. "Do you remember when you were last here you were stuck in those cramped quarters out by the barn?" The governess laughed at the memory of cold nights and a leaking roof. "Well, no more of that for you my dear, for tonight I think my parents' room is the suitable place for a guest of your standing." She rose and, with Adele following her, made her way down the hallway that had been lit by the warm glow of Catriona's lamp.

As they made their way through the house Catriona was suddenly made aware of Adele's close presence through a hand that reached out gently touching her arm. Catriona halted and turned questioningly to the older woman.

"While I'm flattered at you putting me in the comfort of your parents' room, I think I'd be much more comfortable in this one," she suggested and Catriona realised they were standing outside the door to her own room.

Adele's fingers gently traced a trail down the other woman's arm until their fingers were interlaced with one another. Raising her eyes to Catriona, Adele opened the door and led her through it. The two rekindled memories long dormant through 10 years of separation.

Catriona awoke the next morning, languishing in the feel of being in another woman's arms. Thinking on the night's events, she was touched by the tenderness of their lovemaking. There had been no urgency, unlike the lovemaking she had shared with

Adele years ago. It was a more mature ritual, like two friends renewing an old acquaintance. As Catriona lay spooned in the other woman's embrace, Adele, still in a deep sleep shifted her body and her hand found its way to Catriona's breast. Catriona felt her body react to the warm hand and, aware that Adele was still asleep, allowed herself the luxury of the peaceful moment.

Laying there in the early morning light, her thoughts guiltily strayed to Katherine and the morning they had shared together. She had reacted to Catriona's touch, for that there was no doubt, and that all too brief contact lingered in the grazier's memory. As she thought about the Irishwoman, she felt the stirrings of desire in her own body and was at once ashamed. For here she was in the arms of a woman who had educated her well in the arts of love and Catriona repaid her by filling her own mind with the thoughts of another woman.

She shook her head as if to dispel the thoughts. In reality she could indulge in any number of fantasies involving Katherine; however, that may well be as close as she ever got to reality. Despite her responses on that morning, it was Adele who was now holding her not Katherine. As she lay in her arms the younger woman wondered about her reluctance to share with Adele what had occurred between her and the nun. *Why haven't I told her?* Part of her mind answered her question suggesting that her lie by omission was to protect the nun who, in truth, hadn't initiated the actions of that morning. However if she was honest with herself, a selfish and secretive part of her didn't want to share the surreality of that relationship with Adele.

Over the next few days the grazier didn't stray far from the homestead, finding one excuse or another to stay in close proximity to Adele. It seemed so strange not to have to think twice about embracing her in the morning, or worry about the fact that they lay in each other's arms recalling the stories of the past during their evenings in the parlour.

Adele was surprised and touched at the number of watercolours that adorned the house. As the governess of the small wealthy family she'd seen many painters during her frequent visits to Paris. Those artists were extremely skilled in portraying a landscape or face, however their paintings were all one-dimensional. In contrast Catriona's conveyed an emotion which seemed to capture the essence of the moment. She could feel the same light breeze on her face as the one that tenderly blew the grass in the younger woman's watercolours. Her sunrises radiated warmth far beyond that merely created by the brush. She couldn't help but think that if Catriona had pursued the profession, she would have profited greatly from her endeavours.

Friday morning arrived all too soon and Adele reminded the grazier of Susan's parting comments, unaware of the real intent behind the words. Aware of what awaited her, Catriona delayed her departure and set out late in the morning for town with the necessary answers that she knew the shopkeeper would ask for.

When she arrived at the store on lunch she found the front door locked. She walked to the rear of the store and stopped as she came across Susan and Me-Lin in what could only have been a passionate conversation. There was no physical contact between the two, yet the depth of love and emotion was evident. As Susan quietly spoke, delight and laughter seemed to flit across the Chinese woman's features and it was obvious that the bond between the two ran strong. Watching them together, Catriona couldn't help but wonder if Katherine could ever feel for her the way Me-Lin felt for Susan and she found herself landing back in reality with a thud. What was it about the Irishwoman that she seemed to have enmeshed herself so deeply in her thoughts, despite the fact that the relationship between herself and Adele was again blossoming? Shaking her head in confusion, she made a pretence of rattling the back gate before walking through it.

"Good afternoon, you two," she smiled as she walked toward the two women. As a result of years of cautious instinct, both women took a step back from each other before fully realising whom their visitor was. Chuckling at the guilty looks that crossed their faces Catriona continued quietly, with humor in her voice, "Yes, and well may you look like that. What would happen if I had been Katherine and interrupted you speaking in such a manner with such looks of adoration written on your faces?" She placed her hands on her hips.

Susan, noting the lightness in the grazier's tone, parried her thrust with one of her own. "Well, I suspect no sillier than you would have felt had she been at the homestead and saw the look on your face the day of Adele's arrival." The shopkeeper laughed as she saw that her arrow had hit its mark. Catriona, blushing a shade of crimson, was lost for words. "Come on inside. By the look on your face you look like you're ready to pass out at that last comment." Laying an arm across the shoulders of a still stunned woman, the three of them moved inside. Me-Lin gave Susan a soft kiss before making her way upstairs. Susan closed the back door behind her.

"So tell me, what's going on and how is it that Adele has found her way back into your life after so many years?" Susan asked, motioning the younger woman toward a waiting chair.

Catriona baulked as she looked around the house and as if Susan had read her thoughts she reassured her, "There's no need to worry. Katherine set out very early this morning for the Connor farm and I don't expect her home for a while yet." The shopkeeper seated herself, making herself comfortable.

"That's strange, I didn't see her on the way into town." Catriona's brows creased, realising that they should have passed each other seeing how the Connor property was the next one from her own.

"Well, I expect that's because she left early. You're uncommonly late this morning," the other woman replied, a twinkle in her eye.

Catriona again felt a red flush take over her features and Susan laughed as she reached across and grasped the grazier's hand in her own. "If you could only see the look on your face; it's precious. I'm sorry I shouldn't be teasing you like that. How about you start at the beginning? I promise not to tease." She patted the other woman's hand.

Catriona relayed to her how Adele had once again found herself in the Australian countryside by sheer luck. The shopkeeper's eyes widened in surprise as she heard the full story in regard to Mrs Greystone's actions. She found herself laughing at the delicious irony of the situation, wondering the woman's reaction now if she knew what was going on. Shyly Catriona told her of the rekindling of a relationship she thought was all but lost. Susan smiled seeing the happiness in the other woman's face and yet she was worried—there still seemed to be something missing with the woman in front of her.

"And so what are Adele's long term plans?" Susan asked casually, carefully trying not to place too much emphasis on "long term."

Catriona shifted in her seat, taking time to think on that prospect. It was certainly something that the two hadn't discussed; yet she was sure that if she asked Adele to stay she would. As she thought on the question a little voice in the recesses of her mind spoke, *But is that what you want?* Realising Susan was still waiting for an answer she replied, "We haven't really spoken about her plans. However I'm fairly sure if I asked her she would be more than willing to stay. Her tenure as governess to her family is complete, so I get the feeling she's a free soul."

Rather than verbalizing the obvious, Susan raised both eyebrows in question.

"I don't know. It's as if for the first time in my life I've within my grasp what I really want. Adele knows me. She's warm, humorous, exceptionally good looking, well educated, and an extremely sensual woman." She paused as she felt a hotness in her cheeks. "I haven't really thought on that yet." She lied knowing that a great deal of her days since the other woman's arrival had been spent pondering just that question.

Sensing the turmoil Susan sat back and looked at the woman opposite her. She did seem happy and peaceful, yet there was something missing despite her new found happiness. She sensed that the "something" was about 5 foot 6 inches, with brown curly hair and sparkling green eyes. "So where does that leave Katherine?" she asked quietly.

Catriona's head jerked up as if struck. Was she really that transparent? Angry at her friend's apparent ease at reading her thoughts, she retaliated. "Where does that leave Katherine? She knows all too well how I feel and still she moved out. Of course she still painfully figures in my daily thoughts, but hell Susan, what else can I hope for with her? At least with Adele I've a reciprocation of feelings. God, I could spend the rest of my life pining after that woman and she may never bloody well know what she wants. What I have now may be as good as it gets," she finished, exasperated by her emotions.

"Are you really sure Katherine does *not* know what she wants?" Susan continued in a level tone, attempting to calm the grazier's agitated state. It didn't work.

"For Christ's sake!" Catriona pushed the chair out from under her, her voice raised. "What's that supposed to mean? She's *here*; I'm *there*. I really don't think I can expect any more than that."

"If you're so damned sure, then why does she spend the evenings here boring me to bloody distraction with words of you? And how is it that despite living *here* she seems to spend an inor-

dinate amount of time out at *your* property? And don't tell me
it's got something to do with those damn books; they're nothing
more than a lame excuse at best." Susan attempted to rein in her
temper at the stubbornness of the woman in front of her. "God, if
you're so sure then answer me this. Have you spoken to Adele
about Katherine yet? Yes, well I can see by the look on your face
that you haven't," she finished, her anger barely restrained.

Both turned as the door to the upper floor opened to admit a
concerned Me-Lin. "What's going on? I'm upstairs with the bedroom door closed and yet I can hear you both as if you were
standing beside me."

Susan moved to her and hugged her fiercely. After whispering reassuring words that everything was fine, Me-Lin again left
the two, but not before casting a glance of warning in the grazier's general direction.

"I'm sorry, I didn't mean for my words to be so harsh or so
loud," Susan said embarrassed at her outburst.

Catriona hung her head and slumped into her chair. "No,
I'm the one who should be apologising. You're right about
Katherine and it's driving me crazy. She does come and visit,
and we talk about all number of things but it's like she's walking
on coals. She starts to bring barriers down between us and just as
I move closer she puts them back up again. It's as if she's afraid
of herself and her own feelings. And yes, you're right. I haven't
spoken to Adele of her, well not in that sense anyway."

"I think Katherine feels something that her religious teachings say she shouldn't feel and she's as scared as hell, Catriona.
Not from eternal damnation but how to deal with the emotions
which are pulling her apart. Just remember she has never been
with anyone, man or woman, and in matters of the heart I believe
she's relatively naive. As for telling Adele, that's up to you,
however is that fair to her?" She moved around the table to kneel
by the silent woman's chair. "Can you truly be happy with what
you have with Adele? If you can that's all good and fine, but
don't end up despising her for something you never gave yourself the chance to have."

Catriona ran her hands through her hair. "You said she
speaks a lot about me and yet she doesn't know what she wants. I
don't know what to do. I've thought long and hard on the idea
and, I'm sorry, I'd sure like some answers if you have any."

"Well, I do have an idea; however, there are no guarantees
that it will bring her any closer to reconciling her feelings one

way or another." Catriona nodded, urging the other woman to continue. "I believe that part of her problem may be coming to grips with the notion of a relationship between two women. So how about we show her that there's nothing wrong with this?" Seeing the shocked look on the grazier's face, Susan held up her hands. "Don't mistake me, I'm not suggesting you fall into Adele's arms in front of her. You mentioned the possibility of a dinner party over a month ago, have you given it any further thought? I believe it would be an excellent opportunity for Katherine to witness social interaction between women and maybe it will set her thinking. What do you think?"

Catriona took time to ponder the idea, playing through the evening in her mind. Her heart stopped as she realised that she would have two women who she had a deep emotional attachment to under her roof at the same time. Despite this it was a risk she was willing to take.

"Well, given the current circumstances, I suppose things can't get any worse. I'll speak to Mrs Johnston and see if she can prepare a meal for us. I'm afraid that if it was left up to me, dinner would be very Spartan." Catriona's thoughts again strayed to the evening ahead.

The shopkeeper looked at the woman in front of her, eyebrows creased in thought. "I do think it would be a good idea if you first spoke with Katherine and made her aware of your visitor. I'm not saying tell her everything, but at least prepare her for the evening."

Catriona was rapidly becoming wedded to the idea of a dinner party. "Yes, I'll do that next time she's out at the house. After all, as you say she seems to always incorporate a trip to the farm whenever she's out that way."

Catriona paused, her eyes rapidly seeking out Susan's. "Shit!" they said in unison, both remembering at the same time that Katherine's homeward trip that day would certainly bring her past the Pelham homestead.

Chapter
Thirteen

As Katherine began her journey home she couldn't help but reflect on the smiles that had lit the Connor children's faces as she gave them their books. The reverence with which they treated them had spoken volumes to her. *It was obvious that the receipt of such books was something that was few and far between.*

She caught herself and smiled at her use of the last saying, for it was one of Catriona's favourites. Despite the contact she maintained with the grazier, she did miss their evening discussions and the humour the other woman managed to inject into a story about the day's events. That wasn't to say she was uncomfortable staying with Susan and Me-Lin. They were the perfect company and on three occasions now she'd managed to hold a conversation with the exceptionally quiet Me-Lin. During one such discussion they had spoken about the different philosophies of religion that existed between western and eastern societies. She was surprised at the contrast, with the west seemingly having its foundations in fear and damnation and the east on peace and acceptance. While Katherine had been given a devoutly Protestant upbringing, she couldn't help but be deeply moved by the calming spirituality of Me-Lin and her religious teachings. It was something she reconciled to learn a lot more about.

Despite her relationship with Susan and Me-Lin, in the evening hours Katherine found herself missing the contact she and Catriona shared. She blushed as she realised how such a thought might be interpreted. It was nothing physical; it was moreso an almost invisible link between the two that made her feel at home in the other woman's presence. For once she didn't have to conform to the expectations of others. She wondered how Catriona was faring with her return to loneliness, for despite her being a regular visitor, Katherine felt that the evenings must be interminably slow. Nodding her head in resolution, she decided it wouldn't hurt for her to pay Catriona a visit. After all, it was on her way home and she did need to pick up some more books. She laughed to herself, thinking of what excuse she would have used to validate her visits had the books been held at the store. Smiling, she shook her head as she turned the wagon into the driveway of the Pelham property.

After tethering the horse in the shade of the trees by the barn, she made her way to the back of the house and walked through the unlocked back door. This was another custom which never ceased to amaze her. In Ireland, no family would entertain being away all day and leaving the house unlocked; however, out here this seemed to be the norm. In fact she remembered a day when Catriona and herself had returned from being out all day to see a swagman patiently waiting on the back steps. In the time he had waited for the owner's return he had chopped enough wood to last a fortnight as well as clean all the leather harnesses in the barn. Having done so he waited patiently for the owner's return and payment in food for his efforts. Catriona's largess again came to the fore as she gave the man enough food to last him a week rather than merely a day.

Walking though the house, she made her way to the study and, making herself comfortable on the floor, started sorting through the books she would need for the next few days. As she did so, she became aware of footfalls in the house and a smile rose unbidden to her face. "Well, I didn't expect to find you at home at this time of the day." Despite that being the intent for Katherine's visit, she would refuse to admit it to anyone. She turned to the door and her face moved from happiness to shock. Standing in the doorway was a woman who appeared to be in her mid-thirties. Her face had a paleness about it that hinted at a more genteel life; however, what illuminated her somewhat pale features was the presence of a pair of inquisitive violet eyes. Looking at Katherine was a figure, short of being called Rubenesque, capably aided by her height that served to add further refinement to the woman. Katherine couldn't stop herself before she blurted out: "Who are you?"

The violet eyes crinkled in a smile making the governess' appearance more youthful than her years. "Well, it would seem that I have an advantage over you, for you could be no other than Sister Flynn." Stepping through the doorway to the still prone figure on the floor, she extended her hand. "Sister, my name is Adele Cooper."

A look of recognition crossed the nun's feature. *So this was Catriona's last governess. But I thought she'd gone to England— what's she doing here?* "Pleased to meet you," she said standing and taking the proffered hand. "I'm sorry, if I'd known that Catriona had guests I wouldn't have been so quick to barge through the house."

"Oh, no harm done. She's told me of your arrangement," the older woman said, watching as Katherine's green eyes widen slightly at her last remark before managing to gain composure. As Adele watched she sensed a discomfort in the slight woman who was now nervously trying to find something to do with her hands.

Clearing her throat, Katherine answered. "Yes, well, she told me all about you as well." This time it was the other woman's turn to blush for she reasoned no matter how close the Sister and Catriona were, she didn't think for a minute that the grazier had disclosed the nature of their relationship. The nun continued, oblivious to Adele's reaction, "She told me that you were the one who taught her how to paint the lovely watercolours around the house. She has a real eye for detail and her mixing of the colours seems to make the paintings come alive. They're truly wonderful."

"Yes, she was a good student with an eagerness to learn. I don't think anything I taught her about painting helped her though; the talent was always there. It would have been uncovered sooner or later at an opportune moment in time."

"That may be so, Miss Cooper, but that's certainly not how Catriona tells it. When I was living here she spent many an evening discussing your influence." The Irishwoman motioned toward a chair.

Adele took the time in seating herself to reflect on the other woman's last words. *Katherine had lived out here and yet Catriona had neglected to mention it. It was obvious from what Susan had mentioned on the day of her return that Katherine was now living elsewhere. This is something I'll have to speak to Catriona about.* Smoothing out the front of her dress she said subtly, "Well it's a shame you're still not out here, Sister. I'm sure we could have had some wonderful discussions during the course of an evening. Between the two of us we may even convince that stubborn woman to paint again."

Concerned at where the conversation might be heading Katherine attempted to redirect it to safer ground. "Miss Cooper, I'd really feel a lot more comfortable if you'd call me Katherine. Sister Flynn really does seem out of place out here."

"I'm sorry where are my manners? Please, you must call me Adele. I believe there's enough formality in the world without imposing it where it needn't be imposed," Adele replied, a smile lighting her features.

Katherine could feel herself warming to the woman in front of her. Given the older woman's previous employment, it would be very interesting to spend the rest of the afternoon speaking with her. She was sure that she would have some wise words on the ways of teaching children; however, the afternoon was growing late. Looking at the clock about the mantelpiece she turned her head again to meet Adele's inquiring eyes. "I'm sorry to head off so abruptly, but if I'm to get to town before dark, it's best that I leave now." Rising out of her chair she stooped and picked up the books she would require for the day's ahead.

Adele rose also. "Yes, it's a shame as I'm sure we would have had a lot to talk about." *Like why are you so uncomfortable?* Moving through the house to where the nun's wagon was tethered she continued, "If you find yourself out this way in the near future, please call again. I'd love for us to sit down and talk some more." *And find out just what Catriona has been telling you.*

Katherine was grateful that her back was to Adele with those last words spoken. She could feel her features change to petulance, somewhat annoyed that Adele had seemed to have taken her place in the grazier's household. She seated herself and reined in her emotions before replying to the patient figure below her. "Yes, that would be wonderful. Although I don't think I'll be out here in the next week or so. Thank you for the offer all the same." Pulling away she waved to the standing woman and started her journey home.

As she headed toward the entrance, she took stock of her meeting with the older woman. For all intents and purposes Adele was a lovely lady. However, if this was the case, why did

Katherine have this niggling feeling about her? *Was it because she has usurped my position or is it because I'm resentful of the fact that Catriona now has a guest and therefore no need of my frequent company?* She shook her head to clear her thoughts. *What makes you think you have sole ownership over Catriona's company? Those are selfish thoughts. But they're more than that,* a little voice inside her intoned. *They're the words of a jealous woman.* Angry at the stupidity of such thoughts, she urged the horse into a canter, nearly causing it to collide with the rider coming toward her.

"Slow down! At that pace you'll do yourself some damage, knock someone over or both."

Katherine blushed as she watched Catriona struggle to keep her horse's head still. "I'm sorry, I was just in a hurry to get home before it got too dark and I suppose I wasn't looking where I was going. How are you?"

"Oh, not too bad. I'm keeping myself busy with the current crops and new planting at the moment. Between that and going into town there doesn't seem to be enough hours in the day." She sufficiently managed to calm the horse.

Katherine made pretence of wiping dust from the front of her habit. "Well, it must be a relief to have someone in the house then."

Catriona was grateful for the long shadows of the afternoon as a blush rose to her cheeks. "Yes, Adele's visit was unplanned, but I'm thankful for her company all the same."

Katherine attempted to judge whether the grazier's last comment was related to her exit. She dismissed the thought in the same breath. While Catriona had a sharp tone, it was never used with malicious intent. "Yes, she seems like a lovely woman. She was your last governess, if I remember correctly? It's a shame I had to leave so soon as I'm sure we could have found a number of things to talk about."

Thank God for small mercies and long trips back into town, the other woman thought. "Funny you should say that. I was speaking with Susan this afternoon and she mentioned a wonderful idea. She suggested that we all get together for a dinner party. I've organised the meal preparation side of things."

"That's a relief." The Irishwoman laughed. "The idea of you serving steak and eggs up to your guests is probably not what they may have had in mind for a dinner party."

"Yes, well that's organised. Thank you very much for your

vote of confidence." Catriona chided humorously, and then in a much more subdued tone, "So, will you come?"

Katherine looked at the hopeful pleading in the other woman's eyes. Gently leaning over she touched Catriona's arm. "Of course I'll come. Just because I no longer live here doesn't mean we can't be friends." However, the feelings welling inside her at the sudden contact spelt something more than friendship. Removing her hand gently she continued, "And besides, it will give me an opportunity to get to know Adele."

Catriona sat back on her horse, suddenly distant. "Yes, I expect it will. Could you tell Susan I've organised with Mrs Johnston for the dinner to be this Friday? That's if it suits you all. If not just let me know and we'll arrange it for another time." Drawing the reins of her horse toward her Catriona waved good-bye and continued on her way toward the house.

Katherine shook her head at the grazier's sudden distance and, at a loss to find a root cause for it, turned horse and wagon for home.

Catriona sat at the kitchen table and attempted to gather her thoughts. The idea of having Katherine out here for dinner had seemed like a wonderful one when she spoke with Susan, but where did that leave her and Adele? Was she chasing something she could never have when what she really wanted was with her now? As she sat and thought on the dilemma, a soft pair of hands came to rest on her shoulders and they gently kneaded the knotted muscles there.

Leaning down Adele gently kissed the seated woman's cheek. "Well, hello stranger. You've been gone a fair while. I had a visitor while you were gone."

Turning around Catriona placed her hands on the older woman's waist and traced a lazy path up to the fullness of her breasts. Pulling Adele to her, Catriona rested the side of her face on a soft stomach, momentarily enjoying the feel of the smooth fabric on her skin. "Yes, I know. I saw Katherine on her way home."

Adele idly traced a pattern in the grazier's hair. "Yes, she seems like quite a nice woman, a bit nervous though. She seemed to be surprised to find anyone out here. She mentioned that you had told her all about us. I trust you weren't completely candid about our relationship?"

Catriona raised her head to look up at the other woman's face. "No, of course not, she's a nun for heaven's sake," she finished somewhat defensively. She returned her face to the planes of Adele's stomach, her hands now tracing a casual pattern across her back.

In concert with those of the younger woman, Adele's own hands continued to toy with Catriona's hair as she mentioned conversationally, "Katherine mentioned she used to live out here. Funny, I don't remember you mentioning that."

Catriona was glad for the security of Adele's stomach, suddenly afraid of that which her eyes might betray. "Yes, she did, but it was a temporary arrangement. She now lives with Susan in town. This gives her the freedom to tend to the families of the district without interference from the Ladies Committee."

Adele had noticed the slight pause in the grazier's hand as she had asked her question and a niggling thought took shape. "That's strange, I thought that she would have been able to achieve the same out here."

Catriona removed her hands and stood up, now looking into the other woman's eyes. "Yes, she did. However, she decided to move into town."

Adele struggled to inject diplomacy into her next words, but lost the battle. "Catriona, was there anything between the two of you?"

The younger woman's eyes widened at the question. Reticent to admit what had occurred between them, Catriona tried to answer as truthfully as possible. "We are close, yes, but there'll never be anything more between us than a close friendship. She's a nun and I wouldn't jeopardise our friendship for something I can't have."

Adele leant against the table and drew the grazier into her arms. "So, now she's living with Susan?" Catriona nodded her assent. "And so does she know about Susan?" she asked candidly.

Catriona blinked, the look of surprise plain on her face. "How did you know about Susan?"

"Well, let me say that I know the difference between a look and the fine appraisal of another woman whose tastes are the same as mine. Let's just say that on the day of my arrival your shopkeeper friend was very appraising."

The grazier threw her head back and laughed. "Oh, I can't

wait to tell her that she's been caught at her own game. She always reads me so well. It will be ever so delicious to tell her that she's been caught out for once."

"Well, I must say in her defence that the appraisal was reasonably mutual," the governess added with a twinkle in her eye.

"If that's the case you'll get a second look this coming Friday. She's coming out to dinner, as is Katherine. However, be aware that she's bringing her partner and I don't think she'll be as receptive to your roving eye as Susan."

Both women laughed as they prepared supper for themselves before sitting down and discussing the day's other events in greater detail.

In the ensuing days leading up to the dinner party Catriona found her time preoccupied with tending to the needs of her crops and herd of cattle, and again she found herself touched at the pledges of support she'd received from the farmer's cooperative. In turn, Katherine found her days occupied with the teaching of children on the farms surrounding the small town, leaving her little time for the persistent Ladies Committee or Father Cleary. She knew that she should allocate her time more evenly, but as her stay in the town lengthened she'd realised that her focus had shifted. She was well aware of her calling as a nun and that certain things were expected of her; her habit reminded her daily of the religious demands on her life. However, when she had a few precious moments to herself, she couldn't help but start to question her initial decision. The recent week's moments of reflection had been scarce and before too long the night of the dinner party was upon her.

As they arrived at the doorsteps of Gleneagle, Katherine found herself trying to remember the last time she'd been invited to an evening such as this. She chuckled ruefully as she remembered how long ago it had been and how many things had changed since then. Alighting from the buggy, they were greeted at the door by Adele.

Katherine took the time while introductions were being made to look at the woman in front of her. Her black hair had been gathered fashionably into a chignon, raising it clear off her long slender neck. Her dress accentuated her figure perfectly, with its gold hues dancing in the porch light. She ceased her mental meandering as the woman turned her attention toward the nun. "Hello again, Adele. At least this time we haven't surprised each other. Hopefully you won't think me too forward, but that's a beautiful dress you're wearing." The nun finished, extremely conscious of her own drab attire.

"Thank you. Why don't we all go into the parlour? Catriona is just checking on the meal and will join us shortly." The older woman turned and moved through the open door.

"I don't mean to sound rude, but before the evening starts completely would you mind if I gather some books from the study? It would be silly to waste an opportunity to pick up some more books while I'm out here."

"Certainly," Adele replied. "You know where the study is, why don't you just come on through when you're finished?"

The Irishwoman continued down the hall, happy to have been given breathing space to gather her thoughts which, to say the least, were at war with one another. An irrational part of her mind kept insisting that the role of hostess the governess had been so capably filling should have been hers. Shaking her head in agitation, she raised the light on the trimmed lamp by the study door and moved inside, grateful for the solitude.

"Good evening, ladies," Catriona said as she moved into the parlour with the rest of the group. Taking Me-Lin's hand she placed a gallant kiss in it. "Me-Lin, you bring light to what would otherwise be a dull occasion."

"I expect that you radiate enough of that yourself—sometimes more than you can handle." The small group laughed and Susan's eyes twinkled at her partner's repulse of Catriona's mock pass.

Moving to the cabinet the grazier poured herself a drink. "Well, tonight should be a fine evening thanks to Mrs Johnston's good cooking. I must tell you though something interesting occurred when I was organising for her to do the cooking." Seeing she had the attention of the others she continued, "Susan, I decided after we spoke that I'd take the opportunity to speak with Robert Johnston and ask if his mother was available to cook for us tonight. Well, as you know he's the blacksmith's apprentice. When I went to speak with him I found him in what could only be, by the body language of the two, in close conversation with the caretaker's son, William Gilchrist. When they heard me approach they both stepped clear of each other looking rather guilty as they did so."

The shopkeeper nodded, taking a sip from her sherry. "You know, funny you should say that. I've seen them together on a number of occasions and they certainly look like a lot more than just friends."

As the group shared a knowing laugh the door opened admitting Katherine. "Who looked like more than just friends?" Pausing at the door she took in the occupants of the room. Her eyes travelled to Susan, whose beauty was captured in a blue silk dress that would have done any English drawing room justice. Seated close by her side was Me-Lin whose exquisite maroon dress served to highlight her delicate features. Adele in turn conveyed an air of confidence, radiated by the burnished gold of her dress.

Moving her gaze to the fireplace, Katherine felt as if she'd momentarily lost her breath. Standing with her hand casually resting on the mantelpiece was Catriona. Unlike the three women, Catriona was dressed in black trousers and dress boots which served to complement her figure and her toned yet sleek legs. The shirt she wore was a full sleeved creme silk shirt, opened at the neck and highlighting her tanned skin. Around her neck she wore a simple diamond pendant, its facets catching the light of the room. Realising she was staring she continued into the room. "What a lovely group for a dinner party. I'd almost forgotten what fashion looked like. And your trousers Catriona, where did you get them?"

Catriona was flattered by the Irishwoman's obvious pleasure at her attire. "Me-Lin made them for me. It's just a little difficult for a lady to walk into a tailor and ask for a pair of trousers, especially out here." The gathering shared a laugh. "You were asking about who it was that looked like more than just friends. I don't think you've met them yet, so never mind. Now, can I offer you a watered down whiskey perhaps?"

The nun laughed at the suggestion. "Miss Pelham, you must know that as a Celt the only way I'd drink good scotch is in its purest state, not tainted by water." Seeing the look of surprise on the grazier's face she continued, "However, given that it's been quite a long time since I took a 'wee dram,' I feel I'll have to refuse. Besides, between that and the wine with dinner, I believe by the end of it all I'd be a right royal mess." The women again laughed at Katherine's response and the idea of a drunken nun.

Placing her glass down beside her, Adele rose. "Speaking of dinner, I believe it's my turn to check on the meal. I expect it shouldn't be too long before serving, so if you'd make yourself comfortable I'll let you know when it's ready."

Katherine also moved toward the door. "Let me help you, surely it's too big a job for just one." Both women left, closing the door behind them.

Susan waited until the sound of their footfalls had diminished before turning to Catriona. "If you think that woman doesn't know what she wants then you're wrong. Given what I've just witnessed I'd have to say there goes someone who has made up her mind, she just doesn't know how to ask for it," the shopkeeper declared and took a sip from her sherry.

Dinner that night was a simple fare of individual Beef Wellington accompanied by a range of roast vegetables and suitably complemented by a couple of bottles of claret which were Susan's donation to the meal. The pure lines of the dining room were ones of understated elegance, with it being dominated by a simple yet elegant red cedar table and a matching hutch. As was the case throughout the house, Catriona's watercolours adorned the walls, their soft vistas visible through the light of three silver candelabras.

From her place at the head of the table, Catriona was the ever-attentive host and drew Katherine into conversation when she felt she'd been too silent. Truth be told, the Irishwoman preferred her silence as it gave her the opportunity to view the social interaction occurring around the table. She'd noted that as they had entered the room, Catriona had moved ahead of Adele and her to ensure their seats had been drawn and waiting for them. Susan did the same for Me-Lin. Susan seemed very caring of Me-Lin, drawing her into conversation when she fell silent. The looks that passed between the two women surprised the nun. They were looks of comfort and happiness and obvious commitment toward each other. Katherine was surprised that she hadn't noticed the interplay between the two women sooner. She found herself confused at the closeness shown between the two women. *Was this what Catriona and I shared?*

Thinking on the two women, Katherine turned her attention to the other two at the table. It was obvious that there was a closeness between them and yet it was different to the one she sensed between Susan and Me-Lin. She searched her mind for words to compare the two and found that she was at a loss. What wasn't lost on her were the frequent light touches of Adele to Catriona when she was emphasising a point or questioning the grazier who, at times, seemed to be somewhere else. These touches bespoke familiarity and comfort and Katherine found herself missing such touches that she'd shared with the other woman.

Katherine wasn't the only surreptitious spectator that night, for Adele watched with interest the looks that passed between the grazier and the nun. No amount of shadows could hide the look on Catriona's face as she teased the Irishwoman or drew her into conversation. Sitting beside the Sister it was difficult to clearly judge, without being too obvious, what Katherine's reactions were to the grazier's comments. However, the few times she stole a glance toward the nun, she seemed to be engaged in a private struggle. Adele found herself wondering if Catriona had been entirely honest with her.

As the dinner drew to a close the party rose to adjourn. Katherine waved away the governess' attempts to gather the dessert plates. "No, it's only fair that I help a little here. Why don't you go into the parlour and I'll meet you there? I'll just put these in water before I join you. If they're left they'll be rock hard by morning."

"Just like your scones I expect?" Catriona said, moving to help the nun.

Susan took the plate out of the Catriona's hands and made the motion of ushering the people out of the dining room. "No, you three go into the parlour, I'll help Katherine with these. Just make sure there's a port waiting for me when we bring in the tea," Susan warned, picking up the jug of cream and the remains of a Mulberry pie.

In the kitchen, the shopkeeper placed the cream on the counter. "Well, I think that was a most successful evening. What do you think?"

Preoccupied with her own thoughts, Katherine put the bowls in the washbasin. "Yes, it was a lovely evening and such nice company." Moving over to pour milk into the jug of the tea service she said as casually as possible, "You and Me-Lin seem to be good friends. Between your busy schedules and her recent trip to Sydney, I think that this evening was the first time I've really seen the two of you relax together. Catriona told me that she came with you when you left the goldfields."

Moving to the washbasin, Susan busied herself with pouring hot water over the bowls. "Yes, we're good friends and we run a very successful business. She's a seamstress of some skill while I tend to the front counter. In all it's a very comfortable arrangement," she chose her words carefully. Placing the kettle back on the stove she turned to find that the Irishwoman had closed the distance between the two of them and was looking at her with curious eyes.

"Susan, do you mind if I ask you a question?"

Sensing what was coming next, she replied as calmly as possible, "Of course you can and if I can answer it I will."

Searching the older woman's face Katherine asked, "Are you and Me-Lin lovers?"

Expecting such a question and having it raised in such a manner were two different things and the shopkeeper, finding herself taken aback at its bluntness, returned a salvo of her own. "Are you and Catriona lovers?" Katherine stepped back as if she'd been slapped and the older woman hurriedly regained her composure. "I'm sorry, Katherine. Forget my last question. It was rude, presumptuous and inappropriate. I trust what I'm about to tell you won't be repeated, except perhaps to Catriona, as it would cause great pain to both Me-Lin and I. Yes, we are and have been so for some time." She took a seat at the table, hands in her lap and waited for the nun's reaction.

Instead of the expected religious condemnation, Katherine took a seat beside her. "But how did you know? I mean, what happened for you to know that you felt this way for each other?" She questioned, as if desperate for simple answers to what was an infinitely complex question.

The shopkeeper took her time to answer, trying to remember what it was that first brought the two of them together. "That's not an easy question to answer. You know I've been married and that provides a convenient cloak of respectability for me, yet I was never really happy with the arrangement. Somehow I felt that there must be more to relationships. Shortly after the death of Me-Lin's husband I persuaded my husband to employ her. I knew of her skill as a seamstress, as she had been a great help to many of the women on the goldfields. However, this had not been her sole employment, it had been moreso what she loved to do. Of greater profit to her and her husband was the laundry that they both ran. Dirty men have very little time to look after such matters, despite the importance in cleanliness warding away disease. My husband could see the financial return in such a venture and so she worked under my supervision. In the quiet moments of the day we would sit and talk and I think it was then that I felt a connection that I'd never felt before. After my husband died and I decided to leave the goldfields, it was only natural that she would accompany me. Over the months our friendship grew stronger with the passing days. There was no great incident; rather it was a gradual development and recognition of deeper feelings than those of merely friendship. One night she came to my room and has been there ever since." Touching the chest of the other woman, Susan continued, "The feeling comes from within, Katherine. No-one else can tell you. It's how you feel."

The nun digested the information, her features a study of introspection. Looking up, she smiled at the woman beside her. "Thank you for sharing that with me. It's obviously a very personal thing between the two of you. Rest assured your secret is safe with me and it certainly won't be discussed with anyone in town." The younger woman finished, looking at the relieved face of Susan. Realising that the conversation had taken a serious course she added lightly, "So, I expect your confession will make the, er, night time arrangement between the two of you more amenable."

A surprised yet furiously blushing Susan breathed a sigh of relief. "You can't begin to imagine how relieved I am that you're happy to stay with us. But, we would never do anything which would make you feel uncomfortable."

The Irishwoman laughed. "Don't you think I'm running out of houses? If I was to move out of the store, can you imagine what the reaction would be? No, if you're happy to have me stay, I'm comfortable where I am. After all, where else would I go?" she asked, a hint of wistfulness in her voice.

Sensing her loneliness Susan placed her hand over the other woman's. "Katherine, is there anything you wish to speak with me about?" She watched the indecision cloud the younger woman's features. She seemed almost on the verge of disclosure when the laughter of women wafted through the house.

Katherine turned toward the door from where the sound had come and then back to the shopkeeper, her mask once again in place. "No, everything's fine. Though I think you've spent enough time in here. Why don't you rejoin the rest with the tea? I'll put the salt and pepper tray away." Susan reluctantly nodded in agreement and left for the parlour.

Katherine gathered the platter and a small lamp, and headed for the dining room. The light from the candelabras had since been extinguished. Katherine worked silently by the lamp's warm glow, first removing the candles from their place and then returning the salt and pepper tray to its place within the hutch. Finishing her task, she turned to join the party but instead found herself taking a seat at the vacant table. With her elbows resting on the red cedar, she placed her head in her hands. How did she really feel about Catriona? Was it the same as what Susan felt for Me-Lin? Rubbing her face vigorously she reconciled that she couldn't have those same sort of feelings for the grazier; after all she was a nun. *Isn't that excuse wearing a little thin?* the small voice inside of her challenged.

Running her hands through her hair she replayed the inter-action between Catriona and Adele. It was suddenly very obvious to her that there was more to their friendship than what she'd first presumed. As she struggled to comprehend how she felt about this development the door to the dining room opened and Catriona entered, closing the door quietly behind her.

"What are you doing in here all by yourself? Haven't you enjoyed the party?" she asked, taking a seat beside Katherine. It was obvious to Catriona that the younger woman had been preoc-cupied on her entrance and this was conveyed by the tension that radiated from the woman beside her. She was glad that as she sat by Katherine she could feel some of those tensions dissipate.

"I'm sorry. I've very much enjoyed myself and the dresses everyone wore. It's been a while since I've seen evening gowns and they made quite a sight." She looked at the woman beside her. "And you look beautiful, Catriona. It's just a shame I made the evening dull with my habit," she finished self-consciously, her face cast downward to her hands in her lap.

Catriona knelt beside Katherine and lifted her hand to the Irishwoman's face to look into her eyes. "Beauty is not made by someone's clothes, Katherine; they just serve to complement it. Don't ever think that you're not beautiful because of the habit you wear. It's what is underneath that makes you beautiful and how you feel about yourself." She took a breath before adding quietly, "For what it's worth, you're very beautiful to me, Katherine."

Both women were silent as they looked into the eyes of one another. What was reflected back through the shadows at Katherine was the controlled face of a woman hungry for the

fleeting intimacy they had shared together. In comparison, what
Catriona saw was a woman indecisive over her emotions; the turmoil was plainly evident on her face.

Breaking away from the older woman's hypnotic stare
Katherine whispered, "Oh my God, please don't, Catriona."

"I'm sorry, Katherine. You know I'll never do anything to
offend you either by words or by action."

"I know that. It's just that you ask too much," the nun
replied, barely keeping her emotions in check.

"I ask for nothing that you won't willingly give. If that
means all that we will ever have is friendship, then I'd settle for
that rather than a lifetime without you," she said quietly, stroking the nun's arm in an attempt to calm her.

"I just need time to find my own way on this. I value our
friendship as well. Trust me when I say that was one of the main
reasons I moved in with Susan and Me-Lin. I needed the space to
seek my own counsel over what had happened, was happening
between us, without being so close to a key object of that counsel. I wanted to be able to do this without the risk of endangering
our friendship. I've no intention to stop visiting you unless you
wish me to."

The grazier shook her head vigorously in denial and, before
she could say anything further, a shaft of light split the two
women. Turning around Catriona looked at the figure of Adele
silhouetted in the doorway.

Adele felt like an intruder, for it was obvious she'd walked
in on something. If the proximity of the two wasn't an indica-
tion, the look on Catriona's face at her arrival was enough to seal
it. As hard as Catriona tried, she couldn't conceal the shadow of
guilt that crossed her features, before the mask once more
slipped into place. Keeping her emotions in check, Adele
adopted a conversational tone. "I'm glad I found you both.
Unfortunately, the wine has given Me-Lin a headache and Susan
is keen to get her home."

Both women rose as one and made their way to the door. As
Katherine silently made her way past the governess and toward
the direction of the parlour, Catriona avoided Adele's inquiring
stare. Goodbyes were said and the three women climbed into the
buggy. Katherine couldn't help herself in taking one last look
back to the house as they made their way down the driveway. Lit
in the light of the doorway were the figures of Catriona and
Adele and, just before the light gave way, Katherine saw the arm

of Adele possessively clasp Catriona's waist before they moved inside. The Irishwoman was shocked but not from the display of intimacy. What shocked her was the bolt of irrational jealousy that had surged through her at the closeness the two women shared. Settling herself back in the buggy, Katherine spent the return journey attempting to reconcile what it was in life she actually wanted and what she now undeniably felt toward Catriona.

Chapter
Fourteen

Adele awoke the next morning with her limbs still entwined with those of a somnolent Catriona. Staring at the peaceful features of the sleeping figure beside her, she cast her mind back to the passion of their lovemaking. The trail of discarded clothes from the front door to the bedroom was a testimony to the urgency of last night. Adele had barely managed to close the door when the younger woman was upon her, Catriona's lips desperately seeking those of Adele's. No uncovered flesh was safe from the grazier's passionate onslaught as she feasted on the bare shoulders and half clad breasts of her lover. From the front door the trail began, piles of discarded clothing identifying a sudden pause, before the two finished their journey to the bedroom.

Despite immensely enjoying the ardour of the occasion, Adele couldn't help but be concerned by the desperation of the act. It was as if the emotions shown to her were meant for some-one else and, as she lay there, she reminisced on the intrusion she'd made in the dining room the previous evening. It was clear to her even in such dim light that the friendship between the two was more than just platonic, but how much more she didn't know. She'd been very aware of the nun's eyes upon her during the dinner and Katherine's interaction with Catriona. From the look of guilt on Catriona's face when she had entered the room it was clear to her that she hadn't been privy to the whole truth.

As she thought on the night's activities, the woman beside

her slowly began her ascent from sleep. "Good morning, sleepy head. I didn't think you were ever going to wake up."

Catriona gracefully stretched her limbs before enclosing the other woman in her arms. "Yes, well it was a long night after all." She laughed gently.

Laying within the younger woman's arms, Adele knew that was where she wanted to be, but did Catriona really want her there or was she merely a substitute for someone else? Gently extricating herself from the comfortable embrace, she looked into Catriona's relaxed eyes. "I know I've asked you this before, but I need to ask you again. Was there anything between you and Katherine?"

The grazier's eyes widened as she sought an appropriate answer. She quietly admitted, "Nothing that was reciprocated."

Adele smiled at the other woman's averted features. Touching her chin with her fingers, she tilted Catriona's face up to her own before gently saying, "I've been a governess all my life and I'll always remember you as one of my most intelligent students. Your ability to use words to suit your own purposes never ceases to amaze me. But a lie by omission is still a lie. Now, how about you tell me what passed between the two of you?"

Slumping her shoulders in defeat, Catriona relayed the events of Katherine's arrival through to what had occurred around the time of Alexander's death and up till the present day. Strangely enough she felt the better for telling Adele, for it was as if a wall had been lifted between them. She finished with, "So, now you know it all. For all that's happened, nothing more can or will happen. She's made that clear on a number of occasions now."

The governess looked at the woman in front of her who in some matters possessed maturity beyond her years, but in matters of the heart she was still incredibly naive. "Catriona, I've watched the two of you together and I know what I saw in the dining room last night. Katherine may be in the grip of a great struggle, but trust me when I tell you she does want you."

Catriona rolled away from the older woman. "Why in the hell does everyone except Katherine keep telling me that? What makes you so sure?"

Adele thought back to her own indecision concerning Catriona ten years ago. "You seem to have that effect on people, for after spending time with you as your governess I felt much the same way. I found myself in a daily struggle, trying to maintain a professional distance for fear of the ramifications of my actions." She smiled wryly. "In the end, it was a distance I must add that I was woefully inadequate at keeping. Although you didn't know it at the time, little by little you broke down my defences. Slight touches here and there. A smile that had the potential to light a whole room. That first day, I was so afraid I'd lost you as you almost drowned in that waterhole. Until you spoke, I had no idea of what your true feelings were for me. But times change and you now find yourself in a similar situation. The major difference is you know how she feels about you and more importantly how you feel about her." Adele's eyes searched troubled blue eyes for some hint of denial of what she'd just said.

"How can I want her when it's you I love?" Catriona challenged.

Adele placed her hand on the grazier's shoulder and shook it gently. "I know you love me and I love you, that's beyond any doubt. But search your feelings. You may love me, but you're not in love with me." She placed a hand to the woman's lips to halt the cry of protest about to burst forth. "What we had and what we have is special and no-one can take that away from either of us now. No matter where I am, I'll always be there for you, if not in body then in spirit. However, while I'm here you'll never have what you really want and, more to the point, Katherine won't come looking for it. That's why I must tell you that I've made up my mind to return to England." The words once spoken couldn't be recovered and yet they hurt Adele far greater than they could have ever hurt the woman beside her. She'd been less than truthful with Catriona, for the passion and the love she had for Catriona burned as brightly within her as it had done so eleven years previously. It would have been easy for her to stay for she believed that in this strong and proud woman she'd found someone she could be truly happy with. She saw a girl who had grown into a woman and while what they shared would always be there, Catriona's love now rested with someone else.

"Has this got something to do with my house manners? Why is it that every woman I love decides to get up and leave me just when things seem to be going so well?" Catriona joked covering her hurt, confused by the older woman's comments.

"It's not like that and you know it. If I stayed we would have wonderful times and revel in each other's company. But for you that would always mean having to settle for second best. When I left all that time ago I neglected to tell you one thing and that was don't sacrifice your own happiness just to suit the expectations of others. At least this time give yourself a chance to be truly happy. This is something you can't achieve with me here. Don't mistake me, I'd happily stay, but after a time you may grow to resent me for never really giving you the opportunity to pursue what you really want and that's Katherine."

Catriona looked deeply into the older woman's eyes as tears started in her own. "I don't deserve you, Adele, and knowing that, I only hope for two things. If I can give Katherine just half of the love that you've shown me, I'll be eternally grateful, and I just hope that the woman waiting for you in England knows how very lucky she really is." She closed the distance between the two and for one last time, they made tender love.

Barely a week had passed since the dinner party and still Katherine found her thoughts occupied with a continual replay of the evening. It so happened that, as she was tending the store replaying the night yet again, the central character appeared. Making her way to the counter, Catriona removed her hat and characteristically ran her hands through her hair. "Well, well, you are a woman of many talents. Not only are you a nun, teacher, and part time healer, but you're now a storekeeper. So, where is the proprietor on this fine day?"

The Irishwoman bent down to return a jar of nails to their place below the counter. "She and Me-Lin have gone on an outing. It seems that it's been a long time since they've both been able to get away and have some time to themselves. So I told them that I'd look after the store if they could trust me to do so." She straightened up and looked into the surprised face of the woman in front of her.

Katherine laughed to herself as she realised that Catriona was obviously not aware of her newly acquired knowledge regarding the two women. She sought suitable words to allay the grazier's obvious shock. Casting her eyes toward the door of the empty store she said, "Don't tell me I've surprised the unflappable Catriona Pelham, surely not." Leaning across the counter she gently patted the shocked woman's arm. "Susan has told me the nature of her relationship with Me-Lin. Surely you don't think me that self righteous to condemn their obvious happiness out of hand?"

Catriona shook her head, amazed at the words coming from the nun's mouth. "No, I don't think that at all. It's just I'm lost for words. I mean, what they have is genuine love for each other. I didn't expect that sort of reaction from you, Katherine, that's all."

"Obviously from the perspective of the Church what they share can't be condoned, but as you so rightly pointed out to me, sometimes things are not what they seem. Maybe I'm just learning to live with that," she finished quietly.

"I didn't mean for it to sound as if I was making fun of you. I'm sorry that wasn't what I intended." She tried to steer the conversation onto smoother waters. "So, did you enjoy the other night?"

"Yes, and thank you for the invitation. It does make a change to be able to chat in good company, and Adele is such a lovely woman to talk to. Speaking of Adele, did she come with you today?" Katherine queried, busying herself with clearing stock off the counter.

The older woman shifted uneasily. "Well, yes, she did, but she's left for Sydney. It seems her trip out here was on an opportunity basis only. She has business dealings she must attend to in Sydney before returning to England." Catriona wandered to a far part of the store to gather her thoughts. While their goodbyes at the stagecoach had been formal, stilted, and that of friends, their farewell at the homestead had been otherwise. Again the grazier's courage had failed her and she'd again questioned the older woman's decision to leave. As Adele held her in her arms, she reassured Catriona that everything would turn out for the best, and if it didn't then maybe it was her turn to visit next time.

Catriona's thoughts were interrupted by the close presence of Katherine who had placed a hand on her shoulder. "Is everything all right?"

She shook herself out of her depression. "Yes, it's just that I thought that she might stay here a little longer." Then realising how that may have been interpreted by the other woman, she hurried to add, "What with the harvest upon me I barely have enough time to do everything. It was good to be able to come home to find company and a cooked meal. However, I expect I'll adapt," she finished and realised that with her last comment Katherine had removed her hand. Again kicking herself at her thoughtlessness she continued, "At least I can look forward to your visits and, speaking of which, you've been suspiciously absent of late. When can I next expect you to grace the Pelham household with your presence?"

"Well most of my work for the next few days is on this side of town. However, by next Thursday, I'll need to pick up some more books to take to the Connor clan. By all accounts they've just about read their way through the last ones I gave them. If it suits you, I might drop out to the Connor farm early and then I'll return and we can have some lunch and catch up on matters."

Catriona made a quick calculation. "Yes, I expect by then the harvesting will be finished and the crop under cover. I'll look forward to your visit then." She placed her hat on her head.

Katherine made her way to the front of the store to open the door for the other woman. "Well, Thursday it is. I'll be out early to pick up some books and if you're not there I'll leave you a note. That should have me on my return trip by 12.00pm at your place for lunch. Until Thursday then." The grazier nodded her assent as she walked down the stairs. With a final wave between the two, both returned to the business at hand and their own private thoughts.

Katherine set out early on Thursday morning and already the heat and humidity of the day were making their presence felt. Catriona had mentioned to her early in her arrival how hot the days became out here, but only now was she truly beginning to understand. *It wouldn't have been so bad if it was only the days that were hot,* she thought, *but the occasional humid evenings accounted for many a sleepless night.* On speaking with Susan that morning even she had commented on the extreme heat and hoped fervently that the clouds that had teased the town for the past week promised rain. While the nun would welcome the relief, she hoped it didn't occur before she returned home. For again, and despite continuous lectures from both Catriona and Susan, she'd forgotten a raincoat.

Arriving at Gleneagle she was disappointed to see that Catriona already left. Surmising that she was checking the last of her harvest, the nun didn't wait and instead preferred to leave a note advising Catriona that she still wished to have lunch together if she was not too busy. Remembering the farmer's pre-

disposition to timings, she made a quick mental calculation
before leaving a return time of 12.30pm Placing the note prominently in the centre of the table, she left the kitchen and set out
for the Connor farm.

Arriving home Catriona called out Katherine's name before
she noticed the note. It was in the other woman's fine hand,
appropriately demonstrating many years of schooling and disci-
pline. Catriona laughed out loud when she read the specifics of
Katherine's return. It seemed that the Irishwoman had learnt
from her previous ventures and was indeed making a light-
hearted jab at her. Shaking her head she placed the note back
down on the table and washed her hands, still dirty from seeing
the last lot of wheat onto the large carts that would take it to
town for storage before it started its long journey to Sydney.

Glancing at her fob watch, Catriona cringed at the thought
that she had ample time to start on the farm's books before the
Sister returned. Bookkeeping had never been one of her
strengths and yet Katherine had displayed a true aptitude for the
required double entry bookkeeping of the farm. Within days of
Katherine's arrival the farm's accounts had progressed from a
series of debit and credit notes in the top drawer of the study to a
pristine book detailing receipts and expenditure of the last three
months. While it would have been nice to have Katherine do this
again, Catriona sadly realised that this might be something she
could never again hope for and resignedly made her way to the
study and the stubs of paper that awaited her.

As she pulled away from the farewelling waves of the Connor family, a light rain fell and Katherine silently cursed herself
for yet again forgetting her raincoat, or as they were more correctly known in country Australia, a drizabone. Thinking about
how she would look by the time she reached Gleneagle, she visualised Catriona's reaction. Catriona would again lecture her on
why she seemed so hell bent on giving herself pneumonia before
disgustedly going for towels with which to dry her with. She
smiled at the thought, for despite the ranting and raving of the
older woman, she believed they both quietly enjoyed it. She was

glad that Adele wouldn't be there to witness the tirade, for she
felt that it was a game better played between the two of them
without a spectator present.

As she rode on she reflected on the governess' all too soon
departure which had again left Catriona alone in a house too big
for merely one occupant. Katherine was grateful for this busy
period with the farm, for at least this boded some company, with
the farmers true to their word in assisting the grazier to deliver
the crop. Despite how deeply she hid the feelings, Katherine
remembered the lightness of her heart when Catriona had told
her of Adele's departure. She sensed a closeness between the two
which she found she resented as she felt her position in Catriona's life somewhat subordinated by Adele's presence.

Thinking further afield she reflected on the change of
friendship between her, Susan, and Me-Lin. Since the night of
the shopkeeper's disclosure, things had been definitely more .
relaxed in the Crosier household. Whereas before, when after the
evening meal Me-Lin would make polite conversation before
retiring, now she would sit by her partner, her hand shyly
clasped in Susan's while they talked of the day's events. Susan
was an attentive listener, occasionally pausing in her listening to
fetch Me-Lin a cup of her treasured green tea or to place a cush-
ion under her aching feet sore from a day's standing in front of
laundry tubs. It was at these times that the Irishwoman felt like a
privileged spectator to the interaction between the two women. It
was a gentle and familiar closeness; not that dissimilar to the
closeness that she'd shared with Catriona. It was a closeness that
Katherine was missing and, indeed, she was missing the woman
who shared that closeness with her.

Katherine drew the wagon to a halt in the rain. What had she
just said to herself and what did it mean? Casting her eyes
around a softened landscape she sought an answer and found one
coming from a quiet place deep within. *You want the closeness;
you know you do. And what's more, you want the same sort of
intense, comforting, and passionate closeness with Catriona that
you now witness every night between Susan and Me-Lin. You can
run from the truth but when you stop running, you'll turn around
and it will still be following you. Don't you think it's about time
you stopped running and just turned around?*

Katherine felt her own tears mix with that of the water
already dripping down her face. Regardless of all the religious
excuses in the world, this was what she wanted. She just hoped

that she hadn't left it too late to tell Catriona. Feeling as if a great weight had been lifted from her shoulders, she again urged the horse forward with a greater purpose than ever before.

Rounding a bend she found herself staring into the eyes of the young male bushranger she'd helped that night which now seemed like an eternity ago. Despite his sudden intrusion she refused to allow it to dampen her now high spirits. "What is it about you people? Do you keep constant tabs on me or something?" She stopped her chastising, seeing something other than defiance in the boy's eyes. "What's wrong?" Eagerly she leant forward to catch his reply over the noise of the downpour.

"We raided a homestead yesterday and it went horribly wrong. Before we could make our escape a posse of men arrived and we had to fight our way out of there."

Katherine felt an uneasiness settle in her stomach. She struggled to calm herself and the boy in front of her. *Remember his name.* She asked hurriedly, "Joshua, what of injuries? Did you all manage to get away unscathed?" She gripped the reins tightly, somehow sensing what the answer would be.

"We lost three dead almost immediately before we could escape." The boy hesitated, swallowing a lump that had risen to his throat. "But Mary wasn't so lucky. She's been badly wounded and has been asking for you ever since."

Her thoughts of a warm homecoming with Catriona were put to one side as she queried Joshua on the location of the head of the bushrangers. Turning the wagon, she followed his lead.

Breaking through the clearing half an hour later she was surprised to see a small grey upright slab hut, smaller than that of the Connor's if that was at all possible. Looking around its general surrounds she noted a conspicuous absence of horses and activity. Alighting from the wagon she turned to Joshua, "Where's the rest of your, er, gang?"

"Gone to the four winds. As soon as they saw Mary's injury they split our gold amongst them and took off," he replied, tethering his horse to the closest tree.

"So it's true as the saying goes, there's no honor among thieves, present company excepted of course," she finished hurriedly, seeing the boy's face whip around in defiance.

They moved toward the hut with Joshua opening the door to allow her to enter and before closing it behind her. Adjusting her eyes to the interior light, Katherine could just make out a bed on the opposite wall and the pale figure of a woman lying upon it.

Sensing the nun by her side, Mary's face lit up as she managed a weak smile. "I told him you'd come, but he didn't believe me. All I needed was for him to find you and I knew that you'd come." She winced, her breathing hampered by the obvious injury to her groin. Watching the nun's eyes travel from her face to her bloodstained sheet that concealed the bushranger's legs, she attempted to sound nonchalant. "It was a lucky hit, really. The bullet ricocheted off the pommel of my saddle and got me in the thigh. Fortunately they didn't follow us and I had time to stop and tourniquet it before we continued on home."

Katherine pulled back the bloodstained sheet to get a better look at the wound, sucking in air through her teeth as she did so. Kneeling beside the woman, she attempted to make out where the bleeding started and where it stopped. "God in heaven, you don't do anything by halves. If you're going to survive this wound, we've got to get you into the back of the wagon and into town now." Her attempt to rise was halted by the bushranger's restraining hand.

"Now why would I want to go all the way into town, have it tended to by a doctor and healed so they could hang me? Even if it were a possibility, you know I couldn't do that. The wound's too far gone for that and both you and I know it. I've managed to slow the blood, but I've lost far too much to recover from this. I know it's only a matter of time," she finished gently, a sense of finality in her voice. "However, before I went to wherever it is I'm going to end up, I had to speak to you once more and clear the air between us."

Katherine held up her hand to stay any further discussion. "Before you start at least let me look at the wound and clean it." The bushranger nodded her head in tired acquiescence and settled back down on the makeshift cot.

Katherine used a knife to quickly tear the trouser leg away in an attempt to get a better look at the injury, and in doing so she knew the woman's words to be true. The wound was high up on the thigh and, despite a tourniquet, was still slowly oozing blood. The flesh immediately surrounding the wound had become reddened, an obvious indicator of the onset of infection. Rising to fetch Joshua she instructed him to fill one of the pots with rainwater and heat it by the fire. As he did so, she tore the now discarded trouser leg into strips with which to dress the wound. As soon as the water was warm enough, the boy silently left the two women to allow the nun the privacy to tend to the bushranger. Having dressed it as well as she could, Katherine took the remains of the water from the kettle and made some tea with the gang's meagre rations. For her ministrations Mary at least looked a little more relaxed but there was no fooling either of the two—the wound was mortal. Pulling a chair from the table, she sat beside Mary and handed her a cup of strong black tea.

Mary gratefully took the warm liquid, allowing herself a sip before she eased her head back onto the pillows. "Thank you. I've no right to demand your help especially since the way I behaved last time we met. I should never have intruded on you as I did that day and for that I'm sorry. On top of that, you were right about my questions in the kitchen. They were both rude and presumptuous, and for that I'm also sorry."

Katherine gently stroked the bushranger's arm before quietly saying, "No, they weren't presumptuous. You were right. Something had occurred between Catriona and I. It just seems that for so long I've been denying it to myself and on that day your questions were a little too close to the mark."

The dying woman smiled a knowing smile. "Yes, I knew they were by the way you reacted and what I heard about her actions on your safe return after the first time you, er, visited me. In truth, I was jealous at what the two of you had. She obviously cares for you very deeply."

The Irishwoman mutely nodded her head. Reaching out Mary gently covered the small hands clasped firmly in the nun's lap. "Katherine, you and I both know that I'm dying and at times like these there's no time to mince words and dance around innuendo. So I'm going to be honest with you. Can I expect your honesty in return?"

Katherine looked first to the hand resting over her own clenched fist and then to the bushranger's pale features. Unclenching her hand, she turned it up to gently clasp Mary's own before quietly uttering a single, "Yes", as other words failed her.

"I've been around lovely women all my life, from casual liaisons to the look of hopeful expectation in rich grazier's wives who I've divested of money. But by far you're the most beautiful woman I've ever known. Your beauty is not just skin deep, for God knows that any man, or woman for that matter, would risk life to win just one smile from that face. It's more than that; it's within you as well. No matter how well you hide your beauty behind that habit of yours, it won't be hidden from no man nor beast." The nun blushed at the other woman's candid comments. A familiar fire again ignited itself in her stomach as Mary continued.

"Every time I'm close to you I sense an energy between us that's almost palpable. I felt it that night when we argued by the fire, I felt it in the kitchen when I held you that morning, and I feel it radiating from you now. Katherine, do you not feel the same energy?"

Katherine's eyes moved from the dying woman's face to the hand she was holding and back to the expectant face of Mary. She nodded. "I felt it, too. It confused me for before I came here to Australia I'd never been exposed to such feelings. Then suddenly both you and Catriona produced the same reaction." She took a deep breath. "That day in the kitchen when you held me I thought you were going to kiss me and, while I was afraid, I was excited at the same time. After you left all I felt was ashamed," she finished, at last relieved to speak to someone about how she felt about that morning but ashamed at the same time. Turning her head, she looked away from the searching eyes of Mary.

Removing her hand from the younger woman's grasp, Mary eased herself up on her elbow before reaching up to tenderly touch the averted face. Turning it to her, Mary said softly, "What you felt were your own emotions, Katherine, and they're powerful ones that won't be constrained by social or religious mores no matter how hard you try. That day there was nothing to be afraid of for I never would have hurt you." She searched the woman's face before her hand found its way to the back of her neck. "Here, let me show you," Mary uttered huskily and guided the Irishwoman's face to her own.

The lips of the two women had barely touched when Katherine felt as if a lightning bolt had passed through her. Leaning into the kiss to gain greater contact between the two, she trembled at the feel of Mary's tongue lightly teasing her upper lip as if in question. In answer, Katherine lips parted slightly to the gentle exploration of the other woman's tongue.

Mary broke contact and eased herself back onto her pillows, uncontrolled tears now falling from her eyes. In confusion Katherine reached for the woman's hand. "Are you all right? Are you in pain?"

The bushranger laughed a shallow yet bitter laugh. "Yes, I am, but it's pain of the heart I suffer. Life is cruel, Katherine.

I've waited since that first night to be able to do that to you and now it's too late. I once told you that I could have never changed my ways. I'd have given this all up to spend my life with someone as beautiful as you, and now it's too late. But it's not too late for you; things can be different. Promise me you won't wait until it's too late to finally admit what it is you've always wanted."

Katherine looked down at the pleading eyes of the bushranger. "No. No, I won't. Now please rest for a while and conserve your strength." With that the bushranger's eyes closed, the shallow breathing of her chest barely visible. As the rain fell outside the nun shed her own silent tears for a woman whose life was almost over before it had barely even started.

Catriona cast her disgusted eye at her attempts to maintain a halfway decent set of books. It was easy to discern Katherine's last neat entries, for in contrast hers looked as if a cat had dipped its paws in ink and walked across the page. Seeking an excuse to break away from the tedium, she glanced at the clock and frowned. It was 2.00pm and, by the time given on her note, Katherine should have been well and truly here by now. What concerned her more was the steady fall of the rain on the corrugated roof of the homestead. If the nun had been her normal self she would be out in the weather without a drizabone and, despite the heat of the day, a rainstorm could quickly chill a person to the bone. Pushing herself out of her chair she made her way to the barn, grabbing her hat and drizabone as she went. Striding across the yard she rationalised her actions by silently insisting that she would ride out in such a rainstorm for anyone. An inner voice laughed mockingly in return.

As she rode toward the Connor property her concern grew. The rain was falling in steady sheets by now, making it difficult for her to see the muddied track in front of her. At one stage her horse temporarily lost its footing before regaining it under the skillful horsemanship of the woman astride. *Anyone in a wagon would have found it nigh on impossible to recover from that,* Catriona thought, reaching forward to pat her horse's neck in reassurance. All she could hope for was that the nun had displayed the sense to wait out the storm with the Connor's.

A dripping Catriona knocked hard on the door to the small hut to have it opened by the surprised face of Aiden who, at seven, was the Connor's youngest boy. Stepping aside he allowed the woman to enter.

Her sudden entrance equally surprised Mrs Connor. "Miss Pelham, 'tis foul weather to be out riding. What can I do for you?" she asked motioning toward a chair.

Catriona shook her head politely. "I'm sorry to bother you like this, but I was looking for Sister Flynn. She left me a note saying she was visiting you and that she would return via my farm for lunch around 12.30pm. So far she hasn't turned up. I didn't pass her on the road and now it's getting on late afternoon; have you seen her?" she queried, apprehension seeping through her bones.

"But my dear, she left here just after eleven," Mrs Connor said seeking confirmation from her eldest. "Yes, it was just after eleven. I wonder where she's gotten to?"

Chapter
Fifteen

Katherine spent the last hour valiantly trying to stem the life force that was slowly seeping its way out of the bushranger's body. The trouser leg she had stripped and used for bandages was now soaked in blood and Katherine knew that regardless of her efforts Mary wouldn't last the afternoon.

Whether it was the loss of blood or onset of infection Katherine didn't know, but Mary seemed to pass from a calm state into one of delirium. It was obvious from the words flowing from her mouth that Mary was once again on one of her bushranging escapades. Occasionally her eyes would open and she would sit up, urging this man or another onto greater feats of daring. At these times the nun would gently ease her down onto the cot and for a small period of time Mary would once again be at peace.

It was late in the afternoon when Mary opened her eyes and with surprising clarity reached for the Irishwoman's hand. "Thank you for coming and helping me this afternoon." She gave a humourless laugh. "It seems that even the majority of my supposedly loyal followers couldn't hang around till the end."

Katherine attempted to comfort her, but the other woman gently waved her hand away. "No, that's all right. I always thought that it would end somewhat like this. I'm just glad you came." She closed her eyes, her face a concentration of effort. "Katherine, I've got to go now. It's time for me to move on."

The younger woman attempted to soothe her. "Just lay back

and conserve your strength. You need to rest."

The bushranger sighed. "Oh my dear, you make a great helper but a woefully poor liar. It's time and we both know it. Know that in another time I would have loved you with all my heart, if only things had been different. Please go before I die. The boy knows what he has to do."

"Let me stay; I've seen death before. Do you think I'm afraid of it?" Katherine chided gently.

The bushranger shook her head. "No, my love, it's not you I'm afraid of; it's me and my actions. I want you to remember me as I was, not with a face contorted by fear when I die. Please, I beg of you, go now," she finished, falling exhausted back into the cot.

A steady stream of tears fell down the nun's cheeks as she leaned down to kiss the woman now lying in undisguised pain. Raising herself up she cleared her throat. "I'll always remember you. I'll remember your pride, your stubbornness, your bravery, and your courage. But most of all I'll remember the love you had for other people. That I'll always cherish." Leaving her bedside vigil before separation became too much to bear, she made her way to the door of the cabin. With one last look at the other woman's features, Katherine opened the door and stepped outside.

The boy was where he had sat all afternoon—on the bench on the small front verandah out of the rain. "Mary hasn't got long before, before," she struggled with the words, "before she's gone. She told me you have instructions?" The boy nodded silently.

She was reluctant to leave, seeking excuses to remain behind. "I can help you if you like. There'll be things that need to be done to prepare her..."

Joshua held up his hand to halt the woman's words. "I'm sorry, Sister, I have my orders. Mary was adamant that you weren't to be here when she died. I was to show you to the main road and send you on your way. She made me promise that and it's a promise I'll not break. Now if you'll wait here, I'll bring your wagon around."

She nodded mutely, suddenly feeling terribly inadequate and frustrated. To go against Mary's wishes would be wrong, yet it was taking every element of her willpower not to do just that. Stepping into the rain and up onto the wagon, she followed her guide back to the main road.

She began to rue her forgetfulness regarding a drizabone as a steady stream of water made its way down between her shoulder blades. The rain was coming down with such force that Katherine could barely see the road in front of her. Shivering, she urged the horse onward.

Her thoughts were still focused on a cabin and the words spoken between herself and Mary when the wagon lurched sideways, losing its footing on the slippery road. With very little time to spare she managed to bring the wagon to a halt before she got off to inspect the damage. Jumping down she found herself sinking into the quagmire that once formed a road and, trudging around to the side of the wagon, she shook her head angrily. The pin that had been holding the wheel had dislodged, with the rear wheel now more off than on. Grasping hold of the wet and muddy object, she struggled with all her meagre strength to push it back on but to no avail.

With a shivering look of disgust she turned to the horse. Riding it bareback would be uncomfortable but at least it was better than dying of cold. As she got closer to the beast, she shook her head in disbelief. He was balancing the greater amount of his weight on three legs and despite her gentle coaxing wouldn't put any more weight on the fourth. Crying in frustration she stomped her foot, only to have mud spatter itself up the front of her habit. Laughing through chattering teeth at the picture she must be presenting she began the slow walk home.

Catriona barely allowed enough time for the words of Mrs Connor to sink in before she was once again on her horse, wheeling it away from the small home and back from where she had come. *Where is she?* A sudden thought dawned on her. This was the same road where the bushrangers had previously kidnapped Katherine, so maybe this had happened again. *At least*, the grazier thought, *she would be out of this interminable rain.* However, as her horse precariously made its way around the next bend the rider froze. Sitting off to one side of the road was the unmistakable horse and wagon so frequently used by Katherine and she was nowhere to be seen.

A quick inspection of the wagon confirmed her concerns

that the wheel was indeed broken. Looking toward the horse she could clearly see that it was favouring one front leg over the other. Quickly un-harnessing the beast, she ran an expert hand down its lame leg and gently coaxed its hoof off the ground. Deeply embedded in the hoof's centre was a sharp white piece of quartzite, a stone that regularly plagued the horses of the region. Using her knife she carefully removed it and allowed the beast to test its weight on the now unencumbered hoof. Satisfied he was no longer impeded and would find its own way home when it was good and ready, she mounted her own animal.

As she made her way carefully down the road her mild concern developed into an outright fear for Katherine's safety. Clearly the wagon hadn't been there on her outward journey and that could only mean that the nun lay somewhere ahead of her. Urging her horse into as much speed as she dared, she made her way through the steadily falling rain. She struggled to keep her horse in check on the liquid road. As she rounded a bend, her face changed from a study of concentration to one of shock, for staggering along the road under the weight of her habit was Katherine.

Pulling her horse to a halt beside the soaked woman, she leapt from her saddle. "My God, are you all right? You're drenched," Catriona yelled, so as to be heard over the relentless sound of water.

Grabbing the nun Catriona turned her gently, and her heart turned cold at what she saw. The other woman's eyes were glazed as if in sleep and her lips already a tinge of blue. Catriona immediately thought back to a time when as a child she had nearly died after falling in one of the property's dams in the middle of winter. Her father had found her in the nick of time but still it had been touch and go. For years after that he would tease her about how blue lips never really did suit her.

Shaking Katherine gently, she attempted to rouse the woman. Momentarily Katherine's eyes took on a fuzzy focus as she looked at Catriona. "Ccccold," was all that she could manage.

Divesting herself of her drizabone Catriona wrapped it around Katherine's shivering form. Then with a fair degree of manoeuvring she managed to get them both on her horse before starting their journey home. The hard riding she had already done combined with the added weight made the return journey a painfully slow one and, by the time they arrived home, Katherine had progressed from cold to delirium.

Wasting no time Catriona guided the horse toward the kitchen entrance, managing to bring the beast to a halt before dismounting both her and Katherine. Elbowing the horse toward the stable, she quickly mounted the stairs and carried Katherine through the house and into her old room. Placing her in a chair Catriona tore the top bedcover off the bed and swaddled the nun in it. Looking at the delirious form in front of her, the grazier struggled to remember how she had been saved on the day of her mishap. One thing that remained in her mind was the all-night vigil of her parents ensuring she was constantly warm. *Warmth is obviously key to Katherine's survival,* Catriona thought as she unwrapped her from the bedcover.

This was the first real opportunity Catriona had to appreciate how well soaked the woman really was. Moving toward the habit, Catriona tried to remove it from her only to be met with resistance—not from the nun but from the infernal object itself. It had been quite a while since she had worn a dress and finding her way into this one was like trying to find her way out of a maze. Concerned over Katherine's increased shivering, Catriona resolved that a new habit could be made anytime, but it was unlikely that she would ever find another Katherine. Removing her clasp knife from her pocket she tore the front of the dress from neck to waist and literally peeled her from it and her drenched underclothes before roughly drying her wet form with the bedspread. Catriona carried Katherine to her bed and lay her in it before going in search for more blankets.

Her vigil beside Katherine stretched throughout the night. On one occasion when she Catriona had left her side in search for more blankets, she took the opportunity to change herself into her dressing gown. It would do no good to either of them to have her stabilise Katherine only to make herself ill. Aside from her quick change and a warming glass of scotch, she spent the rest of her night seated by the nun's bedside gradually peeling off blankets as her condition improved. Despite her efforts to stay awake, sometime in the early hours of the morning, Catriona too, drifted off to sleep.

Katherine abruptly awoke the next morning aware of familiar yet most recently unfamiliar surroundings. As her mind woke from its stupor, the events of the previous day came back to her. She had a fairly good recall of events up until the point when her horse and wagon had left her stranded. From that moment on, her memories were like scenes on post cards—static moments in time. She remembered Catriona finding her and raising her up onto her horse and then carrying her through the house. She also remembered Catriona coming at her with a knife and a ripping sound. Glancing at the black and white heap in the corner of her room, she realised that she had been physically extracted from her habit. Creasing her forehead she foggily recalled losing her underclothes as well. Moving a tentative hand across her body, she found herself completely naked. As she did so, she noticed out of the corner of her eye a shape and, turning her head ever so slightly, she saw that Catriona was asleep in a chair by her bed, her head lolling forward. She was dressed in some form of a men's dressing gown and, by the looks of her uncomfortable position, she'd been there for quite a while. As the memories came flooding back, she recalled the older woman's presence at various times removing blankets from her and forcing her to stay in bed. Catriona seemed at peace now, getting some well-needed sleep. If Katherine was honest with herself, she was content to languish in bed and watch Catriona all day.

Catriona's face was a study of tranquillity making her younger than her years. There was no creased forehead or bitterness around the mouth—her face was at peace, radiant in the beauty it conveyed. The Irishwoman ran her mind over the previous day and the feelings she had admitted to, concerning Catriona. She'd harboured these feelings and fought against them for so long.

In a sudden movement, the grazier's head jerked uncomfortably forward causing her to wake with a start. Grabbing onto the sides of her chair for stability, Catriona blinked twice, momentarily taking her bearings. Remembering what had occurred, she looked toward the bed to find a pair of now alert green eyes watching her. She rubbed her face with her hands to shake off the sleep. "How are you? You had me worried last night. At one stage you were a shade of blue. Do you feel okay now?"

Katherine smiled at the seated woman's concern. "I feel fine, considering what I can remember going through. But the horse and wagon, I think they're somewhere out there still and I think the horse has broken its leg."

Attempting to allay her fears Catriona placed a reassuring

hand on the nun's arm. "I wouldn't worry about it if I were you. You're right about the wagon, but all the horse had wrong with him was a piece of quartz stuck in its hoof. I fixed that and I don't doubt that once he gave himself some time he started home for Susan's store and a warm stable for the night. Why I'd be surprised if he's not there by now, demanding his oats." Catriona's attention strayed to the pile of what were now rags before returning her gaze to Katherine. "And besides I think you should be more concerned about yourself. I couldn't get you out of that damned habit last night. I swear you must lock yourself in it every day. I had to cut you out of it, so I think I owe you a new one."

"I don't think you owe me anything, Catriona. If it hadn't been for you, I'd have probably died last night. Any action you took I'm sure you had good reason for," she replied, her green eyes locked with the grazier's deep pools of blue.

Embarrassed by Katherine's words of thanks and her hypnotic eyes, the older woman cleared her throat and shifted to stand. "Well, I'm sure you must be hungry after your most recent adventures. Why don't I fix us both some breakfast?"

Before she could fully rise, Katherine caught hold of the hand that had been resting on her arm. Perturbed that her quick exit had been thwarted, Catriona looked down questioningly at the woman on the bed. "Catriona, I have to tell you something and I think now is the time to tell you." She took a breath, while the other woman held hers. "I've made a decision."

The grazier didn't need to think twice on what decision she'd made, for Katherine could only be referring to one. While maintaining a tight hold on Catriona's hand, Katherine sat up in bed fully aware that in the process the bedclothes tumbled away from her naked body. Catriona was glued to the spot alternating her eyes between the seated woman's face and the alabaster form in front of her. Slowly reaching forth with her free hand, Katherine reached for the belt holding Catriona's dressing gown closed. After a slight resistance it gave way, revealing to Katherine a break in the cloth and the beauty concealed within. Words were not needed between the two as Catriona shrugged herself out of her robe and it silently fell to the floor to expose her body fully to the Irishwoman's admiring glance. Pulling back the bedcovers Katherine shyly moved across the bed to allow space for the other woman to join her.

Catriona's heart was in her mouth as she finally found herself lying naked beside the woman she loved. After all the pain she had been through in her life, at last something wonderful was happening to her. She had every intention of very slowly making love to the woman beside her lest Katherine shy away as she had done so previously. But as her lips brushed over Katherine's, a fire flared between them and the passion they had concealed from each other for so long was fully ignited. Catriona began a passionate assault on Katherine's mouth while allowing a hand to meander it's way down the other woman's back to finally rest on the softness of the younger woman's backside. Katherine gasped at such intimate contact but, rather than pull away at this heightening of her own desire, she returned the kiss fully and explored the older woman's mouth as she had done so once before.

Catriona moaned as she felt Katherine's tongue on her own and her delicate hands chart their own course along the muscles of Catriona's back. She couldn't help but think that for a celibate woman Katherine knew how to please well. Moving her hand from its resting place, Catriona traced a lazy line up the Irish-woman's side. She eased Katherine onto her back as she trailed her hand until her fingers came into contact with the outer full-ness of Katherine's breast. Deliberately avoiding their more sen-sitive centre, she gently stroked the breast; her fingers teased and barely touched the tender aroused flesh. In response, Katherine arched her body into the teasing hand, only to feel it removed before once again continuing its tantalising assault.

Breaking the kiss, Catriona looked deeply into the eyes of the woman beside her and was surprised at the raw desire she saw there. With a smile, she lowered her head and made a trail of kisses down the Irishwoman's throat to her breast. Lightly teas-ing the erect nipple, she barely allowed her lips to touch the sen-sitive piece of skin. Katherine moaned and arched her body in an attempt to capture the busy lips. Sensing the woman's need, Catriona's mouth closed on the eager nipple and firmly teased the erect bud with her tongue.

Katherine couldn't believe the wonderful sensations she was feeling. It was as if her body had taken on a mind of its own. The feel of the grazier's tongue on her skin caused a wave of desire to shudder through her body. She had barely managed to recover herself from the sensual touch of Catriona's electric tongue when she again heard herself moan in pleasure as Catriona's teeth lightly grazed the hard nipple. Again she arched her back toward

Catriona's busy lips, drawing Catriona's head to her breast eagerly increasing the contact between the two.

Lightly nipping her way to the other breast, Catriona allowed the hand that had been resting there to dance its way down Katherine's body. Her hand drew feather light circles on Katherine's stomach before turning its attention to the sensitive crease of skin where leg meets hip. Playing a delicate tattoo with her fingers, Catriona teasingly encroached on the outer regions of Katherine's hair before slowly retracing her way to the safer ground of Katherine's hips. "Oh God, please, Catriona, please!" the Irishwoman groaned in sensual anguish, unsure of what she was asking for, yet seeking deliverance from the exquisite tension she was experiencing.

Catriona chuckled deeply as she brushed her hand over the pleading woman's mound and allowed it to come to rest on the inside of Katherine's thigh. With a deeper primal sexual instinct, Katherine parted her legs ever so slightly to allow Catriona to continue in her explorations. As her fingers trailed ever so slightly over Katherine's lips, Catriona felt the woman raise her leg in invitation. Delicately parting the soft folds of flesh, her own excitement mounted as she felt how ready Katherine was. Breaking contact with the taut nipple, Catriona moved up Katherine's body to close again on her lips. Catriona allowed her fingers to play with sensual strokes in Katherine's wetness, listening to the moans of excitement emanating from the woman beside her.

Katherine couldn't believe the pleasure that she was feeling, for it was as if wherever Catriona's touch lingered, her own skin was ignited. The sensation that had started as butterflies in her stomach had now progressed to a horde of stampeding elephants. Unconsciously her hips moved in concert with the grazier's touch, whose fingers beat a relentless tattoo in Katherine's readiness as her tongue still languished in the comfort of the younger woman's mouth.

Breaking contact with the now swollen lips and pausing her fingers, cerulean eyes locked on emerald pools of desire. "Trust me," Catriona entreated huskily.

Katherine, her breathing ragged, struggled to answer, "Trust you; I trust you with my life," before again passionately seeking the contact between their two lips. There was a resistance and a slight pain as she felt Catriona enter her. Catriona's fingers quickly recommenced the symphony they had started as

Katherine arched her hips in rhythm. Maintaining a constant rhythm inside her lover, Catriona delicately accompanied her motions with her thumb, again cresting the Irishwoman to new heights of excitement and pleasure.

With the sensual overload she was experiencing, Katherine found it hard to concentrate and, as her passion continued to mount, her body seemed to disassociate itself from her mind. With a will of their own, Katherine's hips were now thrusting uncontrollably with Catriona's increased strokes. She was remotely conscious that the voice urging Catriona on was her own. Forgetting everything else, Katherine completely focused on the mounting excitement radiating from the older woman's touch and suddenly, as if breaking through an invisible barrier, her body shuddered and thrust itself uncontrollably. Calling out Catriona's name repeatedly Katherine held Catriona's head to her breast as she regained control over her body.

As the grazier's strokes slowed, her lover laid herself back on the bed and wiped her face from the heat of their efforts. Moving back up the bed, Catriona let her eyes rest on her lover's face. The older woman's breathing was ragged and her face aglow from her delicious exertions. Katherine cupped Catriona's face in her hand and her thumb traced the gentle line of the other woman's cheek before the Irishwoman finally found the words to encapsulate the emotions she was feeling. "If someone had tried to explain to me what just happened between us, I wouldn't have believed them. I don't think I've ever experienced anything so, so passionate and frenzied and yet so beautiful. Thank you." She was unable to control the tears springing from her eyes as she pulled Catriona into her embrace.

For Catriona the moment was almost too much too bear. Resting in the Irishwoman's arms she felt tears spring to her eyes as she realised how long she had waited to love this woman. She cast her mind back to the recent rekindling of her relationship with Adele and there was no comparison. This is where she wanted to be, now and always.

After Katherine managed to regain a sense of composure, she idly stroked Catriona's strong arm and continued, "Not in all my imagination would I have thought that loving you was like this. And I do love you. I know that I hid it for so long behind religion, society, propriety and any number of convenient excuses. It wasn't until I saw Susan and Me-Lin together that I began to fully realise how special my feelings for you are."

The older woman laughed, brushing a stray hair from Katherine's face. "I think I've loved you from the moment I set eyes on you all dusty at the train station. You frustrated me at first with your anger and your pride, but I later realised that was what made me want you so desperately." She fell silent, searching the other woman's face as if she were taking in every element of beauty captured in Katherine's features. Earnestly looking up into her eyes, she was exposed to the love held within. "Be my partner, Katherine, and I promise you my home, my security, my friendship, and my love for as long as I live."

Words failed her so the younger woman let her actions speak for themselves. Taking the grazier's face in her hands, she kissed her deeply. Gently easing Catriona onto her back Katherine played her hands lightly over Catriona's stomach, dancing a line up to her breasts for it was her turn to do the teasing. Using her open palms, she made small circles over Catriona's breasts and felt them respond to her touch. "Yes," was all the older woman could muster, her body finally assuaging the thirst for which it had been afflicted with for so long.

Taking Catriona's lead, Katherine lowered her head until her tongue was barely in contact with the woman's excited nipple. She brushed it lightly with her teeth and heard Catriona gasp with pleasure. Suckling it as a baby would, Katherine soon had the nipple hard and erect. She trailed kisses across her chest and started on the other sensitive nub. In doing so, she felt Catriona's hands entangle in her hair as she uttered words of endearment and encouragement.

Remembering the trail the grazier's hands had blazed on her own body, Katherine started a similar one of her own and was surprised at Catriona's wetness. Playing on the peripheries of her passion, Katherine could sense Catriona's impatience building as her hips sought the inquisitive fingers of the Irishwoman beside her.

Covering Katherine's hand with her own, Catriona gently guided her to the sensitive bud that was the font of her pleasure. Taking her lead from the experienced hand enveloping hers, Katherine gently stroked the bud, occasionally dipping into the other woman's passion. As she did so, her hand developed a rhythm with the thrusting hips of the grazier. Somehow realising that Catriona craved deeper contact, Katherine tentatively teased the older woman's opening. The moan from her lover was enough for her to realise Catriona's need. With two fingers she entered her to the emphatic "yes" of the grazier. Mirroring the motions of the woman's hips, Katherine used her thumb, teasing the bundle of nerves that seemed to send Catriona to greater heights of passion. As Katherine watched the heavy lidded eyes of her lover, Catriona's breathing deepened as her body lost all control and crested in the sensual waves of her passion. As her hips slowed, Catriona again guided the hands of Katherine away from where they had been previously preoccupied.

As the two women rested in each other's embrace from their exertions, Catriona's hand gently stroked the head of the other woman. "My love, no-one has ever made me feel so complete. It scares the hell out of me when I think about how close I came to losing you last night." Kissing the top of the Irishwoman's head, her mind went over where she'd found Katherine the previous night. She slightly frowned in confusion. "Love," she paused until the woman in her arms mumbled in response. "I'm just doing the sums here and I can't seem to get it right. You left the Connors, but Mrs Connor said that was hours before my arrival at the farm. But then I found you not all that far down the road, in the bigger scheme of things. What happened?" Catriona fell silent as she felt Katherine pull away from her.

Searching the grazier's features, Katherine decided that despite the reception of her next words, they needed to be said. "I was on my way home when one of the bushrangers—" she got no further as the other woman sat up in bed.

"What! What do they think they're doing? They've got no right to prey on anyone who travels that road. What did they think they were doing?" This time her protests were halted by Katherine's fingers upon her lips.

"Please, let me explain." Seeing the compliance of the grazier, Katherine collected her thoughts in an endeavour to try and reason where to start. "The gang was involved in a botched robbery two day's ago. In the process a number of the gang was killed with Mary, the leader, being seriously wounded. I couldn't refuse to help her." Her voice lingered away as her face turned away from that of Catriona.

Watching the other woman's actions, concern raised its head within Catriona's mind. She gently guided the averted features of the Irishwoman back to her own. "Katherine, what is it? Did something happen out there?"

"Yes, no." she added as she saw the surprise on the features of the woman beside her. "Please let me tell you from the beginning, before you say any more." Seeing the grazier nod in assent the Irishwoman continued.

"That day when I was captured by the bushrangers and I first met Mary, I knew something wasn't quite right. I couldn't put a finger on it, it was more of a feeling really. She made me feel, well...strange, scared and exhilarated all in the same moment. I had really no idea of what was going on with me. As we sat and spoke she told me of...of her love for other women." She smiled ruefully as she remembered her outburst. "I told her that I thought it was unnatural, and that women shouldn't live together. That's when she challenged me over our living arrangement. I was outraged and yet it was strange. At the same time I wondered if that was how other people saw us. Anyway, the moment passed and the next day I was given my freedom. Do you remember our argument in the study?" The recognition by the other woman was enough for her to continue. "When you touched me, I felt the same sensations that Mary had evoked in me. I found myself wondering if there was something between us. It confused me; I didn't know what to do or who I could speak to, so I hid the feelings deep down, hoping that they would pass.

"Shortly after your brother's death Mary visited the homestead. Again she challenged me on my feelings. It scared me so much. That's why I had to move in with Susan and Me-Lin. I didn't know what to do and I felt that some distance between us might put the whole issue in better perspective." Katherine laughed ruefully. "I shouldn't have bothered. Every time I visited you I felt the same feelings. Then there was the dinner party and, well, I think I began to see things a lot more clearly. I had every intention of speaking with you about it yesterday, that was until I was waylaid by a bushranger." The Irishwoman paused, shifting uncomfortably. "Mary and I spoke yesterday and she told me how she felt for me. We, that is, I kissed her."

A look of hurt crossed Catriona's features. "Do you love her?" she asked hoarsely.

"No! I don't love her, although I think she has strong feelings for me. The kiss, it just seemed natural given the situation."

Catriona's thoughts raced through her head like a team of wild brumbys. She calmed herself before asking the obvious question. "What sort of situation would have precipitated you kissing a bushranger?" Try as she might she couldn't keep the anger out of her voice.

Sensing the other woman's displeasure, Katherine took Catriona's hand and placed a kiss in the upturned palm. "She was dying, Catriona. Her dying words were of her feelings for me. We kissed and then she told me to not wait too long to find what it was in life that I really wanted. What she was doing was sending me to you. Please understand me when I say the feelings I had for Mary are nothing compared to the love I have for you." As she finished tears began to fall unbidden, their tracks noticeable on her face.

Seeing the pain in the Irishwoman's features, Catriona drew her into her arms. "I'm sorry that Mary had to die, but she always knew the risks a bushranger takes, you know that, don't you?" Feeling the head of the other woman nod against her chest, she continued. "I understand what you must have gone through. Between Mary and I, your life over the past weeks could not have been easy."

Katherine raised her head from the chest of her lover and lowered her lips to capture those of the woman underneath her. "It hasn't been easy, but I can honestly say that the outcome is more than I could have ever hoped for."

Moving out of Catriona's embrace, the Irishwoman's face had suddenly taken on a pensive visage. "Can I ask you a question?"

The contemplative look on the younger woman's face hadn't escaped Catriona. "My love, you can ask me anything you wish."

"Were you and Adele lovers? Is that why your mother originally asked her to leave?" she asked watching the interplay of emotions on the grazier's features.

Catriona looked at the face in front of her and knew that avoiding the answer wasn't an option. "Yes, we were. How did you know?"

Katherine smiled gently. "The night of the dinner party she was very attentive to you and your needs." She searched for the right words. "And the glancing touches she gave you; they were so intimate. I couldn't help but feel frustrated by her actions." Feigning preoccupation with the line she was trailing down Catriona's thigh she continued, "Did you renew that acquaintance when she returned?"

Catriona looked at the green eyes searching her own, suddenly fearful of the next words she would utter. "Yes, we did," she said quietly. "But somehow it was different. Different to back then and different to this. It wasn't so much a great passion as a rekindling of an old friendship." Her eyebrows creased, "It's hard to describe."

"So, why did she leave again?"

She chuckled and pulled Katherine to her. "Well, it seems you weren't the only one people-watching that night. Adele spent the greater part of the evening trying to figure out where you fitted in the puzzle of my life. Her suspicions were confirmed when she walked in on us in the dining room." She paused, looking at the colour rise in Katherine's cheeks. Kissing her gently she continued, "When she asked me, I couldn't tell her anything but the truth. Despite my protests, she said you felt the same way but while she stayed nothing would happen between us. So she left and I let her go."

Katherine's eyes avoided those of Catriona. "Do you regret your decision? That was a large gamble on your behalf."

"I know," she answered quietly. "And yet in truth, it was a gamble I was willing to take. As for my decision, I don't regret it in the least. In all honesty, I know Adele and I could have been content with what we had, but she was never who I really wanted and she knew that as well. I think she was right when she said I would have gradually begun to resent her for that. For there's only one person I truly want and love, and that's you." Gathering the younger woman into her arms Catriona once again kissed the waiting lips of Katherine.

Catriona broke the kiss between the two women, leaving Katherine with a confused look on her face. Catriona managed a small laugh before saying, "Have you any idea how beautiful you are? You're like wine that I can't get enough of, woman." She gently brought Katherine's hand to her face, smelling her own scent on the Irishwoman's fingers. Taking a finger in her mouth, Catriona sensually toyed with the digit before offering the fingers to the woman beside her. Without hesitation Katherine's lips closed over the grazier's fingers evoking another groan of pleasure from the older woman.

"I need to feel more of you," Catriona managed and straddled one of Katherine's thighs to begin a rhythm matching her mounting need. As Catriona reached again for the younger woman's eager lips, she felt Katherine's hands move instinctively to her backside, her hips moving in motion with Catriona.

As their pace increased Catriona was absorbed in the feelings flooding through her body. Gazing into Katherine's eyes, Catriona saw the reflection of her own passion and excitement,

steadily building in the younger woman's features. Bending her
head, Katherine's mouth ravaged Catriona's neck, alternating
between kissing and lightly nipping it with her teeth. In a cre-
scendo of thrusting hips Catriona felt her body override her mind
as she exploded with pleasure. Katherine sensed the change and
locked her arms around the moaning woman's hips to heighten
the sensations. Arching her neck, Catriona cried out Katherine's
name, as they came together with a depth of passion neither of
them had ever experienced.

Spent, Catriona lowered herself onto her lover supporting
the better part of her weight with her elbows. Katherine's hands
gently wiped the perspiration from the grazier's forehead. Easing
herself off the beautiful body underneath her, Catriona lay
beside the Irishwoman, their legs entwined. In the space of such
a short time, Katherine's facial features had undergone a meta-
morphosis. Gone was the apprehension and confusion of the past
weeks and for once the younger woman seemed to be at ease and
relaxed. Smiling at her the grazier commented, "I'm looking at
someone who for the first time looks relaxed and happy. She
looks as if she's found a place where she feels she really
belongs. Am I correct?"

Katherine smiled. "I feel happier than I've ever felt, and
you're the reason for this. For once I think I'm home and, having
found my home, I'll never leave you, my love, no matter what
may happen." She again covered Catriona's body with her own
and kissed her deeply, all sense of time and chores forgotten.

Catriona awoke with the calling of her name and the sound
of footfalls in the house. As Catriona shifted out of the embrace
of the Irishwoman, Katherine eyes had also opened and in unison
they exclaimed to each other: "Susan!"

Before the Irishwoman could utter anything else, Catriona
bolted out of the bed, grabbed her robe, and was out the bedroom
door. Looking around, Katherine realised the grazier had left
with the only intact piece of clothing in the room.

Coming through the kitchen door, Susan barely avoided col-
liding with the robed Catriona. "For Christ's sake, what are you
doing still in bed? Are you ill? Never mind that now. Katherine
didn't come home last night and my horse turned up less harness
and one Sister. With all that rain last night I fear that she may

have come to no good...." The last words trailed into silence and Catriona realised the shopkeeper was no longer looking at her face but over her shoulder. Following Susan's gaze Catriona turned her head, to see Katherine, wrapped in a blanket, her hand furiously trying to bring some order to her hair.

"Morning, Susan," Katherine uttered somewhat sheepishly.

Dumbstruck, Susan looked at Catriona and then Katherine and back to Catriona before she could manage to frame a sentence. Stepping forward she hugged her long-time friend and in her excitement said, "Oh, I'm so happy for you both." Then, as if realising the original intent of her visit, she slapped Catriona on the arm. "For God's sake, I've been worried sick! Here I was thinking the worst and instead nothing's happened at all. Well, something has, but nothing dire," she scolded, her thoughts alternating between joy and remonstration.

Katherine moved around her bemused lover, who was more disposed to taking in the reaction of Susan, and gently manoeuvered the still stunned shopkeeper to the kitchen. "Well, that's not exactly the case. In fact, I got caught in the rain and if it hadn't been for Catriona, then I most likely would have died. She found me wandering the road, somewhat the worse for wear I fear. So now that we've sorted that out, how about we have some lunch?" Casting a sideways glance at Catriona she commented, "I'm starving." Katherine was pleased at the blush that rose unbidden to the grazier's features.

"Yes. *No!*" Susan said almost instantly. "You don't understand. Katherine, when I couldn't find you I spoke to the town constable. When I left, he was getting together a search party and we were to meet here. They should be here any minute."

A look of horror passed between the two women before Catriona collected her thoughts. "Okay, okay. There's a way through this. I'll explain it just as it happened." Seeing the look on the Irishwoman's face, she held up her hand, "Less a few pertinent details. Susan, can you keep an eye out for the constable and his group?" the shopkeeper nodded and moved out the kitchen door and onto the verandah. "You, Katherine, need to go back to bed until they've left." The younger nodded, turned, and made her way back from whence she came. Opening the bedroom door, the Irishwoman felt the gentle restraining hand of Catriona come to rest on her shoulder. Katherine turned to the other woman, a questioning look adorned the younger woman's features.

"Katherine, you can't sleep in your room," Catriona offered gently.

A look of pure naiveté crossed the Irishwoman's features, "Why not? This is where I always sleep. I'll just hop back in here and everything will be fine, you'll see." Patting the grazier's arm in reassurance, she made herself comfortable in the centre of the bed.

Catriona took the younger woman's hand in her own. "Well, not exactly, my love. This bed, well, it doesn't exactly look as if one person has been sedately lying in it close to death, does it?" Seeing the look of shocked recognition on Katherine's features, she laughed. "Now come on, I'll place you in my parent's room and you can use one of my mother's old nightgowns. I'm sure that the doctor would have a number of questions if he found you sleeping in the nude." Taking the smaller hand in her own Catriona led her down the hall.

Catriona barely had time to affect a fast change before the small group of men were upon them. Fortunately, Susan had managed to heat some water and was busily feeding the men when the head of the house came through the kitchen door. Retelling the story to the collective audience, Catriona reassured them that Sister Flynn was all right, but was now resting. In reassurance, the doctor who had travelled with the group performed a quick examination on the nun before returning to the kitchen and declaring her fine if not a little tired and hungry from her exertions. Catriona barely managed to stop herself from choking on her biscuit and, looking up, noted the laughter present in Susan's eyes. Before more was said Susan rose and arranged a tray of food for the Irishwoman. Leaving Catriona to any further explanations, she took the tray to Katherine.

It took some time and another lot of lengthy reassurances before Catriona could get the group of relieved men from her home. Waving the last one off, she turned to a smiling Susan.

"Oh, Catriona, I can't begin to tell you how happy I am for you. When she didn't come home last night, I feared the worst and it seems that was almost the case. She's a beautiful woman from what I saw this morning." The shopkeeper laughed at the blush creeping across her friend's features. Prodding her arm she continued gently, "Just make sure you take care of her."

· Catriona grabbed the other woman in a hug before releasing Susan. "That's one thing you can be sure of."

The shopkeeper made her way down the steps and climbed into her own buggy and, with a wave, was on her way.

Walking back through the now quiet house, Catriona opened the door to her parent's room and the woman she loved reclining in the centre of the bed. Quietly Katherine whispered, "Are they gone?"

Closing the distance between the two Catriona placed a kiss on her forehead. "Yes, and thank God for Susan's early arrival. Otherwise it could have been disastrous. Well, so much for that episode," Catriona said raising herself from the bed.

"Where are you going?" a voice asked quietly.

Turning around Catriona caught her breath. Katherine had sat up, allowing the bedclothes to fall, in turn again revealing her naked body to Catriona.

"What happened to the nightgown?" She asked lamely.

Katherine smiled. "With everyone gone, I didn't think there would be a great need for it, would there?" she paused, seeing the reaction in Catriona's face. She leant forward, very aware of the reaction she was evoking in the grazier. "Now, where are you going?"

"I, er, have work to do. Those books haven't been the same since you left; they're the bane of my existence." As she uttered the words, she felt herself drawn to the woman on the bed until she was again sitting on the coverlet beside Katherine.

Katherine's arm draped itself casually on a moleskin clad leg as she looked into Catriona's eyes. "What about a deal? How about you leave those books to me and you look after your patient here?"

Catriona was momentarily surprised by the brazenness of the younger woman's words and she knew she wasn't doing a good job of concealing her amazement. As a smile gathered at the corners of her mouth, Catriona leant toward the woman she loved. "Deal, Katherine, deal." She agreed as she claimed the woman's waiting lips with her own.

Chapter
Sixteen

From that day on Katherine's life changed. Much to the confusion of Father Cleary and the town's ladies, Katherine returned to the Pelham property. On her homecoming, sleeping in separate rooms was dispensed with and with each passing night Katherine became more accustomed to falling asleep in someone's arms. Strangely, the idea of going to bed naked was something Katherine struggled with. She couldn't believe Catriona's brazen way of strolling around the bedroom and sometimes the house naked while she preferred to maintain some air of modesty with her nightgown.

Such modesty didn't last long, with her gown being shed by Catriona shortly after they retired for the evening. The grazier had promised to share her knowledge of the delights and intricacies of lovemaking with Katherine, and that she did. She in turn was surprised by the eagerness of her pupil and at times wondered if she too had been as eager to learn with Adele.

The change in Katherine's life wasn't merely limited to the further intimate relationship shared between the two women; it was something more. For the first time she had a sense of belonging. Katherine thought about the relationship she'd shared with her parents and saw it as one of typical Victorian restraint in which emotions were rarely expressed between parents and siblings. In retrospect, she wondered whether her parents truly loved each other with the same feeling she felt for Catriona, or whether their marriage was purely one of social convenience. Her newfound feeling of at last finding a home was accompanied by new feelings of freedom and strength. This was a source of more than one heated discussion between the two lovers, especially when Katherine suggested that Catriona had given her that feeling. Catriona denied she had, arguing the feelings had been there all along just waiting for the right time to surface.

That same freedom allowed Katherine to voice opinions on subjects, where previously she would have remained diplomatically silent. One such occasion involved her scheduled saga with the Ladies Committee. The nun had decided to broach with the ladies the possibility of them supporting the purchase of additional books to assist in the education of the less fortunate children of the district.

Mrs Greystone reached forward and patted Katherine's hand in her normal condescending manner, an action that was really beginning to grate on the younger woman's nerves. "Well, my dear, your little project is all very commendable; however, don't you feel your time could be better spent attending to your religious duties? After all, are you offering these young children false hope by giving them such education?"

The Irishwoman barely bridled her rising temper. "How do you know whether the education is worthwhile if you never allow them the freedom to learn in the first place? In Ireland, under the class system, working class children rarely get the opportunity to learn and, therefore, never break free of the educational bonds that constrain them. I was led to believe that one of the true benefits of Australia was its relative freedom from such archaic thinking. Surely I wasn't misinformed?" By the embarrassed looks on the faces of the women she realised she had spoken too freely, something that she continually fought against. She expected that her religious duties were suffering at the expense of education; strangely enough it didn't gravely upset her.

The rest of the afternoon with the women was rather frosty and Katherine was relieved at being able to pay a quick call on Susan before returning home. As Katherine relayed the events of the afternoon to the shopkeeper, she couldn't help but laugh. "Oh Katherine, you'll find yourself off their Christmas list now. They rarely like being put in their place by anyone, let alone a foreigner. But enough of such talk." Pausing she cast an eye around the store before continuing, "So, how are things between you and Catriona?"

The mention of her lover's name brought a smile to

Katherine's lips. "They're wonderful. I feel that she is the happiest I've seen her since my arrival."

Susan thought on the blossoming relationship the two women shared. Her happiness at finding the two had finally accepted their true feelings for each other brought tears to her eyes. "I'm so happy for you both. Catriona has been so lonely for such a long time. It pained me to think that when she did find someone to love it was a nun. After all the heartache she's experienced over the past few months it's about time something good happened to her." The shopkeeper chose her next words carefully. "I hope you don't think me intrusive, but what made you make up your mind? I don't mean to pry and I don't want to know what happened to make you initially move in with Me-Lin and I. It's just on the night of the dinner you were acting so strangely. Then your mood on the journey home was dark to say the least. At that moment I thought neither of you would ever arrive at a logical solution to your relationship."

The nun smiled and suggested to Susan that they go into the kitchen, given that her story was quite a long one. There she relayed to the older woman her realisation after leaving the Connor farm and her subsequent seizure by the bushrangers, or what was left of them. She recalled to Susan the clandestine kitchen visit by Mary, and the confused feeling she'd experienced as a consequence of the visit. It wasn't until the bushranger was dying that she fully understood the depth of feelings she shared for both the bushranger and, more importantly, Catriona.

"So, how did Catriona react to the news about Mary? I'm assuming that you've spoken with her?" The shopkeeper queried.

Katherine nodded. "Yes, she does know; we spoke about it the day that we admitted our feelings for each other." The Irishwoman's blushed, strangely shy regarding speaking about that morning with Catriona. "I think she was concerned at first, however, now it's as if that's in the past and all that she's living for now is the present and future. There's something else you won't be aware of; Mary, the leader of the bushrangers, passed away from wounds she received in her last robbery. I don't expect there'll be any bushranging in this part of the countryside for a long time."

Susan nodded soberly. "Despite the threat that she posed to the district, I can't help but feel saddened by Mary's passing. She did a lot to help the poor people of the district. It's just a shame that we can't get the same type of help from the more

influential members of the town. That aside, I think it's wonderful that you two have finally resolved your feelings for each
other. I don't know how much more subterfuge Me-Lin and I
could have coped with."

Katherine smiled, belying the lurch she felt her heart make.
For despite her dismissal of the religious innuendoes made by
the Ladies Committee and her newfound relationship with the
grazier, there was one element of her changed life that disturbed
her. That concern revolved around her status as a nun. She felt
her solution would have been reasonably simple had the same
situation occurred whilst she was still in Ireland—for she would
have returned to the convent and made up some sort of reason for
not staying with her Order. She felt in Ireland it would have been
made easier by the fact she was just one of many sisters. In truth,
she'd never really been made to feel as if she was part of a group
of women who dedicated their lives to God. In retrospect she'd
always felt as if she was no more to the convent than a means to
an end, with it allowing her to escape the clutches of her family
and marriage.

But having arrived in Australia the situation had changed.
She was now no longer one of many, but a sole representative in
a small country town. Unlike the cold religious distance she'd
experienced at the convent in Ireland, these down to earth people
had welcomed her with their hearts. They had put their own and
their family's faith in her, trusting her with the guidance she
gave them and the education she gave their children. The respect
the townsfolk had for her was something she'd never experienced before and that was what pained her most. For she
couldn't help but think how they would feel if they discovered
she was living a far from religious life. The idea of living a lie
and fooling such folk didn't sit well with her.

In the ensuing days she found herself riding the property in
search of an answer, using the peace she felt on these rides to
organise her thoughts. One thing was certain and that was whatever the decision, it must involve her relationship with Catriona.
It was during one of her many such outings, while resting in the
shade of a large eucalyptus tree that she hit upon a solution. Taking stock of her work in the district, she assessed what gave her
the most satisfaction.

Quite a while ago she had accepted her joining the Order
had been a means to an end, saving her from her mother's shame.
She didn't dismiss her religious beliefs, for despite her laxness

in exercising the vows befitting her membership to a religious order; she still had beliefs that were much the same as any other person. The Order had enabled her to work with people, especially children, and that was what she enjoyed the most. She smiled as she remembered the joy she brought the children by just teaching them the rudimentary learning skills of reading and writing.

Katherine sat up suddenly. She'd uncovered what she most enjoyed about her time in the town. It had nothing to do with her religious faith—one that had been sorely tested in the unforgiving cruelty of the Australian countryside and its being a land of contrasts. For it was one contrast to her previous private life in Ireland that she greatly enjoyed and that was teaching the children of the district. *So why was it I couldn't just do that?* She was certain she could continue to teach the district families—her assistance to their children didn't have to stop just because her formal religious calling did.

A wicked smile came to her face as she thought of the reaction of the town ladies, especially given the topic of conversation during her last visit. It would be almost worth it to have them in the room when she spoke about her decision with Father Cleary. However, as she visualised his reaction her stomach turned. How was she to explain to him that he had lost another nun? She wondered what his reaction would be if she also added that it was again to another Pelham?

That night, resting by the fire with Catriona, Katherine raised the issue with her. The grazier listened patiently and laughed with her over the suggestion that she have the Ladies Committee present when she spoke to the Father. Stroking her hair, Catriona was pleased that the Irishwoman had made a decision on her future and, despite not having said anything, she was also not comfortable with their deceit of the town's folk.

"I'm glad you've made a decision, my love. You've been preoccupied lately and I expected it had something to do with this. Your idea to educate the children is an excellent one and I'm sure there are many people within the district who could go far given the chance of a proper education. I don't mean to throw a wet blanket on your decision, but don't you think you should first tell the Father about your wish to leave the convent?"

Somewhat frustrated Katherine nuzzled her back into her lover's chest. "I was hoping to lessen the blow through making him realise that while he may be losing another nun, I have no interest in leaving this town. In essence he's getting the best of both worlds. I'm more than happy to continue on with most of my duties, but in honesty I can't continue to perform them as part of a religious order. It's nothing more than living a lie and that's not fair to him and the families, and it's certainly not fair to us." She turned herself in the older woman's arms so that she could face her. "You know I love you dearly but please understand me when I say that while I'm a Sister I still feel as if I'm married to the Church and God. I don't want to share myself with anyone but you, and as long as I'm a nun I can't do that."

Catriona pulled the confused woman to her. "To me you're already mine, but I do understand your feelings on the matter. I know that tomorrow is the day you regularly visit Father Cleary; are you going to speak to him about your decision?" Catriona felt the head against her chest nod silently. "In the meantime, I feel desperate measures require equally desperate actions. As far as I can see, at the moment the only thing that signifies to me that you're a nun is that infernal habit. Now this is one problem that I can solve, and in turn you can fulfill a dream of mine that I've always had." She laughed huskily and, gently pushing Katherine from her, slowly divested her lover of the black and white garment. Having done so, Catriona removed her own clothes and they passionately made love before a simmering fire.

The following day, the two women exchanged a long and lingering kiss before the nun began her journey into town. While Catriona knew she couldn't be with her lover during this difficult task, she hoped that in some way she could transfer some of her strength to the other woman. With a tentative backward wave Katherine was on her way, leaving the grazier to spend her day tending to some of the overdue needs of her farm. Aside from those chores that had taken second place to their newfound relationship, Catriona was expecting two male visitors. The day she had organised with Robert Johnston for his mother to assist in the dinner party, Catriona had casually mentioned that he and the young Gilchrist might wish to pay her a visit and spend a couple of days on the property. A couple of days had passed before Robert sent a reply with a puzzled Katherine. He and William would be visiting the property; however, their stay would only be a short one. Catriona was quietly pleased that she could help these two young men. She was almost certain that they too were in the early stages of trying to gauge their feelings for each other.

During her silent journey the nun mulled over her sleepless night beside the form of Catriona. Having decided the path she wanted her life to take was one thing, but how was she going to explain it to Father Cleary? To date he seemed to be continually pleasantly surprised with her work in the surrounding district, yet now, unbeknownst to him, he was about to lose another nun. Arriving in town she was still no closer to how she would broach the topic with the priest. Pulling up at the front of the accommodation hotel, she took great time in tethering her horse and placing a nose bag on him before reluctantly starting up the steps.

Father Cleary greeted her at the parlour door and motioned her inside. He couldn't help but think that the nun seemed to be very much absorbed in her own thoughts lately. He hadn't raised the issue with her, preferring to allow her to introduce the topic of her preoccupation. And, if he was honest about the situation, despite her rumination, she continued to perform splendid work around the town. *Maybe*, he thought, *my concern over the influence of Catriona Pelham and the protests of the Ladies Committee were unfounded.*

As the nun moved into the room, she took great pains in smoothing out her habit before sitting down. Her calm outward countenance belied the apprehensive feelings currently stirring in her stomach, despite this being, at face value, her weekly visit. Rather than immediately launch into the supplementary and indeed key reason for her visit, she decided to head for what was safe social ground. "So, Father, how are you? I must say there's been a distinct change to the weather over the past week. Where it was merely warm, the weather seems to be a lot more unsettled."

Father Cleary creased his brow in a mixture of thought and response to the question. "Yes, I believe you're right. We're definitely well on our way toward summer. I'm sure at first you'll enjoy the change from the cold Northern hemisphere climate at this time of year, but trust me Sister when I say that when our winter does finally arrive you'll be wishing and wondering if summer will ever raise its face again," he finished as he took a seat.

The nun quietly smiled, disturbed that all she could think of was the prospect of snuggling up close to her lover in front of a roaring fire—much as they had last night. Her face flushed as she reminisced on the evening's activities. She shook herself out of her mental reverie. "Oh, I don't think it will be that bad, Father. You forget that I'm used to the harsh winters of Ireland where it's not unusual to stay beside the warmth of the hearth for days on end. Now surely you can't tell me that Australian winters are that harsh, are they?"

The Father smiled, again realising that the woman in front of him was more resilient than her deceptive slender frame. "No, not at least in this part of the country anyway. But you'll find yourself having to use your woollen habits once again." He paused as there was a knock on the door and a pot of tea and biscuits was set down between them. As this was done Katherine couldn't help but think the Father was wrong; she couldn't honestly ever see herself in those habits again.

As he poured tea for them both, Katherine relayed her progress in the district. She took great pains to emphasise the interaction she had in educating the district's children, again stating her concerns regarding the absence of any formal means of education within the town. She spoke with enthusiasm about the reception her books had received and her intent to circulate them around the families. In an attempt to put in a good word for Catriona, she mentioned the grazier's generous offer to pay for the next order of books on the proviso that the nun didn't turn her house into a library.

Father Cleary laughed at the suggestion, silently reminiscing about the last time he found himself in such an institution as a library. "Yes, that's most generous of her. If I could only convince some of the other affluent families of the worth of these small farmers and their families, then maybe we could have our own library for everyone to use. Unfortunately, I think sometimes they are perhaps too frugal for their own good."

She nodded her assent and took a sip from her tea. Realising that the time of telling was almost upon her, she irrationally wished that she could have just one gulp of scotch to steel her for the next issue she was going to raise. "Father, there's one other matter that I feel I must discuss with you." Raising her eyes she met his questioning glance. "I know this is presumptuous of me but may I ask that you let me tell you what I have to tell you from beginning to end without interruption? I'm sure that you'll have many questions and I promise I'll endeavour to answer them for you when I've finished what I have to say."

Angus Cleary felt a serious pang of concern. Despite not being aware of what the nun was about to utter, he knew whatever it was he wasn't going to like it. However, respecting her decision, he silently nodded his head and settled into his chair.

"Father, I feel you need to know something about my calling as a nun. I'll admit to you that religion has always had a place in my life, but it wasn't my sole reason for pursuing a religious life. I experienced the unfortunate situation of being left waiting at the altar by a prospective husband. For a reason not quite clear to me, my mother seemed to lay the blame at my feet and to escape her continual remonstrations I left home and entered a convent. When they told me a nun was needed in Australia I jumped at the chance. I didn't know what to expect, but in essence it took me away from a place I felt I wasn't part of.

"I know my arrival in town was less than orthodox, but I feel that it has been to my advantage. The friendship and interaction I've managed to achieve with the townsfolk could only have come so easily as a consequence of the tragedy I was thrust into. In truth, I've found my greatest joy has been in the time I've spent with the children and helping them in their education. I feel that the town itself has made me one of their own." She cautiously raised her eyes, trying to read the look on the man's face. Choosing her words carefully she continued, "Father, it's that feeling I wish to formalise. I want to be a part of this town and live just as the other women of this town do. With my feelings so reconciled, I honestly feel that I can no longer be a nun."

Save for the ticking of the grandfather clock in the corner, a silence was cast over the room. Katherine waited, hands nervously clasped, for an answer. In contrast, Father Cleary was fighting to keep his frustration under control. Despite the short period of time he had known the woman in front of him, he knew that nothing would be achieved by showing his anger. Fighting back this urge, he responded calmly, "But Sister, don't you realise you're already part of the town? You're well accepted and respected by all I speak to. Surely you can see this in the people that you work with? Why this sudden need to part from your religious life?" He sought her face for an answer but instead was met by the nun lowering her head toward her hands.

"I'm sorry, but I can't. I don't feel I can honestly look at people and tell them that the loss of their child or the ruin of

their crops is God's will. While I still hold my religious teachings dear, in circumstances such as those, I find myself questioning the holy logic of such actions. If I were to continue as a nun
under my current vows, I'd be committing my own sin of lying to
these people. I'm afraid that after a while I would grow cynical
and I don't want to do that. I want to do what I enjoy most and
that's to work with these people as an educator and a helper, but
not as a nun."

Angus Cleary raised his hands to his face and closed his
eyes, as if to block out the words he had just heard but also to
concentrate. Searching his mind for a reason for Katherine's
change of heart, he wondered about the role Miss Pelham had
played in her decision. Her brother's death had only served to
reaffirm to him that she was no stout member of the Church.
Admittedly though, Miss Pelham still continued to contribute
money to assist those in need, and for that he was glad. But he
couldn't help but think that something wasn't quite right.

"Sister, I'd be lying to you if I said that your decision hasn't
come as a sudden shock to me, but there's something I need to
know. What influence has Miss Pelham had in your decision?
She's an unorthodox woman with unorthodox ways. Her actions
with Miss Crosier on the day of her brother's death, surely they
didn't escape your notice?" he asked searching her face for an
answer.

Katherine felt her heart miss a beat for she wasn't about to
tell him that the grazier was in fact the catalyst for her decision.
"I'll be honest with you; I've discussed this with Miss Pelham.
Her response was that she respected any decision I made. As for
her actions on the day of her brother's death, I can only say that
what I saw was perfectly reasonable given the circumstances.
Miss Pelham and Miss Crosier are close friends and I feel that
it's only right that she should comfort her when she refused any
comfort that we could give her," she concluded as reasonably as
possible.

Father Cleary rose from his chair and paced the room. He
couldn't help but think that he had already played out this scene
once before with Sister Coreen. *What was it about this town that
resulted in Sisters behaving in the way they did?* The best he
could do was to postpone her decision in the hope that she would
change her mind. "You must be aware I don't have any power
over your presence here and I also have no power over the decision you've made. I feel that you should at least advise your

Mother Superior of your decision and await her response. There are formalities that must be addressed if you're to do this and they can't be done here. Will you at least do this?" He asked, hoping for at least a small degree of respite on his behalf, that might, in turn, cause her to reconsider her decision.

The nun was momentarily taken back. He was right; she would need to advise the convent. She'd completely forgotten there'd be formalities that would need to be finalised before she was no longer formally regarded as a nun and she shuddered at the thought of having to return to Ireland for this to occur. In theory her decision had seemed all too easy. However in practice she realised that it wouldn't just be a case of mailing her religious belongings back with a letter. Reluctantly she turned to the man standing in the corner of the room, waiting for an answer. "Yes, Father, I will write to the Mother Superior and let her know of my request and wait her response. You must be aware though, I've made my decision and despite what the Mother Superior has to say I won't remain a nun in name's sake only. If I have to return to Ireland for the formalities of leaving the convent then I'll do so. However, take heart, Father, for if that's the case I'll definitely be back. My ties with this town are far too great to leave it forever," she finished somewhat enigmatically.

Catriona had spent her morning tending to the needs of the farm, and became so engrossed in her paperwork that it wasn't until she heard the knock at the back door that she remembered the guests she was to have for the day. Arriving at the kitchen entrance, she found Robert Johnston awaiting her, hat in hand. Looking around him, she could just make out the other figure of William Gilchrist still sitting on the wagon they had travelled in. Returning her gaze to Robert she smiled welcomingly. "Welcome to my home, Robert, and thank you for bringing out that blade for the stump plough. I swear with the ground out here, it's a wonder I don't go through more of the blades. Won't you come in? And tell William to come in also. I don't expect my reputation would be enhanced greatly if I left one guest outside while I entertained the other."

Robert motioned to the other man who alighted from the wagon and, upon paying his respects to the grazier, followed the two of them inside. On showing them into the parlour she temporarily left them as she made tea, happy that her lover had found time to make up a batch of what were becoming increasingly respectable scones. Settling down with the two men she noticed a note of discomfort on Robert's behalf. She casually poured tea for the group and handed both men a cup. "Robert, is there anything the matter?"

The young blacksmith shifted uncomfortably in his seat. It seemed strange to be treated as a visitor in such a grand house, given the comparatively rudimentary abode he shared with his parents. "I'm sorry, Miss Pelham. It's just that I've never been invited into a house like this, and well, it's just so big." He shifted on his seat at a distinct loss for words.

Sitting back in her chair, leg slung casually across one knee she replied, "Well, I think that you should know that you're welcome at any time in this house, and that goes for you as well, William. And while you're at it, when you're a visitor here I'd prefer if you call me Catriona. Calling me Miss Pelham all the time makes me feel fifty years old and that I can assure you I am not."

"Thank you for your offer, Miss, er, Catriona." Robert stumbled, finding it difficult to break with the formalities so often addressed to people more influential than himself. Having corrected his error he turned to William. "I'm sure that I speak for both William and myself when I say that we'd be happy to visit again, possibly on a day when there isn't work to do—a social visit perhaps?"

The grazier smiled, feeling a common bond with the young men in front of her. There was no need to spell it out, for she was sure by the silent looks that passed between the two that they were indeed lovers. Looking at the two, she leant forward to retrieve a scone. "Yes, that would be very nice, very nice indeed."

The rest of the conversation revolved around the work that was overdue in the family graveyard. William had kept his responses to her questions short and business like. *Far too serious for such a young man*, she thought. However, given the reputation his father had around the district, she sympathised with him trying to carve a niche of individuality representational of his own distinctive work. She signaled the end of the morning by rising and advising her two visitors she'd paperwork to attend to in the study. Taking their lead from the woman, they too rose to attend to the day's tasks.

As they left the house, Catriona set about tidying up the parlour before her lover's return. Although she wouldn't call
Katherine a fastidious woman, she did seem to have a nervous
habit of cleaning even the smallest mess left about in the house.
Smiling to herself, she placed the plates, cups, and saucers on a
tray and took them out to the kitchen.

From behind the curtains of the kitchen window she
watched as the two men lifted the additional plough blade she
had made by the blacksmith from the rear of the wagon and carried it toward the barn. As they finished their efforts and made
their way back into daylight, William looked around him before
reaching up and gently wiping sweat from Robert's forehead.
With a smile on his face, Robert also carefully looked around
before pulling a laughing William back into the darkness of the
shed. Catriona wondered if she acted the same way around
Katherine. With a chuckle she headed back to the study, realising
that she was now well and truly relegated to bookkeeping duties,
at least until her visitors started for the family cemetery.

After her visit with Father Cleary, Katherine left the main
part of town in haste for fear of encountering one of the members
of the Ladies Committee. It had been a stressful morning for her
and the last thing she wanted to do was to have to endure inane
pleasantries and false smiles. After the Father's success with the
ladies, firstly in allowing her to remain where she was and, sec-
ondly, supporting her decision to return to Gleneagle, relations
between her and the Committee had been somewhat strained. Not
that this bothered her in the least; she really didn't care for the
opinions of women whose values were so shallow.

Having not visited Mrs Connor since the birth of her last
baby, she took the time to ride past the homestead and on to the
Connor property. On arrival, she was amazed to find that, despite
the difficulty of the birth, Mrs Connor was again knee deep in
manual labour with a smiling Katie on her hip. She was greeted
warmly by mother and children alike. It was this family that
she'd bestowed the initial majority of her books upon, amazed at
the speed in which they learnt. Her heart ached at the idea of
such keen seekers of knowledge resigned to working on a farm.
She felt at least two of the children showed sufficient potential
to pursue a more formal path of education. However, such insti-

tutions were places for the wealthy, not struggling farmers who needed every hand to help them to survive.

Satisfied their learning was progressing well and after lecturing Mr Connor on the strain that continual births were having on a woman aged beyond her years, Katherine set her wagon for home. She smiled at the thought that for the first time she genuinely felt she had a home to go to, rather than just a temporary arrangement.

Heading toward the front gate she was at first surprised to see the happy faces of Robert Johnston and William Gilchrist leaving the property. They seemed to be sharing a joke and weren't yet aware of the wagon approaching in the opposite direction. As she reined in closer to the two men, William, upon recognising the Sister, slid himself from where he was sitting to be as far away from Robert as possible. Robert, on looking up, blushed as he saw the wagon of Sister Flynn almost beside them. Drawing on Catriona's teachings, she drew the horse to what she considered an expert halt. "Good afternoon, gentlemen. You look as if you've had quite a pleasant morning's work. I trust that Miss Pelham hasn't worked you too hard?"

The faces of both men reddened as she finished her sentence, which she found strange. Robert was the first of the two who managed to regain his composure. "Oh no, Sister, not at all. We were happy to help Catr, er, Miss Pelham. She's also invited us back in the near future to finish our work."

"Well that's nice. Perhaps we can have lunch together next time you return?" she asked innocently.

"Yes, thank you, Sister, that would be nice," Robert said and smiled. "I must be on my way as there's still plenty of work to be done at the foundry before my day is finished. We hope to see you soon." He finished the conversation and motioned the horse forward.

Katherine creased her forehead in perplexity, feeling as if she'd missed something but she wasn't together quite sure what. Turning the wagon onto the property, she headed toward the house to tell her lover the result of her visit with Father Cleary.

She smiled as she looked toward the house, seeing a waiting Catriona on the verandah. It was so nice to come home to someone who was more than a friend, who would hold you and love you no matter how difficult times were. She surprised herself by saying a small blessing that it was the grazier who had been at the station that day and not Mrs Greystone.

After unharnessing the horse she moved to the verandah and a woman very eager to learn the result of her day's discussions. Moving inside out of the afternoon sun, Catriona listened quietly as Katherine relayed the essence of the morning's meeting. However, her face fell as the younger woman relayed the news that she may have to return to Ireland to formalise her departure from the convent.

"Can't anyone do it out here or can't they just send a letter saying that they respect your decision? It seems a long way to go just to have someone tell you that you're formally released from your vows," she queried, somewhat confused and frustrated by the formality of the situation.

"Cat, I'm not quite sure myself how this is done. It only makes sense that the Mother Superior may wish to speak to me about my decision before she makes hers. As for somebody else doing it in her stead, I suppose I'll know this once I hear from her. Rest assured that if I have to return to Ireland to see an end to this situation, then I will. But don't worry, the minute the matter is resolved I'll return to you on the next available ship," she promised, stroking her lover's face.

"Return to me, be damned. If you think that I'm going to let you travel all that way without me, then you've got another thing coming woman. If you have to go half way around the world, then so will I. Besides, it's about time I broadened my horizons," Catriona declared, holding tightly onto the younger woman's hand.

Katherine was somewhat surprised by the vehemence of Catriona's reaction. "But if you do go, who'll look after the property? The visit could take over a year."

The grazier thought back to the two visitors she had that day and smiled a secret smile. "Oh, I think I've just the people in mind for the job who would be more than willing to look after the property." Before the Irishwoman could question her further, Catriona moved from her seat and, taking Katherine in her arms, gave her a lingering kiss.

In bed that night, the younger woman remembered the reaction she'd evoked in the two men that afternoon and relayed the incident to Catriona. As she did so her lover started laughing. Katherine raised herself on her elbow and looked indignantly at the chuckling woman opposite her. "And what is it that you find so funny about what I've just said?"

Catriona, who had managed to gain control of herself, looked knowingly into the younger woman's eyes, evoking a warmth that stirred deeply inside Katherine. "You mean you really don't know?" She chuckled as she reached for the lithe body of the woman beside her.

Katherine luxuriated in the feel of her skin against her lover's. "Mean I really don't know what?"

"Well, unless I'm extremely wrong, which as you know I very rarely am," the Irishwoman mockingly punched her at that comment, "I believe young Robert and William are lovers." She declared smugly.

Katherine was shocked and felt her face redden. It was all so obvious to her now. The laughter they had shared and the look that passed between them as she approached, not to mention William's move to the extreme side of the wagon. Catriona watched as the realisation was reflected in the younger woman's features. Temporarily lost for words, Katherine looked at Catriona and giggled. "Oh my, the shock they must have got, seeing the pious Sister Flynn approach. I wonder what their reaction would be if they knew the brazen and wanton side of my life." She locked her legs around the grazier's.

"Well, at least for the moment, I think the less said the better," Catriona advised huskily, bringing her lips down to meet a laughing Katherine's.

Chapter
Seventeen

It took Katherine the better part of a week to find the words to write to the Mother Superior. It proved to be a lot more difficult than she'd expected. She honestly wanted to tell her she felt she'd joined the Convent for all the wrong reasons, but all the same she didn't want to sound ungrateful for the help the nuns had given her. After a lot of wasted paper, Katherine felt she had succeeded in conveying her request as tactfully as possible. She reassured the Mother Superior that despite her decision to leave the convent, her intent was to remain in the district and continue her work. In closing she sought the Mother Superior's advice on what she was expected to do next.

Catriona was relieved Katherine had managed to complete the letter, for the past week her lover had been on edge with her demeanour resembling that of a bear with a sore head. Every time the older woman offered help she was met with a terse refusal. Exasperated, she focussed her efforts on planting the wheat and barley crops for the oncoming season. Again, she was grateful for the small group of helpers that had made a potentially difficult task easy. She made a note to herself to ensure that she was extra generous with her Christmas hampers she regularly gave out to the less fortunate. This was really the only way that they would openly accept recompense from her—under its thin disguise of a present. When she found herself within the house, the Catriona would retreat to the solitude of the study, away from a frustrated Katherine, and somewhere at least no-one yelled at her.

Katherine's finish was heralded by a quiet knock on the study door and a sheepish request that the grazier cast her eyes over the letter. Catriona solemnly took the letter from her lover and read it in its entirety before meeting the eyes of the woman in front of her. "But it doesn't say anything about you and I in here." Her face was a picture of innocence.

Katherine snatched the letter back from the seated woman, her tongue clicking in disgust. "If you're not going to treat this seriously, then I'm not going to waste my time." Wheeling, she started for the door.

Catriona was out of her chair before the Irishwoman could reach her destination and placed her hand on the door to halt her dramatic departure. "Oh, Katherine, for heaven's sake I was only joking! I didn't expect that you'd tell the Mother Superior about us and, as you say in your letter, there are a number of reasons why you've made your decision." Grabbing her hand reassuringly she continued, "The letter's fine. When are you going to send it?"

The nun relaxed her body from its tightly coiled disposition. In all honesty, she'd known that Catriona was merely teasing, but with all the letter meant and the substantial recent changes in her life, it was hard for her to see any humour in the matter. She was relieved that Catriona liked the letter, the house was running out of writing paper. Smiling ruefully, she gave her partner a hug. The calming effect that this woman could sometimes have on her was amazing. "Well, I'd like to send it as soon as possible. The sooner I do this, the sooner I'll get a reply. Then we can honestly get on with living our own life together. Are you going into town tomorrow?" The grazier nodded. "Good, I'll come in with you and give it to the postmaster. Now how about we get some of the work done that's been waiting and tolerating my mood for the past week?" Giving the older woman a quick kiss, she opened the door.

Both women spent the rest of the afternoon riding the property to check on the status of the newly planted wheat and barley crops. Catriona was pleased the recent continual rains had helped greatly when it was most needed and there were already good signs of healthy growth throughout the paddock. *It wouldn't be long before the kangaroos sought out these sweet*

grasses, Catriona thought. She'd have to begin riding out early in the mornings to see to the pests.

When she voiced her intentions to the rider beside her, Katherine was shocked. "I can't believe you're planning to kill those creatures! They're only small; surely they don't eat much?"

Catriona turned in her saddle. "Yes, you're right. One kangaroo doesn't eat much, but unfortunately these animals don't travel alone. They travel in mobs. It's these mobs that can ruin a farmer's livelihood in less than a week. But rest assured, I only cull as much as I need to. I don't do it for sport, as some of the richer families of the district do."

Katherine was silent. She'd never understand why such creatures needed to be killed but then she'd never had to rely on the land for her livelihood. This was a concept she was going to have to get used to. "Well, if you have to do it, then so be it. But don't expect me to help you. I honestly can't see myself killing such beautiful animals."

The next morning both women rose early and after tending to morning chores set off for town and the postmaster. Katherine had to laugh at the formality of such a name; after all it was simply an additional job given to Mr Tanner, the man who managed the travel to and from the town by the stagecoach. For this was how her very important letter was to travel. Given that the train still only ran once a week it seemed the fastest way to have her letter reach Sydney and then inevitably Ireland. Catriona had explained to her that despite the round about trip it would take, the coach would still beat the train. It was still the most relied upon means of transportation. When the grazier had casually mentioned the cost of such a letter and the younger woman found herself quite shocked by the expense. It was only when she paused to think about the journey that the letter had to take that she appreciated the expense. She was resolved that the money had to be spent, despite the fact that it would herald the end of her precious cache of money.

With Catriona's thoughts somewhat preoccupied on cattle, crops and kangaroos, the nun took the time to view the changes to the countryside since her arrival. With the onset of regular rains, the yellow brown grass was now interspersed with a carpet of green, on which cattle were happily grazing. One thing that struck Katherine as being truly beautiful were the blossoms that were now opening on the huge eucalyptus trees. It was as if all the time that she'd been there she'd pictured these trees as steadfast, reliable, and somewhat decidedly masculine in their visage, but now they were revealing their true beauty to her. She smiled to herself, thinking that these trees reminded her a little of Catriona. Strong, silent, and unapproachable at first, an appropriate mask to hide the true tenderness in the woman. She again whispered a silent prayer of thanks before reaching across to place a comforting hand on the other woman's knee.

Shaken out of her reverie, Catriona turned and smiled at the woman beside her. Returning her smile, Katherine asked, "A penny for your thoughts?"

The grazier chuckled at Katherine's use of an Australian euphemism. "Oh, I was just thinking about how many times we've made this trip together, you sitting on your side and me on mine. I must admit I prefer the closeness rather than the distance option." She took the other woman's hand in her own, "I was also thinking about something else. You've told me your intentions regarding the letter and that's to seek removal from the convent here or in Ireland, but what happens if the Mother Superior refuses to allow you to be released from your vows? What will you do then?"

The nun sat back in her seat. She hadn't really thought about the possibility of what would happen if her request to leave the convent was refused. She just expected they wouldn't want to hold onto someone who didn't actually want to be part of a religious order. "To tell you the truth, I haven't thought of it. Why wouldn't they want to release me if it's what I want to do?" she asked with a frown creasing her features.

"Well, to play Devil's Advocate, have you thought about the fact that it mightn't suit them? I've no doubt that they've expended a great deal of money to send you out here and they'll be looking for a return on their investment. And besides, the idea of them having to send out another nun so soon to replace you, for financial reasons may not be an option open to them. In one of your more *delightful* moments, you once reminded me that nuns are married to the Church. Despite the fact that in a normal relationship which has turned sour it's possible to get a divorce, this option is only open to the very rich and barely religious. After all, aren't you breaking a promise in seeking out what you wish?" Catriona queried, pained by the worried expression that clouded over Katherine's features.

Katherine was silent for a moment as she thought on her lover's words. Although she didn't expect to feel as if she had an answer to everything, Catriona had come up with questions she hadn't really thought about. What would she do if the Convent refused her request? As far as she was concerned there was really only one option open to her. "I think we should first wait to see what her response is before we start seeing only the bad in things. Besides, it mightn't occur. However, if they refuse my request, then I'll have to take an alternate course of action. I'll just pack up everything I have that belongs to the convent and return them to Ireland. I've no intention of living as a nun for the rest of my life and I also have no intention of living the rest of my life without you. If that's what it takes then I'll do it," Katherine declared, looking for a response from the other woman.

Catriona drew the wagon to a halt short of a bend in the road. Once stopped, Catriona secured the reins and brake before turning to the woman beside her. "You don't know what it means to me to hear you say that. I've never had anyone who was so willing to take risks for me like you are, not even Adele. I honestly hope everything goes smoothly and turns out for the best. Just be aware that whatever the result I'll be here for you, and I hope I can live up to what you want and need from me." Closing the distance between the two of them, Catriona glanced around before taking the younger woman's face in her hands. Gently pulling her face toward her, Catriona tenderly kissed her.

Both were so engrossed in each other's actions that it wasn't until the phaeton buggy was almost on them that they registered its presence. Pulling away suddenly Catriona turned to see the shocked faces of Elsbeth Greystone and a male friend staring back at them. Given their reaction, the grazier was in no doubt they had witnessed them kissing, and Catriona cursed under her breath. How had she managed to allow herself to do that in full view of anyone who should ride along? It would have been bad enough if the kiss had been exchanged between a male and a nun, but two women was abominable. Before the grazier could say anything more, the phaeton's horse had been urged forward at a canter.

Katherine's thoughts were racing. Like the woman beside her, she had no doubt their kiss had been witnessed by the two and she groaned inwardly at the face in the phaeton. *Of all the people, why did it have to be the daughter of the head of the Ladies Committee?* She'd no doubt that young Miss Greystone would waste no time on her return to tell her mother what she'd seen. Fortunately this was the only road she could return on and she had been heading in the opposite direction. This at least gave the two lovers some time.

Catriona looked at the younger woman. "Well, I suppose that's torn it. It won't be long before the Ladies Committee have their suspicions of me confirmed." She laughed bitterly. "It's a shame really. I'd been leading them on such a merry chase for such a long time. I'm sure Mrs Greystone will waste no time in advising Father Cleary of the horrendous actions of the two of us."

The grazier watched as Katherine's face ran the gamut of emotions from shock to anger. Her eyes, usually so calm, were now a brilliant green and her hands were balled into white fists as she fought a barely controlled rage. "I'll be damned if I'm going to allow our happiness to be disturbed by that intrusive woman. I haven't come half the way around the world to find love and then be cheated of it before it's barely begun. We'll mail that letter and then wait for a response. In the meantime, if the town is about to know all, then I might as well be hung for a sheep as for a lamb." With that the Irishwoman reached over, drew her lover into her embrace, and kissed her roughly but passionately on the mouth.

Catriona pulled back to look at the woman she admired, respected and loved and started laughing. Katherine's eyes still held the green fire but it was now more a look of passion than of anger. She never ceased to amaze and shock the grazier with her actions and for that Catriona knew that there would never be a dull moment between the two of them. "Well woman, I suggest we get into town and mail that letter. If you do that to me again, I'm just as likely to disrobe you by the side of the road, which will really give them something to talk about. I suggest we let Susan know and then return home. We may have a long wait before the dust settles over the both of us, that is if it ever does." She motioned the horse back on to the centre of the road toward the direction of town.

Katherine used the last of her savings to send what she hoped would be her lifeline out of the Convent. The "postmaster" assured her that it would reach Sydney within four days and it would then be on a vessel bound for Ireland shortly thereafter. Given that all mail was sent by steam packet, the earliest she could expect a response was four months. Catriona gasped at the time period, only now realising the distance between Ireland and Australia. *Well, if we have to wait then that's exactly what we will do.*

Leaving the makeshift post office, they headed for the store where, while the nun relayed the morning's events to Susan, Catriona loaded the wagon with sufficient provisions to see them through the next month. She wasn't sure if this would be enough time for the incident to pass, but Catriona had no intention of adding fuel to the fire by having to come into town for anything other than urgent matters, not in the short term anyway.

Dusting her hands as she finished the loading, the grazier moved toward her friend to settle the bill of sale. As the shop-keeper took the notes from Catriona's hand, she looked at the woman across from her. "Have you any idea what the reaction of the town will be when this news gets out?"

Catriona shook her head. "I've a pretty good idea of the reaction of the Ladies Committee. There'll be celebrations and 'I told you so's' all round. As for the rest of the town, I can't be sure. I don't think they'll be too receptive to the concept that I've ravished their nun, but whether or not they will continue to think along these lines, I just don't know. I'll tell you one thing though, and that's I'm willing to sit this one out for as long as it takes. This is my home and will always be my home. I don't intend to leave here merely to satisfy the prejudices of others. You never know, after a while they may get used to it."

"Well, I don't know that there's much I can do for you except to point out to people that who you love doesn't change the person you are. You have the respect of a lot of people in this community who serve to lose out if you're forced to leave. I don't think they'll want this but I've no doubt that they'll be angry about your actions with Katherine. I'll endeavour to keep my ear to the ground and let you know which side of the fence the town is sitting on. However, I don't think their acceptance is going to occur over night." Susan finished as Katherine returned from her discussions with Me-Lin. Susan squeezed Katherine's arm in reassurance before smiling at the determination reflected in the features of the women that stood before her. The women remained silent, each too preoccupied in their own thoughts.

Sensing it was time they started for home, Catriona began to say her goodbyes. However, before she could finish her sentence, the shopkeeper swept around the counter and gave Catriona a hug. Leaving what might potentially be the last friendly face they would see in a while, Catriona and Katherine headed out of town and back to the farm.

Their journey home took them past the spot that had started the chain of events that morning, they didn't spot the returning phaeton of Miss Greystone and company. So unless it had been a short trip and she'd returned past the store unnoticed, both women surmised that the town was still ignorant of that morning's incident. On returning to the farm, the provisions were unloaded and packed in their respective places. Having finished what had started out as a routine trip to town turned into completely something else, they sat beside each other at the kitchen table and shared a pot of tea. Both were aware of the storm that was about to descend upon them and were lost in their own thoughts.

Shaking herself out of her pensiveness, Catriona rose out of her chair with determination and strode toward the pantry. "Well, we can sit around this house all day and wait for the recriminations to commence or we can get out of here. At least in the short term if anyone calls they won't know where to find us. I suggest that we pack a picnic and I'll take you somewhere special," she offered, amidst the noise that she was creating in the pantry. On coming out, she held a picnic basket in one hand and was using the other to dust herself down.

Katherine gazed at the woman in front of her who was preoccupied slapping her pants free of the dust they had accumulated, looking all of thirteen instead of twenty-nine years old. Rising from her seat, she took Catriona's preoccupied hand. "You know we can only run from the inevitable for so long, my love. It will eventually catch up with us both."

Placing the basket on the table Catriona replied, "Don't you think I know that? I just don't want to have to sit and wait for it to happen. Damn them, damn them all. This is my property and if I want to take you on a picnic, then I damn well will. Let's live for now for once, not for what may arrive tomorrow." She gathered her lover into her arms and fiercely hugged her.

The Irishwoman gently pulled herself back from the embrace. "All right, but let me prepare the hamper. I don't want to spend the afternoon having to eat your interminable steak and eggs." Katherine said trying to inject some levity into the situation. She dodged a mock swipe from Catriona as she took the basket.

That afternoon Catriona took the nun to the waterhole where her own voyage of self-discovery had started so long ago. She'd very rarely returned there since Adele's initial departure and felt it fitting that the next person she took there was someone who she genuinely loved. The waterhole hadn't changed with the exception of the growth of the trees. The spring still ran with the water as fresh as ever.

The raw beauty she found herself in took Katherine aback. Catriona had explained to her on the trip out the circumstance surrounding the waterhole, and she was touched that she'd been brought here. She couldn't help but wonder if this was what God had in mind when he created Eden.

After having a late lunch both women enjoyed the cleansing waters of the spring, luxuriating in its relative warmth and privacy. As they left the water, the older woman spread a blanket and pulled her lover to her. They made tender love as Catriona had done so many years before. *Their lovemaking again was different than they had shared before,* the nun thought. *It was as if there were no secrets now.* In retrospect, there weren't. Regrettably, they couldn't stay in this idyllic setting forever and as the last of the suns rays filtered through the trees, the time came for them to return home and to the reality that awaited them.

The following day Catriona had no particular work at the house, but she had a distinct feeling that it would be in her partner's best interests if she didn't stray far from it. With this feeling, she worked on superfluous paperwork in the study. When she heard the sound of a carriage coming up the drive, she looked out the window and smiled grimly. *It hadn't take the Greystone girl long to tell her story, for what other reason could there be for this particular visitor.* Katherine, who was preoccupied in the parlour, hadn't yet heard the carriage and so it was the grazier who moved to the front door to open it.

Standing at the foot of the front steps bearing a grim countenance was Father Cleary. Seeing the Pelham woman in the doorway he was momentarily taken aback, for he had presumed that he would be able to speak with Sister Flynn without encountering this woman. As this was obviously not going to be the case, he busied himself with tethering his horse and collecting his thoughts before turning to Miss Pelham, saying, "I've come to speak with Sister Flynn, is she in?" He barely met Catriona's eye.

Despite her initial instincts to physically remove him from her property, Catriona maintained a level head. "Yes, she is. If you'd like to move into the parlour I believe you'll find her there." As she turned she came headlong into Katherine standing silently with her full gaze on Father Cleary.

"It's okay, Catriona, I'm here. I heard the front door open and wondered who was visiting us at this time of day. Won't you come in, Father?" She stood aside for him to enter.

Seeing him begin his ascent up the steps, the nun moved toward the door of the parlour without bothering to see if he was indeed following her. Waiting at the door, she stepped aside, allowing him to move in ahead of her. As Catriona made a move to follow her, the Irishwoman stopped her. "No, Catriona. I've no doubt there are things that Father Cleary wishes to discuss with me in private." She gave her a reassuring look before gently pushing the grazier back through the door and closing it behind her. Turning, she found Father Cleary hadn't taken a seat, preferring to stand as he said what he wanted to say. As calmly as possible she took a seat in anticipation of his onslaught.

"When Mrs Greystone came to me yesterday afternoon with her wild tale, I was ready to dismiss it as yet just another example of her overactive imagination. In fact, on the ride out here all I could think of was the perfectly reasonable explanation you'd be giving me for what occurred yesterday. Yet when I arrived and saw how the two of you interact together, I chastise myself for not seeing it sooner." Father Cleary paced the room in an attempt to rein in his anger.

The nun didn't offer an explanation, instead she allowed him to continue. "Young Miss Greystone saw you and Miss Pelham exchange a kiss, a kiss like one that is exchanged between man and woman. Is this true? Are you two intimate in that manner?" Father Cleary stumbled over his words, not quite sure of how to form such a question. Looking directly at the woman in front of him, he saw her head give a barely perceptible nod. This was the trigger for him to completely lose his temper.

"And you have the audacity to call yourself a nun! Is it not sufficient that you should break your vows of celibacy, but you do so with a woman? What you both are doing is sacrilege not only in the eyes of the Church but this town as well. Not one week ago you stood before me and said that your leaving the Church wasn't that woman's doing. You even said to me that you couldn't bear to sin by living a lie any longer. So what kind of lie is it that you're living now, Sister?"

Katherine had heard enough and crossed the floor to meet Father Cleary face to face, barely managing to keep her own anger in check. "Yes, Father, I remember what you asked me that day and everything that I told you was true. My leaving the Church has never been Catriona's doing and despite what you may think, with or without her I would have eventually left the Church. And as for my living a lie, it was true. How can I serve out religious humble pie when I find myself gagging at its taste? My lie had nothing to do with the relationship between the two of us; it was the relationship between the Church, myself, and the townsfolk that I found deceitful." She paused to collect her breath. "And as for our relationship being sacrilegious, I'll ask you just this, Father. How is it that something which involves love and commitment on both sides can be seen as something sordid by such an all loving, all caring God?"

"I'm not about to get into a theological debate with you. You know or should know your Scriptures better than most people. Such acts are regarded as unnatural. Just stop for a moment and think about what it is that you're doing. If you think for one moment that the town is going to accept what's going on out here as natural, then you're wrong. Why, as we speak, Mrs Greystone is petitioning for your removal from the town. And as far as I'm concerned that's the only way there can be an end to this. Furthermore, I feel that I can no longer trust you with the well being of the children of the district. You're released from your requirement to work with them and I'd advise you not to try and approach them or I'll personally see to your removal!" Father Cleary finished, realising that his last arrow had found its mark.

Katherine turned from him in an attempt to have him not see the pain in her face. She didn't care about his opinions on the relationship, but his warning regarding the children hurt her deeply. This was one of the things that had truly given her pleasure and now he was taking it from her. Gathering her thoughts she turned once again to face the Father. "You once told me that you've no direct authority over my being here and if you've no direct authority on my being here then you also can't order me to leave. As for the children of the district, I can't believe that you think that I'd ever do anything to hurt them. What you're saying will hurt them. What do you think will happen to their education without someone to teach them? It will wither and die. You've allowed me to build up the hopes of these children and now you're going to ruin it with one decision? If that's what you really want then so be it. However, I warn you I won't turn away any mother or child who approaches me."

"You're right. I can't have you thrown out of this town, but I doubt I'll have to. This is one time when I'll be happy to have the Ladies Committee do my work for me." Without waiting for the nun's reply, he strode toward the door pausing long enough only to open it and headed straight for the front door.

Catriona had come from the kitchen, arriving just in time to see the front door slam and the figure of her lover slump against the hallway table. "Well, that was a short trip. I gather good news doesn't travel fast."

"No. You're right, it doesn't. He accused you of having an influence over my decision to leave the Church and called our relationship sacrilege. He then called me a liar and followed that by telling me Mrs Greystone was organising to have me thrown out of town. And if that wasn't enough, he has taken all my responsibilities off me, including the education of the children. Catriona, he's set me adrift and taken from me one of the things I love doing most," the Irishwoman finished, moving into the comfort of the older woman's arms.

Catriona held onto her tightly. "Well, at least you still have me. Think about it, he could have brought the Greystone lynch mob with him."

"I'm glad that I still have you, but what kind of life can we expect with that woman ranting and raving all over town? I know her type; she's just like my mother. She'll never let up until she gets her own way. How are we going to cope with that?" Katherine asked, desperate for an answer.

Pulling her tighter, Catriona was ashamed that she didn't have one to give. "I don't know, my love. I don't know."

That night, despite being in the comfort of Catriona's bed

and her arms, the nun found that she couldn't sleep. *Was this the sort of isolation I really wanted?* She'd never be able to show her face in town again, knowing that around the corner lurked one of the Ladies Committee, ready to spit invectives at her which were undeserving. She couldn't help but think of the life Catriona would have. Despite her brave reassurances that the feelings of the town didn't matter, she still had a lot of dealings with it. How would the farmer's cooperative react to the news and what impact would that have on Catriona's crop and cattle sales? There were so many questions to which there were no answers. Sometime in the small hours of the morning, beside a sleeping Catriona, the nun made her decision.

Katherine was unusually silent and distant that morning with Catriona, attempting to avoid contact where at all possible. She prepared breakfast for the two of them, eating hers in silence, refusing to be drawn into a conversation with the other woman. By mid morning the silence had become unbearable and taking the nun's protesting hand, Catriona led her into the parlour. "What's the matter with you? You've hardly said two words to me this morning. What's wrong?" The grazier searched her face for any clues of an answer.

The nun stood and moved away from the older woman before saying quietly, "It can't work like this. My work here has suffered and your work is bound to suffer because of the pressure the Ladies Committee will bring to bear on the town. They'll ostracise us both. We'll never be able to show our faces, or go out anywhere; we'll be like prisoners to the prejudices of others. I don't think I can live like that."

The colour drained from the grazier's face. What Katherine had said had come entirely unexpectedly to her and she found herself seeking her mind wildly for an answer. "What do you mean it can't work? It *is* working, Katherine. Why does it have to matter what the town says or how they feel about us? We still have each other no matter what."

The Irishwoman moved quickly to her lover's side. "Yes, but is that enough? Maybe it is for today, next week or next month maybe, but what happens if it's not enough? What happens if you can't get help during the harvest? We couldn't possibly do the job ourselves. And what happens if you can't sell your crop because no-one will buy it or muster your cattle for sale? How will you live then? I couldn't bear to see you or your farm suffer for the love that you have for me and I couldn't bear to see you grow bitter and resentful because of it. There has to be more, and this has been taken from us. I don't want to see us end up hating each other for it."

Catriona shook her head as if she were waking herself from a bad dream. Seeing Katherine still in the same position, she heard herself utter the words she dreaded. "So what are you saying?"

The nun took a deep breath, not breaking contact with the worried eyes of the woman opposite her. "I think that it would be best for both of us if I leave."

She didn't get any further before Catriona wheeled out of her chair, letting out a groan of pain, as if she'd been wounded deeply. "How can you say that if you really love me? How can you? You once told me that you'd never leave me, but now things are getting a little hard you're just going to walk out? Yesterday you were adamant that we would see this through. We *can* make it through this, Katherine. I know we can. Just try a little harder," she pleaded.

It pained Katherine to see her lover so badly hurt, but there was no easy way of saying what had to be said. As she moved toward her, the grazier recoiled like a child who had been given a beating and wasn't sure why. Halting her movement the nun replied, "I love you and I'll always love you. If I didn't, I wouldn't be doing this; can't you see that? I can't bear to see us grow apart from each other. You're right when I said that I'd never leave you. I never will; I'll always be here with you in some form or other. Please trust me when I tell you that there can be no other way to end this without further pain for both of us." She stopped as Catriona's shoulders rose and fell as she cried. Moving to her, Katherine took her in her arms and gently held her as she wept.

It wasn't until later in the morning when she had put an emotionally exhausted Catriona to bed, that Katherine hitched the wagon for a trip into town that wasn't going to be easy. Aside from the cold reception she was sure she'd receive from the townsfolk, her emotions were strained to breaking point. She had to stop the wagon twice to shed her own tears before continuing on.

As she entered the town she was conscious of the eyes that judiciously avoided her. She felt that before she approached the Father she at least owed Susan a reason as to why she was about to do what she was. Negotiating the wagon to a stop in front of the store, she encountered difficulty in getting off. The more she tried to pry her habit loose from its place, the more flustered she got. She was aware of people watching her but no-one moved to help her, almost as if to touch her would herald the same contagion that she was obviously inflicted with. Barely holding back tears of rage she felt the hands of someone loosen the cloth from its sticking place. Turning around she looked into the quiet eyes of William Gilchrist, who was waiting to help her from the wagon.

No words were exchanged between the two even though both felt the surrounding crowds were waiting for some. Instead a look of gratitude and acknowledgment passed between them before the Irishwoman moved into the store. Susan, having witnessed the incident, finished with her customer as Katherine walked in. The shopkeeper moved to close the door. "What are you doing here? I thought it was agreed that you'd wait until a little time had passed."

Katherine told Susan of the Father's visit and the words she had with Catriona. The shopkeeper couldn't help but think Katherine was right, despite how much it pained her to say so. She grew angry at the narrow-mindedness shown by a town that had benefited so greatly from the work of both these women. And now it had come to this. *Would there ever be a time when women could live together without the judgement of others?* Susan thought. *It was unlikely while the likes of the Greystone's and Monteith's prevailed.*

"I'd ask one thing of you if I may," the nun paused, looking at the woman opposite her, "that you take care of Catriona, especially in the first few days. She doesn't understand that I do this out of my love for her; I don't want to see her hurt by these people. She has essentially closed herself to me and apart from her initial silence has been almost puppet-like in her actions. On top of that and given what has happened in the past month I'm not sure how she'll cope."

The shopkeeper squeezed Katherine's arm reassuringly. "Of course I will. I'd be lying if I said that this isn't going to affect her deeply. But are you sure that this is the only solution?"

The younger woman turned away from Susan, attempting to hide the tears in her eyes. "Don't you think I know that? I hope what I'm about to do works out for the better but I expect all that I can ask of you at this time is for you to trust me and most of all take care of Catriona for me." She pleaded with her back to

Susan.

Sensing the nun's resolution Susan found herself fumbling for the right words to say, and in doing so she fell back on safe ground. "So, when are you going to leave?"

"I hope to secure a berth on the train which passes through here in two days time. I know that doesn't leave me much time, but I'd prefer it this way. I couldn't bear to watch Catriona suffer any longer than is necessary." Katherine turned and saw the look of shock that passed over the shopkeeper's features.

"It seems so sudden, but I expect that there's not much more to say. I'll be at the train on Saturday to see you go, but don't expect too many others." She opened the door to allow the nun to pass through.

Katherine turned to her as if she'd forgotten something. "I want you to know that I'm grateful, Susan, for the friendship you and Me-Lin have given me and I'll never forget it. I wish you both the best and hope that you never find yourselves in a similar situation," she finished quietly and moved before the shopkeeper could reply.

At last, there was one final person she had business with. Having spent the last of her funds on her letter to the convent, she found herself in the ironic situation of asking for money so she could leave. Father Cleary gave her barely enough money to see to her boat and train fare, letting her know that the funds were not his and had been raised by the Ladies Committee with specifically that intent in mind. However, if she needed lodgings in Sydney she'd have to approach the sister convent and ask for their charity. There were no more words left to be said between the two of them. Katherine gathered up her meagre funds and left to book her passage at the train station.

Despite the fact that the two women continued to share the same bed, there were very little words exchanged between them in Katherine's remaining hours in the house. Catriona moved around the house in a catatonic state barely responding to the nun's questions. On their last night together, Catriona made love to Katherine, bringing her to climax again and again in hopes of changing Katherine's mind about leaving. Katherine responded by giving to the grazier all that she could, hoping to convey with her actions the deep love that she felt for the only true love she had ever known.

When morning came, Catriona was again sullen and distant. Katherine had packed what little there was of her possessions the night before and was surprised to see that the wagon hadn't been prepared for the journey. The older woman instead sat on the verandah, looking ahead. "I may have to live with the fact that you're leaving this town, but if you think for one moment that I'm going to help you, then you're wrong. You can leave the wagon at the train station. I'll pick it up in good time."

Katherine felt her legs almost buckle from under her for, until now, she'd not realised that Catriona wouldn't be coming with her to the station. Holding onto the doorpost for support, she steadied herself before resolutely heading for the stables to harness the horse. Coming back from her task, she knelt before the older woman's statue-like form and spoke carefully. "I know you find this hard to accept, but what I'm doing now I do for both of us. Remember two things if you forget everything else. Remember that I'll always love you no matter what and that I'll always be with you, if not in body, then certainly in spirit." Katherine took Catriona's unresponsive body in her arms one last time and kissed her. Moving quickly lest she change her mind, she mounted the wagon and, without a backward glance, drove into town.

As she approached the station Katherine was relieved to see Susan waiting for her. It was bad enough that Catriona had refused to see her off, but to leave the town alone would have been too much to bear. Pulling the wagon to a halt, she applied the brake. "Thank you for coming. As you can see Catriona hasn't accompanied me. I left her sitting on the back verandah."

Susan, having alighted from her carriage, helped the nun with her meagre two bags. "I didn't really think she'd have come in. It's probably for the best, given the possibility that some of the Ladies Committee may have shown up. I doubt she could have coped with them seeing her cry. Oh, by the way, I almost forgot. Me-Lin said to give this to you." The shopkeeper handed a parcel to the younger woman. "She said that she felt that you might be needing it."

Katherine hurried a thank you before placing the package in one of her near empty suitcases. She looked up at Susan whose eyes were beginning to water and, sadly smiled. "You know this is for the best. Trust me when I tell you that only good can come from this." She reached out and grasped the other woman's hand.

Susan managed to choke back her emotion before reaching into the folds of her skirt she pulled forth a small purse. "And this is from me to you. Now take it and be done with it. I know you can't have much money left and I'm sure that you'll be needing it," she finished, placing the purse in Katherine's hand and closing her fingers around it.

Katherine nodded wordless thanks and the two of them moved through the doors of the railway station. Katherine paused as she came out the doors on the other side which led to the tracks, for standing next to the door in what must have been their best set of clothes were the Connor family. Seeing them the nun felt her own eyes water at the people that she was leaving behind. Mrs Connor, seeing her distress, moved forward and comforted her.

"Now there's no need for tears. What kind of friends would we be if we didn't come and say goodbye? There have been a lot of things said about you and Miss Pelham over the last few days and they don't need to be said again. I'm grateful to you, Sister, for the help that you've given me and my family and I feel that it's important that you know this. Not everyone feels as those women do. I also want you to know that my Daniel will keep an eye out for Miss Pelham to make sure that she doesn't come to any harm." She brought a handkerchief up to her own nose, blowing it before adding, "Some people may be quick to forget the good she has done, but that won't be said of the Connors."

Katherine quietly thanked her before taking the time to say her goodbyes to all the children before the train arrived. Reaching Aiden, he held out a bag containing pasties and cakes to see her on her journey. As she turned to hug Susan one more time, she saw the unmistakable plume of train's smoke heading in their direction.

It was only then that the nun began to cry. She'd come so far and achieved so much, and now it was finally time for her to leave the town. As the train pulled into the station, she gave her farewell party a final hug before receiving her ticket from Jim Nelson, who took her bags and saw her to her seat. The last view she had of the Connor family and Susan was of little Aiden, running down the platform as if to catch up with the metal beast, before the train rounded a bend and took her out of their sight.

Chapter Eighteen

The sun's rays beat down relentlessly on a seated Catriona. Since the nun's departure the day before, she had taken up her old chair on the back verandah and refused to move from it. As far as she was concerned, there was no purpose of moving. She couldn't help but feel that every time the glow of happiness entered her life, it was soon reduced to nothing more than ashes. She had often thought she had loved Adele, yet the depth of emotion she had for Katherine was beyond words. She knew the Irishwoman felt the same and yet she'd left. The more Catriona thought about the entire situation, the more betrayed she felt.

It was this same stoic figure that Susan came across when she rode out the early afternoon after the nun's departure. She could understand why her friend hadn't farewelled her lover at the train, but for her to cease to speak to Katherine in the manner she spoke of through the few words they had exchanged at the station the previous day was insanity. Reining in her horse, she alighted from the buggy and approached the non-responsive grazier.

Moving to the woman's side, she knelt beside her. "Catriona, don't you think it would be better if we got out of this sun?" Reaching up, she brushed a stray hair from her unresponsive friend's forehead. "Have you eaten at all in the past 24 hours? Why don't you come inside and I'll fix you something to eat? After my ride I'm looking forward to a nice cup of tea." Still the woman beside her refused to answer. In exasperation, the shopkeeper tried another approach. "I know this is a hard time, but you must go on. You have responsibilities to your farm and your livelihood. Aside from that, if you continue like this and make yourself ill, who do you think is going to help the less fortunate in the district? You are their shining light. Who do you think is going to help them if you don't?"

A flicker of recognition swept across Catriona's face. "Help them? Are these the same people who have been more than happy to cast me out over the past few days?"

The shopkeeper shook her head. "You don't know that Catriona. Certainly the Ladies Committee was vociferous in their demands for Katherine's removal, but I saw no immense interest shown by the greater townsfolk or the smaller landowners to support such a decision. Don't punish them for something they didn't do."

Catriona's blue eyes flashed in anger. "But don't you see? That's just it! They didn't do anything either way. They were more than happy not to voice their dissent. It was easier just to let her go."

"What, in much the same manner as *you* did with Katherine?" the older woman challenged. "I didn't see you at the railway station asking her to stay. And from what she told me regarding your actions on the morning of her departure, you didn't seem to have raised a finger in her defence."

This finally provoked a full reaction from the seated woman. Rising from her chair, Catriona wheeled on Susan. "How dare you! You know how much I felt for her; I've told her often enough. She knew and yet she still left; nothing I could have said would have stopped her. So if you've come to tell me what I should and shouldn't have done, it's too late. Go home, Susan, and leave me. I'll survive, I always do. And if I don't, I doubt anyone will weep a tear for my passing anyway." Catriona laughed bitterly.

Susan shook her head in disgust. "My God, listen to yourself wallowing in self pity! Your life hasn't been easy, I'll grant you that, but there have been many others who have had it a lot harder. At this first real test of adversity you falter. Maybe it *is* for the best that Katherine has left."

Moving away, Catriona angrily strode off the verandah. "I don't have to listen to any more of this. If you're not going to leave, then I will." She reached the barn door before the strong hand of her friend stopped her.

"You're right, you can go where ever you like. But before you do, just answer me this. You said she knew how you felt about her, but did you *tell* her when she needed to hear it most? Did you tell her yesterday before she left for the train station?" Not waiting a response Susan continued, "No, you didn't, and I believe that was all it might have taken to get her to stay. The town's folk would have eventually come around, and if they didn't then to hell with them. Now this might only be supposition on my behalf and, if you continue the way you are behaving, then I suppose you'll never know."

Catriona hung her head, her emotions barely in check. "Well, I suppose we'll never know. It's too late; she's gone."

Susan grasped the other woman's shoulders. "Catriona, look at me." She waited until Catriona's distraught face looked into her own. "It's only too late if you allow it to be. Go after her, bring her back."

"And how do you expect me to find her? Sydney is a damn site larger than this small town. I wouldn't know where to start. It would be tantamount to looking for a needle in a haystack. And what about the farm while I'm gone? I can't just drop everything and leave."

"Strangely enough you seemed content to allow the farm to go to ruin when first I arrived this afternoon." She grabbed the grazier, impeding her escape before gently continuing. "Can't you see the only barriers that will stop you from finding her are the ones *you* place there? Do you remember the dinner last year when after one too many bottles of claret we became very philosophical about life and love?" Seeing the recognition on the other woman's face she went on. "You said then that you believed in Fate. Well, if that's the case then look at the chain of events over the past few months. It was you who went with Jim Nelson to look at any possible damage to the railway station, and it was you and he that found her. If it had been any other day than that of the dust storm, then the Ladies Committee would have greeted her and you would be none the wiser. Had they greeted her, there was no way you would have got a look in regarding her staying with you. If this had been the case, neither of you would have discovered how you felt about each other.

"Love like that shared between the two of you is precious, Catriona, and it's sure worth going after. If you believe in Fate, then you'll find her in Sydney and if you don't then you were never meant to. However, there's one thing that's a certainty in all of this. If you stay here you'll never find her, and she'll leave never really knowing the depth of your love for her. Go after her, find her, and tell her how you feel; tell her that you want her to stay. As for the farm, I'm sure there are two young men who could capably manage its affairs during your absence."

Catriona sadly shook her head. "She is already a day ahead of me and the next train's not due for another week..."

Before she could continue the older woman held up her hand. "Yes, that's right, she does have a day on you and if you wait for the next train then you may well be too late. However, the Sydney coach comes by here in the next couple of hours, does it not? Haven't you told me that given its more direct route it usually beats the train into Sydney? What are you waiting for?"

Catriona paused, her thoughts in turmoil. *Why hadn't I asked Katherine just one more time to stay? Would it have made any difference? Susan was right, I will never know unless I try.* If she could just beat the train into the central terminus, she could meet Katherine there and tell her one more time. Despite the crowds it would be easy to pick her out in that infernal habit. It would be one time that she would be happy to see her wear that painful attire. Sighing she met the eyes of the woman in front of her. "You win. I'll give it one more try, God only knows. I love her, Susan. I've never felt this way for anyone before and I'm unlikely to feel this way ever again."

Both women spent the next hour packing and hoping that, for once, there was at least one seat left on the coach. Catriona reconciled that if need be she would ride on top of the luggage, if for no other reason than to give Katherine just one more chance.

Katherine awoke to the gentle shaking of her shoulder and the quiet lilting sounds of the Irish woman beside her. The voice belonged to the mother who, with the nun and her small family, had shared the small third class compartment over the past three days. After three days of relentless silent rattling, Katherine was grateful at the need for a three-hour stopover. Saying farewell to her companions for the first part of her journey, she set out to find somewhere to eat, as well as somewhere she could attend to her ablutions. Of greater relief, the stop presented the first opportunity for her to rid herself of her habit. Only now had she realised how fortuitous her request to Me-Lin had been. In anticipation of her leaving the Order, Katherine had asked her if she could possibly make a few simple dresses for her. Refusing any payment, Me-Lin had been happy to comply with the nun's request. Given the circumstances, she had just finished them in time and an unknowing Susan had delivered the parcel on the day of Katherine's departure.

Returning three hours later to her cabin, she found her entrance blocked by a small redheaded boy, his face a patchwork of freckles. "Ma says this is our cabin and until she returns I'm to make sure no-one else tries to take it from us."

Katherine had smiled at the young boy's defiance. "And a good job your doing, too. However, if you look in the corner you'll see a small suitcase and it's a match to the one I'm carrying." Holding up the bag she continued. "You see, I've been on this train for three days already and have been in this cabin. However, I'm sure there's enough space for all of us to share for the rest of the journey. What's your name?"

Relaxed by Katherine's manner, the boy offered the information willingly. "Ned O'Riordan; and who are you?"

"My name's Sister," Katherine stopped herself and looked down at her clothing. Too many questions would be asked of a nun traveling in plain clothes. Maybe it was time she started her new life—the one she wished she could have started with Catriona. "My name's Miss Flynn, and by the sound of you we both started off in the same place. Where in Ireland are you from?"

Before the boy could answer, a flustered woman with another child in tow arrived at the door of the carriage. Katherine introduced herself and before long the small group was Sydney bound yet again. During the remainder of the journey she learned that the O'Riordan family had been prospectors out west. However, after the unfortunate death of their father in a mine cave in, the family was now returning to Sydney before securing passage to Tasmania and to Margaret O'Riordan's sister and family.

The same polite questions were asked of Katherine and she found herself in a quandary. She could hardly tell this other woman who she really was or what had happened to take her to Sydney. Embellishing the truth somewhat, she told Margaret that she was a teacher who had been visiting friends and was now returning to Sydney. The relief in the woman's eyes was apparent and, at least for a short while, she could rely on the other woman to assist her in keeping the children occupied.

Just when she thought her body could take no more of the continual rattle of the train, they finally approached the outskirts of Sydney. Passing through the small train stations along the track to their final destination, it was not long before they reached the large town of Sydney. As she did so she found herself looking at the Gothic arches of the Redfern Mortuary Station. This certainly meant she was very close to seeing the end of the first part of her journey home, and in an attempt to avoid conversation, she continued to peer at the young city landscape while pondering what to do next. Mentally calculating her savings, she assessed she had enough money left to get to the Circular Quay to book a berth to Ireland, pay for a small amount of provisions for the journey, and pay for one night's accommodation in the city. She silently prayed that there would be no delay to an immediate return home, for if there was she would have no other choice than to again don the garb of a nun and seek temporary accommodation in the convent—something she wasn't comfortable with.

Helping Mrs O'Riordan and her children from the carriage, Katherine again graciously refused her offer of temporary stay with relatives of hers. As she was making her excuses one final time, a solid and yet gentle faced man grabbed young Ned. It was obvious through the likeness of the two that he was a relative of sorts. "Sean, set the boy down and behave yourself," Margaret O'Riordan insisted, laughter in her voice. "And where are your manners? Introduce yourself to *Miss* Flynn here."

Pausing, the man turned toward Katherine, placing Ned down in the same motion. The emphasis that Margaret had placed on "Miss" was not lost on Katherine and she found herself somewhat embarrassed by what she saw in the man's eyes as he introduced himself. There was nothing sordid, moreso he was shyly interested by the features of the woman in front of him. Removing his cap, he offered his hand, "Sean Doherty, Miss Flynn. I'm sorry if I seemed rude. It's just it's not often that I get to see my sister."

Katherine accepted the apology before politely listening to an overview of what he did for a living. In doing so, Katherine found herself somewhat bemused. When, as a nun, she had initially arrived in Sydney, she had received nothing but respect and assistance. This was still there in the eyes of the man in

front of her, yet there was also something else. It was a regard of
a more personal nature, and for the first time since the debacle of
her engagement, she saw interest reflected in the eyes of another
man. It was only then that she realised just how careful she
would have to be in Sydney and on her homeward voyage.
Before her habit had acted as a sort of religious shield. Now
there would be nothing to protect her from the prying eyes and
hands of men. Respectfully refusing one final attempt by Mrs
O'Riordan to invite her to stay, Katherine managed to extricate
herself before finding a Hansom cab to deliver her to the Circular Quay booking office.

Traveling down George Street, which she presumed to be
one of the major streets of Sydney, Katherine found herself
amazed by how the city itself seemed to be a series of contradic-
tions. The buildings lining the road heralded the availability of
sandstone in the Sydney environs, with most of them being elaborate works of sandstone architecture. The newly built Sydney
Town Hall laid testimony to an architectural style more reminis-
cent of Ireland, and the paved footpaths carried men and women
bedecked in the latest fashions of the day. However, in the presence of such civility was a visual reminder of the rural nature of
this town. Halted in the shadow of such a refinement of people
and architecture was a heavily laden bullock dray. The driver,
casually attired, paid little attention to the passing men and
women; his focus more trained on adjusting the harness of his
team before continuing on his journey. Just as Katherine began
to determine exactly what he was carrying, the Hansom cab she
was travelling in lurched sideways. Obviously the town's coun-
sellors had expended all their available funds on building and
pavements, for the street itself was no more than a hole-ridden
dirt road, not at all like the cobbled streets of Ireland. Paying
greater attention to hanging on, she passed the equally large and
elegant Post Office before finding herself at the birthplace of
this country— Circular Quay.

Politely manouevring her way around the numerous spruik-
ers, selling their wares and pausing only to ask directions of a
soldier in charge of a work gang, she finally arrived at the booking office. She straightened her bonnet before entering.

Looking up from the charts in front of him, the middle aged
bespectacled man greeted her. "Good morning, miss, may I help
you?"

Katherine baulked at the man's use of "Miss" as opposed to

what she was more used to and gathered herself. "Good morning and, yes, I hope you can. I'm looking to book a passage to Ireland as soon as possible. Could you please tell me when the next available boat departs?"

The man in front of her smiled. Well, ma'am, firstly it would be better for you to refer to these fine vessels as ships, unless of course you want to raise the ire of their Captain." He paused as the Irishwoman nodded her head in mock chastisement. "And in answer to your query, yes we do have a ship due to leave port for Ireland. She's set to sail on the 14th."

The look on Katherine's face caused the man to pause. "But that's not for another seven days. Surely you have something leaving sooner?"

"I'm sorry, ma'am, but that's the best I can do. If I might be so bold, I'd suggest that you book now. It doesn't take long for these passages to be quickly filled up. If you miss this one, it will be another month before a ship is due to sail to Ireland."

Resignedly taking the man's advice, Katherine parted with enough money from her meagre savings to book a shared cabin for the long sea journey home. Thanking him for his assistance she turned, and in the process of securing her ticket, she walked straight into someone in front of her. Stepping back and raising her face to apologise, Katherine's jaw dropped in shock. "Adele?"

An equally surprised Adele looked at the woman in front of her not dressed in her normal habit. Adele could quite clearly see the beauty that had so captured Catriona. Despite the wisps of hair struggling to free themselves from her cotton bonnet, Katherine's emerald green eyes capably accentuated the nun's delicate features. Regathering her composure, Adele chose her words carefully. "Katherine, what are you doing here? Have you been called home early? Is everything all right with, er, the town?" She caught herself before she posed the question she really wanted to ask. *What had happened between her and Catriona?*

Katherine took in Adele's refined features, her mind creating a rather intimate image of her ex-lover and the governess. She shook herself from her reverie. "Well, yes and no. However, what of you? I thought you were due to return to England. What happened, did your business keep you here?"

Adele laughed, her eyes crinkling in delight. "Well, yes and no. My business affairs did keep me a little longer than what I'd expected, however my delay has been imposed by the vagaries of the sea. The ship I was due to sail on foundered in Bass Strait and barely managed to limp into Port Phillip Bay. I'm now not due to sail for another ten days and that's what brought me here this morning. I was just about to check with Mr Jamieson to ensure my return journey had not again been delayed." Adele's last words were said loudly enough within the small office to ensure that their intended recipient heard them.

Doffing an imaginary cap, the man, who had previously served Katherine, replied, "No, ma'am. I've heard no reports that this ship has encountered any difficulties. She's due to arrive in Sydney on the 17th, weather permitting."

She nodded her thanks before again focusing on the nun. "So, where are you staying? I'd very much like to catch up on any news you might have of the town, and maybe we might take tea. I don't know about you, but this sea air has a tendency to make me quite hungry." She looked at the downcast features of the woman in front of her. Ushering her out of the office and the prying ears of Mr Jamieson, Adele took the nun's hand. "Katherine, what's wrong?"

"It's a long story. Yes, I'd like to speak with you about it, but firstly I've got to find somewhere relatively inexpensive to stay. I didn't figure on a seven day wait in Sydney. My funds should be just enough to secure me a room in an inn for the intervening period."

The older woman shook her head. "The inns of Sydney are not like the inns of Ireland. They're no place for a woman, much less a nun. I'm currently staying at Petty's Family Hotel and I've more than enough room for us to share. I'd be very offended if you refuse. After all, I couldn't bear to think what might happen to you if I let you stay in one of those inns. I don't think the Church would ever forgive me," she finished light heartedly, still somewhat confused over the Irishwoman's lack of religious attire.

"Thank you, maybe that would be for the best. I promise I won't be much of a nuisance. Maybe after I'm settled we can get something to eat and I can tell you what's happened since your departure." Adele strove to read the other woman's features but found them masked. Something fairly significant had occurred, of that she was sure of.

The trip to the small, yet exclusive, hotel was relatively silent with both women engrossed in their own thoughts. Casting her mind back to the first time they made love, Katherine recalled the discussion regarding Adele's somewhat sudden departure. Catriona had told her that the governess had guessed some sort of an involvement between the two of them at the dinner party and left to give it the chance of blossoming. Katherine blushed at the thought that the woman beside her had read her so well. Even though embarrassed, she was relieved. At least with Adele she would be able to express what had occurred without shocking the other woman.

Adele looked out the window as she tried to collect her thoughts. It was obvious that something had occurred, for why was Katherine in a dress rather than her habit? Finding her in the booking office could only mean that she was booking a passage to return to Ireland. Was this to finalise matters with her convent before returning to Australia? Despite the nun's silence, her non-verbal cues spoke volumes. *This woman is desperately unhappy*—that Adele was sure of.

Arriving at the hotel, the nun trailed Adele to the rented room and quickly attended to the accumulated dirt and grime of her train journey. Both women left for the tearooms of George Street and a well-deserved meal. Taking a wide berth of the busy reception area in the foyer, neither woman noticed the presence of a somewhat bedraggled traveller, her normally white pants covered in the dust of a coach journey. And the traveller, preoccupied in securing a room and a bath, failed to notice the presence of anyone but the manager in front of her.

Catriona had no sooner alighted from her bone-jarring journey when she hailed a cab and made her way to Central Station and, hopefully, Katherine's train. Cursing the state of the roads, she and the rest of the passengers had been forced to take an unscheduled overnight halt at the foot of the Blue Mountains due to a broken rear axle. After a sleepless night and the fitting of a new axle that took the greater part of the night, the coach was again on its way. Catriona prayed that the delay wouldn't hinder her finding Katherine and trying to convince her to return to Gleneagle one last time. Pausing only long enough to pay the driver, she grabbed her bag and ran for the station. However, arriving at the platform her heart sank, for despite the presence of a train, there was no-one in sight. Collapsing onto one of the railway seats dotted along the platform, she struggled to come to grips with what she could do next.

"Excuse me, sir, can I help you?" Catriona looked up at the porter in front of her. During her journey it hadn't been the first time she'd been mistaken for a man and, given her clothing, it was an easy if not wrong assumption to arrive at. Given the greater freedom of men to move unhindered through such a large town she saw no need to correct him. After all, her voice had always held a low timbre–something her mother had regretted but was potentially now to her benefit.

"Yes, thank you. Has the Western weekly arrived yet?" A sinking feeling took hold in the pit of her stomach as he nodded.

"Yes, sir. It arrived about half an hour ago. We're just cleaning it for the return service. Would you like to book a return passage? It's due to leave at about 12.15pm."

For a fleeting second she was tempted to call an end to it and just book her trip home. How in the hell was she supposed to find Katherine in a city the size of Sydney? Mentally cursing Susan's suggestion, the coach's broken axle, and her own stupidity she almost didn't hear the porter repeat his question. "Sir, do you want me to book you a journey home? There are still a number of first class carriages available for the return journey."

Suddenly a light came on in Catriona's eyes. If she'd been in Katherine's position, the first thing she would have done on arriving in Sydney would have been to book herself a sea passage home. If that were the case, then it was just possible that she may still be doing just that. Politely refusing the porter, she thanked him before grabbing her suitcase and leaving the station at a run and into the nearest cab she could find.

Paying the driver to get her to the Quay as fast as possible had almost resulted in them causing an accident. As the cab entered the enclosure of the booking office they almost careened into a cab containing two women, who had been in the process of departing the yards. Dismissing the curses of the other driver, Catriona sprang down from her cab, hoping the two women had not been harmed. Not halting to see if any damage had been caused, she strode toward the booking office.

The attendant again gazed up from his tables. "Good morning, sir, can I help you?"

Placing her bags on the floor and looking at the man's

nametag, Catriona forced a degree of calmness into her voice. "Yes, Mr, er, Jamieson I'd like some information on a passenger if I may."

The man in front of her creased his eyebrows in concern. "I'm sorry, sir, but it's not the policy of this office to provide information regarding the nature of people booking passages."

Catriona forced herself to maintain a calm exterior while deep down all she wanted to do was reach across and grab this man by the shirt and shake him senseless until the information she wanted fell from him. "And a sensible policy that is. After all, the privacy of your passengers must be maintained at all costs. Would it be possible then for you to tell me when the next ship is due to sail for Ireland?"

"Why yes, sir, indeed I can. The next ship to Ireland is not due to sail until the 14th. Do you wish to book a passage?"

She shook her head. The last thing she wanted was to be potentially stuck on a ship with a woman who didn't necessarily want her there. "No, thank you. If I may, one final question." She paused until the man nodded and then she continued. "Have you had any nuns booking a passage to Ireland?"

Mr Jamieson again looked at the man in front of him, momentarily wondering if this person had lost his senses. Deciding to err on the side of caution, he replied, "No, sir, I can't recall that I have."

"The person I'm looking for is a nun. Would it be possible that you could keep an eye out for her? She's a friend of the family and I missed saying goodbye to her before she left." Catriona reached into her pocket and pulled out a roll of notes. "I know a man like yourself may be too busy to look for someone so specific as a nun; however, I'd be willing to cover any inconvenience this may cause."

How hard could this be, looking out for a nun? the man thought to himself. *And if the man in front of him was willing to pay, then he was more than willing to help.* "Yes, it's a busy job, but I know what it's like when you don't get to say goodbye before family sails overseas. I tell you what. The *Elizabeth* sails at 4.00pm on the afternoon of the 14th. If you return here before the ship sails, I'll let you know if there have been any such passengers."

Thanking the man, she handed over what she thought was an adequate sum to cover any "inconvenience" caused. "Just one more matter if I may. It looks as if I'm going to be here in Sydney at least until the ship sails. Could you recommend a place where I might stay?"

"I certainly can, sir. There are a number of taverns about the town that would be more than suitable for you with the Princess Royal on Hunter Street being one of the more reputable establishments." Seeing the man shake his head, Jamieson persisted, "Of course that's a little loud at night. Possibly a hotel would be more to your taste? In that case, might I recommend the Petty's Family Hotel? Any driver will be able to take you there; it's on Church Hill."

Thanking the man again she left the office, wondering when Katherine was going to book a passage home. Maybe she'd been side tracked? If this were the case then Catriona's last chance would be on the day the boat was sailing and that was seven days away. How was she to occupy her time until then? Hailing a cab she made her way to Petty's Family establishment where, tired and bedraggled, she booked herself a room for the week and ordered a well-deserved bath. Preoccupied with signing the register, she didn't see the two women she had nearly crashed into at the shipping yards cross the reception room and leave the hotel.

Following the waiter, Adele made her way through the other diners before arriving at a relatively quiet corner of the tearoom. Taking a seat, she ordered for them both and paused until the waiter was a safe distance before returning her gaze to woman opposite her. "Please don't think me bold, Katherine, but what's going on?"

The Irishwoman looked down at her tightly clasped hands, wondering where she should begin. She found the words were out of her mouth before she could recover them. "Catriona told me about you and her."

The older woman's eyebrow raised in surprise before she managed to regain her composure. Laughing to herself, Adele wondered how Catriona had tolerated such candour. Casting her eyes in the direction of the other diners and satisfied that they were preoccupied in their own conversations, she returned her gaze to the woman opposite her. "If she told you then that could naturally only mean one thing." She chose her next words carefully. "Do you and Catriona share a similar relationship?" The younger woman didn't need to say anything for the blush that radiated from her face to her neck spoke volumes.

"Yes, we did." The younger woman said quietly, her face downcast. Looking again at her hands she found them clasped by Adele.

"Katherine, you needn't be worried; I'm not about to leave in disgust. That would be a little hypocritical, don't you think?" Seeing the other woman shyly nod she continued, "I sensed there was something between you in the few times the three of us were together. And the night of the dinner; I'm terribly sorry I walked in on you two like that. It was unintentional I assure you." Pausing once again she looked at the confused woman. *What was Katherine doing here?* She was sure that any such feeling would be reciprocated by Catriona. Had the strength of emotion been too much for the woman opposite her to bear?

"You don't have to answer me if you don't want to; however, were Catriona's feelings for you not the same as you felt for her?"

Katherine looked at the woman across from her. How could she tell Adele that in Catriona's arms she had finally felt at home, and despite feeling that way she had left her. She shook her head. "No, the feeling was mutual." She laughed ruefully. "It seemed that after a number of occasions of avoiding the subject we finally admitted our feelings for one another. It was after this that I decided to leave the convent and approached Father Cleary about it." She looked at the shocked face of Adele. "Sorry, I didn't mean it to sound like that. I certainly didn't tell him the whole truth regarding leaving the Order. I told him I was no longer comfortable in continuing my religious calling." The Irishwoman paused as the waiter returned with a plate of sandwiches and refreshments.

Waiting until the man was a respectable distance, Adele again turned to the younger woman. "So, is that why you're returning to Ireland, to get dispensation to leave the Convent?" She had barely got the sentence out when tears welled in the other woman's eyes.

"No, that's not exactly the truth although that will be one thing I'll see to on my return. We were caught by the young Greystone girl kissing on the way to town." Hearing Adele's intake of breath she paused to gather herself. "I know, it was a foolish indiscretion and given that same day again we would have never let it happen; but it did. I'm sure you can imagine the reaction of the Ladies Committee. I truly believe that if they could have organised it, they would have seen to the lynching of Catriona and myself. Instead they settled for me leaving town."

"What was Catriona doing through all of this? She's never struck me as the type of woman who would take such treatment lying down."

"You're right, she wouldn't if she had been given the choice. If you could have seen the reaction of the Father, you would have understood what I had to do. Catriona's livelihood relies on her receiving a good price for her crop and her cattle. That was unlikely to occur if I remained. I couldn't bear to see her and the farm waste away because of me. I didn't want her to carry the simmering resentment that might have arisen from her being made an outcast." Katherine looked into the violet eyes of the woman opposite her. "It was my decision to leave. I knew Catriona would never ask me to go and if I stayed I don't think she would have managed to keep the farm."

The governess was shocked at Katherine's revelation and leaning across the table she took the smaller hands of the other woman. "Did she try to stop you? Surely she didn't take this in her stride."

Katherine smiled ruefully. "Well, at first she did when I tried to explain to her why I was doing what I was doing. However, as it came closer to my departure, it was as if she didn't care anymore. She stopped speaking to me and refused to take me to the station. On my last day it was all I could do to get any words from her at all." She paused before adding quietly, "I think she was glad to see me gone."

Adele sat back in her chair. She had dealt with her stubborn charge often enough to recognise a defence mechanism when she saw it. As a teenager, withdrawing into herself had been Catriona's way in dealing with pain. Feigning indifference had caused many a frustrating time when she'd been the young woman's governess. "Are you telling me that she made no move to tell you to stay and that she made no move to drive you to the station?" Seeing the other woman nod, Adele gently asked, "Do you love her?"

Silent tears fell down the other woman's face. "Yes," was all Katherine could manage before reaching into the folds of her dress for a handkerchief.

"Believe me when I tell you she loves you as well and the

last thing she would have wanted was for you to leave. Go back, Katherine, tell her how you feel, and be damned with what the townsfolk feel. If you feel half as much for her as what she feels for you, there'll be no issue with your return."

"How can you say that? You weren't there, you didn't see how she acted on the final day. And what about the farm? If I return I doubt the feelings of the townsfolk will have changed. And what if she doesn't take me back? I've barely enough funds as it is." Shaking her head she again met the distressed eyes of Adele. "No, I'm sorry, Adele. As much as this hurts and believe me when I tell you it's like a suppurating wound, I can't return. It's for the best that I return to Ireland. In time Catriona's life will go on and as days pass her memories of me will fade along with the pain she is currently suffering. It's for the best," Katherine finished, wondering who she was trying to convince— herself or Adele.

"I don't think so, Katherine. I really don't think so." Sensing closure to their discussion, at least for the moment, Adele shook her head and took a sip from her now lukewarm tea.

Over the ensuing days Adele tried on many occasion to convince the nun to try at least one more time with Catriona. Despite her protestations, her pleas fell on deaf ears. In response, Katherine tried to detract the conversation back to Adele and her time as a governess in both Australia and England. The Irishwoman found herself thinking that this might at least be one way that she could achieve at least some happiness in her life.

When not drawing Adele into conversation regarding her times as a governess, Katherine fell back on the safe ground regarding the governess' imminent departure and her plans on returning to England. Strangely enough, Adele had become evasive on the matter, preferring not to discuss her travel plans with the other woman. Even on the second day of their stay, when she had left the nun at the hotel under the auspices of a visit to the booking office, Adele had mentioned very little on her return. Sensing that the governess may have an aversion to long journeys, Katherine ceased to quiz her on the topic.

In her remaining days in the country it was as if Adele couldn't do enough for Katherine. Sensing the woman's lack of suitable attire for such a journey, she had taken her shopping at the David Jones Emporium, politely but firmly refusing any form of payment from Katherine for the goods purchased. Visiting the gardens of the Domain, they strolled in the imposing crenellated shadows of Government House, talking on just about every topic possible except Catriona. The governess shared with Katherine tales of her life, one of a different path to Katherine's. Reassuring the younger woman, Adele advised her that she was not alone and that within London society relationships such as the one she and Catriona had shared were, if not common, at least present.

When they weren't taking in the sights of Sydney, both were content to spend their evening hours at the hotel, taking tea in the parlour before retiring early for bed. In passing their time in such a manner, it wasn't long before the day of Katherine's departure was upon them.

The Irishwoman woke very early that morning and gazed across at the form in the other bed. She was relieved that Adele wasn't yet awake. *She had been a godsend over these past few days*, Katherine thought. However, all she wanted on this last day was to be alone with her own thoughts. She knew that once she stepped on the ship she would never return to Australia and to her Catriona, and she found herself silently grieving at the thought. Would she ever again find anyone who would affect her the way that Catriona had managed to do? In all honesty she doubted she would ever experience that depth of emotion again. At least if she could find a job as a governess, she could continue to have at least some small spark of joy in her life. Quietly Katherine dressed herself for the long journey ahead.

After what had been a trying day and despite her protestations, Adele was adamant in seeing the nun to her ship. After all, the older woman reasoned, she knew what it was like to embark on such a journey with no-one to say goodbye. Shaking her head in resignation, Katherine allowed the governess to call a cab to start her final departure from a country and people she had learnt to love.

As they entered the shipyard, Katherine could see the three tall masts of what could only have been the *Elizabeth* and all of a sudden her departure seemed all too real. Using every last ounce of her composure Katherine thanked the driver, who had taken up a position on the cab rank. Katherine and Adele made one final journey to the booking office. They hadn't gone far when a rather burly porter approached them.

Doffing his cap he introduced himself. "Afternoon, ladies. Would you be travelling on the *Elizabeth* this fine afternoon then?"

Smiling in return, Adele replied, "I won't be but my friend here is one of the passengers. Could you please arrange for her luggage to be stowed on board?"

Once again doffing his cap in obeisance, he moved to take the luggage from Adele and Katherine. He had barely taken the luggage from them when the Irishwoman looked around herself, as if trying to find something. "Heaven's! I've left my book on the seat of the cab. Adele, I'll go back for it before our driver gets another fare. I'll meet you at the booking office." Without a backward glance the Irishwoman made her way back into the throng of people.

After paying the porter a small gratuity to ensure Katherine's entire luggage was loaded, Adele made her way to the Booking Office. Stepping through the door she gazed across the room straight into the eyes of a woman she would continue to love all her life.

A surprised Catriona closed the distance between the two women. "Adele, what are you doing here? I thought you'd be on your way by now."

Grabbing the other woman's arm, Adele guided her outside and away from the prying ears of Mr Jamieson. "What am I doing here? Who cares what I'm doing here? Did you get the telegram I sent you?"

Catriona's face took on a puzzled expression. "What telegram? I didn't receive any telegram. What are you talking about?"

"I sent one to you five days ago, advising you to come at once if you wanted any chance of a relationship between you and Katherine." Adele paused as she took in the surprised features of the woman in front of her. "I can't believe you let her walk out without trying at least one more time. Shame on you, Catriona. Didn't I teach you better manners than that? And you should think yourself lucky that I perchance was in this yard the day Katherine booked her passage for Ireland. God knows where she would have ended up staying. As it was she's been sharing a room with me at Petty's Family Hotel for the last seven days."

Adele didn't think it was possible that anyone could look so incredulous as Catriona did at that moment in time. "Petty's on Church hill? My God, I've been there for the past few days, trying to work out a plan to get her to return with me to Gleneagle. My last chance was to speak with her today when she came to board her ship." Catriona struck herself on the side of the leg. "If I'd just spent a little more time in the parlour than moping around in my room, this might have been solved by now."

The older woman steadied Catriona's ramblings. "This is your last chance to try and convince Katherine to stay. Be patient, but persistent, Catriona. I honestly believe she wants to stay but she needs to hear it from you and in a manner that doesn't resemble you talking to one of your blessed cattle."

Unable to control herself Catriona closed her eyes as she wrapped her arms around the somewhat startled woman. "Thank you. You don't know how much I wanted to hear those words. I honestly think today signals a new start for us."

"Yes, I've no doubt it does," came the voice from behind them.

Catriona opened her eyes to find herself staring back at the angry form of Katherine. Breaking away from their embrace, Adele also turned to see barely controlled emotions of the younger woman. Raising her hand, the Irishwoman pointed a finger in Adele's direction. "You! After all I told you about Catriona and I, and this is how you pay me back! Is that why you've been so elusive about your travel arrangements? And your surreptitious trip to the booking office. That wasn't to confirm your trip, it was to cancel it!"

The governess attempted to placate the temper of the younger woman. "That's not it at all. The times when I left you were not to go to the booking office, although this proved a convenient excuse. I went to the post office to telegraph Catriona. Katherine, there's a reasonable explanation for what you just saw and heard—"

The Irishwoman cut her off before she could go any further. "Oh, yes, I'm sure there is. With me out of the way you could return to Catriona. I'm sure today does signal a new beginning for you both. However, it will definitely be one without me in it." Turning on her heel, Katherine made her way back into the crowd and toward the waiting ship.

Both women were momentarily stunned by the vehemence of Katherine's words, before Adele began to laugh. "Oh God, Catriona, she's a fine one. Go after her before it's too late. Tell her what that was about and what you mean to her. Now, go!" she ordered, physically pushing the shocked woman in the direction of the retreating back of Katherine.

Galvanised into action, the grazier took after the woman she wanted to share the rest of her life with. If she physically had to restrain Katherine and carry her from the ship, she resolved she would do this if not for anything else than to give each of them one more chance. She became frustrated as her progress was impeded by the men and livestock moving in the same direction. She arrived at the gangplank in time to see the figure of Katherine move to the other side of the ship.

Reaching the railing of the gangplank, she found her progress again halted by a slightly built porter. Struggling to go around him, he persisted. "Excuse me, sir, can I see your ticket?"

"I don't have a ticket, but I do need to just speak to someone on this vessel. It will only take a minute and then I'll happily get off and you can be on your way." Again the man in front of her blocked her passage.

"I'm sorry, sir, but without a ticket you can't board the ship. How do I know you're not a stowaway?"

"You don't know that I'm not a stowaway, but here's something you should know. If you value your life you'll let me board this vessel. I'm going up that gangplank come Hell or high water. I must speak to the woman who just boarded." With one mighty shove Catriona moved the man and ran up the entrance to the ship. Closing the distance between the two of them, she managed to call out Katherine's name before her progress was yet again halted; this time by two extremely well built sailors.

"Now where do you think you're going then? Do you think you can thump people and board a ship at a whim? If you're not a paying passenger then you're an attempted stowaway and we hand your type over to the constabulary."

The grazier wrestled to break free from the vice-like grip of the two men holding her. "Don't be absurd! All I want to do is have a few quiet words with that woman over there." Catriona inclined her head in the direction of Katherine's shocked features.

The older of the two men answered her. "Strangely enough, she doesn't look as if she wants to talk to you. What sort of man are you, accosting fine ladies in such a manner—?"

He hadn't finished his sentence as Catriona brought down a booted heel on the foot of the vile smelling man, causing him to yell in pain and loosen his grip. "You bastard, I'll make you sorry for that!"

Before she could get any closer to Katherine, Catriona's stomach was impaled on the hand of the angry man. Doubling over in pain with stars dancing in her head, the last thing Catriona heard before she was soundly hit across the head was Katherine screaming her name.

On the fringes of consciousness, Catriona could just make out the heated conversation between an angry Katherine and a somewhat contrite sailor. Adele's voice was also there, trying to calm the angry woman.

"I'm sorry, ma'am, but with her dressed the way she was and all; I thought she was a man aiming to do no good. I'd never have hit her if I knew she was a woman." He paused as he looked at the seething features of Katherine and as if in his own defence pushed on in attempted defiance. "After all, how could anyone tell? Women shouldn't dress like that; it's not natural."

"What's not natural about it? She's a grazier for heaven's sake!" Katherine looked at the tied back hair of the sailor in front of her. "And what about your pigtail, is that natural? I thought only little girls wore pigtails." Sensing that her arrow had hit its mark she calmed down. "I know that's how sailors have worn their hair for many years, and how she's dressed is how farmers have dressed for many years. Just as hair in your eyes would hinder your ability to work, so would her wearing a dress in her line of work. I thank you both for coming to my defence. Just don't be so eager in the future to jump to conclusions." Katherine paused as yet another man entered the scene.

Consulting his fob watched he addressed the group in front of him. "By my reckoning, it's now 3.55pm and this ship sails at 4.00pm sharp. If any of you are staying, then stay. If you're not then get off my ship or *I* will have you thrown off, female or otherwise."

Before the Irishwoman could take issue with the man's tone, the crowd had quickly dissipated leaving just Adele, her, and Catriona. Feeling the weight of Catriona shift in her lap Katherine looked down into the face of the woman she loved to see Catriona open her eyes.

"Katherine, I love you and I don't want you to leave. I'm sorry I acted the way I did before you left. I really didn't handle the situation at all well. We'll work through this, Katherine, I promise." Taking the Irishwoman's hand in her own she placed a small kiss in the palm. "Come home with me, Katherine, please."

She looked down on the pleading eyes of the woman she loved. "I'm already home, my love. Wherever you are, be it Gleneagle, a shack, or the deck of a ship, as long as I'm with you I'll always be home."

Epilogue

While the scandal of Katherine's return with Catriona to Gleneagle did take more than the better part of a month to die down, an even greater one replaced the fracas caused by the two women. It seemed that young Miss Greystone had done more than just go riding on that fateful day she'd made her shocking discovery. Six weeks after the Irishwoman's initial departure, young Miss Greystone began to develop a small bulge consistent with someone expecting a child. While the Greystone family hung their heads in shame, there was quiet cheering by the poorer families of the district.

So great was the ignominy Mrs Greystone felt, she packed herself and her daughter, and left for Sydney and a trip to the continent or somewhere till at least Elsbeth's size was reduced. Without the presence of the outspoken and waspish Mrs Greystone, the remainder of the Ladies Committee seemed to lose its momentum. They became content to busy themselves with small tea parties, leaving the rest of the town, and in particular the two women, to their own devices.

Almost three months had passed when Catriona held a dinner party, inviting Susan, Me-Lin, William, and Robert. The dinner was of even greater significance, for it was one of the few times that Me-Lin treated the group to a traditional repast of her own, surprising even Susan with her culinary skill. Robert and William had become regular visitors to Catriona and Katherine's home, and had on more than one occasion spent the night. Sometimes the grazier found herself shaking her head at the greater freedom of men to women.

It was almost five months since Katherine's initial departure when the postmaster received a letter from Ireland addressed to Sister Flynn. A tireless supporter of the work of the Ladies Committee, he elected to redirect the letter to where he felt it was most appropriate—Father Cleary. The Father smiled sourly as he read the contents of the letter that first mentioned how sorry the Mother Superior was about Sister Flynn's decision. However, as she wasn't in the habit of tying people to something they didn't want to be associated with, she told the nun that she'd honour her resolution to leave the convent. The Mother Superior went on in her letter to praise Katherine's choice to remain in the district and advised her that when it was possible they would send another nun out to the town.

It was at the nine-month mark that the new nun arrived in the town. Unlike as with Katherine, both the Ladies Committee and Father Cleary afforded her a great reception at the train station before she was whisked off to the home of Mrs Monteith. Sister Gordon was a woman in the twilight of her years who was quite taken by the reception she'd received from the Ladies Committee. In return she seemed quite content to spend the better part of her days regaling the ladies with stories of the "Mother Country."

With Sister Gordon's time occupied on such matters, there was little time for her to care for the less fortunate families of the district. As Susan had correctly surmised, it didn't take long for the poorer families to come to grips with the somewhat bohemian relationship shared between the grazier and the Irishwoman. After some initial misgivings, and at the prompting of the influential Connor clan, families within the community again accepted Katherine's teaching of their children. As the years passed and more children found doors opened to them by virtue of the education this fine woman had provided, they wondered what had been the major issue in the first place.

As time went on, the town accepted the two eccentric women who lived just outside of town. Unlike the Ladies Committee, which eventually petered into obscurity, their love for each other grew. They spent the rest of their lives in blissful peace surrounded by true friends.

Jacob's Fire
By Nan DeVincent Hayes

Jacob, a university professor/scientist has found a formula to cure AIDS—a formula that causes mass destruction if improperly used. The government and a private pharmaceutical firm want Jacob's formula, and go to brutal, vicious, murderous means to get it. But Isleen, the pharmaceutical rep who is assigned to cajole him into selling the formula to her firm, refuses to exert unethical means, and, instead, she and Jacob eventually become friends and allies who try to fight "Big Government." Isleen tries convincing Jacob that world events are following biblical prophecy, the end time is near, and that he should reconsider his staunch Judaic position. She wants him to believe that the Second Coming of Christ is at hand.

Mystery, intrigue and suspense intertwine with secret societies and politics while the global leaders attempt to form a "New World Order" on the political, religious, and economic levels. Jacob innocently gets caught up in this web of shadow organizations and soon finds himself trying to find an antidote for the plague that has been unleashed on the world, all the while watching as the prophecies Isleen told him about continue to unfold. In the end, Jacob must make a decision on the Truth before it is too late.

Other titles to look for in the
coming months from
RENAISSANCE ALLIANCE

You Must Remember This By Mary A. Sannis

Restitution By Susanne Beck

Full Circle By Mary A. Sannis

Bleeding Hearts By Josh Aterovis

New Beginnings By Mary A. Sannis

A Sacrifice For Friendship By DS Bauden

Born and residing in Australia, Helen specialises in lecturing and tutoring in a variety of human resource development/ management subjects, including communication, leadership and management studies. Currently based in Canberra, she is working as the operations and business manager within a major organisation. When she isn't tied to her work she enjoys traveling, reading, writing and bushwalking. She is an avid sportswoman, having competed in softball and soccer at a representational level, although recently she is more of a spectator than a participant. She currently lives with her partner of eight years and their two cats.